The
Seventh
Unicorn

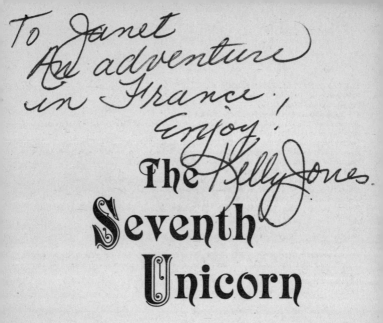

To Janet
An adventure
in France!
Enjoy!
Kelly Jones

The
Seventh
Unicorn

KELLY JONES

BERKLEY BOOKS, NEW YORK

THE BERKLEY PUBLISHING GROUP
Published by the Penguin Group
Penguin Group (USA) Inc.
375 Hudson Street, New York, New York 10014, USA
Penguin Group (Canada), 90 Eglinton Avenue East, Suite 700, Toronto, Ontario M4P 2Y3, Canada
(a division of Pearson Penguin Canada Inc.)
Penguin Books Ltd., 80 Strand, London WC2R 0RL, England
Penguin Group Ireland, 25 St. Stephen's Green, Dublin 2, Ireland (a division of Penguin Books Ltd.)
Penguin Group (Australia), 250 Camberwell Road, Camberwell, Victoria 3124, Australia
(a division of Pearson Australia Group Pty. Ltd.)
Penguin Books India Pvt. Ltd., 11 Community Centre, Panchsheel Park, New Delhi—110 017, India
Penguin Group (NZ), Cnr. Airborne and Rosedale Roads, Albany, Auckland 1310, New Zealand
(a division of Pearson New Zealand Ltd.)
Penguin Books (South Africa) (Pty.) Ltd., 24 Sturdee Avenue, Rosebank, Johannesburg 2196,
South Africa

Penguin Books Ltd., Registered Offices: 80 Strand, London WC2R 0RL, England

This is a work of fiction. Names, characters, places, and incidents either are the product of the author's imagination or are used fictitiously, and any resemblance to actual persons, living or dead, business establishments, events, or locales is entirely coincidental.

THE SEVENTH UNICORN

A Berkley Book / published by arrangement with the author

PRINTING HISTORY
Berkley edition / October 2005

Copyright © 2005 by Kelly Jones.
Cover design by George Long.
Interior text design by Stacy Irwin.

ISBN: 0-425-20625-4

BERKLEY®
Berkley Books are published by The Berkley Publishing Group,
a division of Penguin Group (USA) Inc.,
375 Hudson Street, New York, New York 10014.
BERKLEY is a registered trademark of Penguin Group (USA) Inc.
The "B" design is a trademark belonging to Penguin Group (USA) Inc.

PRINTED IN THE UNITED STATES OF AMERICA

10 9 8 7 6 5 4 3 2

ACKNOWLEDGMENTS

Thank you to The Log Cabin Literary Center in Boise, Idaho, and my fellow writers who continue to inspire me. I am especially indebted to Coston Frederick, Frank Marvin, Byron Meredith, Maria Eschen, Liz Goins, Bud Pembroke, and Terry Wibbels for their thoughtful critiques of *The Seventh Unicorn*. I would also like to acknowledge friends and family members who read early drafts of the manuscript, offering suggestions and sometimes just much-needed reassurance. Thank you to Renie Hays, Maggie Saunders, Mrezzie Putnam, Paul Van Dam, Carolyn Hartman, Carol McFarland, Peggy McMahon, Lori McFarland, Ariana Hays, and Lynn Marinko Ruoff. A very special thank-you to my mom and dad, Mary Alice and Otto Florence. You have always believed in me, yet have never denied me the pleasure of surprising you. I hope you don't find anything too surprising within!

I am grateful for two special women who have worked with me to make my story a book. Thank you to my agent, Julie Barer, for encouragement, for generosity, and for being so clever. Thank you to my editor, Leona Nevler, whose wisdom and kindness have made this seem almost easy. I would also like to thank Peter McGuigan and Kirsten Neuhaus for their support and for handling foreign translation rights.

And finally, I acknowledge my husband, Jim. Thank you for being at my side and for bringing out the best in me. Thank you for *Le Toucher*. Thank you for Paris.

The Seventh Unicorn is fiction inspired by *The Lady and the Unicorn* tapestries in the Musée National du Moyen Age-Thermes de Cluny in Paris, France. Most likely created for the Le Viste family of Lyon sometime in the late fifteenth century, many art historians believe the tapestries are allegorical representation of the five senses. The artist who designed them remains a mystery, providing fertile ground for storytelling. I have used several sources in my research, including *La Dame à la Licorne* by Alain Erlande-Brandenburg (Edition de la Réunion des musées nationaux, 1989), *The Unicorn Tapestries* by Margaret B. Freeman (The Metropolitan Museum of Art, 1976), *Tapestry* by Barty Phillips (Phaidon Press Limited, 1994), *Tapestry Mirror of History* by Francis Paul Thomson OBE (Crown Publishers, Inc., 1980), *The Unicorn* by Lise Gotfredsen (Abbeville Press Publishers, 1999), and *La Dame à Licorne: A Reinterpretation* by Kristina E. Gourley (*Gazette des Beaux-Arts*, September 1997).

PROLOGUE

THE PAIN CAME in the night as the old nun said it would. Adèle sat up, placing her hand over the swell of her belly, feeling frightened and unsure, though the discomfort itself was no greater than the cramps of her monthly bleeding. And then the pain subsided. She lay again, the rhythmic breathing of the young novice sleeping nearby filling the void in the tiny cell they shared. "Not yet," Adèle whispered to herself. "Wait."

She tried to return to her sleep, but could not. She had been dreaming. It was the dream that had come to her each night since she'd arrived, a scene so familiar she could pull it up with ease, a dream that did not require slumber. Each detail as clear and precise as the drawings she had carried to the garden that day tucked inside her book of prayers.

The air is ripe with the clove scent of carnations, the fragrance of the orange trees, the damp earth. Adèle has come to the garden to draw, as she often does, under the pretense of prayer and meditation. She slips one of the drawings, which she had begun during her last visit, from the prayer book. It is a drawing of her sister Claude playing the harmonium, attended by a handmaiden who works the bellows. With pen and ink Adèle has created the texture of the satin and velvet of their garments. On the right she has placed a unicorn, symbol of a maiden's purity, an animal that could be tamed only by a virgin. She has drawn a lion, the symbol of strength, on the left. The family arms—*gules, a bend, charged with three crescents argent*—is hoisted on banners held by the two beasts. Now Adèle takes out pen and ink and with skillful strokes she encloses these figures inside a garden that resembles an island. She draws rabbits and a dog within the island, then places several of these small creatures, adding a fox and sheep, in the background as if floating in air. She sits for a moment examining her work, quite pleased, and then she places the drawing on the sun-warmed bench to dry while she goes to gather flowers to complete her scene.

When she returns, a man stands near the bench. He has picked up the drawing and examines it with great concentration.

She knows he is the tapestry weaver. She had watched as he and the older man arrived from Brussels this morning. Have they completed their meetings with her father?

Suddenly she feels very bold. "You are the *tapissier* from Brussels?"

She has startled him and he turns. "I am."

"Please," she says, reaching for the drawing. He places it in her hand and for several moments they stand not speaking.

"You are an artist of impressive skill," the man says. She smiles but does not reply, though she can see he is entranced.

"The woman in the drawing," he asks, "a woman of fantasy?"

"My sister, my eldest sister, Claude."

"Your sister is very beautiful."

"Yes."

"And a musician?"

"My father has encouraged her musical talent to attract and entertain a young knight, or a nobleman, perhaps even a prince. Our family is of humble origin. Merchants, drapers from Lyon."

The weaver nods as if he has heard the stories, but he seems as surprised as Adèle that she would speak of such private family affairs. Yet, isn't it well known that the Le Vistes had attained great wealth and property in Lyon, then advanced their political position in Paris and married well? And isn't it known that despite Jean Le Viste's rapid ascent in the administration, as far as he has risen in the service of the king, he has failed to attain the noble status and royal title he so desires? Her father, Adèle muses, is no more lord or knight than a simple *tapissier* from Brussels. Yet she knows her father would not approve of this intimacy they now share.

"My father," she asks, "he will use an artist from Paris to design the tapestries?"

"It is his wish. There are many skillful painters in Paris."

She picks a daisy from her bouquet and holds it to her nose for a moment, then studies it carefully. "But the finest workshops, the weavers, are in Brussels?"

"Yes," he answers, "the finest weavers are in Brussels."

"Has a theme been chosen?"

"There has been much discussion. Your father is one to think on a grand scale. He wishes to celebrate the family's accomplishments, his appointment as *présidente de la Cour des aides,* but also the anniversary of his marriage to your mother."

"Politics," she says, slowly shaking her head as she scatters the flowers she has collected on the bench. She sits, pulls a large book from below, nestles it in her lap, and places the parchment upon the book. Then, using the flowers as a model, she begins to draw, arranging pansies and daisies around the small animals in the background. "And how many pieces will my father commission?" she asks. "Does he wish to cover all the walls in the château? Or will this be a simple *chambre*?"

"There has been talk of seven panels."

"Seven is a good number." She pushes back her long hair, which has fallen across her cheek.

The *tapissier* watches as she fills the background with flowers. *"Mille-fleurs,"* he says, and she smiles, aware it is a style currently fashionable in the design of tapestry. When she has finished, she reaches down, picks up a wooden box below the bench and takes out a soft cloth. She wipes the ink from the point of her drawing pen. As she places the pen, ink, and cloth inside the box the weaver asks, "May I?" He has noticed the prayer book at her feet and the other drawings slipped between the pages.

"You may." She picks up the prayer book and hands it to

him. And then, with a shameless gesture that again startles them both, she brushes the flowers to the ground, inviting him to sit beside her. He hesitates for a moment, then he sits.

There are four more drawings, five total, each depicting a woman on a garden island with a unicorn and lion. He examines each with great interest.

He holds up the drawing of a woman weaving a caplet out of flowers.

"My sister Jeanne," she says.

"Your sister Jeanne is also very beautiful."

"Yes."

He studies the drawing in which a hunting bird is perched on the gloved hand of the young woman.

"My sister Geneviève," she says. "And, yes, she is also very beautiful. And a skilled hunter."

He comes to the drawing of a woman holding a mirror in which she has caught the image of the unicorn cradled in her lap. The lion to the woman's right supports a banner embellished with the Le Viste family arms.

"My mother," the girl says.

"There is great sadness in her eyes," the weaver replies thoughtfully.

"Alas, what is there but sadness for a woman who produces no sons?"

"A woman who produces but four daughters?" he says with a smile. "Four beautiful daughters." And even now she feels her own smile, a rise of warmth and, then . . . great pain as this image fades.

She is back in the tiny cell, the scent of the garden replaced by the dry scent of stone. The cramps have come again, this time harder, deeper. Yet still she thinks, *it is not time*. She pulls up the memory once more, the final drawing as the *tapissier* studies it carefully.

The woman in this drawing does not possess the delicate countenance of the others; her face is long and drawn. She stands, holding a lance in her right hand, her left hand caressing the horn of the unicorn, which more closely resembles a goat than the elegant beasts in the other drawings. The small animals in the background are collared or chained.

"The young woman in this drawing?" he asks, his eyes moving from the parchment to Adèle's face. His brows rise and his eyes tighten, revealing his confusion, as if he understands she has drawn herself but cannot see the likeness. Perhaps he wonders why she has chosen to portray herself in this manner.

And then, again, the pain. She feels the break of water between her legs, the bedclothes damp. The smell of blood. She calls to the young nun, who awakens. "Now," Adèle whispers.

The old nun arrives quickly. The pains are closer now and more intense. Adèle sees the horror in the young nun's eyes. And the blood, deep red, and then Adèle cries out.

She sees the tapestries, brought from the workshop in Brussels. Six now, her impatient father unable to wait for the complete set, and Adèle has yet to see the seventh.

She can no longer hold these images. The pain has overtaken her, so fierce it demands her entire body and spirit.

The old woman stays with her, as does the young nun, through the morning chants coming from the chapel, through the midday, the evening. Adèle sees the fatigue in the old woman's eyes. Just inches from her face, the nun's lips move in silent prayer, and Adèle's prayer is only that she will have the strength to bring this innocent child into the world. But the pain takes so much from her, she cannot pray in a proper way. Words will not form. Again it is night; the only light comes from the flickering candles in the cell. Adèle has an urge to push, to push with all her might.

"Not yet, my daughter," the old woman says, and even this seems to be a prayer. She touches Adèle's face with a damp cloth and massages her legs, her arms, her stomach with warm oil, speaking always in a soft, steady voice. She presses a cup to her lips. Wine with herbs to sate the pain.

Finally, the woman commands, "Now, Adèle, push." There are others in the room, holding her arms, her legs, pulling her up as if this child is a ripe fruit ready to drop to the earth. "Push," the old nun whispers, and Adèle does, again and again until the woman exclaims, *"Deo gratias, Deo gratias!"*

With a strength that seems to rise from outside her, Adèle gazes upon the child. He is so very small, but when he gives off a hardy cry, Adèle's heart leaps and she whispers her own prayer of praise.

The old nun is bathing him. The early morning light reveals blood everywhere—on the child, on the bedcovers, on the rushes that have been placed on the floor, on Adèle's legs, on her feet. The woman swathes him tightly for warmth, and when she hands him to the young nun who carries him from the room, once more Adèle cries out.

"Rest, my daughter, rest," the old nun says, and Adèle closes her eyes. Again, she sees the crimson red. At first it is blood, but then . . . she can see how pleased her father is when first he gazes upon the tapestries, the rich red threads, the blue, and gold. And then his discovery, and then the rage. But now it is gone. She no longer feels the anger, or the pain, but a peaceful calm, and she is walking once more in a garden.

1

THE CONVENT OF Sainte Blandine, a two-story structure of rustic stone, appeared to be abandoned. Weeds and wild vegetation rose up on either side of a narrow dirt path leading to the front door and reached their way into a small orchard of unpruned fruit trees. Rows of dilapidated trellises, choked with grapevines, stood among discarded wooden crates on the opposite side of the path. The north side of the building was covered with ivy, eating away at the brick chimney, which must have been a more recent addition, as it did not match the rest of the large stone structure. Several bricks had worked their way loose and had tumbled to the ground where they lay in a pile. The air, still except for the slightest breeze rustling through the trees, gave no indication of recent life or occupancy.

Alex Pellier stood in the path and examined the map again. She'd followed the directions precisely—south from Lyon, past the village of Vienne. The highway from Lyon was carefully labeled, then every turn and jolt and bump—and there had been many—on both the gravel and dirt roads marked and identified. The map had come tucked inside the letter from the Mother Superior.

Alex approached the large wooden door, perplexed by the deserted appearance of the building and grounds. She knocked and waited. No answer. She knocked again.

Surely someone would come; she had an appointment.

The letter from the Mother Superior, in an unsteady yet still graceful cursive hand, written with an old-fashioned ink pen, had arrived at the Cluny addressed to Madame Demy, the Director of the museum. The language of the letter was as ornate and embellished as the script: "Elegant embroidered altar linens trimmed with exquisite handmade lace, priceless tapestries of the finest quality dating back to the convent's founding in the thirteenth century, an extensive library, including medieval manuscripts of great value." According to Reverend Mother Alvère, the convent wished to dispose of the properties before the move to Lyon. All items would be available for viewing the last weekend of May.

Alex knocked again, but still no answer. Had the nuns already left for the retirement convent in Lyon? It had been just two days since Alex received a second letter from the Mother Superior, a reply to Alex's request for a date to visit. An appointment had been set for this very evening at seven P.M. It was now ten after.

She knocked again. Had she driven all the way from Paris for nothing?

After several more minutes, she walked to the side of the building and put her face to a window, which was boarded up from inside, and peered between the gaps. She could see nothing but the faintest sliver of light cast on a dark wall.

She returned to the front entrance and knocked again with greater force. Still, nothing. She was about to try the door when a small window on the upper portion opened. The face of a woman appeared, small and wrinkled, framed in a stiff white hood and wimple.

For several moments the woman stared, then in a raspy, irritated voice she said, *"Bonjour."*

"Bonjour," Alex replied. She introduced herself and explained that she was from the Musée National du Moyen Age, the Cluny in Paris, and that she had an appointment with the Mother Superior.

"Elle est malade," the old woman replied tersely. There

was no indication that the nun would invite Alex in. It was clear she would not be able to speak to the Mother Superior, who, according to the nun, was ill.

Alex unlatched her briefcase and pulled out the first letter from Mother Alvère. She handed it through the small window to the nun. As the woman read, her eyes squinting into tiny slits, Alex explained that she was staying in Lyon that evening, and it was a good one-hour round trip. Couldn't she come in and take a quick look?

The old nun did not reply, her eyes moving slowly across the page, her thin lips set in a scowl. She looked up once at Alex, then back to the letter as if it contained some secret code or hidden meaning.

"Madame Demy?" the woman asked.

"Madame Pellier," Alex replied. Perhaps she should have presented the second letter, the most recent, addressed to Alexandra Pellier.

She pulled it from her briefcase. The old woman reached out and took the second letter, not bothering to return the first. The downward turn of her mouth remained fixed.

Alex stood, her face growing warm with impatience while the woman read the letter as tediously as she had read the first.

Finally, the woman handed Alex the letters, gazed at her for a moment, then said in a low voice, "Madame Pellier," as she motioned with a gnarled hand.

The door swung open, Alex stepped inside and followed the stooped little body, which moved surprisingly fast, through a vestibule and down a dark hall. With her old-fashioned habit, yards of coarse black cloth, hood, and wimple, the woman looked nothing like the modern nuns Alex saw in Paris with their knee-length skirts and permed hair.

The place smelled of old stone and something else . . . a nursing home, Alex thought as they continued down the narrow hall. Yes, the scent of ancient bodies, triggering a memory from years ago, a visit to her great-grandmother in a nursing home. Yet there was no evidence of other inhabitants. Alex knew the order itself was dying, that there were fewer than a dozen remaining nuns, ranging in age from sixty-nine to ninety-two. They were to be sent to a retirement convent owned by another order in Lyon, by directive of Philippe Bonnisseau, Archbishop of Lyon. Sainte Blandine's was to be renovated and converted into a hotel.

They turned into a second hall, as eerily quiet as the first, the stillness disturbed only by their soft footsteps on the stone floor, the slightest *click-clack* of rosary beads hanging from the nun's belt. Abruptly, the woman stopped and motioned Alex into a small room.

Alex's eyes moved quickly, taking in as much as she could in the dim light. The walls were covered with shelves, some sagging in the middle from the weight of hundreds of books. A table and chair sat in the middle of the room, a wooden desk in front of the bookshelves on the opposite wall. The air was thick and smelled of dust. Tiny motes floated in a narrow stream of light coming in from a single small window. The nun lit two wall sconces, a lamp on the desk, another on the table. As Alex scanned the shelves, a knot of anticipation tightened inside her. Could the Convent of Sainte Blandine truly possess authentic medieval manuscripts, as Mother Alvère had implied in her letter? She turned to explain that she was particularly interested in earlier works dating back to the convent's founding, but the nun had somehow managed to slip out of the room.

Alex approached the first shelf. Books were crammed in, one on top of another. She pulled one out and dusted it off. *Théologie de la Trinité,* published in the early 1930s, with the proper *Nihil Obstat* on the back of the title page. Probably of value to a book collector, but not a medieval museum. As her eyes moved up and down, she wondered if there really was anything old enough to be of interest to the Cluny. Nothing specific stood out, but ancient manuscripts were often rebound. Yet finding anything here without some kind of guide or catalogue would be almost impossible. *Needle in a haystack.* She glanced back at the door, but the nun had not returned.

She pulled off a couple more books and could see others jammed behind these. She lifted several out, taking only those that appeared to be the oldest, and carried them to the desk. Quickly she flipped through them and found nothing. She moved on to the second wall. She glanced at her watch. She had no idea how long she would be allowed in the library, and she also wanted to look at the tapestries described in the Mother

Superior's letter. Her thoughts turned to her young daughter, Soleil. It was the French word for "sun," and she truly was the light in Alex's life.

Alex had dropped her off with Simone and Pierre Pellier, Thierry's parents, in Lyon. She had told Simone to put Soleil to bed by eight-thirty, though Alex knew that Simone would most likely keep her up, simply for the pleasure of her company. Simone doted on her granddaughter—the only child of her only child.

Alex sat now, her eyes moving up and down the shelves. She liked the idea of actually *discovering* a medieval treasure. Madame Demy generally turned any invitation that seemed somewhat dubious over to Alex. She'd been to homes in Paris and the French countryside where the items purported to be of medieval origin turned out to be nothing more than latter-day imitations. Yet there was always the possibility. During times of political upheaval in France, property had been confiscated or looted and items ended up in the most improbable places. A set of tapestries now displayed in a New York museum had been found in a barn, used to wrap produce. And who knew what might be discovered in a remote monastery or a convent undergoing renovation . . . a manuscript or altarpiece seen by the monks or nuns solely as an object of religious inspiration, but truly a work of art hidden away for centuries. Possibilities excited Alex, whereas Madame Demy preferred a sure thing— a printed catalogue with proper description and provenance noted. They both knew there was a finite number of authentic medieval items of museum quality, and there was fierce competition for acquisition. Once a piece entered a museum's collection, it was basically off the market forever. That in itself was enough motivation for Alex to check out every prospect, however unlikely.

As Alex scanned the shelves, a group of worn leather covers on the upper shelf in the middle section caught her eye. She walked over and, standing on tiptoe, attempted to pull down one of the books. They were so tightly packed it was a struggle. Finally, she worked one loose. After a good yank, the book fell from the shelf, hit Alex on the head, then came apart, sending pages and dust flying.

Alex dropped to her hands and knees and began gathering

pages, which, she could see from the print, were not any older
than anything else she had found. Then her eyes rested on a
page that didn't appear to be the same as the others scattered
about the floor. It was penned by hand, the ink faded and
browned with age. It was written on parchment, the bottom
ripped off. Alex picked it up. It had the texture of ancient
parchment, almost a brittle feel. She placed it on the floor in
the light coming in from the window, hunched over it, and began to read.

The language was archaic French. Some of the words she
could decipher, others she could not. In places the ink was
faded, the script unreadable. It appeared to be a poem. She
read, translating the words:

> She met him in the garden
> A chance encounter
> But drawn as if by fate . . .
> . . . amidst the scent of . . .

The garden itself was described in detail—daisies, pansies,
lilies of the valley, carnations, periwinkle, and roses.

> He a simple tapissier, she a maiden fair . . .
> . . . the most fragrant blossom of them all . . .

Alex laughed quietly. Rather "flowery" language. She continued to read a lengthy description of the trees in the garden,
which included, among those she could translate, oak, pine,
holly, and orange.

Then something about the young woman . . . well . . . as
close as Alex could translate it into modern terms—she laughed
out loud at this thought—*a fruit ripe for plucking.*

Interesting. But hardly a medieval manuscript. It was a little poem, scratched out on faded parchment, and not a particularly skillful literary achievement at that. She should get
back to her work. Yet she was curious. She read on.

> To deny this love no truer sin
> so unto the house of the women
> who loved the Lord . . .

The convent? Alex wondered. Here the verse was torn. She glanced at the pages scattered on the floor, wondering if the piece torn from the bottom had also been tucked away in the book. The corner of a sheet stuck out from behind several pages. She pulled it out. It appeared to be a second page to the poem.

> *The labor of their love . . .*
> *buried there beneath the stone . . .*

More faded words.

> *and once more their love to blossom,*
> *the fruit, the passion of their love*
> *to be found in the village near . . .*

As Alex sat on the cold stone floor, staring down at the parchment, she wondered—was this merely a romantic little verse, penned by some sexually frustrated nun? Or was it more? It was very old. She could tell—from the language, from the parchment.

She heard a movement in the hall and looked up as the wrinkled, frowning nun entered the room. The woman's eyes darted across the floor. She glanced at the pile of books on the desk, made a clucking sound, then mumbled something like, *"Monsieur le Docteur Henri Martineau,"* or was it Marceau? *"est arrivé."* Alex was unsure of the nun's exact words, but it was quite clear, as the old woman stuffed the books back on the shelf, that Alex's time was up.

Alex gathered the pages from the floor. The nun stooped with surprising agility and picked up the torn poem as if it were just another page. She reached out for Alex's pages, inserted them all back inside the leather cover, placed it on a lower shelf, then motioned for Alex to follow her once more.

"Perhaps I could take a look at the tapestries?" Alex asked.

"Non aujourd'hui," the nun replied. Not today.

In the hall, a nun in a wheelchair appeared, pushed slowly by another nun. Alex and the old woman stepped aside to let them pass. The pushing nun nodded. The woman in the wheelchair looked up and smiled. So, Alex thought, there were other

residents still in the convent. She had wondered if the old wrinkled doorkeeper was the only inhabitant.

"*Demain?*" Alex asked. "Could I return tomorrow?"

No reply from the nun as they turned into the first hall and
ran into another nun, escorting a tall, thin, angular man. They
both wore somber expressions and neither spoke. The man
was young, probably in his mid-thirties, and pale, with blond
hair and a thin mustache, so light in color it nearly blended in
with his skin. *The doctor attending to the old Mother Superior?* Alex wondered as they passed.

"*Merci,*" Alex thanked the nun as she was led to the front
door. "*Demain?*" she asked again.

"*Au revoir, Madame Pellier,*" the nun said, and nothing
more. She opened the door.

Again Alex found herself standing outside the convent, a
warm irritation rising along the back of her neck. She wanted
to take a look at the tapestries, so she would have to return the
following day. Maybe Mother Alvère, who had issued the invitation, would be available tomorrow.

Alex started toward her car. A second car, a dark-green vehicle, was now parked beside hers.

IT WAS HALF past eight when Alex arrived at the Pelliers'.
She was greeted at the front door by Marie, the Pelliers' nurse
and caregiver. Pierre, who was not well, had retired, but Simone was sitting in the kitchen with Soleil. They were eating
chocolate ice cream and gingersnap cookies. In her arms,
Soleil cradled a beautiful porcelain doll that looked surprisingly like a real baby. With a tiny silver spoon, she lifted small
scoops of melting chocolate ice cream up to the doll's little
rosebud mouth.

Soleil bounced up and ran to her mother. "Mama, Mama,
regarde ma belle poupée!"

Each time they visited the Pelliers', Simone would present
Soleil with an expensive gift. Simone and Pierre had spoiled
Thierry, who came to them late in life, and Alex did not want
this for her daughter. Yet she said nothing. After Thierry died,
Alex swore they would stay close to Soleil's grandparents, but it
seemed, particularly since Alex had taken the position at the

Cluny, they had so little time to visit. Because of Pierre's ill health, the Pelliers were unable to travel to Paris. He had recently suffered a second stroke. He could no longer speak and was now confined to a wheelchair. Yet there was still something in his eyes, an alertness, and Alex knew that he still cherished these visits.

"*Oui, elle est belle, Sunny,*" Alex said to her daughter. "*Grandmère est très genereuse.*"

"*Oui, très genereuse,*" the child replied, smiling at her grandmother as she stroked the doll's cheek. "*Merci, Grandmère.*"

Marie had saved dinner in the oven. Alex thanked her, then sat down to eat as the older woman and Soleil finished their ice cream. As Alex visited with her mother-in-law, Soleil spoke to the doll in a soft voice. "You are a very special child," she said in English. "And I will speak to you in English so you will be bilingual."

Soleil's words made Alex smile. Since she was a toddler, just learning to communicate verbally, Alex had encouraged her daughter to speak both French and English.

After tucking Soleil into bed, Alex sat with Simone in the living room. Marie brought in a tray with cups and a carafe of coffee, then excused herself.

The room was large and elegant, yet comfortably furnished with authentic antiques—Louis XIV chairs, an Aubusson tapestry, imported oriental carpets, a large marble fireplace, and several paintings and sculptures Pierre had collected over the years—a Rodin, a Poussin, a small Delacroix drawing.

Simone rose to refresh their coffee. Even as she aged, Madame Pellier was a beautiful woman, with a regal, graceful posture. As a young woman, she had been an actress, but had given up the stage when she married the wealthy, dashing Pierre Pellier. Snowy white hair swirled around her face. Her wide-set blue eyes still shone, not only with outward beauty, but also with a deep inner strength and splendor. *Belle-mère,* the French word for mother-in-law. "Beautiful mother," the literal translation, and with Simone Pellier, Alex thought it truly fit.

"*S'il vous plaît,*" Alex said, rising. "Please, Simone, let me get that."

Simone motioned Alex to sit. "Relax, Alexandra. You've been working all day. I've spent the day playing with Soleil."

"*Merci.*" Alex sat, although she wondered if Simone wasn't tired from spending the day with her granddaughter. Simone was not a young woman, and Soleil was a rather rambunctious, active six-year-old.

But in truth, Alex *was* exhausted. She was frustrated by her experience at the convent and annoyed that she would have to return the following day. She had hoped to spend Sunday morning and early afternoon with Simone and Pierre before driving back to Paris.

"I'm afraid I must return to the convent tomorrow," she told her mother-in-law.

"Soleil is fine here with us. You know how much we enjoy having her. Perhaps we can plan another weekend when you're free of your business obligations."

"Yes, Simone, we should. Thank you for your help."

The following morning, Alex and Soleil walked with Grandmère the two blocks to the cathedral for Mass. When they returned, Marie had brunch set out on the sideboard in the dining room. Fresh peaches and strawberries, apricot cream-filled crepes, scrambled eggs, fresh orange juice, and dark rich coffee with milk and sugar sat alongside fine china and silver. Grandpère was waiting for them.

Madame Pellier prepared two cups, mixing sugar and milk into her husband's, then her own. She held the delicate cup up to Monsieur Pellier's lips. She didn't fuss, but performed this little task effortlessly, then visited with Alex and Soleil as she fed small bites of everything to Grandpère, carefully wiping his chin when he dribbled. They had always been devoted to one another. When Alex met them fourteen years ago they were elderly but, even then, their dedication to one another was evident. She had once hoped she and Thierry would share a long life together as his parents had, but Thierry had been gone for almost four years. The ache Alex felt now was not because of this loss, but because she had come to know that, even if Thierry had survived that fatal accident, there would never have been this deep love that Simone and Pierre Pellier shared. Even now as the old woman carefully wiped the spittle from the quivering chin of the frail, worn man in the wheelchair, Alex envied them.

Shortly after noon, Alex left again for the convent. She turned on the radio to help pass the time, feeling little enthusiasm for the drive, though she was eager to take another look inside the convent. Simone had packed strawberries and cookies, and Alex nibbled on a gingersnap as she gazed out at the vineyards running up and down the hillsides. Alex's father had told her the family had its roots in this rural area between Lyon and Nimes. According to his great-grandfather, the last of the Benoits to pronounce the name *Ben-wah*, they had immigrated to the States in the late 1700s to escape the political turmoil. The Benoits had supposedly descended from nobility, a belief upheld by nothing more then family tales passed down through the generations.

The sky darkened with clouds. Alex turned off the main road and onto the gravel road to the convent. It started to sprinkle. By the time she reached the dirt road, the rain was falling in thick sheets. The regular motion of the windshield wipers kept a steady beat as the heavy rain pelted across the window. She turned off the radio, nothing but static now.

Vaguely, through the rain-spattered window, she could make out the form of another car coming toward her—the same dark-green vehicle she had seen the day before—the doctor's car. But he was coming much too fast. She slowed almost to a stop as the other car continued straight at her and then at the last moment swerved, nearly running into her as they passed. Alex took a deep breath and glanced back. The man had slowed down too. He looked back. Was he waving at her? No, she could see now, his hand was raised, not in a wave, but a clenched fist as if the near accident had been her fault!

She stopped the car completely and watched as the vehicle disappeared into the mist. Road rage on this little dirt road? What kind of idiot was he, driving so fast? She took another deep breath, then cautiously continued up to the clearing outside the convent gate.

She parked, debating whether she should wait until the rain let up, or dash to the front door and hope someone would answer without the long wait she'd had yesterday. If she stood outside for more than a few seconds, she'd be drenched. Alex sat, trying to decide exactly what she should say. First, she would inquire about Mother Alvère's health, then politely request that she be allowed to speak with the Mother Superior if she was well, or at least be allowed inside to take another look, as she must return to Paris that afternoon. After a few minutes, the rain still pouring down, Alex reached over and picked up her briefcase. She put it over her head and ran. Puddles of water on the dirt path, which was now a river of mud, splashed up on her legs. She knocked on the door, her hand dripping wet. As the day before, no one answered. She knocked again. Then again. Finally, the window on the upper portion of the door slid open and the old wrinkled face appeared. The woman stared, her deep-set black eyes hollow and lifeless. And then, just as Alex was to inquire about Mother Alvère, but before she could speak, the old nun said, *"Elle est morte,"* and the window closed.

2

GAZING OUT INTO the dark tunnel, Jake listened to the rhythmic swishing of the rails as the train moved beneath the English Channel. He pulled out the breakfast Paul's wife, Dora, had packed for him that morning in London, cracked and peeled an egg, then ate it slowly. Halfway through the tunnel, he set his watch ahead an hour.

The shuttle emerged in France at daybreak, the sky a pale pink as they passed the soft undefined edges of Calais-Fréthun, then shifting to a thin yellow as the train moved rapidly through the French countryside, past textured fields of green and gold, touched by the low angle of the morning sun. Vehicles along the highways were vague, indistinct forms, and bridges flashed by. Full-length trains moving on rails in the opposite direction passed in a matter of seconds.

Three hours after leaving London, the train pulled into the terminal on the upper level of the Gare du Nord. Jake walked down to the lower level where a group of people stood, waiting for the next Métro train to arrive. It rumbled into the station, the doors slid open, a few people got off, and Jake stepped inside. He found a seat next to an old man clutching a worn leather bag. A pale girl with dyed black hair, too much makeup and a rose tattooed on her plump left upper arm took the seat next to him. Several tourist types who'd gotten on with Jake settled in across the aisle. It was Monday morning, the last week in May, and Jake could see that the summer visitors were already flooding into the city. At the next stop he stood, too antsy to sit. The tourists studied the map along the upper inside wall above the windows. Jake tightened his grip on the overhead bar as the train jerked and stopped at the next station. Two women chatted and laughed as they boarded. The taller had a head of ginger-colored hair, and it made him think of Rebecca and their last fight when he told her he was going to Paris.

"I thought it was something we'd do together after we had some savings. Doesn't it take several weeks to get a passport?" she asked, attempting to steady her voice.

He'd sent for the passport two months ago.

And then he told her he'd resigned his position as instructor of art at the university. He couldn't bring himself to tell her he'd cashed out his retirement account. Now that they were having this conversation, he could see how unfair he was being. He hadn't included her in this decision. Yet he felt some part of her had to know how controlled and stifled he'd felt these past few months, how their relationship had been suffering from his frustrations. They had talked about his teaching, how it hadn't been about the art, or even the students, for a long time. And his own painting wasn't going well. For months now he'd produced nothing.

He'd told her long ago about those days in Paris when he was a student, the only time he'd ever truly felt any freedom in his work. And yet he had produced nothing of significance during that year. He had been young and the world was big and filled with opportunity for adventure. If only he had settled down and harnessed that gift of creativity, which at times seemed to boil up and overflow. It wasn't until those last few weeks that he had latched on to whatever it was that was moving inside him, but by then he was almost out of money, his father was not well, and he knew he had to return home to Montana. The day after finals he left Paris.

Maybe it was a creativity that belonged only to the young, something that couldn't be relived or retrieved. Maybe this sudden, yet persistent urge to return to Paris was fueled by some kind of midlife crisis. He often found himself asking, "Well, Jacob Bowman, what the hell have you accomplished in these thirty-five years? What do you have to show for it all?"

"You could go with me," he told Rebecca, but even as he said it he knew it was an offer she would refuse, and perhaps this was the reason he placed it before her.

"Quit my job?" Her voice rose. "At least one of us should show some sense of responsibility." She was twisting the ring round her finger, a ring she had been wearing for over a year. They had yet to set a date. "I'm trying to understand."

Understand? It was a word that had entered their conversations repeatedly over the past few months. Rebecca would show up at his apartment unannounced, while he was trying to work, with good intentions and freshly baked bread, or cookies, or his favorite sandwich, as if she could nurture his talent and creativity. Couldn't she understand it was something he had to do himself, and didn't she realize when he was working he needed to be left alone? He tried to explain, but often ended up hurting her feelings, and he wondered if life with Rebecca would consist of apologies piled upon explanations and misunderstandings.

Just before he left for Paris, she told him she would join him for her two-week vacation in August. She still wore the ring.

And now he was here, walking along the quays next to the River Seine. Cruise boats and shuttles moved slowly through the dark waters. Vendors arranged their wares at the book and souvenir stalls—postcards, art prints, colorful coasters decorated with Monets and Manets, photos of Gothic gargoyles. He took a deep breath and sucked in the scents of the city, the cleansing smell of recent rain. Damn, he felt good! So free, as if a weight had been lifted. Even his bag felt light. He'd packed only essentials—socks and underwear, two pairs of jeans, a few shirts, running shoes and shorts, a pair of dress slacks, a semirespectable sports jacket, and shoes to wear on more formal occasions, though he had no plans for formal occasions. And his sketchpad and brushes. Paint and canvas he could get in Paris, but he'd brought along several brushes—worn just so, like old leather shoes, broken in to a comfortable fit.

When he reached the Pont D'Arcole, he walked over to the Ile de la Cité, then continued across the small island to the other side of the river—*La Rive Gauche,* the Left Bank—where he would look for a room. He stopped and rummaged in his wallet for the address of a hotel Paul had given him that morning in London. Paul said it was cheap, "not the Ritz by a long shot," but they could give him a weekly or monthly rate, and the location was good.

After a short distance, he realized he was just blocks from the International School of Art and Design, which he'd attended years ago. As he continued down the street, a ridiculous thought came to him—he would see someone he knew. He studied the faces of those he passed, and imagined they were old friends, students, grown up now. Then, just as he told himself how inane this thought was, he saw her.

A young woman, tall and slender, with long blond hair flowing down her back, exited a building. She had a familiar stature, a familiar gait—quick and graceful and elegant. Could it be? Jake felt something push deep inside his chest. He picked up his pace, walked past the woman, turned and looked. She smiled and nodded; so did he. She was attractive, but it was the face of a stranger. It was not Alex.

During his three-day stopover in London to visit Paul and Dora, they'd gathered one night with a group of old friends from their days in Paris. Frank Mason was in the city, working, also Fiona Grady, and they got together at a neighborhood pub—Paul; his wife, Dora; Frank; Fiona; and Frank's wife, Carolyn, whom Jake had evidently met at one time, although he couldn't recall. Names came up and Frank mentioned Alexandra Benoit, said the last he heard she was working somewhere in Paris, he thought at that medieval art museum on the Left Bank.

"The Cluny?" Fiona asked, and Carolyn said she thought the name had changed to something with *Moyen Age*—"Middle Ages"—in it.

"Musée National du Moyen Age, Thermes de Cluny," Paul said.

Fiona asked, "Didn't she marry some Frenchman from a wealthy family?"

"Thierry Pellier," Frank said. "I heard he was killed a few years ago in a speedboat race."

Jake didn't know about the accident, not that he'd have shed a tear for Thierry. But he did know that Alex was in Paris, working at the Musée National du Moyen Age. He had known that for the past six months.

There was a student he had been mentoring, a young man from Idaho. He was a brilliant painter. One day he had come to class ranting and raving about a paper he was writing for an art history class. His subject was "The Five Senses in Medieval Art." He'd requested an article at the library from a magazine called *Gazette des Beaux-Arts* to use in his research. It was an article about a set of tapestries called *La Dame à la Licorne—The Lady and the Unicorn.* The library did not subscribe to the magazine, but the librarian had ordered a copy through an interlibrary exchange. Much to the chagrin of the young artist from Idaho, when it arrived, it was in French. Jake offered to help with the translation.

The following day the student had dropped it off at his office. When Jake came in later that day, checked his box, and pulled the article out of the envelope, her name on the byline stared back at him, as vivid as if it had been outlined in bright yellow marker. *Alexandra Pellier,* Curator, Musée National du Moyen Age, Thermes de Cluny, Paris, France.

He found the address Paul had given him on Rue Monge, just off Rue des Ecoles. A weathered sign hung from the building two stories up. *Le Perroquet Violet.*

Jake entered and climbed the stairs. In the lobby a man sat at the counter, reading a rumpled newspaper. A parrot in a large wire cage sat at the end of the counter. *Le Perroquet.* But red and green and yellow, not purple as advertised. The parrot cocked its head and ruffled its feathers as it moved back and forth in the cage along the narrow wooden bar of a swing.

The man glanced up over his reading glasses. *"Bonjour."*

"Bonjour," the parrot screeched. Jake jumped, then laughed. The bird continued moving back and forth, rocking the swing.

The man smiled. His bushy white eyebrows rose as if he was waiting for Jake to speak. Crescents of doughy flesh, like puffy half-moons, created dark shadows under his eyes.

"*Un chambre avec salle de bain?*" Jake asked.

"*Combien de temp?*" the man replied, and Jake said at least a month, maybe longer. The man nodded, told Jake the price, said it included breakfast. "*Votre passeport, s'il vous plaît.*" He pulled an enormous leather-bound book out from under the counter.

"*S'il vous plaît,*" the bird mimicked in its high-pitched tone. "*Merci, merci.*"

Jake laughed again. A well-mannered bird. No rude pirate's parrot here.

The man's smile widened, a practiced smile. Jake imagined he wasn't the first guest entertained by this bird.

He asked if he could see the room before taking it. The bushy eyebrows rose—puzzled, insulted almost. The smile faded. The man took a key, which was hooked on a plastic key chain, from a slotted box behind the counter, then called out in a loud voice, "André."

"André," the parrot squealed.

A young man appeared and after a rapid conversation with the old man, in which the keys were handed over, something said about the "young American," the boy motioned for Jake to follow him.

They walked up one more flight of stairs. A hint of lemon cleaner lingered in the air, mixed with the smell of cigarette smoke.

Young American. Jake shook his head, finding this as delightfully absurd as the purple parrot that wasn't purple. Yet it was nice to think that he was still considered young. When he was in his teens, and even into his twenties and early thirties, people had mistaken him for much younger. He was tall and had, he knew, on occasion been referred to as gangly, perhaps a little unsure of himself, which probably contributed to his being taken for younger. He'd filled out over the years, a little thicker through the middle, and hoped he'd taken on a certain air of confidence. There was a hint of premature gray in his dark hair.

The boy unlocked the door and motioned for Jake to enter while he waited in the hall.

The room was small. One bed, a double with a dingy blue bedspread. A tall narrow window with a wooden shutter. Jake opened the shutter. Light fell into the room. Morning light.

Painting light. The price was right, the location good. He walked back to the door where the young man waited, cleaning his fingernails with a pocketknife, somehow managing to look bored and amused at the same time.

"Je la prends," Jake told him. He would take the room.

After completing the registration form, Jake got the key, returned to the room, and unpacked. Carefully, he unwrapped his brushes, which he'd covered with a soft cloth and enclosed in a narrow wooden box. In the bathroom he found a drinking glass, placed the brushes in it, bristles up, then set it on the bureau. He showered, dressed, and left his room. He knew he was just a short distance from the Cluny, Alex's museum. He considered walking over.

"I'm working in the city now," he could tell her casually, "and I heard you were here as well, at the medieval museum." He might mention visiting Paul in London, getting together with Frank and Fiona, how her name had come up in conversation and how he just thought he'd drop by and say hello since he was in the neighborhood.

It had been fourteen years since they had seen each other. During that time she'd married and been widowed. She had a responsible position at a respected museum, specializing in medieval art, the very era in which she'd shown an interest as a student. She was a grown-up now, and what was he? No job. Painting in Paris. In fact, not even painting, yet. Contemplating painting. Maybe he was still the kid he'd been those many years ago, as unlikely to impress her now as he had when they were young.

He would get his supplies. He could go to the Cluny later, after he was settled.

He remembered an art co-op near the school and found it just off Boulevard Saint Michel, the same location it had been years ago.

"Vous désirez?" the clerk, a pretty young Asian girl, asked.

"Merci," Jake replied. He asked about the co-op, how did one join, what were the arrangements.

"You're American?" she asked in English.

"Yes."

"You've not been in before." She spoke with a British accent. She was a pretty girl, though very thin.

"Just arrived."

"Welcome to Paris," she said with a smile.

He filled out an application, then wandered around the store, looking, thinking, rejoicing in the fact that he was here once more in Paris. He selected several tubes of paint, one new brush. He bought two medium canvases, a palette, and a small easel.

As he walked out and down the street, he felt a surge of energy pump through him. Panic or elation, he wasn't sure which. Sometimes there wasn't much difference. What if he couldn't paint? He had dreamed of this for years now, returning to Paris. He'd quit his job, taken the money from his retirement account. This was it. He was here. Here in Paris. And another thought, no matter how much he tried to dislodge it from his mind, kept returning. He was here. And so was Alex.

3

IT WAS LATE Sunday evening when they arrived home from Lyon. Sunny had slept most of the drive but was grumpy when Alex woke her Monday for school. Alex would have to admit she was rather grumpy herself, and tired from the long weekend.

Shortly after she arrived at the museum Alex sorted through her mail and checked her calendar for the week. A special tapestry exhibition would open Friday at the Grand Palais with an invitation-only reception on Thursday evening.

The pieces included in this retrospective were primarily museum-owned, out on loan, and Alex had seen most of them. The Cluny had loaned *Le Toucher,* a piece from *The Lady and the Unicorn* set. The Cloisters, the New York Metropolitan's medieval museum, had sent over a piece from *The Hunt of the Unicorn* series. But another tapestry in the exhibit, a work produced in the late fifteenth or early sixteenth century, was privately owned and had never been publicly displayed. Alex had seen photographs—in fact had used the piece in a comparative study because of similarities in style, color, and theme to the set of unicorn tapestries in the Cluny—but she had never seen the tapestry itself. It depicted a mythological scene featuring

Pegasus, the winged horse. Alex was thrilled when she learned
it would be displayed. Perhaps she could speak with the owner.
If she could learn more about its history, it might provide a clue
regarding the creation of *The Lady and the Unicorn.* The meaning and origin of the six-piece set had been debated by art historians for centuries. But when she spoke with Madame Demy,
who had been instrumental in obtaining *Le Pégase* for the exhibition, Alex learned that the tapestry would be displayed only if
it could be done anonymously. Madame Demy would reveal
nothing about the mysterious owner.

About midmorning Alex left her office and walked down
the hall. She wanted to talk to Madame Demy about a possible
return to Sainte Blandine's. Even after the semidisastrous
weekend, Alex was eager to go back. It had become almost a
challenge, to have a closer look inside the convent, to get by
that witch at the gate.

Madame Demy sat at her desk. She was a plain woman—
small with brown hair just starting to gray, pulled back in a
tight little bun. She wore nothing but gray or black, and Alex
thought she looked more like someone's nanny than the distinguished, well-educated Director of the Musée du Moyen Age,
Thermes de Cluny. Other than some type of decorative brooch
pinned to her right lapel—today a pink enameled rose—she
was devoid of any ornamentation.

"*Bonjour,* Madame Pellier." The two women had been
working together for almost three years now, and Alex had
known Madame Demy for over twelve, but they always addressed one another with the formal *Madame.* Alex couldn't
imagine anyone calling Madame Demy by her given name,
which was Béatrice. If it hadn't been for her published works
and guides put out by the museum, Alex wouldn't even know
her first name.

"*Bonjour,* Madame Demy."

The older woman motioned Alex to sit.

She told Madame Demy about her trip to the convent. "I
would like to take another look in the library. I was surprised
at the number of volumes, though most of them appeared to
be more recent publications. But I was there for such a short
time, and I wasn't able to examine the textiles or tapestries
that Mother Alvère spoke of in her letter."

"And yet you think there might be something for us?"

"I do. Perhaps we could contact the Archbishop of Lyon," Alex suggested, "to make arrangements for another visit."

Madame Demy opened a desk drawer and pulled out a folder, then reached for the reading glasses hanging from a gold chain around her neck and perched them on her small round nose. She opened the file and ran her finger down the first page. "The building, as I understand, has been owned by the archdiocese for the better part of the past hundred years. The contents are still the property of the order. It is, or was, Mother Alvère's wish to defray the expenses at the retirement home with proceeds from the sale. . . ." She closed the folder. "The archdiocese would certainly be obligated to take care of the nuns. Perhaps the implication that Blandine's holds a wealth of medieval treasures was wishful thinking on the old nun's part, involving some degree of pride." She removed the glasses and let them fall over her heavy bosom. "Or perhaps . . . at ninety-two, the mind is not always clear. Some confusion. But now . . . now that the Reverend Mother has passed on."

Alex nodded.

"These older orders . . . often quite autonomous. But who knows what might be going on at the convent now, if there is any kind of leadership."

Alex nodded again, thinking of the difficulty she had had in gaining entry to Sainte Blandine's. "That's why I thought it best to give the Archbishop a call. Communication with the nuns has been through our letters, which can be time consuming."

Madame Demy thought for a moment. "Yes, if you think it might be worth the effort."

"*Oui,*" Alex answered, "I do." She pushed her chair back.

"You're looking forward to Thursday evening?" Madame Demy asked.

"Very much."

"You are bringing a guest?"

"No," Alex answered. A guest? That was almost funny. She hadn't had a date in months.

Madame Demy had always been especially kind to Alex, interested in the younger woman's social life and Alex's daughter, Soleil. The woman had a way of drawing one into conversation, but giving little of herself away. Alex had had lengthy and intimate conversations with her superior, only to realize later that Madame Demy had said little about her own life. On a personal level, Alex knew no more about the woman than she had when she met her years ago. She knew the Director had no husband, that she lived with an elderly uncle. He was said to own the château where they spent weekends. Alex had learned this from other members of the museum staff. The old uncle was enormously wealthy, also somewhat eccentric. Of course, no one had ever met him, and Alex sometimes wondered if he existed. It sounded like such a cliché—the wealthy, eccentric, old uncle.

Alex went back to her office. She called Lyon and was told the Archbishop was in Italy and wouldn't return until midweek. When she asked if someone else could arrange a meeting at Sainte Blandine's, she was put on hold for several minutes, then spoke with a woman who had no knowledge of the situation at the convent, but would have the Archbishop call when he returned.

JAKE WOKE, CONFUSED, in a dim room, thinking he was back home in Missoula, then at Paul's flat in London. He'd had little sleep in the past few days, and he didn't think his body had adjusted to the time change or recovered from the jet lag. He rolled over, reached for his watch on the nightstand, and checked the time in a thin stream of light filtered through a gap in the shutter. Almost noon, two hours late for breakfast at his hotel. He'd go out, get something to eat, then maybe check out a museum or two.

He stopped for café au lait and brioche and sat outdoors, then headed down Boulevard Saint Michel, then along the Seine to the Musée d'Orsay.

He wandered through the lower level, the Delacroix, the Ingres, the early Degas and Manets, for over an hour. After skimming the Art Nouveau on the second level, he climbed to the third where he spent the next three hours lingering over the Impressionists and Post-Impressionists. He studied van Gogh's portrait of Madame Ginoux, recalling a paper he had written comparing this work to a portrait of the same subject by Gauguin. He remembered standing in front of this very painting with Alex, comparing the work of the two artists, and he wondered if there was anywhere in Paris he could go without thinking of her.

After dinner he returned to his room and lay on his bed. He felt tired, but couldn't sleep. He opened the shutter and gazed out the window. There was an interesting play of light on the building across the street, the reflection of the evening sun. He moved closer and studied the light, which moved and shifted until it turned an evening blue. He walked over to the dresser where he had stacked his canvases and paints. He put up the easel and squeezed a snake of ultramarine blue onto his palette. Then, using a thin wash of turpentine and paint, and a fine-pointed sable brush, he began to sketch in an outline.

4

EARLY THURSDAY MORNING Jake put on his shorts and running shoes and left the hotel. He generally liked to get in a run three or four times a week, but hadn't been out since he left Montana. He'd spent the past few days visiting museums and attempting to paint—with frustrating results.

He ran down Rue Monge to Saint Germain, then toward Boulevard Saint Michel. Other than a few delivery vans dropping off vegetables and bakery items, there was little traffic. It felt good to get out, to work up a sweat. He turned onto Rue des Ecoles and ran along a small grassy park enclosed within a circular fence. Wasn't the Cluny on the other side of the park? He glanced over and saw the crenellated wall, the stone tower and dormer windows of the two-story building.

Maybe he should drop by the museum later today, ask about Alex, say hello. It was his fourth day in Paris, surely a respectable amount of time to wait before casually looking up an old friend.

Old friend? Well, they had been friends, at first. Best friends. She was eighteen when they met, yet intellectually and emotionally mature beyond her years. He was twenty, probably somewhat lacking in maturity, or at least lacking any sense of responsibility. He had been madly in love—with Paris, with the life he was living, with the freedom of being young, in a foreign land, in love with having no responsibility or obligation to anyone or anything.

He had been in love with Alex, and at times he thought she loved him too.

It wasn't until second semester when they were in the same art history class that they started spending time together, though he'd had an eye on her since the first day Paul introduced them. They would go to the museums and libraries together and sometimes just sit and talk. She confided in him that she was on scholarship, that her father was the principal at a Catholic grade school in Baltimore in a financially depressed parish, and it paid very little. This surprised Jake, as he'd assumed she came from money, just something about the way she carried herself.

She was good for him, serious about her studies, organized and reliable. She was competitive when it came to grades, and collaborating on a project with Alex was a sure A, though she never let him slide by on her efforts. He had to do his share of the research and work.

Often, particularly if it was dark out, he would walk her home to the student pension where she shared a room with three other girls. She'd invite him in—not to her room, but to a small lobby where guests and students would sit watching TV. One night, after everyone else had left, he kissed her teasingly on the neck, nibbled her ear, then kissed her on the cheek, the forehead, then on the lips. Slowly, then passionately, she responded. But then, abruptly, she pulled back. "I've still got studies to do. Thank you for walking me home."

During the day, they became inseparable, studying together, visiting the museums, talking. It seemed they could talk about anything other than how they felt about each other. One night as they sat alone in the lobby, they started kissing, deeply, intimately. He slipped his hand inside her blouse. At first, she didn't resist. He felt her soft, small breasts, the nipples firm. Then she placed her hand over his. He could feel the tremor. She said, "Not now," as she removed his hand.

Yet several nights later, he noticed she had failed to button the top two buttons on her blouse. An invitation surely. That evening she didn't resist when he touched her breasts, and when he slowly slipped his hand inside her pants, her entire body tensed, then relaxed. He was sure she wanted this as much as he did. Then as his fingers moved down, she grasped his wrist, and murmured, "Please, . . ." then, "no."

He wanted more than anything to make love to her, to tell her he loved her. But the words wouldn't come. He had so little to offer her.

"I . . . I . . . ," she stammered, "I want to wait."

Wait? he wondered. Wait for what? For love? He was in love. He'd never felt like this before. Didn't she feel the same?

"I want to wait," Alex said, hesitating, "until . . . until, I'm married."

He didn't even know how to respond to that. *Married?* They were too young, at least he was. There were too many things he wanted to do before thinking about something that serious.

The following Friday night he dropped by Alex's pension to see if she'd like to go over to a café on Rue Saint Jacques where students from their school hung out.

Anna, one of Alex's roommates, said she wasn't in. When Jake asked if she'd gone over to Saint Jacques, Anna hesitated, then said, "I'm not sure where she's gone," and it occurred to Jake that Alex had gone out with someone else. He and Alex never went on real dates. He could barely afford to feed himself and buy his art supplies. And verbally they'd never made a commitment. But did she think this was perfectly okay, going out with someone else?

The following afternoon he called, and again he was told Alex wasn't in. He walked over Sunday afternoon to see if she wanted to go to the library to work on a report for class. It was then that he saw her stepping into a shiny new Alfa Romeo, a tall handsome man—shit, he must have been over thirty—holding the door for a smiling Alex. She didn't see Jake.

The next day at school, after class, she asked if he'd meet her for lunch. She sounded very serious.

At lunch after they had eaten, talking about absolutely nothing important, she said, "I've met someone."

"What do you mean?" But of course he knew.

"He's from Lyon."

As if this was some kind of explanation.

"It's just that I'd like to get to know him better."

"What about us?"

"Oh, Jake, I just . . . I . . ."

He could see she wanted him to say something, but she was the one who'd called this meeting.

For several moments they sat staring at each other.

What was he to say—*this is okay with me, Alex?* Did she expect him to give his blessing? "I thought maybe you'd give us a shot, Alex. I mean we're just getting to know each other too." He was thinking of those nights in the pension lobby, his touching her, her response, yet always pulling back, always stopping him. And now she was formally announcing it—she was telling him to go away.

"I'm confused, Jake." She said this as if she wanted him to console her, as if he should offer some comfort at her distress. She stared down at her coffee cup now. She couldn't continue this conversation eye to eye.

"So you're dumping me for some rich guy?" He was shaking so badly he could hardly speak.

"Rich guy?" She looked up, puzzled, but at the same time it appeared she might cry.

"Alfa Romeo and all," Jake hissed.

"You've been spying on me?"

"And you've been sneaking around behind my back. I thought there was more to you than that, Alex. I thought you . . ."

She was crying now. Part of him wanted to put his arm around her and say, *Alex, I love you, don't you love me?* But he was so angry he couldn't speak. For several moments the silence was so severe he could hear the clanking of the silverware at the next table, a child fussing across the room. He got up, threw his napkin on the table. "Well, let me know how things work out, Alex, let me know when you decide there's more to life than fancy cars and rich old men."

He walked out, thinking, *this isn't the end, Alex will come to her senses*. But it was the last real conversation they had.

WHEN HE GOT back to the hotel, Jake studied the painting he'd been working on for the past few days. The composition included the window in his room and the building across the street, because he liked the lines and angles. He'd added the form of a woman sitting naked before the window, the softness of her body contrasting with the sharp angles. He could see now that the woman wasn't right, her proportions wrong. Had he already forgotten the shapes and curves? He needed a live model.

He walked over to the co-op and found a bulletin board just inside the front door. Handwritten ads and computer-produced notices advertised models' fees and studio space. Jake pulled a pen out of his pocket, a scrap of paper from his billfold.

"Could I be of assistance?" A voice from behind.

He turned. It was the young Asian woman who'd helped him several days earlier.

"I need a model for a painting I'm working on."

"I've been going to a studio up at Montmartre," she said. "There are classes during the day. Live models Monday, Wednesday, and Friday evenings, but no instruction. We share the fee. It's quite a good price."

She wore a black turtleneck and tight black pants. Jake didn't think she was wearing a bra and he could see the outline of her nipples under her shirt.

"Do you need the instruction?" she asked.

"Just the model," he answered.

"There's a male on Monday, female on Wednesday and Friday."

"I'm looking for a female."

She grinned as if he'd said something amusing.

"A female model," he said.

"Yes, of course." She gave him a phone number and address and he scribbled it down. "Do come by," she said, again with a smile.

"Thanks," he answered.

She turned and he watched as she walked back to the counter in the middle of the store where another customer was waiting. She had a small waist, a nice curve to her hip.

He left the co-op without bothering to take any additional information from the board. Maybe he'd give it a try, go up to Montmartre Friday night. He hadn't thought about going to a studio, and he certainly didn't need instruction. What he had in mind was a model coming to his room. He glanced at the number and address she'd given him, then stuck it in his pocket. Maybe he'd take today off, get some distance from the painting. Today he'd drop by the Cluny.

The entry to the museum was a bright red door with black iron hardware and ornamentation, leading into an open cobblestone courtyard. Gargoyles reached out overhead, protruding from below the decorative stone parapet of the two-story medieval building.

Jake bought his ticket and inquired if Madame Pellier was in. The girl at the desk asked him to wait while she sold tickets to the man and woman standing behind him, then she picked up a phone and spoke to someone and told him Madame Pellier would not be available this morning. Would he like to leave a message?

"Merci, non," Jake said.

After a quick run through the first level, he climbed the stairs. He wanted to take a look at the medieval tapestry set, *La Dame à la Licorne, The Lady and the Unicorn,* which was displayed in a large round hall on the second floor. Since reading Alex's article he'd been eager to take another look at the tapestries.

He had come here often with Alex when they were students, although Jake had never thought of tapestries as real art. Textiles. Handicrafts. But Alex had loved them.

Jake stood, looking around the room. Four tapestries hung on the opposite wall. There was a large empty space where a fifth tapestry had obviously been removed. He read the notice, which said the piece called *Touch, Le Toucher,* was out on loan and could be viewed at a tapestry exhibition at the Grand Palais from June fourth through August sixth.

A single tapestry hung on the curved wall between the two entrances into the room. All of the tapestries were immense— each with slightly different proportions, but Jake guessed they ranged in size from ten or twelve feet in height, the width varying from ten to at least fifteen feet. All done in rich reds and blues—a limited palette, a skillful use of color—they were exquisite. He didn't remember this, how truly elegant they were, and he couldn't help but wonder if perceptions

change over time. He tried to recall details of the article he'd
translated for his student, Alex's article. He remembered that
five of the tapestries represented the five senses. Each was labeled with a small illuminated plaque, the title in several different languages.

His eyes moved from tapestry to tapestry. Each incorpo-
rated a garden island and a slender, ornately clad maiden.
In four of the tapestries, another woman, a servant, stood by
her side. A lion and unicorn appeared in each, and flowers and
miniature animals—rabbits, monkeys, dogs, goats, and foxes—
all were on the island and scattered in the background. A coat of
arms, three crescents on a band of blue, adorned banners and
shields prominent in each piece.

Jake studied the first four tapestries, picking out details in
each depicting the sense it represented. The maiden in *Le Goûte*
held a bird in one hand and reached into a dish offered by the
handmaiden with the other, obviously picking out something to
taste, maybe for herself or the bird. In *L'Ouïe* the maiden
played a portable organ. The unicorn in *La Vue* perched its front
hooves on the fair maiden's lap as she held up a mirror in which
the animal studied its reflection. It appeared docile, content, as
the woman placed one hand lovingly on its back, and Jake remembered Alex's explanation of the symbolism of the unicorn.
The elusive unicorn could be captured only by a virgin. In
L'Odorat the maiden was weaving a wreath of flowers, the tiny
handmaiden holding a tray of blossoms.

Several people had gathered in the circular hall, quietly
viewing the tapestries, moving from one to the next or sitting
on the small metal benches, which were arranged in the middle of the room so you could sit and contemplate the tapestries
on the wall opposite the entries, then turn for a perfect view of
the piece hanging alone.

As Jake turned to study the final tapestry, *A Mon Seul
Désir,* a group entered the hall. They didn't look like typical
tourists. Some of them carried cameras, but the men all wore
suits and ties, the women dresses, business suits, and heels.

"The visual delights of the tapestries alone make the set a
fascinating study," the guide said, "but the history, both known
and speculated, the theories and conjectures, the possible origin
and meaning, their discovery in the Château Boussac in the

mid-1800s by the popular French novelist George Sand only enhance the mystery and romance of the six-piece set." She spoke English. Jake couldn't see the guide, hidden by the group gathered in front of *Le Goûte*. But he recognized the voice.

He stood, feeling a force, first in his gut and then higher as if he had been hit violently in the chest, as if the air he breathed was being forced out of him.

It was Alex.

"The more recent history since their discovery in Boussac," she continued, "is much easier to trace. In a historical study, it is often easiest to start from what we know as fact and work back from that point."

A tall man in the group moved over and Jake now had a perfect view of her, though Alex didn't appear to see him. Jake was stunned to be so close, though he knew this was exactly why he had come. Yet he didn't feel prepared, and for some strange reason he hadn't fully realized that after fourteen years she might have changed.

The lithe, slender body he remembered had taken on the more mature, fuller shape of a woman. She was still slender, but there was a fullness in her breasts, a roundness in her hips. She wore a pale-blue business suit, short enough to show off her shapely legs, long enough to be respectable. What shocked him most was the fact that she had cut her hair. Her long blond hair, which had fallen past her waist, now barely reached her shoulders.

Jake stared at Alex, no longer a pretty nineteen-year-old girl, the image he had carried with him all these years, but now a stunningly beautiful woman.

"George Sand discovered the tapestries in the castle of Boussac in the Department of Creuse probably sometime between 1835 and 1844, while visiting the subprefect whose apartment and offices were located in the château." Her voice sounded so familiar, yet that unexpected mixture of sweetness and authority took him by surprise. "Their existence was brought to light in her writings, most notably in her novel *Jeanne,* published in 1844. The tapestries had been privately owned by descendents of the Comte de Carbonnières until the purchase of the château and its contents in 1835 by the parish of Boussac. In 1882 the six tapestries were acquired by the

State and publicly displayed the following year in the Museum of the Thermae and the Cluny, at the time under the control of the Commission for Historic Monuments. After the Liberation of World War II, the museum was renovated and the circular hall where we now stand was constructed. A recently installed lighting system combines optical fibers and lenses to ensure the preservation and also bring out the natural textures and colors of the tapestries."

Jake moved in closer. Several others who'd entered the hall earlier crowded closer too.

Alex explained that *Le Toucher* was out on loan and could be viewed at a special exhibition opening Friday at the Grand Palais.

"Based on the family arms," she continued as she turned and pointed to the crescents on the unicorn's cape, "it is now generally agreed that the origin of the set goes back to the Le Viste family of Lyon, and they probably arrived in Boussac as the property of an estate passed through two centuries of descendents. They were most likely created for Jean Le Viste in the late fifteenth or early sixteenth century.

"One can't help but believe, on observing the tapestries, that they were created to celebrate a romance." She looked briefly at the group, still not seeing him, then turned back to the tapestry *Le Goûte* and motioned with her hand. "The lion and the unicorn suggest strength and purity of the marriage union. The garden setting, the flowers, the trees have often been associated in both art and literature with the romantic ideals of courtly love. Even the animals, which appear within the *mille-fleurs* background, take on symbolic meaning. The rabbits suggest fertility, which, of course, in medieval days was an important aspect of the marital union. The dogs are symbolic of fidelity. The oak trees represent strength and perseverance; the orange trees, fruitfulness."

She turned back to the group and it was then that her eyes stopped, her voice faltered for a mere second. "And, and . . . this, the belief that they were created to celebrate a romance, has been a theory held by many." Her eyes locked with Jake's. Her calm, controlled, yet slightly mischievous smile had not changed at all.

"The repetition of the family arms," she continued, her

voice composed again, "displayed on lances and shields, implements of battle, strongly suggests a theme of war or combat. An interesting melding of themes—love and war." Alex smiled, not at her group, Jake thought, but at him.

"The Le Viste family came from Lyon, where they had achieved great wealth as cloth merchants," Alex explained. "The family eventually came to Paris, where several members were appointed to high positions in the royal administration, Jean Le Viste being one of the first lay presidents of the Court of Aides. Yet none of the Le Vistes was ever honored with a noble title. The commission of the tapestries may have been an opportunity for the proud Jean Le Viste to display the family arms, a pretension to nobility. The lances and shields fit nicely with this idea, as Jean Le Viste had visions of himself as a knight, even requesting in his will that he appear in a stained-glass window in the family chapel of Vindecy in a coat of mail, although he was never knighted.

"The obvious display of the family arms suggests they were created for a special occasion, sometime after the death of Jean's father in 1457, when Jean IV became the head of the family with the right to bear the full arms. Perhaps they were commissioned in 1489 in celebration of his appointment as president of the Court of Aides."

A short woman standing in the front asked if the tapestries weren't created to celebrate a marriage.

"If we accept the theory that they were created as a marriage gift," Alex answered, "several problems arise. Jean Le Viste married the noblewoman Geneviève de Nanterre most likely in the 1470s, but the style of the tapestries suggests a later date. Looking within the time frame generally accepted for their creation, we find no documented marriages of male members in the Le Viste family. Jean Le Viste had three daughters, Claude, Jeanne, and Geneviève, but no sons. If created to celebrate a daughter's marriage, the bridegroom's family arms, as well as the father's, would be represented. As you can see, the only arms are those belonging to the Le Viste family."

Jake stood and stared and watched Alex as she smiled, pointed, and answered questions put to her by several members of her group who were quite obviously British. He remembered that years ago, just days after they were formally introduced, she had accused him of staring at her. He had indeed been staring at her, but hadn't she been staring at him too?

"You've been staring at me," she'd said.

"Yes," he had admitted. "I'm an artist. I look at things. I study things."

"Things?"

"You've got an interesting face. I'd like you to pose for me someday."

She'd looked at him as if he'd just asked her to take all her clothes off.

He studied her now. She had a lovely face, but he still couldn't determine exactly how all the parts came together so beautifully. Her nose was narrow and a little long, with a slight bump that showed up in profile. It was not a beautiful nose. If plucked from her face and lined up with a random group of freestanding noses, you certainly wouldn't choose it as the most beautiful. And her eyes were perhaps a bit narrow, her lips rather thin. Yet all the parts came together. There was almost a regal look about her.

"The final piece," Alex said, "is the most mysterious of all. Is the tapestry an introduction, or perhaps a conclusion, to the set representing the five senses? Or is it the only remaining piece of another lost set? How do we interpret the inscription, *A Mon Seul Désir?* 'To my one desire'—a dedication? A gift to a maiden, one's true love? Or could the tapestry, which pictures the fair maiden returning a necklace to a jewel box, represent the renunciation of pleasures evoked by the senses?"

The woman in the sixth tapestry stood before a tent, which Alex described as the type that would be set up at a battle encampment. The small handmaiden held a box that resembled a miniature treasure chest, and the woman appeared to be taking or replacing jewels from the box.

"A Neoplatonic theme has often been given to the set of tapestries. The ancient philosophy of Plato suggests that man is engaged in a constant struggle between senses and reason, the soul chained to the body in an unceasing quest to attain the 'Higher Good.' Only through reasoning could order be brought to chaos, a spiritual liberation through voluntarily renouncing the passions of the senses. Might the final tapestry represent freedom attained only by renunciation of these pleasures? And wouldn't this fit nicely with the theme of war?"

When the group had finished studying the final tapestry, Alex led them toward the exit, introducing them to Dominique Bonnaire, who would escort them through the remainder of the museum.

Jake stood back from the group. When the last of the British tourists left the room, he and Alex were alone. She walked toward him.

He had an urge to reach out and touch her, kiss her on the cheek. No, fully on the mouth. She was wearing the most luscious shade of lipstick. But as they looked at each other, he couldn't help but remember. She had dumped him. Dumped him for Thierry. It had been fourteen years now, yet the image of the last time he saw her was still vivid. It was the end of spring semester. He was sitting in class, hunched over his last final. Alex had finished her exam, and was waiting outside the classroom. He glanced out into the hall. He knew she wanted to talk to him. There were so many things left unsaid. He didn't want to hear a "we can still be friends" speech, so he took his time, his eyes back on his paper. He knew she had one more final. When he looked up again, she was gone.

"I didn't expect to find you here," Jake said. "Well, here, but not *here*. I thought they'd have you locked away in an office somewhere."

"I don't usually do tours, but it was a special group, British dignitaries. VIP treatment."

Jake nodded and smiled. "You look good, Alex."

"So do you, Jake." She smiled too. "I like your hair." He knew she was referring to the gray that had started to appear in the past few years. "Very dignified."

"Yeah." He laughed nervously, running his hand through his hair. He was tense as hell, and Alex looked so damn calm. Like she had been expecting him, or maybe this just wasn't a big deal to her, his showing up in her museum. "You cut *your* hair," he said, then added, "It looks nice."

"About six years ago, just after my daughter was born. It was too much, with the new baby and all."

"Daughter?" For some reason Jake hadn't considered this.

He knew she had lost her husband, but it hadn't occurred to him that she might have children.

"Soleil. She's six."

"Soleil? Sun? Sunshine?"

"She's very bright," Alex said and smiled again. "I generally call her Sunny."

Yes, Jake thought, Alex's daughter would be bright.

They stood silently for a few moments, then Alex asked, "How long will you be in Paris?"

"For a while. I'm not sure how long."

"Are you alone?" Alex's eyes scanned the room. There were a few other people, moving about the circular hall.

"Yes."

"You didn't bring along a wife?"

"No wife."

"Married?"

"No."

"Ever?"

"No." He thought it only fair that he mention Rebecca. "Engaged."

Alex looked around the room again. A group of tourists with a guide stood before the first tapestry. "So where is your fiancée?" she asked.

Before Jake could reply, Alex laughed. She had the most delightful laugh. "Oh, Jake," she said, "you never were big on commitment. You didn't bring her with you to Paris, did you?"

He laughed too. "She's a nurse." As if this were adequate explanation for why she wasn't here with him in Paris. "She's joining me late this summer, in August."

"In Paris, or in holy matrimony?" Alex smiled again, a teasing smile.

"In Paris." He smiled.

"A nurse? A responsible, kind woman. Good. That's good."

Jake wasn't sure what she meant by that. Good that he had found a responsible woman? As if that's what he needed.

"Let's go to my office where we can sit and visit." Alex motioned, and he followed.

When they got to her office, she asked if he'd like coffee, and he said yes. As she got up, then left the room, Jake looked around. The walls were covered with certificates and diplomas. A large dark antique-looking file cabinet stood against one wall. A few folders were arranged in a neat pile on one corner of the desk. Large art books filled the bookshelves. Everything was tidy, just what he would expect of Alex. Photos of a beautiful little blond girl sat on the desk. She looked very much like her mother. She had Alex's eyes, her hair.

Alex returned with coffee. "You knew I was here, at the Cluny?"

"I spent a couple days in London with Paul Westerman. We went out with Frank and Fiona. Frank said you were working here at the Cluny."

"How are they?" She sounded excited that he had seen these old friends recently. "The last I heard, Fiona was teaching, and Paul and Frank, what are they doing now?"

He told her Fiona was still teaching, that Frank had recently taken a position with an investment firm. "Paul's involved in art acquisitions and appraisals. He works for a company that investigates art fraud and theft and verifies authenticity for clients."

"Really?" Her eyes widened. "That sounds like interesting work."

"You know Paul. He had a few stories to share. We all went out the night before I left London."

"I've lost track of so many of the group," Alex said. "I hear from Anna now and then, and Geri always sends a card at Christmas, but the rest of the old gang . . . Old gang? We sound like a couple old folks sharing memories."

"Lots of memories."

"And you, Jake," Alex asked, "what are you doing now?"

"I was teaching in Montana, University of Montana in Missoula." He paused, took a sip of coffee.

"Was?"

He nodded.

"And now?"

"I'm taking some time off. I'm staying here in Paris for a while. I'm painting."

"A sabbatical?"

"No, not really." He hesitated again, another slow sip of coffee. "I really wasn't that happy teaching. Well, the politics.

I enjoyed the students. But I had little time to paint. I just felt I needed the time . . . to dedicate to my painting, and I felt the only way I could do it was to do it completely."

"What a brave thing to do. Follow your passion. That's good."

Her response surprised him, not at all what he expected. Maybe he was thinking of his mother, or Rebecca, merging all the sensible women he had ever loved together as one. But despite her pragmatism, Alex had always had passion. A passion he thought she often attempted to hide, afraid to give in to feelings over which she might have little control. He remembered that first kiss. Reluctant and frightened, her lips quivered, then slowly, she had responded with an eager, fierce hunger, not unlike his own. What were her thoughts now, meeting again after so many years? Did she still see the young, scrawny, penniless artist? Such a contrast to Thierry who was filthy rich, Thierry who looked like the hero in some romantic movie. Had Alex fully realized her passion with Thierry?

"Frank said you lost your husband," Jake said. It didn't sound right the way it came out. *Lost?* Should he have said *passed away?* No, that didn't sound right either. He felt uncomfortable, but he should acknowledge that he knew. "I'm sorry for your loss."

"Thank you." Alex lowered her eyes for a moment.

"How long have you been here at the Cluny?"

"Almost three years now. I went back to work about a year after Thierry died. Back to work? I can't really say that. I didn't work at all during our marriage. At least not anything I received a salary for. Thierry didn't want me working, but he wanted an educated wife. I finished my master's several years after we married. Then about two years later, I began working toward my doctorate. I was bored sitting home, so I kept going to school. Then Soleil was born . . . I lost Thierry . . ." Alex took another drink of coffee. So did Jake.

"Sunny is precious," Alex said, "and I enjoyed being home with her, but I knew I needed something else in my life. And I was definitely overeducated and underexperienced. I felt very fortunate to get the position here at the Cluny. I had worked with Madame Demy, the Director, on my thesis. She liked my work and hired me first as an assistant, and then, this past year when the curator's opening came up, she encouraged me to apply."

Jake detected the slightest lack of confidence in Alex's voice. He imagined it would be difficult—a young woman with a child, a young woman who hadn't worked for years. He doubted Alex would have been forced to work, Thierry's family being so wealthy.

"You enjoy your work here?" Jake asked. "I felt the enthusiasm during your lecture."

"Yes, I do. I'm surrounded each day by things that I love. Then I go home to my daughter. And mother. My mother came over from Baltimore several years ago, after . . . I needed help with Sunny after I started work."

"Your dad . . . ?"

"We lost him about six years ago. And your folks, Jake?"

"Mom's in Missoula. Dad's been gone about five years now."

"It's tough," she said, "losing a parent."

"Yes," he replied. And what about losing a husband? he wondered. "Your brother Phillip, what's he doing?"

"Practicing law in Boston."

"You always said he liked to argue. Law sounds like a comfortable fit."

Alex smiled and nodded, then glanced at her watch. "My goodness, it's almost noon."

"Would you like to go out, get something to eat?" Jake asked.

"I'd love to, but I have a lunch appointment."

"How about dinner?"

A look of disappointment came over her. "An exhibition is opening at the Grand Palais tomorrow and the reception is this evening. We've loaned one of our pieces, and our Director, Madame Demy, was instrumental in obtaining one of the privately owned tapestries. It's a big event for her and important that I attend."

"Maybe some other time, then."

"I have an idea," Alex said. "Why don't you go with me? I'm leaving from here. I brought a change of clothes and plan to go after work."

She sounded sincere, as if she genuinely wanted him to go. She obviously didn't have a date. "Sure, I'd love to."

"Come by about seven." Alex stood. "The museum closes at five forty-five. I'll wait out front." She reached over the desk and gave him a little farewell hug, the bulk of the desk preventing him from getting too close, making the hug more a slight embrace of his shoulders. But he smelled the sweet scent of her perfume, so light he had barely perceived it as they sat.

And her perfume stayed with him all the way home, and lingered still, as he sat alone in his room.

5

ALEX LEFT THE museum and walked quickly toward Rue Frédéric Sauton, where she was meeting Alain Bourlet for lunch.

She still couldn't believe that Jake was here in Paris. When she saw him standing behind her group of British tourists, her heart had skipped a beat. Her hands were shaking, and she could hear a nervous jump in her voice. She'd drawn a quick breath before continuing her lecture. She wondered if he could tell. There he was—looking as if he'd barely had time to shake out those suitcase wrinkles. His thick, dark hair was neatly combed. That in itself made her smile. His hair had always been so unruly, as if it had a mind of its own. Sometimes she used to wonder if he bothered to comb it, or if he just popped out of bed and headed off to class.

And yet she had fantasies about seeing him again. She'd heard from Anna, who'd heard it from Fiona, who'd probably heard it from Frank, that he was back in Montana teaching. She knew he hadn't married, but she didn't know he was engaged. To a nurse, a woman who had dedicated her life to caring for others. Yet Jake was aware she was here at the Cluny.

He'd come to see her. It was he who'd sought her out. Or had he? He said he'd come to Paris to paint.

He looked so damned good. A definite maturity about him—the gray in his hair, a few extra pounds on his slender frame. His looks had actually improved with age.

She remembered years ago when Paul introduced them. Jake had the most beautiful, deep dark eyes, and he was tall, which she liked right away, being tall herself. "Jake here, he's from Montana, lives on a ranch," Paul said, "and Alex, she's a sophisticated city girl." Alex had reached out for Jake's hand, which was large and a little rough, like a man who could fix trucks, build houses, and ride horses. She said something like, "You're a cowboy?" and he said, *"Non, je suis un artiste."* She liked that too, that he was speaking French, that he was an artist who looked like a cowboy.

It wasn't until they had a class second semester that they got to know each other. But this had been cut short when Thierry came into her life.

She had met Thierry at the Louvre when they began conversing as they stood before the *Nike of Samothrace*. He was very good looking. He asked her to have coffee, and she said no. "Just here in the museum," he said. "We wouldn't even have to leave the building," and reluctantly she said, "Well, okay." He was easy to talk to. He knew a lot about art. He asked if she'd like to have dinner sometime, and she said no.

Several days later as she was walking to school, she heard someone calling her name. She looked over and it was Thierry, hanging his head out of a fancy little sports car. "Could I give you a lift?" he said, and again she told him no.

"How about lunch?" He was driving slowly, keeping pace with her walking, and horns behind him started to honk. "Please," he implored with a flirtatious grin, "before the fellow behind me comes and bashes my head in. I'll pick you up at school, what time?"

"No," she said, and he said, "Then I'll meet you at half past noon, Brasserie Lipp, Saint Germain. Just this once, then after that, if you want, I'll leave you alone."

And that was the beginning, the day she met him for lunch.

She knew she had to tell Jake, but what? She loved Jake, and yet she couldn't stay away from Thierry. Was it possible that she was in love with them both? If she told Jake about Thierry, would he finally make some kind of commitment, would he finally tell her that he loved her? She was so nervous and confused when she finally spoke with Jake that now she couldn't recall exactly what was said. She knew he had accused her of sneaking around behind his back, of going with Thierry because he was rich. She'd cried and he'd stomped out, too immature to even discuss it.

After that she started seeing Thierry often and with little guilt. He was older and much more sophisticated than the boys she knew at school. And yet there was something reckless about Thierry that Alex found inexplicably appealing. He drove too fast and spent too much money, pulling it out of his wallet as if it could regenerate itself like a tail snapped off a lizard. He often gave her expensive gifts for no particular occasion or for the silliest reasons. A bracelet with diamonds, her birthstone, though it was not her birthday. A pale blue cashmere sweater because it matched her eyes. He sent her flowers. He took her to elegant restaurants. He told her she was beautiful, that he loved her. She'd been just eighteen when they met, nineteen when they married. Too young to know anything about true love and real life.

As Alex hurried down Rue Frédéric Sauton toward the restaurant, she could see that Monsieur Bourlet had arrived and was sitting at an outdoor table. He wasn't difficult to spot—a distinguished, well-dressed gentleman with a thick, full head of white hair and a neatly trimmed goatee. He and Alex met each month for lunch, a business appointment, though she thought it hardly necessary for such. They simply enjoyed each other's company.

Alain Bourlet was the trustee of a Pellier family trust from which Thierry had received a generous allowance. He and Alex lived on this, along with a salary he received for the position he held at a Paris branch of the bank Pierre's family had founded years ago in Lyon. In reality, Thierry did little work. Mostly he played, and it was this that eventually killed him— he had been drinking at the time of the accident.

When Thierry passed away, creditors appeared out of nowhere. The debts were paid out of the estate, leaving Alex with very little. Soleil became beneficiary of the trust, which still had a substantial balance. Alex and her daughter lived comfortably, although not lavishly. The mortgage on the apartment was paid by the trust, along with daily expenses, Sunny's tuition at the private school she attended, and a small salary to Alex's mother for caring for Sunny.

"*Bonjour,* Monsieur Bourlet," Alex said as she approached the table.

"*Bonjour,* Madame Pellier." He stood. Alex kissed him on one cheek, then the other. He pulled the chair back for her.

As they looked over the menus Monsieur Bourlet asked about her work. "Any recent acquisitions or adventures?" He enjoyed her tales of attending auctions and estate sales, of visiting ancient monasteries and châteaux.

"I've just returned from an excursion to a convent south of Lyon," Alex said. "A bit of a disaster really, though I've not given up. It's being closed, renovated, and turned into a hotel, the contents to be sold." She told him about the difficulty she had gaining entry, about the Mother Superior's death, how she was making arrangements to visit again, though she hadn't yet heard back from the Archbishop. "Mother Alvère mentioned tapestries, so I'm particularly interested in pursuing that possibility."

"Would it be likely to find a tapestry in a convent?"

"Not terribly. Possibly something displayed in the chapel, but often the term *tapestry* is used to describe any decorative textile hanging. I'm not sure what the Mother Superior was referring to, but I want to find out."

"Never miss an opportunity," he said approvingly. "A treasure might be discovered in the most unlikely place." He always seemed impressed that she would aggressively follow any potential lead.

Alex told him about the special exhibition opening at the Grand Palais, how the Cluny had loaned a tapestry, how Madame Demy had helped obtain *Le Pégase,* which would be shown publicly for the first time. Monsieur Bourlet listened with interest.

"I had hoped I might learn something more about the tapestry's history," Alex said. "It's privately owned."

"A piece that has been in a family collection for centuries."

The man's brow rose with a suggestion of some knowledge of the owner.

"Have you seen it?" She leaned in toward Monsieur Bourlet. "You know the owner?" His client list consisted of some of the wealthiest families in Paris, and he would often share stories, not confidential financial information, but little bits of gossip, which made these lunches all the more interesting. He had described paintings and sculptures he had seen displayed in the finest homes in the city, and he often knew when a valuable piece of art changed hands.

"No, no." He shook his head. "I don't know the owner." But Alex wondered for a moment if he was holding something back.

Over coffee and dessert Monsieur Bourlet suggested several new investments. He treated Alex with the utmost respect, as if she had full understanding of the world of finance. He had advised her on her own private investments—she had established a nice little portfolio with her salary from the Cluny—and had done well listening to his advice.

Alex returned to her office. As she worked she kept thinking of Jake. Wouldn't Madame Demy be shocked when she showed up at the reception with this tall, handsome American? Just before six, Sandrine stopped by to say she was leaving. At half past six, Alex put away her files, signed off her computer, and changed for the reception.

WHEN JAKE ARRIVED a few minutes before seven, Alex was waiting outside the museum. She had changed into a short black dress and had pulled her hair up off her shoulders, exposing her long elegant neck.

"Bonsoir," he said as he approached. "You look very nice." He couldn't help but notice her diamond earrings, at least a carat plus per lobe, each ear sporting a single stone larger than the diamond in the ring he'd given Rebecca.

"Bonsoir, Monsieur Bowman," she said, making it sound very French—*Bow-mah.* She reached out and gave him a hug. She smelled exquisite. "You look very nice too."

He was wearing his sports jacket, which was brown—probably not the most appropriate attire for an evening event in Paris. That afternoon he'd considered buying a dark suit, but decided against spending that much on something he'd get so little use out of.

"I called a cab," Alex said. "I didn't want the driver to wait, so I requested the cab at seven-fifteen."

"Did you think I'd be late?"

"There were times, I recall . . . ," she said with a teasing grin.

"I've matured considerably in the past fourteen years," he said, also smiling. "I've become a responsible adult."

"Oh, Jake, don't tell me you've become boring." Her tone was both flirtatious and mocking.

"Can't a guy show up on time without being labeled a bore?"

"We'll see how you do tonight."

"Some kind of test?"

She laughed. "Thank you for going with me this evening."

"My pleasure."

"I think you'll enjoy the exhibit." As they waited for the cab, she explained how the exhibition was a retrospective of tapestry through the ages, from fifth-century Coptic tapestry from Egypt to modern twentieth-century pieces based on designs by contemporary artists. "Several medieval tapestries on loan from various museums are included, among them a tapestry from the Metropolitan Museum from The Cloisters' collection, *The Hunt of the Unicorn* series. There's also a tapestry that is being shown for the first time, called *Le Pégase.*"

"You've never seen it?"

"No one has," Alex said and laughed. "Well, someone has. But it's privately owned, never publicly displayed. Our Director was instrumental in obtaining the tapestry."

"It's owned by someone here in Paris?"

"I don't know. Madame Demy evidently has been sworn to secrecy. She obviously knows the owner, or at least knows someone who knows the owner."

"Maybe the owner will be there. Maybe we'll meet him, or her."

"The catalogue lists the work as 'private collection.' " Alex made quotation marks with her fingers. "No name. I think it will remain a mystery."

"Nothing wrong with a good mystery."

"No," she said. "Nothing at all wrong with a good mystery."

The cab pulled up. Jake opened the door for Alex. "Grand Palais," he told the driver.

6

THE RECEPTION AREA was filled with an assortment of people. It always amazed Jake that you could go to an invitation-only private showing and half the people in town would be there. He saw right away that most of the men wore dark suits, the women, elegant evening wear. Hopefully there were enough people crowded into the room he wouldn't be noticed. Thankfully, his attire didn't seem to embarrass Alex.

A waiter walked by. Jake lifted two flutes from the tray and offered one to Alex. A middle-aged woman, reed thin, wearing a maroon dress, standing with a man in a respectable black suit, waved from across the room. Alex took Jake's arm and they walked over.

"Bonsoir," Alex greeted the couple.

The woman bent in toward Alex and kissed her on one cheek, then the other, holding a champagne flute out to one side, a square of cheese with a toothpick in it out to the other, as if she might take flight.

"Bonsoir, Madame Pellier." The man held up his wineglass in a sort of salute, then greeted Alex with a kiss on each cheek.

"Monsieur, Madame Genevoix," Alex said. *"Je voudrais presenter mon ami,* Jacob Bowman."

Madame Genevoix nodded, the expression on her face somewhere between disapproval and curiosity. Monsieur Genevoix shifted his wineglass from his right to his left hand and reached out to shake hands.

Alex introduced the Genevoix as great patrons of the arts. Madame Genevoix told Alex how lovely she looked this evening, and Alex returned the compliment. The woman glanced at Jake, and he was just sure she was thinking what a rude American he was, coming dressed so inappropriately. Alex didn't seem fazed. She told them she and Jake had been students together years ago, how Jake was now visiting Paris, that he was an artist. Alex said that Jake was a talented painter. She didn't mention that she hadn't seen any of his work in years. Madame Genevoix's expression softened now, revealing a trace of interest and approval, as if Alex's revelation might have provided a reasonable explanation as to why he had come so poorly dressed.

The woman said she was always interested in seeing the work of talented young artists. Another couple joined the group and exchanged pleasantries. A waiter glided by. Jake pulled a shrimp appetizer off the tray and plopped it in his mouth. Alex placed one on a napkin in the palm of her hand, then they walked through the crowd. Daintily, she wiped her mouth and stuck the napkin in the small evening bag that hung from her shoulder. Jake downed the last of his champagne and placed the empty flute on the tray of the next waiter who passed by.

They walked toward several small, round colorful tapestries that hung on the nearest wall. They were stopped twice before reaching their destination, first by an elegant dark-haired woman in a long red dress, then by an elderly couple.

They continued, viewing the different tapestries, Alex explaining their origins, the method of weaving, being interrupted now and then by other guests, Alex introducing Jake, always as a painter, with a brief description of who the various patrons were, their particular interest in the arts, their position at some museum or department of the government or chairmanship of an important-sounding committee.

After the first exhibition room, they moved on to tapestries from the Middle Ages. They stopped for several minutes to examine the piece from The Cloisters' collection. It depicted the unicorn, dipping its horn in a stream, surrounded by the hunters. Hanging next to this piece was *Le Toucher* from the Cluny.

"It's interesting," Alex said, "to see them displayed side by side."

Jake stared up at *Le Toucher*. The woman in this tapestry seemed different from the others in the Cluny set. Her face was not particularly beautiful, her expression almost stern. The unicorn looked like a goat. There was no handmaiden. The lion's smile was somewhat smug. What was going on? Ah, the maiden reached out and *touched*—no, more like stroked—the goaty-looking unicorn's horn. Was there something erotic here? Jake glanced at Alex, who stood thoughtfully studying the piece from the New York collection.

They moved on to the next room. On the far wall, a tapestry with a rich red background, similar in color to the Cluny tapestries, caught Jake's eye.

"Le Pégase," Alex whispered.

The winged horse looked in ways similar to the unicorns in the Cluny set—the same graceful, elegant white body, tinged with hints of gold. A knight, mounted on the Pegasus, raised a sword in his right hand. The three maidens had the long, lean, elegant torsos of the Cluny maidens. Their headdresses, too, were similar. One of the three had long flowing golden hair, with an oriental-type jeweled wrap, very much like the maiden in *Touch*. The two other maidens also wore headdresses similar to those in the Cluny set. Their hair was pulled up, wrapped in jeweled turbans, with tufts of loose hair framing their faces, similar to the lady in *A Mon Seul Désir*. Unlike the ornately garbed maidens of *The Lady and the Unicorn,* the maidens in *Le Pégase* were nude.

"The colors," Alex said, "the reds, the blues, so much more vibrant than I'd imagined from the photos I've studied. They look as if they come from the same dyes as the Cluny tapestries, yet there is little evidence of fading. The maidens, the unicorn and the winged horse, the flowers, the little creatures," Alex's words came out slowly, reverently, "so much like the Cluny's, perhaps even a more skillful creation. I've always wondered if it didn't come from the same workshop. The style might indicate a later date."

"Some similarities to the New York set too," Jake said.

"Yes," Alex agreed. "The flowers are growing, rather than floating, and the background is similar to *The Hunt of the Unicorn,* not the artificial 'island' of *La Dame à la Licorne*."

Alex's eyes darted around the room. "I'd love to touch it," she whispered to Jake.

He knew the feeling. Whenever he went into a museum, he had that urge. He wanted to walk right up to a painting and run his hand over the brush strokes, feel the texture of the paint beneath his fingers.

Alex looked around again. There were several people in the room, but no one standing directly before *Le Pégase*. They had seen two or three museum guards, but none in this particular room at the moment. Alex reached into her small black evening bag, pulled out the crumpled cocktail napkin, and carefully wiped her fingers. She glanced around the room again. Then, casually, she walked closer. Very slowly, she reached out and touched the fabric. She ran her long slender fingers slowly over the rich deep fabric of the tapestry, in a gesture at once both sweet and tender and yet so sensuous Jake felt a thump in his chest.

She stepped back, took a deep breath, put her arm through his, and then, without exchanging a word, they continued on to the next tapestry.

When they neared the final pieces in the exhibit, Alex said, "Thank you for coming with me tonight."

"I've enjoyed it."

"Maybe we should go back through the exhibition hall to the reception area. I had hoped to see Madame Demy."

They walked back through the hall, stopping again for several minutes to examine *Le Pégase,* then *The Hunt of the Unicorn* and *Le Toucher.* The exhibition rooms seemed much more crowded as they walked through this second time. The larger crowd that had gathered in the reception area was now beginning to file through the gallery halls. They ran into several more people whom Alex introduced. By the time they reached the reception area, they still hadn't seen Madame Demy.

Alex grabbed a couple more hors d'oeuvres off a tray as a waiter walked by. Jake wondered if he should offer to take her to dinner. The hors d'oeuvres were good, but a bit skimpy. Alex continued to scan the room. "There she is."

Across the room, a plain, mousy-looking, middle-aged woman wearing a black dress waved as she stood chatting with two other women.

"*Bonsoir,* Madame Demy," Alex said as they approached. "I'd like you to meet my dear friend Jacob Bowman."

Slowly, Madame Demy reached out for Jake's hand. Her expression revealed a trace of confusion, and she seemed to be looking him over pretty good. She smiled, Jake thought approvingly, as she nodded and said, *"Enchantée."*

Alex introduced Jake to the two women with Madame Demy. A tall, thin man who was conversing with a gentleman standing behind them now turned and stared at Alex, his expression as bewildered and confused as Madame Demy's had been.

"Madame Pellier, Monsieur Bowman," Madame Demy said, "I'd also like to present a special guest." She touched the tall, thin man on the arm.

The man's hair was so blond it was almost white, his puny little mustache so faint that Jake wondered why he bothered. Jake glanced at Alex, whose face had suddenly gone very pale.

"From the Metropolitan, The Cloisters in New York," Madame Demy said. "I'd like you to meet Dr. Henry Martinson."

7

ALEX REACHED OUT to shake hands with Dr. Martinson in a gesture so gracious and controlled, Jake thought he had only imagined that brief moment of dismay on Alex's face.

"So nice to see you again, Dr. Martinson," she said, "and how nice to have you here with us in Paris."

Dr. Martinson's eyes narrowed. He smiled, but it seemed he was engaged in deep thought, as if trying to bring something to mind. "Madame Pellier? We've met. Was it in New York?" he asked, perplexed.

Alex shook her head.

"Recently, somewhere?"

"Yes." Alex smiled.

"Here in Paris?"

"No."

"Somewhere here in France. It was recent?"

"Yes."

"Lyon?"

It seemed the two were engaged in a little guessing game. Dr. Martinson smiled. Flirtatiously, Jake thought. He wondered how the man could have met Alex and forgotten. Alex was not the type of woman a man could easily forget.

Then Dr. Martinson's smile broadened with recognition. "Ah, yes. Saturday. The young woman visiting the Convent of Sainte Blandine."

"Yes," Alex said. "And Sunday. The woman who was almost run over on the road to Sainte Blandine's."

Dr. Martinson shook his head, apologetically. He started to say something else when he was interrupted by one of the women as she attempted to draw the others into a conversation about one of the medieval tapestries on display.

A plumpish woman in a gold sparkly dress said wasn't it lovely to have so many of the world's most famous and beautiful tapestries displayed all in one place, particularly the Gothic pieces. Another woman, touching Dr. Martinson on the arm, commented how nice it was for so many museums to loan their work for the exhibit, and Madame Demy said that several works were on loan from private individuals.

Dr. Martinson said how fortunate they were to obtain such a beautiful piece of late-medieval tapestry as *Le Pégase*. It was the sole reason he had come to Paris for the show. He knew it had never been publicly displayed, and he certainly didn't want to miss what might turn out to be a once-in-a-lifetime opportunity.

"And your trip to Sainte Blandine's?" Alex asked.

"So sad, the Mother Superior's passing," Dr. Martinson said. "And sadder yet, her belief that the convent owned anything a museum might be interested in acquiring."

"Yes," Alex agreed, "but one might expect either from a ninety-two-year-old woman."

Dr. Martinson looked at her, puzzled.

"Death or confusion," Alex said.

"Oh, yes." He nodded and smiled, amused. "But had I known, I surely wouldn't have wasted the time. Time I could have spent here in Paris."

"How long will you be here?"

"Just two more days, surely not enough. There's so much to see here in Paris."

They all chatted a bit more, about Paris, the exhibit, the fine weather they were having this spring. Madame Demy asked about Jake's work, and he told her that he had spent

time in Paris years ago as a student and always dreamed of returning.

"Perhaps we will meet again," Dr. Martinson said as Alex
and Jake were leaving.

"Yes, Dr. Martinson," Alex replied. "So good to see you
again."

"Nice to meet all of you," Jake said.

Alex didn't say another word until she and Jake were out
on the street in front of the building.

"He's lying," Alex said. "He's going back."

"I have no idea," Jake said, "what was going on in there.
You seemed surprised to see Dr. Martinson this evening."

"Yes, very," Alex said as they continued along the avenue
toward the Champs-Elysées. "Could we go somewhere, get
something to eat? I'm starving."

"I was about to make that suggestion myself."

"Over dinner," Alex said, picking up her stride, "I'll tell
you about Martinson and Sainte Blandine—at least what little
I know of each right now, which I assure you is much less than
I will know after I return to the convent."

WHEN ALEX ARRIVED at the museum the following morning, she called the Archbishop's office. She had called twice
earlier in the week, and was getting rather impatient, as she
had yet to hear back from him. Again she left a message.

Alex rose from her desk. She wanted to speak with Madame
Demy to ask about Dr. Martinson. She was quite sure he had
not shared any information with the Director about his trip to
Sainte Blandine's.

Madame Demy was not in her office, which surprised
Alex. It was unlike the older woman to come in late. Alex
laughed at the thought that Madame Demy might have been
out "partying" after the exhibition opening. Alex herself had
returned home early, right after she and Jake finished dinner.
He had asked if they could get together after her visit to the
convent, and she said yes, that would be nice.

Nice? She had waited, it seemed, for years to see Jake
again. And here he was. Here in Paris. She would never have

had the nerve to do what he'd done—quit his job, just pack up and move. Years ago she had seen him as immature and irresponsible, but now this seemed like such a courageous thing to do. She had enjoyed the time they spent together last night. Yet their reunion seemed overshadowed by her intense desire to return to the convent. To get there before Dr. Martinson, to arrive before anyone else, to claim what treasures might lie there at Sainte Blandine's, hidden perhaps for centuries.

Is there something wrong with me? Alex asked herself. Thierry had accused her of being more interested in "things" than the people in her life. It was true that she often found refuge in her studies. Had she been the cause of the unhappiness in their marriage?

When she looked back on those first years with Thierry, surely she must have been happy. She was still in school, yet hardly on a student's budget. Thierry was generous and she knew she could have anything she wanted. But as time went by, she felt something was missing. When she finished school, they talked about having a baby. Thierry said he wasn't ready. Alex sat at home, often alone, and thought, *this isn't what I had expected it to be.* She enrolled in a master's program. She and Thierry spent less and less time together. He went out in the evenings while she stayed home to study. She suspected he was having an affair, and when she confronted him he didn't even deny it. She suggested counseling, and he'd snorted and said she sounded so American, as if all their problems could be solved by counseling. The next day she packed a bag and checked into a hotel. She thought about divorce, but couldn't bear the thought of telling her parents or Thierry's. And even Alex, who considered herself a liberal Catholic, did not believe in divorce. Or, perhaps, it was failure she didn't believe in.

Thierry talked her into coming home. He said he loved her, that he was ready to start a family, that things would change. And it seemed they did, though Alex was unable to get pregnant. She went to one doctor after another and was told there was no reason she couldn't conceive, that she should relax and go on with her life. She went back to school to work on her doctorate. Thierry refused to have any medical tests. Sex became mechanical—not that it had been wonderful before— and Thierry accused her of having no feelings. Again she considered leaving him, but then she discovered she was pregnant.

When they had Soleil, there were brief periods when Alex felt happy again. Thierry doted on the little girl, who was more beautiful than Alex could have ever imagined. Watching the two of them together, she felt a tenderness for this man who had given her such a precious gift.

But these feelings were short lived. Soon Thierry was back to going out in the evenings, sometimes not returning until morning, always explaining it had been a business meeting. Alex knew there were other women, and she hated him for it. At night, when he didn't return, she would lie awake in bed, angry, then thinking he might have been in an accident, he might be dead. Then wishing it were true. And then . . . it happened, almost as if Alex's evil wish had killed Thierry. She had never shared these thoughts with anyone, as she had never shared the truth that her marriage had been so terribly empty.

JUST BEFORE TEN Alex received a call from the Archbishop's assistant with an invitation to visit the convent on Saturday afternoon between four and five. She was to ask for Sister Etienne. Alex left her office and walked down the hall to find that Madame Demy had finally come in.

"It was a lovely reception!" the Director exclaimed.

"Yes, very nice," Alex replied as she sat.

"Your friend, Monsieur Bowman, he'll be in Paris for some time?"

"He's come to Paris to paint." Alex paused. "And your friend, Dr. Martinson? He's come to France to steal our treasures?"

Madame Demy smiled. "Tell me about Dr. Martinson and your meeting him at the convent."

Alex told Madame Demy about seeing Dr. Martinson inside the convent, believing he was a medical doctor who had come to attend to the old Mother Superior, then realizing, when she met him at the exhibition the previous night, that he too had been contacted by the convent to examine the property owned by the nuns.

"Do you think Dr. Martinson knows something we don't?" she asked.

Madame Demy shook her head. "Probably not. He's young and enthusiastic. He's just taken the appointment at The Cloisters. He was thrilled with the opportunity to come for the tapestry exhibition."

"You don't think the good sisters timed this invitation to coincide with the exhibition here in Paris?"

"I don't know that they would be so cunning. For centuries, the order has had little contact with the outside world. Now they're being thrown out of their home. It seems they are trying to salvage their pride by implying the residence holds a wealth of treasures."

"I finally heard from the Archbishop," Alex said. "I'm going to Sainte Blandine's tomorrow."

"If you believe it would be worth another attempt, then yes, you should go."

Of course she would go again. Nothing could keep her away.

8

WHEN ALEX ARRIVED at the convent at three forty-five Saturday, fifteen minutes early for her four o'clock appointment, she was surprised at all the activity. Two small trucks and a van were parked out front. Loud hammering came from the upper level, and as she approached the front door, a wooden board came flying out from above, landing in a mound of rubbish several feet from where she stood. Alex jumped as another board flew down, much closer. She looked up. A man's head popped out of the window.

"Pardon!" he shouted down at her. Then he disappeared as quickly as he had appeared, retreating like a turtle back into its shell.

Alex knocked on the door. Within seconds the upper portion slid open to reveal the same old nun from her previous visits. Alex introduced herself once more. The old woman nodded, as if to say, *Yes, I know who you are.* But she did not speak. Alex explained that she had an appointment with Sister Etienne. The old nun muttered something about the Archbishop, her eyes rolling upward. She opened the door and motioned for Alex to enter. Without another word, she led Alex through the vestibule, down the dark, narrow, musty-smelling hall into what appeared to be an office.

A nun sat at an ancient, worn desk. She stood and introduced herself as Sister Etienne, then motioned for Alex to sit in a chair on the opposite side of the desk.

The nun was a large woman with a face shaped like a full moon. She looked almost jolly, a female Santa Claus, yet after a brief welcoming smile, her cheerful expression turned solemn. She pulled several sheets of paper from her desk and handed them to Alex.

It appeared to be a handwritten list of the convent's inventory. One section listed kitchen equipment and utensils; another, furnishings; another, needlework, embroidery, and tapestry. A final section, which appeared to be the most extensive, was labeled *"Bibliothèque."* As Alex studied the list she could hear the commotion from above.

"The Archbishop," Sister Etienne said. "Already, he has started his renovations. Of course, we are no longer using the second floor. Heaven knows most of the good sisters can no longer climb the stairs. But the racket! So little consideration. It is difficult for our contemplation and prayer." The woman laughed softly. "At least for those of us who still have our hearing intact."

Alex guessed that Sister Etienne was one of the youngest nuns. Perhaps in her late sixties. The woman sat with her hands clasped in front of her on the desk. They were thin and spotted and didn't seem to match the rest of her corpulent body.

"Where would you like to begin?" the nun said, unfolding her hands.

"The library, please." Another quick look in the library, then she would ask to see the tapestries.

"I'm afraid the library is being used now. Perhaps the textiles."

"That would be fine." Why had she bothered to ask? Alex wondered. She smiled pleasantly at the nun.

"Oui, they are on display in the dining room."

Sister Etienne led Alex into a long, narrow room. A large, plain wooden table, at least eight feet in length, stood before a stark white stucco fireplace. A wooden crucifix hung above the mantel. The chairs had been removed from the table, and it was covered with an assortment of altar cloths and embroidered linens, illuminated by a single light hanging from the ceiling. The rest of the room was dim. A distinct odor drifted in the air. Alex couldn't place it at first. Chicken noodle soup! Dinner was probably being prepared in the kitchen, somewhere close by the dining room. Yes, now, faintly, Alex could hear kitchen sounds—the clattering of pots and pans, nearly drowned out by the banging and pounding from the upper level. What a commotion, she thought—in a contemplative convent, no less.

"You'll find everything well labeled," Sister Etienne said. "The numbers on each item correspond to the numbers and descriptions on the inventory list. Please indicate the items of interest and the price your museum would be willing to pay, as we have other representatives who might also wish to make an offer." The nun spoke in a businesslike voice. "If you need assistance, Sister Anne will help you." Sister Etienne motioned toward the opposite end of the room.

Alex looked over and was surprised to see a nun sitting on a high-back chair in a dark corner of the room, her hands folded neatly in her lap. She was a tiny woman, so small her feet barely touched the floor. Her head seemed out of proportion, too large for her body. Alex thought she smiled, though her face was partially hidden in the shadow of the large white hood and wimple of the order.

"*Bien.* I'll leave you here to look," Sister Etienne said. "If you need assistance, please let Sister Anne know."

"*Oui, merci,*" Alex replied, glancing at Sister Anne.

The small nun nodded. Sister Etienne left the room.

As Alex stared down at the table, she could see immediately that there was nothing of interest to the Cluny. Most of it was altar linens, probably made in the past fifty years, or at least within the last century. She picked up a piece that had a border of white lace along the edge and examined it carefully. Handmade bobbin lace. It was beautiful, but nothing the museum would be interested in. She picked up several more pieces, all hand-stitched linens with lace edgings. Fine, delicate work. Alex could imagine the nuns' agile fingers, moving quickly, reciting silent prayers, Hail Marys and Our Fathers, to the rhythm of the bobbins, like rosary beads, as they formed the pattern of the fine handmade lace.

She heard a sound coming from the corner—Sister Anne clearing her throat. The tiny nun pointed at the wall. Alex walked over. On the wall on either side of the nun hung several textiles depicting liturgical and biblical scenes. They appeared to be hand-appliqued and embroidered. They were as beautifully done as the lace-edged altar cloths, and they looked old—probably hanging for years in the convent chapel where endless burning candles had created a dark sooty coating.

One was a coronation scene of the Virgin Mary, another the crucifixion and resurrection combined in one piece. Another depicted the martyrdom of Saint Sebastian, his body pierced with arrows. It was intricate, delicate work, and the smoky patina, which Alex could smell as she examined the textiles, did not distract from them, but had become part of their history, their beauty. They were exquisite creations, but even in the dim corner of the dining room, Alex could see they were more recent works, not medieval treasures.

It was almost four-thirty. She didn't know if her four o'clock appointment was set up for just one hour or if she would be allowed more time. She wondered if she might move on to the library.

Alex turned to Sister Anne. *"La bibliothèque, s'il vous plaît."*

The nun hopped down from the chair and walked across the room. Her gait was uneven, the small black form rocking back and forth as she moved. The woman's legs, hidden under the many folds of the dark habit, were too short for the rest of her body. It appeared as if the upper, larger portion of her body might cause her to tumble over at any time.

She left Alex alone in the room for several minutes. When she returned, she motioned for Alex to follow. *"Oui, la bibliothèque,"* the woman said in a voice as small as the nun herself.

Slowly, they walked out of the dining room, down the hall, into the library. Sister Anne pointed to the small table and chair in the center of the room, then sat again on a chair in the corner. Alex looked around. For some reason, she wanted to find the poem again, but she knew immediately that something in the room had changed. She could see that the books had been rearranged, and wondered if someone else had been in the library. She scanned the shelves for the group of books she had wanted to examine on her previous visit and noticed a large leather-bound volume on one of the lower shelves. She picked it up and opened it. It appeared to be some type of register, a record of the young women who had come to the convent. Alex scanned the first few pages, which had entries beginning in the middle of the 1800s. She read the names, the ages of the young women: *Brigitte Denis, 14. Catherine Chevalier, 16. Elisabeth Maupas, 15. 4 August 1872.*

She flipped over to the last page, which was empty. She turned back several pages until she found the final entry. It was dated one week ago, last Sunday. It recorded the death of the Mother Superior. A sudden sadness came over Alex. She had not been particularly touched by Mother Alvère's death, had never even met the Mother Superior, but now she was filled with an emotion she couldn't fully understand. It came to her that this old woman had at one time been a young girl of fourteen or fifteen. Like Brigitte, Catherine, and Elisabeth—young women who had given up their worldly possessions, come to the convent, dedicated their lives to the service of the Lord, grown old. And now the remaining nuns were being literally evicted from their home, the only home many of them had probably known since they were young women. Alex looked at Sister Anne in the corner, her eyes drooping as if she might doze off at any minute.

Alex closed the book and returned it to the shelf. She walked to the table and glanced over at the old nun again. Sister Anne looked up and smiled. *"Puis-je vous aider?"* she asked.

"Non, merci," Alex replied. She smiled at the nun, then sat and ran her finger down the first page of the library section of the inventory.

The books were numbered on the list, but Alex wasn't sure

how they were arranged on the shelves. She decided she would scan the list first to determine if there was anything that looked as if it might be of value to the museum. If she couldn't find the books on the shelves, she would ask Sister Anne for help.

The titles on the list didn't seem to be in any particular order. Most had dates, but they weren't chronological. Some of them had authors listed, but they were not arranged alphabetically. About halfway down the list, she read, *"Le registre du Couvent de Sainte Blandine, cinq volumes."* Five volumes? Alex was curious; she had seen only one. She wondered how far back the records went. She would love to find the other volumes, just out of curiosity. Yet she knew they would have no artistic value to the museum. Historical value perhaps, but the thought crossed her mind that she might be running out of time, although neither Sister Anne nor Sister Etienne had indicated she would be tossed out of the convent at five o'clock. She couldn't waste these precious minutes; she was here as a representative of the museum and she needed to keep that in mind and put her own interest and curiosity aside. Alex ran her finger quickly over the first page. Nothing. She scanned the second page. Nothing. She moved quickly to the third page. She flipped to the last page and scanned the list from the bottom up, then worked back toward the pages in the middle of the list. There was nothing that appeared to be of any interest. Then her eyes stopped abruptly. *"Le livre de prières du Moyen Age."* Her heart beat quickly. Could this be authentic? Could there really be a medieval book of prayers somewhere on the shelves? Alex's mind filled with the thought of an illuminated manuscript with miniature paintings, an authentic book of hours. Suddenly, a loud crash shook the room. She jumped, startled. She heard a rustle in the corner. Sister Anne looked up, wide awake now. Ah, yes, Alex thought, the Archbishop's men, working upstairs. She went back to her list.

The number on the list, next to the description, *"Le livre de prières du Moyen Age,"* was 347.

Alex got up and pulled the first book off the shelf to see if it was numbered. Inside the back cover, she found a small piece of paper with the number "1" written in pencil. She quickly estimated the books on the first shelf. Forty-five to fifty, she guessed. Number 347 would most likely be on the seventh or eighth shelf. Her eyes raced down the first wall of shelves. The seventh was the bottom on the first wall, the eighth, the first shelf on the adjoining wall. Alex dropped to the cold stone floor. Eagerly, she pulled the first book off the shelf. It was a large book with photos of the Holy Land. She opened the back cover. A small paper fell out and sailed to the floor. She picked it up—number 339. She replaced the number and returned the book to the shelf. Her hand trembled. She reached for a second book, leather-bound, the only one on the shelf that looked remotely old enough to be a medieval prayer book. It was numbered 348. Without replacing it, she grabbed the book resting on the shelf to the left. 346. There was no 347! The thought came to her instantly—Dr. Martinson had already been here!

She jumped up. Her eyes darted to the corner where Sister Anne sat slumped in her chair, asleep now. Alex grabbed the inventory list and walked quickly to the corner. *"S'il vous plaît,"* she said, tugging on the old woman's shoulder. Sister Anne woke, startled. Alex pointed to the list at the description of book number 347. *"Trois cent quarante-sept?"*

Sister Anne rubbed her eyes, stared at the list, then slid down from the chair and walked across the room. Each step seemed an effort and Alex was ashamed at her own impatience. Sister Anne stooped, slowly pulled a book off the shelf. Alex knew it was 348. The nun replaced it, as if in slow motion, then pulled 346 off the shelf. She shook her head, looked at the list again, then walked, rocking back and forth, tediously, across the room toward the desk. She stepped behind the small desk, pulled a key out of the pocket of her voluminous habit, and opened a locked cabinet built into the lower portion of the bookshelf. Sister Anne reached in and pulled out a book. Alex's heart thumped. The nun handed her the book.

Alex carried it to the table. Sister Anne returned to her corner. After studying the cover—vellum, worn and

faded—Alex opened the book slowly. She examined the first
page. It was terribly faded, almost as if it had been water
damaged. She turned to the next page. Also faded. The next
three pages were stuck together. Several pages following had
worm track and others were torn. She turned more pages,
until she found one that was distinct enough to examine.
Late fifteenth century, she guessed. It was a hand-printed
manuscript, on paper, rather than vellum. Not the deluxe
version by any means. Not the rare museum acquisition for
which she would want to be remembered. It had probably
been printed after the introduction of the printing press in
Europe. The competition from the mass-produced books,
unfortunately, diminished the quality of some of the hand-
illuminated manuscripts.

She flipped through several more pages. The borders with
wayside flowers, entangled with acanthus motif, indicated it
had been produced in northern France about 1475 or after.
There were no miniature paintings; it had not been created for
a prince or a king. And it was generally not in good condition.
But it was an authentic late medieval manuscript. Yes, it was
authentic. If it could be obtained for a reasonable price, the
Cluny might be interested. Even a page or cutting from a medieval manuscript was valuable.

She turned several more pages. The middle section was
also stuck together. Alex pulled the corners of two pages,
slowly, carefully—she didn't want to destroy or damage anything. She stopped, wondering if she should continue. Then
she noticed something, a corner sticking out between two
pages. At first, she thought it was a page that had become loosened from the binding, but it appeared to be an entirely different type of paper, a parchment, she thought. The pages were
stuck together in such a fashion that the top and bottom were
sealed. The side had a small opening, creating what resembled
a flapless envelope. Carefully, very slowly, she peeled the two
stuck pages apart a bit more on one side, and slid the foreign
page out. It was actually two papers stuck together. They were
folded into quarters. Cautiously, Alex pried them apart. She
unfolded the first. For a long moment, all she could do was
stare.

She heard pounding again. She knew it came from the men working on the upper level, yet Alex felt as if it were her heart, thumping with the same rhythm and force. She held her hand to her chest and took a deep breath.

It was a pen-and-ink sketch—several small sketches in fact. The detail was surprising, amazing for such a small drawing. But more surprising than the intricate detail was the subject. As she rearranged the sketches in her head, put the parts together, she could see that the small detailed drawings were pieces of the tapestry *A Mon Seul Désir* from *The Lady and the Unicorn* series.

The tent was drawn in one corner. A variation in another. The maiden, placing the jewels in the casket, appeared in the center of the drawing. A sketch of her face with a different headdress appeared on the left, another on the right. There were several sketches of the unicorn in various poses along the border of the paper.

Alex unfolded the second drawing. It was rendered in the same detail. It appeared to be a companion piece to the first. Yet it seemed more complete, a total work, although there were again several small detailed sketches—the unicorn's head at various angles, the maiden's face with different headdresses scattered along the borders. The drawing depicted a slender young woman wearing a turbanlike headdress like the maidens in *Hearing* and *Sight*. It struck Alex immediately how much this young woman resembled the maidens in *Le Pégase,* because unlike the ornately clad maidens in the Cluny set, the maiden in the drawing was nude.

As in *Sight,* the unicorn sat with its front hooves in the maiden's lap, her arm wrapped tenderly around the elegant animal. The lion was not present, nor the handmaiden. A young man, clad in the armor of a knight, stood to the left of the woman and unicorn. He held a lance, directed toward the unicorn cradled in the maiden's lap. Unlike the tapestries in the Cluny set, which floated on the garden island, the drawing seemed to be set in a more natural setting.

What was the significance of these drawings? Alex wondered. She ran her fingers over the drawing, barely touching the paper. It looked old—an ancient parchment, worn thin

along the folds. Could these drawings have been hidden away
in this prayer book for centuries? The thought seemed ridiculous. They had probably been placed here by some artistic
young nun who had at one time seen *The Lady and the Unicorn* tapestries in the museum. But why the sketches along the
border? Why the changes and variations in the drawings from
A Mon Seul Désir? Why would someone do a sketch using the
design in the ancient tapestry, as if they meant to make
changes? Could it possibly be that the drawings had been
done before the tapestry was woven? It was almost as if they
were done as a study, or preliminary sketches for the series.
Could this be possible? And what did the second drawing
mean? Was it a preliminary sketch for an additional tapestry?
A design that had never been executed as tapestry? Or a tapestry that had been lost or destroyed? A tapestry that had yet to
be discovered?

These thoughts sent a chill of excitement through Alex's
entire body.

She reached over and looked at the inventory list once
more. There was nothing on the description of the prayer
book to indicate it contained two medieval drawings, if indeed
this was what they were. Were the nuns even aware they were
in the book?

Alex examined the first drawing again. There were so
many details in such a small drawing. As she examined the
tent, she noticed there was a name, a signature almost hidden
along the top border of the tent, where the logo *A Mon Seul
Désir* appeared on the original tapestry. It was the name
Adèle.

The room was quiet now; the pounding from above had
ceased. Then faintly, Alex heard something. She looked over
at Sister Anne. She was asleep, a faint, delicate little snoring
staccato coming from the tiny nun.

Alex turned back to the drawings. Had anyone else seen
them? The pages had been stuck together. It would have been
difficult, although not impossible, to remove them without
pulling the pages apart.

Alex reached for her briefcase. Slowly, she unlatched it.
She took out a blank sheet of paper, a pencil. She had to have
a copy of the drawings.

Her hand was shaking so hard, there was no way she could do this. She stopped and took a deep breath. Holding the pencil in her right hand, she steadied it with her left. She started to sketch, attempting to duplicate what she saw. Her hand was steady now, determined. She started in the middle of the blank paper. It took but a few minutes to realize what she had known for years: As much as she loved art, the creative process, she was not an artist herself. She couldn't duplicate the drawings, not with any accuracy or authenticity. She sat, trying to decide what to do. Should she ask Sister Etienne if she could take the book? Tell her the museum was definitely interested? She wouldn't have to tell anyone what she had discovered inside the book. But it was unlikely the good sister would let her take the book. It had been locked away in the cabinet. Someone obviously had some understanding of its value. Yet it appeared that no one had examined it closely. The drawings were still sealed in the stuck pages. But then, maybe they were just trying to leave it in the condition in which it had been found.

She knew someone else had been in the library. Had they run out of time, not even looked at the book? Had they missed the drawings hidden in the middle of the book? A thousand questions swirled through her mind.

Alex heard a shuffling just outside the room, and sensed someone was coming down the hall toward the library. Carefully, she slid the drawings under her briefcase. She looked up as Sister Etienne entered the room.

"Will you need more time?" the nun asked.

"Oui, s'il vous plaît," Alex answered.

"We do have others scheduled to come take a look today," Sister Etienne said. "It's only fair we give each interested party some private moments to examine the work."

"Oui," Alex answered. Briefly, she thought of asking the nun if she might take the book. But then she asked, "Perhaps I could return tomorrow?"

"Tomorrow is Sunday," Sister Etienne answered. "Our priest comes early, about six . . . but later in the day, I believe we could arrange that." The nun smiled, then turned and walked over to Sister Anne, who was asleep on her chair in the corner. She knelt down on the stone floor in front of the small nun and gently touched her on the knee. "Sister Anne," she whispered.

Carefully and quietly, Alex unlatched her briefcase and slid the drawings inside.

9

AFTER ARRANGING TO come visit the convent the following morning, Alex got back in her car to leave. She noticed another car parked out front, one that hadn't been there when she arrived. Paris plates. It looked like a rental. Someone else was in the convent right now, examining the nuns' treasures. Would they make it into the library? Would they examine the prayer book? Would they be able to tell something had been removed? No, of course not. She was being paranoid.

Alex had driven just a short distance—she could no longer see the convent in her rearview mirror—when suddenly she felt a wave of nausea hit her. She stopped the car, opened the door, swung her legs around and put her head between her knees, taking in a deep breath. What had she done? She was shaking, her temples pounding. After several minutes, she stood and started to walk.

The scent of lavender filled her nostrils as she walked up the hillside, moving quickly, taking in deep gulps of air. After a short while she stopped and looked down, over the rolling green hills. Vineyards ran up and down the curved surface of the land in even rhythmic rows. The sky was clear and blue. Not a single cloud. She continued to walk, and the fresh air made her feel much better. Made her feel like she might be able to clear her head.

The book. The drawings. What was the meaning? Had she discovered something of significance? And what had she done? She had no intention of stealing the drawings; she just wanted to get a copy. She would return them the following day. No one would ever know they had been removed. The next person to examine the book would most likely find them. But Alex needed to study the drawings before anyone else, try to determine what they might signify. She stopped and sat on a large rock. In the distance, across the valley, tiny dots of cream-colored cattle grazed on the steep hillside. A red-tiled farmhouse balanced on a bluff. Yes, she would get a copy. But how? The first thought was a photo. No, she didn't have a camera with her. Perhaps she could borrow one from the Pelliers or go buy one. It was half past six now. Where could she find a camera this late on a Saturday evening? Particularly one that could record the intricate detail of the small drawings. She would have to use a flash or strong light, but she didn't want to expose the drawings to more light than necessary. She had no intention of putting them at risk. And she had no means of developing the film herself. She would have to entrust it to a complete stranger.

Could she put the drawings in a copy machine? Where? At the library? At the local copy shop? No, she couldn't do that—take a chance someone might see them. And she couldn't give them up even for a moment to subject them to the horrible, bright, blinding lights of a twenty-first-century copy machine.

Then it came to her—her original thought—an artist's rendering. It would have to be a talented artist, someone who could duplicate them exactly, someone she could trust completely. A vision came to her—Paul Westerman and Jake Bowman, as students. They would go to the museums, set up their equipment, copy the masters. She was amazed, particularly with Paul's ability to duplicate just about anything. And what was he doing now? Working for a firm that investigated art fraud. Alex laughed at the thought. When they were students, she used to tease Paul about the millions he might make some day, doing art forgeries.

Paul was in London, but Jake—Jake was in Paris. He could meet her in Lyon in less than five hours if he had a car. Two hours if he took the TGV, the high-speed rail. Yes, Jake could help her.

Alex turned and started back to the car, feeling energized. She would get a copy without causing any harm. She felt it was her duty to protect these drawings. It was the same feeling she had about the tapestries in the museum. It was not that she wanted them for herself. That wasn't it at all. But she felt protective, in the sense a mother might. With Soleil, especially when she began to exhibit her independence and unique personality as a toddler, Alex knew the child was not really hers, not in the sense that she owned this child, not in the sense that a living person could be considered a possession. She knew she had been entrusted with her care. That it was her motherly duty to protect her from harm, to nurture her, to guide her. And in a strange way, she knew this was the feeling she had toward the tapestries, and now these drawings. They were like a child, a gift to her, placed in her care.

And hadn't she been the one to discover them? Hadn't fate placed them in her hands? She walked back to the road. A bird flew overhead. It landed in a nearby tree and its sweet melody filled the air. Yes, Alex felt much better now.

Just as she arrived at the road, a dark-green vehicle came over the rise. It was Dr. Martinson, and he was driving toward the convent. What a terribly uncomfortable situation for them both. He could hardly pretend he didn't see her. Would he pass right by? Or perhaps run over her?

He slowed. The window slid down. "Madame Pellier, trouble with the car?" he asked with a strained smile.

"No." Alex forced a smile too. "Just needed a little fresh air." She felt queasy again.

"Not feeling well?"

"No, I'm fine. Really. I'm fine."

"You've been to the convent?"

Alex hesitated. "And you, Dr. Martinson, you've also taken this valuable time to return."

He shrugged his shoulders and stared at her for a moment. What could he say, Alex wondered, when he'd made such a fool of himself at the exhibition, carrying on about what a waste of time his excursion to Sainte Blandine's had been. "I'm afraid I left my briefcase on my last visit."

"Oh," she said, "I hope you find it."

"Well, yes, you have a nice day."

"Yes, you too, Dr. Martinson."

Yeah right, Alex thought as she returned to her car. Why had Martinson really come back? Had he seen the drawings or possibly found something else? Maybe he knew something she didn't, or maybe, like Alex, he was willing to chase the vaguest possibility, particularly if someone else was also after it.

EARLY SATURDAY EVENING, Jake went out for a run. Sometimes he could lose himself in a vigorous run, and sometimes it just seemed like a good time to think about all the bad decisions he'd made in his life. Was his coming to Paris another one of those bad decisions?

The painting wasn't going well—he'd spent most of his time this first week visiting museums, though he could certainly rationalize that this was one of the reasons he'd come to Paris. Then going out with Alex Thursday night—what was that all about? She seemed happy to see him, they'd had fun, but at dinner all she could talk about was Sainte Blandine's. He remembered how totally absorbed she could become in any project she took on, though she had only the vaguest idea of what she was after at the convent. She told him she had a "feeling" more than anything, which had surprised Jake. As he recalled, everything Alex did was based on reason and logic.

She had only the slightest interest in what he was doing here in Paris. Did she think it was convenient he'd showed up to escort her to the exhibition?

As he rounded the corner at Rue des Ecoles and headed back toward his hotel, he thought of Rebecca and how unhappy she'd been about his decision to come to Paris.

He'd spoken to her only once since he'd arrived. Why did he feel this need for space, for time? Maybe he should have called the whole thing off before he left. But he didn't feel he was ready to break it off just yet. Maybe he just needed more time. Time for what? Here he was, thirty-five years old . . . When he got back to his hotel, he picked up the phone and called. She was still in bed. She'd worked a late shift the night before.

"I wish you were here," she said sleepily. "Here in bed with me."

It was reassuring, hearing her voice. "I'd like that."

"I miss you, Jake."

"I miss you too, Rebecca." And now, hearing her voice, he did. He wished she could be here with him. And for a moment, he honestly wished he were back home in Montana.

He told her about the painting he was working on, but didn't mention how little time he had spent on it and how unhappy he was with the results. She told him what was going on at the hospital. She said she'd had lunch with his mother, who'd received the postcard he'd sent from London. They talked about Rebecca's coming to Paris in August.

"I can't wait," Rebecca said.

"I'll have some work to show you when you get here."

He felt much better after their talk and went out and ate dinner.

When he got back to his room, the phone was ringing. He picked it up.

"I need you, Jake." It was Alex. "I need you desperately."

10

HE WOULD TAKE the next train to Lyon. Alex would meet him at the station.

He could tell from her voice that she was excited. Usually Alex was completely in control, rarely ruffled, but when she called, he knew she had discovered something she felt was terribly important.

She told him she'd found two drawings hidden in a medieval prayer book, and she thought they had some connection with the Cluny tapestries, *La Dame à la Licorne*. She needed to duplicate them as quickly and accurately as possible. The museum would reimburse him for his trip to Lyon and his supplies, and pay a fee for the drawings. But she needed him right away.

Jake threw his shaving kit, an extra shirt, a change of underwear, socks, and his sketchpad in his bag. He had no idea how long he'd be gone. Alex hadn't said where he'd stay, or even if he would stay. Maybe he'd just take the train over, spend the night drawing, and then Alex would return him to the station, send him back to Paris.

He could have told her no. Told her he was involved in a painting, couldn't leave now.

Pen and ink? Couldn't he do them in pencil? Why was it necessary they be done in pen and ink? And on parchment. Sometimes Alex's sense of perfectionism was ridiculous. Even if he duplicated the drawings, they wouldn't be exact copies. Why didn't she just make a copy on a copy machine? He glanced at his watch. Quarter to nine.

He rushed over to the co-op, which he thought was open until nine. From half a block away, he could see the lights were out. Damn! As he got closer, he saw the pretty Asian girl outside locking the front door. She turned. "You didn't come by the studio Friday night."

"No," he said, sheepishly, then, "Are you open?"

She held up the key. "Does it appear I'm open?"

"Is there any chance, well, uh, this emergency has come up . . . I need some ink, a couple pens, some paper."

"An art emergency?" she said, looking up at him, her head tilted, her mouth set in a playful grin. "This sounds frightfully serious."

"I've been asked to rush down to Lyon this evening to do some drawings." He knew he sounded ridiculous.

"Tonight? I expect you can't wait until morning?"

"It's for a museum here in Paris, the Cluny."

"This *is* serious. I take it they are paying you?"

He nodded.

She turned and unlocked the door.

Inside, she helped him find the supplies he needed. When he dug into his pocket, he realized he didn't have any cash. "Will you take a credit card?" he asked.

"I've closed everything down for the night. You'll have to owe me."

"Thanks," he said. "I appreciate it."

"My name's Julianna," she said. "Julianna Kimura." She reached out to take his hand.

"Jake Bowman." Her hand was very small, like Rebecca's.

"I know," she said. "I helped you with your registration for the co-op."

"Oh, right, and thanks, I mean for tonight."

When they got back out on the street, she asked, "Time for a drink?"

"Some other time."

"Oh, yes." She laughed. "That art emergency in Lyon. Good luck."

"Thanks again."

He arrived at the station too late to take the nine P.M. and had to wait until ten. He imagined Alex would be expecting him earlier.

He got on the train and, as it pulled out of the station, he gazed out the window into the darkness. *At her beck and call,* the words came to him. Alex still had a hold over him.

When the train pulled into Lyon just after midnight, Alex was waiting for him. She smiled as he walked toward her.

"Oh, Jake, thank you so much for coming." She gave him a hug, her hair brushing across his cheek. He could smell her scent, not the perfume she wore when he met her in the Cluny or that night at the exhibition, but something simpler and purer that took him back to the first time he kissed her.

"We're going to my in-laws'," she explained as they walked to her car. "I thought we could do the sketches there, then drive down to Sainte Blandine's in the morning. I have an appointment at ten."

So she wasn't sending him right back on the train. She wanted him to go with her to the convent. She'd said nothing about her in-laws over the phone, and he didn't feel particularly comfortable about the prospect of meeting them in the middle of the night.

As they drove, Alex explained in more detail what she had found, what she thought they might signify. "It's almost as if the drawings were preliminary sketches, done before the tapestries were woven. But the second drawing isn't one of the set of six in the Cluny."

"Is it possible there's a seventh tapestry?" Jake asked.

"When the set was found at the Château Boussac in the nineteenth century, drawings were done as part of an inventory. There were only six drawings, matching the tapestries that now hang in the Cluny. But, strangely enough, when George Sand described them in an article, she referred to eight tapestries. Her descriptions were unclear, as if she were combining elements of the six known tapestries to describe additional ones. It's generally agreed she was confused, perhaps had written the article some time after she'd been to Boussac, and her memory of them was not completely accurate. A set of drawings done by her son, Maurice, was published with her article. Two of the drawings were reversed, produced as if in mirror image, and no one, including George Sand, seemed to be aware of this, which might lead one to believe there wasn't a clear recollection."

"But the tapestries hadn't originally hung at Boussac," Jake said. "I seem to remember, during your tour, you said they were created in the late fourteen hundreds, but first appeared in Boussac in the sixteen hundreds."

"You were listening."

"Yes, I was." In truth, he'd been so startled to see Alex in the museum that day, he'd missed details of her lecture, but he did remember that the tapestries had only been at Boussac for about two hundred years. "Could a tapestry have been lost or destroyed sometime during that interval between when they were created and when they appeared at Boussac?"

"It's possible. In fact, I've always rather liked the idea that there were other tapestries. Maybe even tapestries that had somehow become separated from the others and might still exist."

"Waiting to be discovered?"

Alex smiled as if they were sharing a great adventure. He was glad he'd come.

When they reached the Pelliers', Alex unlocked the door and they walked quietly through the dimly lit living room. Even in the faint light coming in from the hallway, Jake could see the room was elegantly furnished. They walked down the hall and entered a room lined with shelves of hardback and leather-bound books. A large mahogany table sat in the middle of the room. The house was quiet, everyone obviously asleep. Maybe Jake wouldn't have to meet the in-laws.

Alex closed the door, then sat and motioned for Jake to sit. She turned on a small lamp sitting on the table. She opened her briefcase and carefully, tenderly, removed the sketches. She unfolded the first drawing and placed it on the table in front of Jake. As he examined it, he could see it contained the elements of *A Mon Seul Désir*. There were various sketches around the borders, in the corners. He could see what Alex meant—they did look more like preliminary sketches, thumbnails as he might call them, although they contained more detail than he would usually put in a preliminary drawing. Yet the idea that this was created by an artist testing ideas and composition before completing a final design seemed plausible. He examined the detail, wondering how he would complete two drawings by morning, particularly if the second contained such detail. And pen and ink. If he made a slip of the pen, he'd have to start over. Should he suggest a pencil drawing?

"I've been studying them ever since I called you," Alex said. "There are so many intriguing details, some identical to the Cluny tapestries, others different. Look at the inscription on the tent." She pointed.

Jake couldn't recall exactly what the original tapestry looked like. He thought the inscription along the upper band of the tent was *A Mon Seul Désir, To My Sole Desire*. On this drawing there was a signature, the name *Adèle,* followed by what appeared to be an initial, stylized almost to look like a design. The two were interwoven with a graceful tendril.

Alex stood and pulled a large book off the shelf. She opened it, placed it on the table in front of Jake. She leaned over him and he could smell her again. She began flipping through the pages. It was an art book with colored reproductions of *The Lady and the Unicorn* tapestries. Alex stopped when she came to the sixth tapestry, *A Mon Seul Désir*.

"I've often been curious if there wasn't more to this," she said, pointing to the inscription on the tent. "It's always been interpreted as *to my sole desire,* the beginning *A* as the preposition *to*. But there's never been an explanation for the letter that follows the inscription." Alex pointed to a letter at the far right on the band of the tent. It looked like a V or possibly a U, maybe even an I. It was partially covered by a rope coming from the top of the tent attached to a tree on the right side. Jake hadn't noticed this final letter on the tent border when he saw the tapestry in the museum. There was so much detail in each piece that it was impossible to take in everything, even after several viewings.

"And look," Alex said, her voice rising, "at the way the A is drawn on the name *Adèle*." She pointed to the drawing. "Look at the final initial on both the tapestry and the drawing."

The A on the tapestry and the A of *Adèle* on the drawing were done in a similar style. Jake examined the final letter on the tapestry in the art book and the one intertwined with the name on the drawing. The last cryptic letter was similar on both.

"What do you think it means?" he asked, turning to look up at Alex.

"It was common in medieval tapestry and art to intertwine the initials of lovers. I think the A and the final initial on the original tapestry are representative of two medieval lovers."

"Adèle and someone whose name starts with a V or U or whatever the final letter signifies?"

"Yes."

"Who?"

"I don't know. The theory that the tapestries were designed for Jean Le Viste seems to be accurate. It holds together based on the heraldic symbols, the time period, the fact they ended up at Boussac."

"Adèle was one of his daughters?"

"There's no Adèle recorded in any family history."

"Couldn't the V be a representation of the family name, *Viste*? Maybe Adèle was the name of a maiden, the love of one of the Le Viste boys."

"Jean le Viste had no sons, only daughters—Claude, Jeanne, and Geneviève."

"No boys, and no Adèle?"

"No boys. No Adèle."

"A bit of a mystery?"

"Yes, definitely. A romantic mystery perhaps. I've always liked the idea of a medieval love affair, always believed the tapestries were created to celebrate a romance." Alex stood for a few more moments, then reached down, set the book aside, pulled the second sketch out of her briefcase, and unfolded it on the table in front of Jake.

It seemed more a complete composition than the first, although there were some drawings along the border. Alex pointed to a sketch of the unicorn at the bottom of the drawing. Almost hidden in the intricate lines making up the tail of the animal was the name again. *Adèle*.

"What do you think is the significance here?" she asked.

Jake examined the name carefully, the way it was scripted. "It appears to be an artist's signature."

"Exactly," Alex answered.

"You think this Adèle, the lady whose name appears on the tent in the drawing, was the artist who designed the tapestries?"

"Perhaps," Alex answered pensively. "Yet she might just be some little modern-day nun, or maybe one from sometime in the past five centuries, who likes to imitate medieval tapestry designs. Some little nun who's taking great delight now, from her perch in heaven, as she watches all this ruckus she's stirring up."

"That's an intriguing thought," Jake said. "I mean that the artist might have been a woman."

"It's a thought that's crossed my mind a time or two. There are so many elements that suggest the tapestries are saying something about a woman's role during the Middle Ages. Look at the setting—a garden island. The aristocratic, medieval woman was basically isolated, a captive in the castle. For a little outing, she could go outdoors into the garden." Alex pointed to the maiden in the reproduction in the art book. "The women in the tapestries are representative of the idealized woman of the Middle Ages—long blond hair, delicate, slender, almost boyish figures. And the way the maidens are so lavishly dressed. Each decorated in finery, gowns and jewels, and hairdos. Each a prize to be won, or a pawn used by the men to advance their political and economic positions."

Alex turned the page in the art book. She moved the drawing aside and placed the book in front of Jake again. It was opened to the reproduction of the tapestry *Touch*, the one that had been displayed at the Grand Palais.

"Does this seem to be saying something about control?"

Alex bent over, pointed to the small animals that were collared and chained, a detail Jake hadn't noticed on the real tapestry.

Alex pointed to the maiden, holding a banner attached to a lance in her right hand, touching the horn of the unicorn with the other. "A woman during this time had very little control over her own destiny."

Again, Jake could see what he took to be an erotic element of the tapestry. The woman wasn't just touching the horn; she was stroking it, caressing it.

"This is the only tapestry," Alex observed, "in which the woman, rather than the lion or unicorn, holds the lance and banner with the family arms. Is the woman trying to say something about power or control?"

"I see what you mean," Jake answered.

Alex turned the pages once more, open again to *A Mon Seul Désir*. "Earlier interpretations of this tapestry assert the woman is choosing the jewels from the casket, but notice the rhythm, the movement; she's obviously placing them in the casket. Perhaps removing the jewels from her body, removing that which adorns her, giving them up."

Again, Jake would have to agree with Alex's observation.

"And her hair," Alex said. The woman's hair was cut short, ragged, barely grazing her shoulders. "No respectable medieval woman would cut off her hair . . . unless . . ."

"Unless she was going to the convent?" Jake asked, looking back at Alex.

"It appears the woman is giving up her adornment," she answered, "perhaps freeing herself in some way."

Jake wondered if this was how a woman in the Middle Ages would find her freedom. In a convent? He closed the book, moved the second drawing back to the table in front of him. "What about this?" he asked, observing the natural garden setting. "No island? And no embellishment. No fancy frocks. The woman is nude. Freeing herself once more?"

"I'm not sure," Alex answered. "And we are assuming this drawing goes along with the others." She paused. "It has so many intriguing elements of medieval art—the garden, the idealized woman, the knight, the unicorn. I need to do some studying, some research. That's why I need them duplicated." Alex took a deep breath. "Oh, Jake, do you think you can help me? Can you finish the two drawings in time to return the originals to the convent tomorrow morning at ten?"

"Not if we sit and chat all night." He looked up and grinned.

"No, of course not," Alex said, but she wasn't smiling. She had that serious, determined look Jake had seen so often before.

"I'd better get started," he said. "If you expect me to finish by morning."

"Yes. Thank you so much for coming."

He opened his bag, took out the ink, pen, and paper.

"Can I get you something, Jake? Coffee? Cookies? Marie makes wonderful cookies. Always fills the cookie jar if she knows Sunny is coming."

"Your daughter's here?"

"I generally bring her when I come to Lyon. Her grandparents so seldom see her."

"Oh, yes," Jake said as if he understood about children and grandparents. "No, I'd better get started here. No distractions."

"You'd like me to leave you alone?"

"I'll probably work better without distraction."

"Let me know if you need anything." Alex walked to the bookshelf, pulled several books off, leafed through a couple, returned them, selected several more. "Sorry," she whispered. "I just feel I should make use of my time while I'm waiting. I wish I could help you, Jake. I do appreciate your coming."

"Pleased I could be of service."

"I'll be in the living room," she said as she left, her arms loaded with books.

Jake settled down, ready to start the drawing. He would begin with the first, at least what he and Alex had determined was the first—the one that contained the elements of *A Mon Seul Désir*. He decided to do a basic sketch in pencil, then fill in the detail with pen and ink. It would take longer, but if he went straight to ink and made a mistake, he'd have to start all over again. He'd have to work on some sort of grid to get them as accurate as possible, to make sure every angle, every line and curve was as close as possible to the originals. He took his pencil and with a soft, fine line, he divided his paper into perfect quarters, matching the folds in the drawings.

As he worked, a thought came to him. Was Alex asking him to do the drawings, being so particular about the pen and ink, the paper, because she intended to return the duplicates to the prayer book and keep the originals? No, this didn't make any sense. Alex was determined, Alex liked to get her own way, but he'd never known her to be dishonest.

He finished the pencil sketch, then began carefully tracing the lines with ink, starting in the upper left-hand corner. After a while, he changed the point on the pen to work in some of the intricate detail. As he worked on the headdress of the maiden, with fine, delicate lines, the thoughts were turning over in his mind—what did the drawings signify? How had they come to be hidden in the prayer book? And, who, if anyone, other than their creator, had seen them? Alex seemed to think no one else had seen the drawings. If this was true, no one would even know if she decided to keep them.

Alex returned. "Anything I can get for you?"

Jake looked at his watch and was amazed it was already half past four. He would never finish in time to make it to the convent by ten. Alex had told him it was at least a half hour drive. "I'd better keep at it if we want to finish and get them back to the convent."

"It's coming along nicely," she said. She didn't seem in the least alarmed that he was only halfway finished with the first drawing.

Alex replaced some books on the shelf, spent several minutes selecting more. "This is all so exciting, isn't it?"

"Very exciting."

By quarter to six, Jake had finished the first drawing. He set it aside to dry. Then he sat for a moment before beginning. He would skip the pencil drawing, he decided. It was the only way he could possibly finish. He dipped the tip of the pen into the bottle of ink and began.

Carefully, he started again in the upper left-hand corner. It seemed to come easily, as if the first drawing were just a warm-up. His pen now moved with a natural rhythm as he duplicated the drawing on his paper. He filled in the intricate detail as if a hand of confidence guided him.

As he worked, Jake couldn't help but notice how this drawing, how parts and pieces of it resembled *Le Pégase,* the tapestry he had seen at the exhibition at the Grand Palais in Paris. The knight with the lance, directed toward the unicorn on the maiden's lap, bore a close resemblance to the knight mounted on the winged horse, the Pegasus. The setting in this drawing was not the garden island of the six pieces in the Cluny, but a more natural garden. Jake couldn't help but notice how much it resembled the background in the tapestry Alex had shown him at the exhibition. Could she see this likeness too?

He had completed a good portion of the second piece when he heard Alex enter the room. In her arms, she held a beautiful little blond girl wearing a blue nightgown. Her long skinny legs and arms were wrapped around her mother; her head rested on Alex's shoulder. The girl looked up and with large searching eyes she seemed to be studying him.

"Jake, I'd like you to meet my daughter, Soleil," Alex said softly. "Sunny, this is my good friend Jake Bowman." The child clutched her mother even tighter. "She's not quite awake yet." Alex smiled at Jake, then Soleil, as she ran her fingers through the little girl's hair. "Could you say good morning to Monsieur Bowman?"

"Good morning, Monsieur Bowman," she said guardedly, then buried her head again against her mother's shoulder.

"Good morning, Sunny."

"My name is Soleil." The child looked up again, something defiant in her eyes. Eyes that Jake couldn't help but notice were the same pale blue as her mother's.

Alex continued to stroke the little girl's hair. "We were just going to have some breakfast. Will you have time to join us, Monsieur Bowman?"

Before he could answer, the child asked, "Did you sleep here at Grandmère and Grandpère's last night?"

"No, I'm afraid there wasn't time for sleep. I've been working all night."

Alex walked closer and looked at the drawing. Soleil glanced down. Alex said, "I could have Marie pack a breakfast. You could eat on the way."

"I think that would be best. I'm not quite finished." Not finished, but it was going much better than he had expected. It was now eight, and amazingly, he could see he might finish by eight-thirty or shortly after.

"It looks very nice, Jake," Alex said. "Isn't it beautiful?" she asked Soleil. The little girl didn't answer. "Monsieur Bowman is a gifted artist," Alex said. "Come, let's leave him alone to finish." Alex smiled at Jake. "You'll never know how much I appreciate your help." She turned to leave the room. The little girl stared at Jake over her mother's shoulder.

Jake continued to work. By nine-fifteen, he had but a few strokes to finish.

"How's it going?" Alex stood behind him.

"Do we need to leave?"

"In a few minutes. We can drive fast and still make it by ten. I know all the dips and turns in the road now."

"This one isn't dry yet," Jake said. "If we leave it flat, we could transport it in the back seat of the car."

She gave him a puzzled look, a wrinkle forming between her brows. "We don't need to take the copies to the convent. I'll let Marie know we've left them out to dry. They'll be perfectly safe here." She stared at him for what seemed like a full minute. "Oh, Jake, you thought I was going to do a little switcheroo. Keep the originals, replace them with the duplicates."

He shrugged his shoulders. Embarrassed. "I still don't fully understand why you wanted them done in ink. Wouldn't a quick pencil sketch have been sufficient?"

"We can talk while we drive. Marie's packed some bread, cheese, and fruit. We should probably leave soon."

"Just a few more strokes of the pen."

Alex paused at the door. "I came up with the most brilliant thought as I sat contemplating, reading in the living room. I didn't want to interrupt and explain while you were working, but I think we've really stumbled on to something here. I have so much in my head right now, so much we need to talk about. I think we really have discovered something important."

"Yes," he said. And he couldn't help noticing that Alex had said *we*.

11

FOR THE FIRST five minutes of the drive, Alex didn't mention the tapestries. They talked about Soleil, about the Pelliers, Alex's in-laws, whom Jake met briefly that morning.

Alex asked about Jake's work. He said he was having a hard time getting into the painting and didn't fully understand why. She said, reassuringly, she was sure it would come.

He pulled an orange out of the bag Marie had packed, peeled and sectioned it, and offered Alex a piece.

She shook her head. "I'm convinced this Adèle of the drawings was involved with the design of the tapestries. I had a long time to think about all this while I was driving back from the convent yesterday, waiting for you to arrive from Paris, while you were drawing. Something else I found at the convent kept coming back to me, as if the two were somehow tied together."

"Another discovery?" Jake wiped his chin, then his sticky fingers on a napkin.

"A poem I found last weekend when I visited Sainte Blandine's. It was intriguing, but at the time, I didn't think it was any more than a romantic little verse. From the language, the parchment, it appeared to be very old, the ink so faded in places I could barely make it out. It told the story of a tapestry weaver and a young woman. A love story."

"Adèle's story?"

Alex shrugged her shoulders. "I wonder . . . a poem about a young woman and a tapestry weaver . . . and now these drawings . . . possibly relating to the design of a fifteenth-century tapestry . . . The poem was difficult to translate, and portions were faded and torn, the bottom of the first page missing. I'm trying desperately to recall what it said. It seems there was some reference to a love denied, the woman going to the house of women who loved the Lord, which I interpreted as the convent."

"A sad love story, then? Girl loves boy, loses boy, ends up at the convent?"

"I'm afraid that might be true."

"What about the prayer book, the drawings, how did they end up at the convent?"

"I think Adèle probably brought the book with her. I don't know if the drawings were done before she entered the convent or while she was there."

"But you think she designed the tapestries?"

"Yes, I do."

"She also wrote the poem?"

"I don't think so. It was written in third person. But somehow, I feel it was about Adèle."

"Not to put a damper on your discovery, but isn't it strange—you go to the convent, this poem, these drawings just fall into your lap?"

"Actually, the poem didn't fall into my lap." Alex laughed. "It hit me on the head."

"Sometimes . . . ," Jake said and laughed too, "we could all use a little whack on the head."

"Yes, I suppose so." Alex smiled, but her tone was serious now. "If we can learn who this woman is, perhaps we can discover something about the possibility of a seventh tapestry."

"How do you intend to discover who this mysterious woman is, or was?"

"I have a plan," Alex said. "When I was going through the library at the convent, I found a book, a record actually of the Convent of Sainte Blandine. It was a document containing information on the nuns who lived and died at the convent during the past century."

"That's interesting, but if the woman was involved in the design of the tapestry, rather than a latter-day imitator, wouldn't you have to find a record from the fifteenth century?"

"Exactly," Alex answered. "According to the nuns' inventory, there are five volumes. Doesn't that seem to indicate that the records go back to the founding of the convent?"

"Did you see the other books?"

"No. But then, I wasn't looking for them. I was there as a representative of the museum, and I didn't see any artistic value in these records. The thought was interesting—that the history of the nuns had been recorded. But I didn't want to waste time with my own curiosities."

"Are you going as a representative of the museum today?"

"Yes, of course."

They continued to drive, neither speaking. Jake opened a package of cheese, sliced off several pieces, and arranged a couple on a piece of bread. He wondered if he had insulted Alex again. First he had suggested she intended to steal the drawings, that her double discovery was just too much of a coincidence, and now that she was putting her own concerns above those of the museum.

"While you were working," she said, after several minutes, "I was trying to figure out the significance of the second drawing. I don't think we fully understand what the six tapestries in the Cluny mean, so that would be quite a feat—figuring out what a seventh tapestry might signify, if indeed this is a design for a seventh tapestry."

Jake didn't say anything. Alex seemed to be rambling, talking to herself.

"I've done extensive research on the unicorn in medieval art," she said. She didn't seem to be paying much attention to the road. Jake had offered to drive when they left Lyon, but Alex said it would be quicker if she took the wheel, and maybe he'd like to nap on the way since he'd been up all night. After they passed several cars just outside the city, there wasn't much traffic. He gazed out the window at a herd of Charolais feeding on the hillside. The motor of the car hummed. Now he *was* getting sleepy. He wondered about

Alex—she'd been up all night too, but didn't seem the least bit tired.

"There are representations where the unicorn is shown with the nude rather than the clothed maiden," she continued. "Perhaps an erotic element, perhaps not. In some interpretations of the symbolic use of the unicorn in medieval art, the mythical animal is taken to be a symbol of purity, chastity, and divine love. The maiden, a symbol of the Virgin Mary. Virgins, purity, chastity were big in the art of the Middle Ages." She reached over and attempted to pull a piece off the loaf of bread.

"You drive," he said, motioning with his head toward the road. "I'll fix breakfast." He pulled off the bread and handed it to her. "Cheese?"

"No, thanks." She took a bite. "The representation of a male figure . . . generally when a single male figure appears with the maiden and unicorn he represents the angel Gabriel. Medieval and even Renaissance art often pictured the unicorn in Annunciation scenes, the unicorn representing both chastity and Christ. It has been suggested by some that the Cluny tapestries have such symbolic meaning."

"But there's no man in any of the tapestries."

"Unless . . ."

"Unless there's another tapestry?"

Alex nodded.

"Do you think the drawing has some religious significance?" Jake asked.

"The religious interpretation of the unicorn in the Cluny set is an intriguing idea. I've always been fascinated by the multiplicity of symbolism in medieval art. But the knight in the drawing . . . and the fact that the maiden is nude . . ." Alex rubbed the side of her head as if thinking so intensely had given her a headache. "I recall a small miniature in a thirteenth-century English bestiary where the knight, the unicorn, and the unclothed maiden were represented. I was trying to find something in Pierre and Simone's library, a reproduction of the work. The Pelliers have always kept a wonderful library, an extensive section on medieval subjects, but I couldn't find anything."

Alex was silent again, deep in thought, running her fingers through her hair now, massaging her left temple.

"There are frescoes in the Camera del Perseo at the Castel Sant'Angelo in Rome," she said, "featuring nude or semiclad, bare-breasted maidens frolicking with the unicorns, stroking their horns, caressing the beasts, seducing them, basically, coaxing the animals toward their laps. Plainly the unicorn's horn takes on phallic symbolism, as it often does as we move away from the religious interpretation of the Middle Ages. These particular frescoes were done about fifteen forty-five and are credited to Pierino del Vaga, a student of Raphael."

"Interesting," Jake replied. Well, wasn't Alex being scholarly and academic—dates and artist's credits and all. But this conversation was certainly perking him up again. Maybe he hadn't been imagining the woman in *Touch* caressing the horn. He wondered if Alex wasn't playing with him a bit, all in the guise of art. "The true derivation of the word *horny*?" Jake said and laughed. Alex laughed too.

"While I was browsing through Pierre and Simone's library," she said, quite serious again, "I came across a book of medieval literature. The garden setting is a frequent theme. The maiden and her lover are always meeting in the garden, a little clandestine tryst. This was the setting of the poem, actually, the one I found in the library. And, of course, the Cluny tapestries. Are you familiar with the Garden of Deduit in *Roman de la Rose*?"

"I don't recall reading that one, but I can't say I paid much attention in literature class."

"I know—you were the fella in the back of the room doodling in his notebook. The artist."

"Yup, that was me." He grinned. "And you were the scholar. Tell me about the Garden of Deduit."

"The garden of pleasure, as they say. The garden of earthly pleasures, the *hortus deliciarum*. Medieval thought has also connected the garden to the *hortus conclusus*, the enclosed garden, relating it to the Song of Songs."

"From the Bible? That one I've read."

"Yes, the Song of Solomon, where the bridegroom speaks of his beloved as the 'garden enclosed . . . a fountainhead sealed.'"

"Another erotic element here?"

"One might think so. The early Christians related the bride

to Mary, the enclosed garden the symbol of her virginity, and also of the Garden of Eden, which is regained by Christ's incarnation and resurrection."

"Eroticism and redemption all in one package."

Alex smiled once more but didn't answer. Jake looked out the window. Two horses galloped down a hillside next to a small stone farmhouse. After a while, he felt his head getting heavy, then dropping as the rhythm of the vehicle and the road lulled him to sleep.

When he woke, they had turned off the main highway and were now bouncing up and down on a rutted gravel road.

"The convent isn't much farther," Alex said, motioning with her hand.

The road was rough and hilly. It didn't appear to have been kept up. Alex was driving much too fast, not paying attention as she kept looking over at him, out at the scenery. "We'll be there soon," she said. "Beautiful country."

"Yes," he answered, looking out the window at the hills and vineyards. So much green, dotted with red-tiled farmhouse roofs.

"Family legend has it the Benoits came from somewhere in this vicinity, from south of Lyon."

"Then you feel at home around here."

"Yes." She smiled.

As they continued to drive, it seemed as if Alex had again picked up speed. He looked at his watch. Three minutes to ten. They were on a narrow dirt road now.

The thought came to Jake that Alex had never told him why the drawings had to be done in ink, why a pencil sketch wouldn't do. She said she would explain on the way, but hadn't mentioned it. He was about to ask, when she pointed down the road as they came over a rise. *"Le Couvent de Sainte Blandine,"* she announced.

A small van, a utility truck, and a dark-green, newer-model vehicle were lined up a short distance in front of the convent.

"Damn," Alex said under her breath. "Martinson's here."

"The curator from New York? I thought he said his trip had been a waste of time. Now he's come back?"

Alex glanced over at Jake with a sardonic smile. "I don't

believe Martinson is a person in whom you'd want to put much trust."

She held her briefcase protectively under her arm as Jake followed her up the path. She walked with the same hurried pace at which she'd driven to the convent.

As they got closer, they could hear pounding coming from the upper level.

"The Archbishop is renovating," Alex explained. "He plans to turn the convent into a hotel."

An elderly nun opened the front door, mumbling something about the Archbishop, "even on *dimanche,* the day of the Lord." She bowed her head, Jake thought in reference to the Lord's name, and then with a scowl she motioned them to enter. They were soon met by another nun, whom Alex introduced as Sister Etienne.

"You've brought a colleague this morning?" she asked.

"Yes," Alex replied, then introduced Jake as an artist from America. "We'd like to take a look in the library."

"Another American," the nun said thoughtfully.

"I see Dr. Martinson has returned," Alex said.

"He's quite interested in the library. If you don't mind, perhaps you could both share the space this morning."

"If that is agreeable with Dr. Martinson," Alex said graciously, but Jake could tell she was not pleased. They exchanged glances of concern.

Sister Etienne led them into the library. A small nun sat in one corner on a large chair. Dr. Martinson sat at the far end of the room at a desk, with a book opened in front of him. He looked up and smiled. Jake could almost imagine the man twisting his anemic little blond mustache in his fingers like the villain in a melodrama.

"*Bonjour,* Sister Anne," Alex said cheerfully, then introduced Jake to the small nun. "*Bonjour,* Dr. Martinson," she called across the room.

The man sat stiff and rigid in his chair. There was something unpleasant about him. Jake didn't like him at all. "You remember Monsieur Bowman," Alex said.

Dr. Martinson looked puzzled. "Ah, yes, we met at the exhibition."

"Do you mind, Dr. Martinson, may we work here?"

"That would be fine," he replied with little emotion.

"Bien," said Sister Etienne. "If you have questions or need assistance, Sister Anne is here to help you." She smiled at the tiny nun in the corner.

"Oui," Alex said. *"Merci."*

Alex and Jake sat at the small table in the middle of the room. Sister Etienne left. A loud crashing noise came from above. Dr. Martinson shook his head, then returned to his book.

"That's the book," Alex whispered. "That's the prayer book. Now how am I going to return the drawings?"

Jake shrugged his shoulders and wondered if maybe Alex shouldn't just keep them. Who would ever know?

Alex opened her briefcase quietly. Another loud pounding noise shook the room. Everyone looked up as if expecting the ceiling to cave in.

"The Archbishop's men," Alex whispered. She removed several pieces of paper from her briefcase. With the slightest shuffling, she sorted through them and set one on the table in front of Jake. She pointed to *"Le registre du Couvent de Sainte Blandine."* Then she picked up the paper, rose quietly, and walked over to the small nun. Sister Anne glanced at the list, then slid off the chair and walked across the room, rocking back and forth as she moved. She maneuvered her small, distorted body behind Dr. Martinson, then unlocked a bookcase and pulled out a book. Dr. Martinson looked over the nun's shoulder, obviously trying to get a glance at what Alex had requested. The nun walked back to Alex and handed her the book, saying something Jake couldn't hear.

Alex returned to the table.

"Can I help?" he asked. "Could you get another volume?"

"She'll only let me take one at a time from the locked bookcase," Alex whispered. "I asked for the first volume. It's probably too early but I don't want to miss anything." She opened the book and ran her finger down the first page, barely making contact with the fragile paper. Carefully she turned the page. She scanned one side while Jake examined the other—faded scratchings that were difficult to read. They continued, attempting to decipher the ancient names and numbers. Some of the pages were torn and stained. It appeared portions of some were missing.

As they got to the last few pages of the book, Alex took a pen and blank paper from her briefcase and started to scribble notes. She had found the name *Adèle* in the register. "Most likely too early," she whispered, shaking her head. She closed the book, got up, and walked to Sister Anne.

The noise from above had subsided. The two women spoke in hushed tones. Jake glanced at Martinson. He was definitely curious, obviously puzzled as to why Alex had returned to the convent. Jake liked this feeling, knowing that he was in on this and Martinson wasn't, that he had at least a vague notion of what Alex was after.

Sister Anne got up again, pulling a key from the pocket of her habit as she traveled with great effort across the floor of the small room. She replaced the first book, withdrew another, walked back, and handed it to Alex. All the while, Dr. Martinson watched.

Just as Alex sat down again next to Jake, Dr. Martinson spoke. "You must be on to something, Madame Pellier."

"And you, Dr. Martinson," she answered, looking up across the room, "you've extended your stay in France to return to Sainte Blandine's?" She glanced down at the floor next to the table where he sat. "Oh," she said, with mock surprise, "I see you've found your briefcase."

Dr. Martinson stared at Alex, saying nothing as if he were trying to find a reply, then without a word his lips turned up in a smug smile. For several moments Alex stared back, and then she opened the second book and began turning pages.

Jake was feeling drowsy again. His head dropped and he drifted off. When he woke, he wasn't sure how much time had passed. Alex looked discouraged as she turned the pages. She closed the book and gazed at the bookcase against the opposite wall. "Am I crazy," she asked in a soft voice, "to think I might find a clue here in the records of Sainte Blandine? Am I crazy to think there is anything to find? That the drawings signify anything other than wishful thinking on my part?"

Then, before Jake could reply, she was up again, returning to Sister Anne, who was looking a bit bored and sleepy herself on her perch in the corner.

Sister Anne retrieved the third book. Alex sat and turned to the first page. Martinson closed his book and stared down at the desk.

Jake felt Alex reach over and touch his hand, then clutch it. He turned to her. A mischievous, yet satisfied, smile turned her lips so slowly it was as if she wanted to hide it, to prevent it from appearing, giving a clue of her obvious delight. She pointed. "Look."

Jake looked down. On the first page of the third book, he read silently, "Adèle Le Viste, 15, 29 décembre 1490."

12

ALEX SAT STARING at the faded script. She looked at Jake and realized she was still holding his hand, unconsciously squeezing it. Without releasing his hand, she turned the page. Halfway down the second page, the name appeared once more. Recorded on 16 July 1491, the death of a young Adèle Le Viste.

An unexpected sadness came over Alex. She knew it was ridiculous—the woman had been dead for over five hundred years. Yet Alex felt she had just found the young woman, only to lose her again. She closed the book, released Jake's hand, and sat staring at the cover. When she looked up, Sister Etienne had returned to the room. This time, Alex hadn't even heard her come in.

"Madame Pellier, Monsieur Bowman, I'm afraid we have others coming this afternoon." The nun spoke in an anxious, hurried voice. She picked up the register Alex was examining and motioned for Sister Anne to come retrieve it. She whispered something to the small nun as she handed her the book. Sister Anne returned to the locked bookcase. Sister Etienne walked over to the desk where Dr. Martinson sat, spoke quietly to him, then picked up the prayer book. She motioned the three Americans out of the library.

"Might I speak with you in my office, Madame Pellier?" Sister Etienne asked as the four of them walked down the hall. It was then Alex realized the nun was carrying the prayer book.

"Please, Monsieur Martinson," Sister Etienne added as they walked, "you might indicate items of interest by using the numbers on the inventory sheet."

"Thank you," Dr. Martinson said. "Perhaps I'll be contacting you soon."

Alex wondered if he really would—had he discovered something she was unaware of?

"In my office, please," Sister Etienne said to Alex as a reluctant Dr. Martinson was led by the old wrinkled nun, the gatekeeper, who had appeared again out of nowhere. "Perhaps, Monsieur Bowman," Sister Etienne said, "you might be comfortable waiting here." She pointed to a wooden bench in the hallway. Jake nodded, then, giving Alex a concerned look, he sat. Alex followed Sister Etienne into her office.

The nun sat. Alex sat. She felt like a young schoolgirl called to the principal's office.

Sister Etienne placed the prayer book on the desk, glanced down briefly, and then looked up at Alex, who was having a hard time meeting the nun's gaze. She looked at Sister Etienne, then stared down at the prayer book

"In all the commotion and excitement," the nun said, her voice calm, "perhaps in gathering up the inventory sheets, perhaps your own notes, it would be understood papers might become inadvertently intermingled." Alex looked up. Across the table, the nun's alert gray eyes, clear and unblinking, met hers. Alex didn't see anger in the way the older woman searched her eyes, but Alex was sure she knew. Yes, Sister Etienne knew she had taken the drawings. But it seemed the good sister also knew Alex had every intention of returning them, that it was only Dr. Martinson's hoarding the prayer book this morning that had prevented her from doing so.

Before Alex could reply, she heard a light knock on the door.

"Oui," Sister Etienne called out. The door opened and Sister Anne's oversized head popped through the opening about halfway down. It struck Alex once more what a strange, distorted little woman she was. "Please, will you excuse me for a moment," Sister Etienne said as she rose. She left the room without waiting for a response.

Alex knew what was expected. She reached down for her briefcase. Slowly, she lifted the drawings out. She opened the prayer book and flipped over pages until she reached the middle section where the pages were stuck together, still forming a protective envelope. Carefully, she slid the two drawings back into the book, then closed it and took a deep breath. She was grateful Jake had made the copies, grateful she had been able to return the originals, grateful for Sister Etienne's kindness. But why had the nun let her return them without any accusations?

Alex sat for what seemed like a good ten minutes. Was the nun giving her time to contemplate her offense? She shifted in the chair and looked around the room, which was very plain—stone walls, nothing but a small crucifix hanging on one wall. The desk was neat and tidy and bare except for the prayer book, a small pad of paper and pen, and a rather large book on one corner. It was leather-bound and looked as old and worn as many on the shelves in the library. She wondered if it had been removed from the library. After waiting a few more minutes for Sister Etienne's return, wondering if the nun would leave her here for the rest of the day, Alex picked up the book and opened it.

Her hand rose to her throat as she took in a deep gulp of air and stared down in disbelief. The poem she'd found on her first visit was inside the front cover. It wasn't the same book she had pulled off the shelf in the library, the book that had fallen apart. This was much larger. Alex guessed the poem had been placed in this book to protect it.

The torn first page was now complete, held together with clear plastic tape. Alex read the faded words.

> *She would not wed the one she loved*
> *Nor he of rank, the father's choice*
> *A bride of Christ and here to die*

To die? It *was* Adèle, and the young woman *had* died at the convent. Alex read the first verses again. As she read, she was even more convinced that the drawings and this ancient poem were somehow related. The description of the garden, the flowers described—daisies, pansies, lilies of the valley, carnations, periwinkle, and roses—were identical to those pictured in the tapestries. Alex's heart beat rapidly as she read the cryptic words. She felt a shiver, a chill of excitement run through her.

She continued to read . . . the words faded, illegible here and there.

> *The labor of their love . . .*
> *buried there beneath the stone . . .*
> *and once more their love to blossom,*
> *the fruit, the passion of their love*
> *to be found in the village near . . .*

The labor of their love? Was the poem referring to the tapestries? Designed by Adèle? Woven in the workshop of her *tapissier*? One buried? Perhaps another in the village? Did Sister Etienne intend for Alex to read this? Did the nun see the connection between the drawings and the poem? The tapestries?

Alex heard a movement in the hall. Quickly she slid the poem back into the book and placed it on the corner of the desk.

Sister Etienne entered the room. The nun sat. For several long moments she didn't say anything. She glanced briefly at the book on the corner of her desk, then looked at Alex. "The book," she asked, "is it valuable?"

At first Alex thought she was speaking of the book containing the poem.

Then Sister Etienne tapped the prayer book, still lying on the desk in front of her.

Of course, she was referring to the prayer book.

Alex took a deep breath and said, "It appears to be an authentic medieval book of prayers."

Sister Etienne continued to tap the prayer book. She nodded, as if she wished Alex to continue.

Alex felt as if she were a college student now, sitting in a professor's intimate little office, taking an oral final. "It's from the late Middle Ages," she said, "not the best example of medieval illuminated manuscripts. It's done on paper with modest ornamentation rather than vellum found in some of the older, more deluxe versions of books of hours. During this period, after the mid-1400s, after the invention of moveable type, books were being produced in larger quantities. Books could be purchased by middle-class laymen at cathedrals and shrines. The competition from printed books, unfortunately, reduced the quality of some of the hand-illuminated manuscripts."

Alex took another breath. Sister Etienne folded her hands in front of her on the desk, the book between the two women.

"The book is hand-scripted text, in Latin," Alex continued, "on paper as I said, with minimal ornamentation, which reduces its value. There are no miniature paintings as found in some of the more valuable illuminations. Some of these have gone at auction for millions, more valuable than many paintings from this period. But this book," Alex said, touching the small volume, "it's not in very good condition—pages torn, possibly missing, some water damage and worm track. But there are several pages still legible. Even single pages of authentic illuminated manuscripts have been sold for hundreds, even thousands."

Sister Etienne paused, thinking. She looked down at the prayer book. Slowly she looked up, directly into Alex's eyes once more. "And the drawings," she said, "are they valuable?"

Alex felt suddenly as if the oxygen were being removed from the small room where she sat with Sister Etienne. As if there weren't enough air for the two women to both breathe at the same time. Why had she taken the drawings? And now, where was this conversation going? Was this where the accusations would begin?

"In themselves," Alex answered, "I'm not sure."

Sister Etienne paused. "But what they might represent?"

Alex stared down at the prayer book, then raised her eyes once more to meet the nun's.

"You've studied the drawings?" Sister Etienne asked.

"Yes." Again Alex felt she should be cautious. Did she owe this good sister more? Did she owe her an explanation, a summary of what she had discovered? But what had she discovered? That the drawings might possibly have some connection to the tapestries in the Cluny Museum? That they might have been designed by a young woman named Adèle Le Viste? That they might have been designed to celebrate a romance? And had she discovered that the romance was the love between a common *tapissier* and Adèle Le Viste? Did all of this mean there might be a seventh tapestry somewhere, hidden for centuries? Maybe even an eighth *in the village near*? Or might it all signify nothing?

"It is correct to believe there is some connection," Sister Etienne said, continuing to look directly at Alex, "the drawings with the unicorn tapestries in your museum?"

How could Alex have thought for a moment that the drawings had not been discovered until she herself pulled them from the prayer book? And even Sister Etienne had seen the resemblance, the possible connection of the drawings to the Cluny tapestries. And what about the poem? Why had Sister Etienne left it on the desk?

"I'm not sure," Alex answered. It seemed there were many pieces to a puzzle, little bits and parts she was trying to put together, but she really had nothing to prove she was following a path that would lead anywhere. So much of this was based on hope. A belief she was in the process of discovering something that would lead her to some treasure.

"Would it be valuable," Sister Etienne spoke slowly, "a tapestry, based on one of these drawings?"

Alex felt her stomach turn, a pounding, throbbing sensation in the back of her head. What was the nun telling her? That a tapestry had been discovered? "An authentic fifteenth-century tapestry would be quite valuable," Alex said. "I can't say exactly how valuable. They are so rare. Now and then, a small fragment will be discovered, but nothing complete. So many were destroyed. And generally the pieces, fragments are not in good condition. But an authentic, complete, fifteenth-century tapestry? In good condition?"

Sister Etienne hesitated again, lightly stroking the silver

cross hanging from her neck. She cleared her throat. As cautious as Alex herself. Yet it seemed the woman was on the brink of making a momentous revelation. "When Mother Alvère contacted the museums to come look at the order's belongings, I don't imagine she truly believed there was anything of great value. Perhaps for a small sum, anything might have been offered, but now . . . if there were anything of great value, perhaps a public offering would be more appropriate?"

Again, Alex wasn't sure what Sister Etienne was alluding to. Had something of great value—a tapestry—been discovered?

A public offering? More appropriate for something of great value? It was true the museums generally had limited acquisition funds and relied heavily on generous benefactors, but if there was something of value, a tapestry, possibly an additional piece to *The Lady and the Unicorn,* it should go to the Cluny.

The two women sat looking at each other across the desk. Alex knew a public offering would greatly reduce the chances of such a tapestry being acquired by the Cluny. How many years in purgatory, she wondered, for lying to a nun?

"Yes," Alex said, "if there were an item of great value, a public offering would most likely bring a higher price."

Sister Etienne stood. *"Merci,"* she said.

Alex stood.

"As I told Dr. Martinson," Sister Etienne said, "you may indicate an interest in any of the items by using the numbers listed on the inventory sheet."

"Will there be other items added to the list? Items that could be viewed at some time?"

Sister Etienne smiled. "Perhaps I will be contacting you. For your expertise again."

JAKE LOOKED UP as Alex came out of Sister Etienne's office. She didn't speak and her naturally pale complexion seemed drained of color, transparent almost. Silently, she and Jake left the convent. He thought it best if he waited until she spoke.

As they drove, Alex kept her eyes on the road ahead, driving much slower than she had on the trip to the convent. "Could I ask another favor of you, Jake?"

"Sure. What is it?"

"I have to stay another day. I can't return just yet to Paris." She looked at him now. "I realize this is an enormous favor, but will you take Sunny home on the train with you? I don't want her to miss school tomorrow and I know you have to get back to work. I'll call my mother, have her come meet you at the station."

"Well, uh . . . sure," he answered, trying not to sound reluctant. He wasn't used to being around kids. Two hours on the train with a six-year-old? He didn't think the child had particularly taken a liking to him when they met that morning.

"Thank you," Alex said. Again she stared straight ahead.

"What did the good sister have to say?" Jake asked. Curiosity had the best of him now. "Did she slap your hand with a ruler for stealing the drawings?"

Alex laughed, as if a lighter mood had suddenly overtaken her. "No. She didn't verbally acknowledge I had taken them, although she suggested papers could have *inadvertently* become *intermingled*. Then she was *unexpectedly* called out of the room. Of course, she left the prayer book, sitting right there in front of me."

"And you put the drawings back."

"Yes, of course."

"Maybe you should have kept them. How would she have known you took them? There were others who came to the convent yesterday. Now she knows you were the culprit who took them."

"She knew I took them. But somehow she also seemed to know I had come back to return them."

"She didn't send you to the father confessor to unload your sin?"

"She pretty much let me off the hook. She left me in the room alone for quite a while, maybe fifteen, twenty minutes."

"You were gone a long time. I was ready to barge in and rescue you."

Alex smiled. "Thanks for coming with me."

"Sure."

"It was so strange. Sitting in the room waiting, after I'd returned the drawings to the prayer book, I noticed another book on the corner of her desk. I picked it up." Alex looked at Jake. "You're not going to believe this."

"Try me."

"The poem. It was inside the front cover."

"The poem you found in the library on your first visit?"

Alex nodded. "The part that had been ripped off was taped onto the first page. As I read it, I was more convinced than ever that the poem and drawings are connected to our Adèle. Unable to marry the one she loved, refusing her father's choice, she went to the convent. She died at the convent."

"Adèle Le Viste?"

"Yes. I truly believe the poem is Adèle's story. It makes sense. She fell in love with the *tapissier,* a choice her father would never have approved. Jean Le Viste would have considered only those of high rank and social status for his daughters. They would not have been forced into a marriage, but a refusal would greatly limit a woman's choices."

"The convent being the most likely?"

Alex nodded.

"Your theory about Adèle Le Viste sure seems to hold up. If she was a nun, maybe that's why her name doesn't appear in any family records. She never married. Isn't that where a woman's name would most likely appear in medieval records—as the wife of so-and-so?"

Again a nod.

"Why do you think Sister Etienne left the poem there for you to read?"

Alex shook her head slowly. "I don't know. But I'm sure she did."

"Did you say anything about it when she returned? Did she?"

"No. But she asked about the drawings. What I thought of them."

"What did you tell her?"

"I told her I didn't know if the drawings were valuable in

themselves, but they might be valuable in what they represent."

"So you told her you thought they might be preliminary sketches for a design that belongs to *La Dame à la Licorne* tapestry set?"

"She seemed to have come up with that thought herself—at least the thought that the drawings were somehow related to the Cluny set."

"What did she say?"

"She asked if a tapestry based on one of the designs would be valuable."

"Jeez, Alex. That's got to mean there's a tapestry. At the convent?"

"I don't know." Alex rubbed her left temple. "Then Sister Etienne asked, 'Wouldn't a public offering be more appropriate if the convent possessed something of great value?' "

"She didn't offer it to your museum?"

"I'm not sure they have it, or if she was just baiting me. Maybe she thinks I know where it is. Maybe she thought I picked up something from the poem, the drawings. My feeling—if they don't have it, she definitely thinks it's somewhere at the convent. And there was something in the poem . . . *buried beneath the stone.*"

"Buried? Beneath the stone? Of the convent? Or maybe a gravestone? Can you picture the old nuns out there digging up a grave?"

"Not a pleasant thought. And maybe there isn't even a tapestry. Maybe both Sister Etienne and I have set out on some kind of wild goose chase."

"Or wild unicorn."

"Yes, wild unicorn chase." Alex smiled. "But if they don't have it, I'm not sure why she would have asked about the possibility of a public offering. I know one thing for sure—this new nun's in it for the money, ready to forsaketh her vow of poverty." Alex's hands tightened around the steering wheel.

Jake couldn't help but laugh a little, yet he could see how tense Alex had become.

They turned off the gravel road onto the highway. Jake reached down and picked up the bag Marie had packed. There was still half a loaf of bread, cheese, and several pieces of fruit. He peeled a banana and asked Alex if she'd like something.

"An apple?"

"Sure," he said as he pulled one out of the bag. "Did you tell Sister Etienne what we discovered in the register?"

"No." Alex took a large bite of the apple.

"If the tapestry exists, if it's at the convent, how did it end up there?"

"I don't know."

"Could it have been created there, at the convent?" Jake asked.

"Not likely. Earlier tapestries with religious themes were created in monasteries and convents, but later works, secular and mythological pieces like the unicorn series, were almost exclusively done in private workshops. And I do believe Adèle's *tapissier* was involved in its creation." Alex bit into the apple with a loud crunch.

"That makes sense, if the poem, the drawing—"

"If it does exist, based on the drawing, it belongs in the Cluny."

"And why shouldn't it be there with the others? Why do you think you won't be able to get it for the museum?"

Alex took another enormous bite but didn't reply.

"You're afraid even if there is a tapestry, even if the nuns have it, they'll sell it off to the highest bidder?"

"Precisely," Alex answered. She took one last bite, then threw the apple core over her shoulder into the backseat, where it hit with a thunk. A startled Jake glanced back. She was obviously upset. Her car was so damned clean, he could see she didn't generally use it as a trash bin.

They rode in silence. She was driving too fast again.

"As I remember," Jake said as they passed the village of Vienne, "you're the girl who always gets what she wants."

"Is that how you remember me?" She looked straight ahead, down the road.

"Yes," he answered. "Haven't you always had your way, Alex? Haven't you always gotten exactly what you wanted?"

He looked at her, she at him.

"I've never been afraid to go after what I want," she replied. There was something both defiant and sad in her voice now, and Jake sensed that something Alex had wanted badly had eluded her. Something much more important than a hidden tapestry.

13

SUNNY WAS NAPPING when they returned to Lyon. Madame Pellier said they'd had a busy morning. After Mass, they'd gone to the Parc de la Tête d'Or, then to the Guignol puppet show, and the little girl was just plain worn out.

"Did your business at the convent go well?" Madame Pellier asked as she led Alex and Jake from the entry into the living room.

"*Oui*," answered Alex, "although my business at the convent, it seems, will take longer than anticipated. I'd like to stay another day."

Madame Pellier smiled. "Monsieur Bowman, will you also be staying with us this evening?"

"No, I'm heading back to Paris."

"Jake needs to return to his work," Alex said. "I'm afraid I've taken up a good amount of his time. I've asked him to take Soleil home on the train with him."

Madame Pellier looked disappointed. "Yes, she shouldn't miss school. When will you be leaving, Monsieur Bowman?"

"Perhaps Monsieur Bowman would also like to rest a while," Alex said glancing at Jake.

"I'm fine." He figured he could catch a nap on the two-hour

train ride home, but then he realized he'd have the kid with him. Would he have to stay awake to keep an eye on her? Hell, he didn't know anything about kids.

"Could I get you something?" Madame Pellier asked, motioning for them to sit. "Soleil and I had a nice little picnic lunch at the park. We could have an early dinner, before you leave, Monsieur Bowman. You will stay for dinner?"

He wasn't hungry right now, and he wasn't sure how soon they'd have to leave for Paris. He glanced at Alex. "What's the plan here?"

"Marie packed an enormous breakfast," she told Simone. "Enough for lunch on the drive back. But perhaps some tea. Could you have Marie bring it into the library? And yes, maybe something light, a small supper before we send Jake and Soleil back to Paris."

"Yes, that would be no problem."

I APPRECIATE ALL the help you've given me," Alex said as she and Jake walked down the hall to the library. "And thank you for agreeing to take Sunny home this evening."

"I'm glad I could help." He felt confident about the help he'd given her by doing the drawings, even his going to the convent this morning, but this babysitting bit he wasn't so certain about. Surely he could get that kid back to Paris without any problems. He opened the door and stood back for Alex to enter. "Tell me," he asked, "why was it necessary to do the drawings in pen? You know a pencil sketch would have been much quicker and easier."

"Now, why would we want to have a simple pencil sketch when we could have an exact copy? I want to study the drawings, have the duplicates as close to the originals as possible. Besides, you finished in time to make it to the convent by ten. And they are practically perfect."

"*Practically* perfect?" Jake laughed.

Alex flipped on the light switch.

They both stood, silently, staring. Jake wasn't sure what he was seeing, but it appeared a mini snowstorm had hit the room. Tiny pieces of pale paper covered the floor.

Alex rushed to the table where they'd left the two drawings to dry. "What the hell?"

Jake walked over. He looked down at the bare table, then glanced again at the floor. "Jeez, what happened?"

Marie entered the room with a tray. The light clink of teapot and cups broke the silence.

"Was anyone in the library while we were gone?" Alex demanded.

Marie looked puzzled, then almost fearful as if she were being reprimanded. "No, Madame."

"No one?"

Marie hesitated. She set the tray on the table, then looked down at the scraps of paper covering the floor. "Oh."

"*Oui?*" Alex was shaking. Jake had never seen her so angry.

"When they returned from the park, the puppet show," Marie said slowly, "Soleil, she wanted to find a book. The story. She wanted to find the story from the puppet show."

"So you came into the library to find a book?"

"No."

Alex stared at the woman. She was small and dark and Alex towered over her.

"*La petite fille,* she came and found the book."

"Soleil!" Alex shouted as she stomped out of the library.

A LATE-AFTERNOON SUPPER of soup and salad was served on elegant china with a full set of silverware in the formal dining room. Pierre was not well and did not join them. Soleil did not join them. She was served in her bedroom. She would not be allowed to leave her room until they were ready to depart for the train.

Jake had not been particularly enthusiastic about the two-hour train ride back to Paris with a six-year-old girl in tow, but now, when it was so obvious she hated him, the prospect was almost frightening.

"I can't understand," Alex said, "why she would do such a thing. Do you know what she said when I asked her?" Alex glanced at Jake. He didn't answer because he was sure he knew—the kid hated him. From their first encounter when she found him, early in the morning at her grandparents' house with her mother, just having completed the drawings her mother said were *beautiful,* he had felt the child saw him as an intruder. As she looked over her mother's shoulder when they left the library that morning, she had given him the "evil eye," if a little girl was capable of such a thing. The child obviously had no use for him, or his *beautiful* drawings.

"Her answer," Alex continued, "do you know what she said? She said she didn't know. She destroyed the drawings, and she doesn't know why."

"Children sometimes do things they don't fully understand," Madame Pellier said.

"It makes no sense," Alex said.

"Are you sure," Jake asked after several moments of thought, "this is a good idea? Sending her home on the train with me?" Maybe this was his out. "She might blame me for what's happened—her being punished, eating alone in her room."

"She needs to go back home," Alex answered. "I don't want her to feel she's controlling the situation. I want her to return to Paris this evening. She'll be okay, Jake. I wouldn't send her home with you if I thought she would be difficult. I've had a talk with her. She's generally a well-behaved child. The worst scenario—she'll give you the silent treatment. But I guarantee, after our little talk, she won't be misbehaving."

ALEX WAS RIGHT about the silent treatment. Jake's attempts at conversation were futile, not that he had any idea how to converse with a six-year-old girl. But the kid was well behaved. She did exactly as Jake asked. Nodding when appropriate. Answering his simple questions with no more than a polite, "Yes, monsieur . . . no, monsieur."

After about half an hour on the train, Jake got out his drawing pad and a pencil. If he couldn't nap, at least he could make use of his time. He would do another sketch of each of the two drawings while the images were still fresh in his mind. He'd gathered the bits of paper scattered on the library floor and found some in the wastebasket and stuck them in his pocket. He would try to patch them together when he got back to Paris, but he wasn't sure if he'd found all the pieces. Who knows, the kid could have flushed some of them down the toilet.

Soleil gazed out the window, her head pressed up against the glass. He thought maybe she had fallen asleep, but then she turned and watched him draw. He wondered what was going through her mind.

"Why did you destroy the drawings?" He was more curious than angry, and tried to convey this in his tone. He didn't want to frighten her. He continued to draw.

"I didn't like them," she answered sharply, surprising him that she would reveal this much.

"What was wrong with them?" He looked up. She had turned back to the window. *Conversation over?* he wondered.

As he sketched, he sensed she was again watching him. When he looked over at her, she turned back to the window.

"Do you like to draw?" he asked.

"Sometimes," she answered, still staring out the window.

"I've got extra paper, if you'd like to sketch."

She didn't answer.

"Helps pass the time," he said.

She did not reply, but after a few moments, she turned. Slowly, he pulled off a sheet of paper, and then, along with a pencil, held it out for her. Reluctantly, she reached over, took the paper and pencil, but said nothing. He went back to his sketching, watching her out of the corner of his eye. She stared down at the paper, then gazed out the window again, clutching the paper to her chest. Again, she turned, then leaned down and pulled a book out of her small backpack. She set it on her lap, placed the paper on the book and started to draw.

She didn't say anything and neither did he. A small triumph? He thought it best to leave her alone. He continued to work on his own drawing. After a few minutes, he glanced over. The little girl had sketched several flowers resembling those in his drawing. Now she was attempting to copy the unicorn. It was a skillful drawing, he thought, for a six-year-old. "It's a nice drawing," he said.

She didn't say anything, but under her hard-set exterior, an exterior strong, yet delicate and porcelain like her mother, he could detect the slightest hint of a smile.

JAKE CALLED FROM Paris as Alex had requested to let her know they had arrived safely.

"Safe and sound," he said.

"She was well-behaved?"

"Yes, fine."

"Thank God. I had second thoughts after you left. And third and fourth thoughts. Maybe I wasn't being fair to either of you. Making her ride back with a stranger, putting such responsibility on you."

"She did fine. And really, Alex, I'm fairly reliable."

"Oh, Jake, I didn't mean . . . it's just that . . . so it went okay?"

"We had a pleasant trip."

"Pleasant?" Alex laughed now. "What's your definition of pleasant?"

"Light conversation. A shared experience."

"Shared experience?"

"We sketched on the train."

"No one tore anyone's prized sketches?"

"She's a good little artist."

"She is. I know. So you bonded in your creativity?"

"I don't know that we bonded. But maybe she doesn't hate me anymore."

"She doesn't hate you, Jake."

"Maybe not."

"I think it's jealousy."

"Of my talent?" Jake asked, laughing.

"Of the attention."

"Yes," he said.

"I think she resented your being at her grandparents' home. She pretty much rules the roost around here, and she wasn't prepared to find you in the library this morning. Perhaps she even misinterpreted why you were here. But I still can't believe she destroyed the drawings."

Misinterpreted why he was there? Maybe the child, Jake thought, was wiser than the mother. "I tried to duplicate them on the way home, and maybe I can piece the torn drawings back together."

"Thank you. I appreciate so much what you did. Coming here on such short notice. Doing the sketches. Taking Sunny back to Paris this evening."

"Good luck at the convent tomorrow."

"Thanks, I may need some luck."

"What's your plan when you go back?"

"Maybe I'll steal the drawings again." Alex laughed, and then seriously she added, "I've considered talking to Sister Etienne, telling her what we discovered. Maybe she will help me. She did, in a way, take me into her confidence."

"Might be worth a try. I'm anxious to hear."

"I'll call when I get back to Paris. You could come for dinner."

"I'd like that."

"What did Sunny draw?"

"Flowers and gardens and unicorns."

ALEX CALLED AND left a message for Madame Demy. The Director was not at her apartment in Paris, and Alex guessed she had gone to the country château with her uncle. Alex wanted to let her know she would be staying in Lyon another day, that she had made what she considered a discovery of importance to the Cluny at Sainte Blandine's. She did not go into detail.

That night, she dreamed. Of flowers and gardens and unicorns. But first she dreamed of the poem. She could see the paper on which it was written. An archaic French penmanship on a pale, faded parchment. She tried to translate the ancient words. She could see the words, finely penned by hand. *Jardin . . . Fleurs . . .* At first the dream contained no images, only words.

> *She met him in the garden*
> *A chance encounter*
> *But drawn as if by fate.*
> *. . . the labor of their love . . . the fruit, the passion of their*
>   *love . . .*

Then the ink became blurry, words fading into one another. But one word remained. *Buried.*

The dream became no longer words, but images. A loom appeared, dressed with warp, threads running up and down. And then the weft, threads of deep rich red madder, gold of weld, and blue from the dyes of woad, began to intertwine, creating a maiden and her lover. The passion of their love recorded in the union of their design. The fruit. The labor of their love.

It was the maiden from the drawing, naked and innocent, and the knight, who was in fact not a knight but the *tapissier,* who had come to claim her innocence, to awaken her passion. They were on the garden island, and then it spread and opened and became a world that was not confined, but a garden that was the world itself. And then, Alex was the maiden. The knight was Jake. He kissed her. Touched her skin. Caressed her naked body. Entered her and they became one.

Alex woke in a sweat. She sat up in bed.

She got up and threw on her robe. She walked down the hall to Soleil's room, although she knew the child wasn't there. She went in. The bed was made. The doll Grandmère had given her on their last visit, which they had agreed would stay at Grandmère and Grandpère's in Lyon, sat on the bed. Alex picked it up.

Soleil was jealous; she always had been. Jealous of Alex's work, jealous of anyone or anything that made demands on her mother's time. Alex had been cautious with men around her daughter. Soleil had never really known her father, but had created an ideal image of him, which Alex would not destroy. But had Soleil seen Jake as more than a business associate?

He had come to Lyon to help her mother, to do the drawings. Couldn't Soleil understand this? She should have explained to her daughter. But how could she explain when Alex herself wanted to believe that Jake's coming without hesitation in the middle of the night was so much more than this? He hadn't even questioned her request that he accompany her to the convent that morning. She thought of what Jake had said that afternoon—that Alex had always gone after what she wanted.

Now what did she want? To discover another tapestry? To

obtain it for the museum? But she knew there was much more. Her deepest desire was to protect her daughter, to keep her safe, knowing that she was loved and cherished above all things.

Alex caressed the doll. She loved her daughter dearly. It was the deepest love she had ever known. But wasn't there more—love between man and woman? Would she ever know this love? And somehow, strangely and unexplainably, it all seemed tied up in the tapestry. As if every wish rested on the search for and acquisition of a tapestry that might not even exist.

14

ALEX ARRIVED EARLY at the convent of Sainte Blandine the following morning. Unable to sleep, she had left Lyon before the sun was up. She knew the nuns rose early—Matins at two-thirty A.M., Lauds at five. How did they ever get any sleep? Sleep—something Alex had had very little of the past two days. Yet she didn't feel tired.

When she knocked on the door, the wrinkled little nun who kept the gate didn't seem surprised to see her, although Alex had not been invited. She asked for Sister Etienne. According to the nun, Sister Etienne was not available at the moment, but Alex could come in and wait if she wished. She was led to the office and asked to take a seat. As soon as she sat, she heard a tiny voice. *"Bonjour,* Madame Pellier." It was Sister Anne.

"Bonjour," Alex replied. *"Comment allez-vous?"*

"Très bien, merci, et vous?"

"Très bien."

"Venez." The nun motioned and they walked out of the room, down the hall. "Your friend," Sister Anne said, smiling, "he is not with you today?"

"I'm alone today."

"Your friend, he is very handsome." The nun's expression was playful, her smile that of a young girl, teasing a friend about her crush on a boy.

Did she think there was something going on between Alex and Jake? Was she expecting Alex to share some intimate little detail regarding her affection for the young man? Alex recalled sitting in the library with Jake, Sister Anne perched on her chair in the corner. What had Sister Anne observed that made her think he was anything but a business colleague? Had the nun, who Alex thought was snoozing, noticed Alex grab Jake's hand when they discovered the name *Adèle Le Viste* in the register?

"Very handsome," the nun said once more.

Alex thought about telling the nun Jake was just a business associate, but instead, she said, "Yes, he is very handsome."

They turned a corner in the dark hall and walked past several closed doors until they came to a stone staircase. There was a rough wooden bench below the stairs.

"S'il vous plaît." Sister Anne motioned toward the bench, then up the stairs as she patted her hip. "Too difficult," she said. She sat down on the bench and Alex understood that she too was expected to sit.

"I once knew a boy," the nun said, adjusting the bulky folds of her habit beneath her. "Oh, a very special boy, like your friend. Many, many years ago. He looked very much like your young friend. Of course, much younger." The nun smiled.

Alex smiled too. "He's an artist," she said, feeling a need to participate in the conversation, but not knowing exactly what to say. Was Sister Anne recalling a past boyfriend? It was a strange thought—this distorted little nun with a man. Alex didn't feel good, having these unkind thoughts, but she couldn't help herself, and she had no idea what kind of response was expected of her. "He's a very talented artist," she added.

The nun must have sensed Alex's discomfort. She smiled again, then said, "Is it too difficult to imagine? An old woman, once young and in love with a young man?"

"No," Alex lied.

Sister Anne sat, a dreamy smile on her face. Alex wondered how long they would have to wait. She adjusted herself on the bench, which was hard and uncomfortable. She guessed the tiny nun was uncomfortable too. Or maybe this was something she'd learned to accept—perpetual penance. Alex wondered where Sister Etienne was, if she would make her wait all day.

A tiny mouse scampered across the floor, startling Alex, who quickly pulled her feet up as her back stiffened.

"We hear them day and night now," Sister Anne said, patting Alex on the knee, "crawling overhead, scratching across the floors." She sighed. "Now that the Archbishop has come in with his men, tearing everything apart." Her eyes lifted upward. "They don't seem to know what's going on. Confused little creatures."

Alex assumed she was talking about the mice. "A disruption, surely."

"Yes, a bit of a disruption." Sister Anne looked up the stairs as if expecting someone. "This has been my home for almost sixty-seven years."

"Sixty-seven years?" It amazed Alex that anyone could live like this for so many years.

"Sixty-seven years this August."

"That's a long time."

"A very long time." Sister Anne continued to gaze up the stairs.

Alex wanted to ask if she had been happy here for the past sixty-seven years, if this had been a wise choice, if she ever wished she had stayed in the secular world, married, had a family.

"You wonder if I've been happy these past years?" Sister Anne asked. "There have been good days and bad days." The nun laughed quietly.

"I suppose," Alex said cautiously, "any choice we make might produce both good and bad. Hopefully, more good."

The nun continued to smile, but did not reply.

"What was it," Alex asked, hesitating, wondering if she was being too bold, too personal, "what was it that made you choose this life?"

"I don't know that it was my choosing." The nun's expression was serious now. "It was the good Lord's choosing me."

"Then you had no choice?"

"Ah, but we always have choice. We always have the choice—do we answer yes, or do we answer no."

Alex heard a rustle on the stairs and looked up to see Sister Etienne.

"*Bonjour,*" the nun said pleasantly.

"*Bonjour,*" Alex said.

"*Merci,* Sister Anne," the younger nun said. "*S'il vous plaît,* Madame Pellier." She motioned to Alex. "Please, come with me." Her voice was friendly and welcoming, almost as if she were expecting Alex this morning, as if she were inviting her up for tea and cookies. Alex followed her up the steps. Once Alex glanced back down at Sister Anne, who stood at the bottom of the stairs. A broad, proud smile covered the little nun's face.

They walked through another hall. Alex could see what the Archbishop's men had been doing for the past several days, what had upset the mice as well as the nuns, what had created such a commotion. Walls, floors, ceilings were being torn out. Alex imagined that the single nun-sized cells wouldn't be large enough to accommodate the tourists the Archbishop hoped to attract to the renovated convent.

Sister Etienne opened a door and they entered a large open space that had probably at one time been several cells. There was a distinct, ancient, musty odor. More so than the rest of the convent. As if opening up the walls had somehow released the scent of centuries gone by.

Sister Etienne stopped and looked directly at Alex. "I know," she said, "I can trust you."

Alex wondered how the nun had come to this conclusion, knowing Alex had taken the drawings from the prayer book.

"We've been praying this past night," the nun said, "praying for guidance."

Sister Etienne walked to a dark corner of the room. She pulled back several sheets of heavy canvas to reveal a long rolled object, at least ten or twelve feet long. It was wrapped again, a rope securing it on either end. She untied the ropes, removed the second canvas, then motioned for Alex to help her move it closer to an open window with better light. Each taking one end, the two women carried the heavy bundle across the floor, then set it down beneath the window. Slowly and carefully, the nun began to unroll it.

Alex's heart pounded in her chest as she watched, then seemed to rise and catch in her throat. An unexpected cry of both shock and joy pierced the silence, Alex barely aware that it had come from her. And then a warm, comforting sensation enveloped her as she gazed down at the large tapestry rolled out on the floor.

It was, of course, the seventh tapestry, based on the second drawing found in the medieval prayer book. The detail was as fine and precise as the delicate drawing—the nude maiden with the unicorn sitting at her side, front hooves perched on her lap, the natural garden setting, the knight with lance—but the total effect was even more powerful. This could have been due to size alone, but here, the elements of color and texture had been added to the composition. The colors were the same as those in *La Dame à la Licorne* in the Cluny, the same brilliant reds and deep blues. Yet unlike the museum tapestries, they seemed barely faded. The Cluny set had suffered terrible damage from hundreds of years of exposure. Three of the tapestries—*Taste, Sight,* and *A Mon Seul Désir*—had been stored for a time in the Hôtel de Ville of Boussac, where they had been attacked by rats and moisture.

"It's beautiful," Alex said, releasing her breath. She bent down on one knee, examining the detail more closely.

"Is it authentic?" Sister Etienne asked. "Is it valuable?"

Alex reached out to touch the tapestry, to feel the texture. She turned and looked back at Sister Etienne. "May I?" she asked.

The nun nodded.

Alex knelt, then ran her fingers across the selvedge. The tapestry seemed to be in perfect condition. The borders in the museum tapestries had all been replaced or reworked, and the earlier restorations had been crudely done, with poorly dyed threads. There had been a total of four cleanings, rewarpings, and darnings, but it was so evident now that the Cluny tapestries were far from restored to their original brilliance. Alex wondered how this piece could have survived in such splendor over the centuries. As she examined the detail more closely, she could see the slight imperfections of a hand-loomed tapestry. She was sure it was real, that it was a seventh piece to the set in her museum.

"Your professional opinion?" the nun asked.

"It's beautiful," Alex whispered.

"Woven at the same time as the others? Could it have survived this long?"

"Where did it come from?"

"Here."

"Has it been here all along?" Alex turned back to the nun.

"It appears it has. If it's true, it would be valuable."

"If it's truly what it appears to be."

"And is it? Is it what it appears to be?" Sister Etienne asked.

"There are chemical tests, chromatography, spectroscopic analysis, nuclear magnetic resonance methods."

"Oh, that sounds dreadful, harmful. But, you, Madame Pellier, aren't you an expert? Do you believe it's authentic?"

"Yes. I do."

The nun smiled triumphantly.

"Why wasn't it on the inventory," Alex asked, "with the other property?"

"We didn't know it was here until yesterday."

"You had no idea it was here?"

"There are legends, stories," the nun replied, thoughtfully. "The order dates back to the thirteenth century . . . some of the stories . . ." She gestured with her hand as if to dismiss such stories. ". . . but when we found the poem . . . perhaps some truth. The young woman, she falls in love with a tapestry weaver. Her father is displeased, as he has arranged a more fitting union for his daughter. She refuses and he sends her to the convent, or perhaps it is her choice."

"Rather live in the service of the Lord . . . than without the one she loves?"

"Perhaps . . . but then, the story . . . before they part, they have created something of beauty together—"

"The tapestries?" The words of the poem went through Alex's mind. One word stood out—*buried*—and a morbid vision came to her. The old nuns out in the middle of the night, digging up the cemetery, the plot of Adèle Le Viste, to find the tapestry. She thought of stories she'd heard of ancient saints, dug up after hundreds of years, their bodies miraculously preserved, exhumed in perfect condition as if they had been just recently laid to rest.

"This part of the convent was built in the late fifteenth century or possibly the early sixteenth," Sister Etienne said, pointing at the wall.

Alex looked around the room. Evidence of the Archbishop's work revealed where walls had just recently stood. "It was buried in the wall?"

"Oui."

Who had placed it in the wall? Alex wondered. A double wall? Constructed to hide the tapestry?

"Somewhat of a miracle," Sister Etienne said.

"Amazing," Alex said as she examined the tapestry once more. The maiden was the slender blond girl of the Cluny set. The unicorn resembled the elegant beast in *Sight*. The flowers in the garden were the same as those found in the other six tapestries—daisies, carnations, roses, pansies, lilies of the valley, periwinkle. The garden island had expanded from the enclosed space to cover the bottom portion of the tapestry in a more realistic setting; a man was represented as a knight; there were no Le Viste coats of arms. Yet Alex was sure it was part of the same set. She knew it belonged with the others.

"Une loupe?" she asked. Sister Etienne left while Alex remained, studying the tapestry. The nun returned and handed her a small magnifying glass. Slowly, Alex examined the detail, then larger areas of color, where she could see the variations in the intensity of the natural vegetable dyes, the uneven colors. She leaned over, touched her nose to the ancient wool and breathed in the scent. Once more she studied the fine detail, the texture and grain of the weaving, the shading and graduation of color created by the skillful hatching. Yes, authentic! She handed the magnifying glass to the nun and explained how the colors, the texture, the depth of the color were

all indications of its authenticity. Sister Etienne grinned, her eyes flashing with excitement.

After several more minutes, both women studying the tapestry, Alex lifted the edge to examine the reverse side. What she saw now caused her heart nearly to leap out of her chest. A monogram, a distinctive mark, had been woven into the back of the selvedge. It was the same as the mysterious letter following *A Mon Seul Désir* on the tapestry in the Cluny, the design that was interwoven with the tendril to the name *Adèle* in the drawing.

Alex ran her fingers across the enigmatic design. There was no doubt in her mind now—it was the signature, the hallmark of the weaver. And there was no doubt in her mind that Adèle and the weaver had been lovers.

"*Merci.* Thank you for coming today," Sister Etienne said, again speaking as if Alex had been invited. "May I?" she asked, bending down to reroll the tapestry.

Alex could have stayed, kneeling on the cold, hard floor, examining the tapestry for the remainder of the morning, but she said, "*Oui. Merci.*" She reached over to help Sister Etienne roll the tapestry. They moved it back to the dark corner and covered it with the canvas.

"The men will be coming soon," Sister Etienne said as she secured the rope. "The Archbishop feels he is behind on his schedule."

Alex knelt and retied the rope on the other end. They covered it with another layer of canvas.

"Perhaps the Archbishop will have to rethink his schedule now," the nun said. "*S'il vous plaît,* Madame Pellier, please come." She stood. "There are arrangements to be made. We must make plans."

Alex followed the nun out of the room, down the stairs, and through the hall into her office. As soon as they were seated, Sister Etienne said, "The Archbishop is not an unkind man. But for him it's a matter of economics. The upkeep of the convent has become too much for the archdiocese. And we are producing so little income now . . . a little from the handmade lace, but we are no longer able to keep up the vineyards. At one time Sainte Blandine's produced a fine altar wine, but now . . ." Sister Etienne stroked the cross hanging from her neck. "The Archbishop feels we need nursing care, as if we can no longer care for ourselves." The nun sighed. "But I am not a woman unable to see, and it is clear the Archbishop is right. We are, indeed, in remarkable health for women our age, but . . . Poor Sister Anne, she does well, yet I'm fearful she will fall one day and break a hip, and both Sister Eulalie and Sister Philomena, in wheelchairs, and Sister Hélène, a sturdy woman, but . . . bones become brittle, eyes start to dim . . ." The nun's voice trailed off. "If we were able to pay for the upkeep, to hire help. A nurse to come tend to our needs. Why, the Archbishop could still have the upper level for his hotel." The nun's voice grew with excitement. "It would all work out." She looked at Alex as if she needed confirmation.

Alex nodded.

Sister Etienne continued. "But we need help. This is why you have come to us."

How had the sister arrived at this conclusion? Alex had not come to the convent out of charity or benevolence.

"We have no idea," the nun said, "how to expose the tapestry to those who would be most interested. How to get the very best price. I wouldn't know what price would be fair."

"Ownership would have to be established."

"But we found it here at the convent. It belongs to the Sisters of Sainte Blandine."

Alex wondered if the Archbishop would see this as property of the nuns, or would he consider this part of the real property, having been pulled out of the wall? The Archbishop's men, who Alex assumed were private contractors, had found it in the wall. Would they be aware of its value? "Has Archbishop Bonnisseau been contacted?"

"I wanted to talk to you first," Sister Etienne said, "to determine if it was authentic."

"When the convent was sold to the archdiocese," Alex asked, "the contents were to remain property of the nuns?"

"Yes."

"There is documentation to establish this fact?"

"Yes, I believe something in writing, a contract. And letters, correspondence from the Archbishop when he decided to convert Sainte Blandine's to a hotel and send us to Lyon." Sister Etienne stared across the desk at Alex. "It is ours, isn't it?"

"It seems the proper documents exist to establish ownership."

"And the value," Sister Etienne asked, "how does one determine its value?"

Again Alex hesitated. "The exact value is hard to determine. So few tapestries from this period, in this style, have survived, let alone in such good condition. It's quite remarkable."

"Remarkable indeed. So, the value?" Sister Etienne asked anxiously.

"Even the art world revolves around economics," Alex answered. "Supply and demand. The value based on desirability, condition, age."

"And the fact that so few of these in such remarkable condition exist?"

"Would make it quite valuable."

"It was Mother Alvère's wish for anything of value to go to the museums," Sister Etienne said, "but . . . she wasn't aware of the tapestry. It seems this has changed everything." The nun cleared her throat, bowed her head, then looked up at Alex. "But now, if this discovery will somehow allow us to stay . . ."

Alex nodded once more, though something deep inside her wanted to protest. "Does anyone else know? Any of the other museum representatives who've come to Sainte Blandine's?"

"You're speaking of Dr. Martinson?"

"Yes."

"No." Sister Etienne shook her head. "You are the only one."

Alex wanted to shake the nun. She wanted to say, *Can't you see it is the seventh piece in* La Dame à la Licorne? *They belong together. Don't you understand? It must go to the Cluny!*

Sister Etienne looked at Alex, deep into her eyes. The nun smiled.

"A reputable auction house," Alex said, "would be most

effective in achieving the greatest exposure to those willing to pay the price."

"Yes, an auction house. You are familiar with these?"

"I would suggest you contact the best—Sotheby's or Christie's."

"And how would one go about this? Can you help us?"

Alex took a deep breath. "Yes, I can help you."

15

AFTER SPEAKING TO Alex, reassuring her the trip with Soleil had gone well, Jake attempted to piece the bits of torn paper together. The kid had done a fine job, but after two hours he had enough to make out the main drawings as well as the details around the borders. He could tape these together and give them to Alex. Yet he felt an obligation to duplicate the drawings again, as Alex had written him a generous check just before he left Lyon. When he protested and tried to return it, she had insisted he keep it. After all, he'd come to Lyon in the middle of the night and completed the requested work, even if Soleil had destroyed the drawings. That was Alex's problem, she'd told Jake, not his. But with the sketches he'd done on the train and these he'd patched together, he figured he could do another set as close to the originals as his first.

He fell into bed and slept until quarter to eleven the following morning. When he woke, he got out his supplies and started the ink drawings for the second time.

Later that afternoon, he left his room to get something to eat. When he got back, he checked for messages; there were none. He knew he should run over to the co-op and pay Julianna for the supplies she'd given him Saturday night, but he still didn't have any cash. He'd go to the bank later with Alex's check. He entered his room and stood, staring down at the drawings. Then he sat, dipped his pen, and started to work. He wasn't sure how long he'd been at it when he heard a knock on the door. Thinking it was André, who said he'd bring clean towels that afternoon, Jake got up and opened the door.

"I thought maybe you'd come by the co-op." It was Julianna.

"It was late last night when I got home."

Julianna looked at her watch. "It's quarter past six now," she said. "Are you going to invite me in?"

Jake motioned Julianna into the room. "I started working and I guess I lost track of the time."

"Your trip to Lyon, did it go well?"

"Fine," he answered.

"Fine? You finished your pen and ink drawings?"

"I'm getting there. How did you know where I lived?"

"The co-op application."

"Oh."

"Are you coming by the studio tonight? I'm on my way up."

"What day is it?" He scratched his head, ran his fingers through his hair.

"Monday."

"Monday . . . male model?"

"Oh, yes . . ." she said with a grin, "I expect you still need a woman."

"Right."

She stared over at the table, and then, before he could object, she walked right past him. She looked down at the drawings. "What happened here?" she asked, gazing at the drawings he'd pieced together.

"Long story."

"Yes, I would imagine." Her eyes moved from the torn drawings to the pencil sketches, then rested on the first ink drawing he'd started this morning. "Quite nice. This is why you rushed off to Lyon?"

He nodded but said nothing. He had no intention of showing the drawings to anyone. He knew Alex would want to keep their discovery secret.

"This is a sketch of a tapestry in the Cluny Museum?" She pointed to the drawing resembling *A Mon Seul Désir,* then reached down and picked it up. "Although there are some differences." She set it down and carefully picked up the second drawing, which was still wet. "And this one?"

He didn't answer. How careless of him to let Julianna in while he was working on the drawings.

"This one, it's a similar style, but not one of the tapestries in *La Dame à la Licorne.* I know those tapestries well. The medieval art, quite lovely. Incredibly romantic. Don't you think?"

"Yes, it is romantic."

Julianna's eyes darted around the room again. He'd put the canvas he'd been working on in the closet, for which he was grateful. He didn't want anyone to see it. He couldn't stand to look at it himself. Julianna walked to the window and looked out. She turned and glanced down at his unmade bed, then her eyes rested on the nightstand where he emptied his pockets each night. It was covered with a pile of change, museum ticket stubs, postcards and receipts, a history of his first week in Paris.

"You'll be there Wednesday? You could pay me back then."

"Yes, I'll come Wednesday."

"You have the address?"

"I'll be there."

After Julianna left, Jake waited for Alex's call, but finally gave up and went out by himself to get something to eat.

Tuesday, he pulled the painting out of the closet and attempted to work on it, giving up about noon when he went out for lunch, then over to the Louvre, where he stayed until it closed. Still no call from Alex when he returned. He was curious to know if she'd discovered anything more about a possible tapestry.

Wednesday morning he went out for a run. He ran longer than usual, realizing now he'd do just about anything to keep from painting. As he caught a glimpse of himself in the window of a store on Boulevard Saint Michel, Jake got a weird sensation, as if it were his father staring back at him. Not that his father would do something as foolish as run down the streets of Paris wearing shorts that looked like his underwear. "Why would a man want to run on the street? A man gets plenty of exercise puttin' in an honest day's work." He could hear his father's deep, rough voice.

There was never a great deal of approval in his father's voice. Jake remembered when he was in graduate school and painting "those pictures," which his father said weren't pictures at all—Jake was deep into abstract at the time—the old man had asked him why he didn't paint horses, like Remington or Charlie Russell. A Remington reproduction of a cowboy on a bucking horse had hung in John Bowman's office for as long as Jake could remember. "You were good at drawing horses when you were a kid."

What would the old man think now about Jake's returning to Paris? Jake had a pretty good idea what his dad would think. Even his mom, who'd always been supportive, didn't have much enthusiasm for this decision. She couldn't understand why he'd give up the security of his position at the university.

BY LATE THAT afternoon, still no call from Alex. She said she'd call when she got back to Paris and have him over for dinner. Was she jerking him around? He waited until almost seven, then took the Métro up to the studio at Montmartre. He wasn't about to drag his paints and canvas along, but he took his sketchpad and pencils.

When he arrived, the model, a young brunette, had already disrobed and was sitting on a chair, staring blankly into nowhere. From across the room Julianna smiled and waved. On the floor next to her, a barefoot young black man with dreadlocks sat, sketching on a pad. A skinny, long-necked girl with short blond hair stood before an enormous canvas propped on an easel. A plumpish, middle-aged woman looked up and smiled at Jake. There were several others scattered about the room, some painting, others drawing.

"Delighted you finally made it." Julianna had walked over to greet him.

"I've got your money."

She waved her hand. "Let's not be concerned with that now. Let's get you set up. You should check in with

Patrice"—she motioned toward the plumpish woman—"when we take our break. You didn't bring a canvas?"

"I thought I'd do some sketches to get started." He wondered if Julianna expected him to make this a regular event.

"You're not painting?"

"Just thought I'd see how things go."

Jake heard someone enter the room. Both he and Julianna turned. It was an old man. He looked around, perplexed. "Madame Lamoureux?" he asked no one in particular.

"*Ce soir, non,*" Julianna said. She walked over to the man. Jake could hear her explaining there was no instruction this evening. The old man seemed confused and said he thought there was to be an instructor. Julianna suggested he set up anyway. There were several in the group who could help him get started. The man seemed hesitant. He wandered around the room for several minutes, looking up at the model now and then.

Jake pulled out a chair, opened his sketchpad, and started to draw. The old man stopped and watched.

Julianna had moved back across the room and was setting up an easel. "*Venez, venez essayer de faire,*" she called to the man. "Come try."

Slowly, the old man walked over, stood, and stared at the paper.

As Jake continued drawing, Julianna and the man spoke softly, but Jake couldn't make out what they were saying.

The students chatted among themselves. The general conversation was in French. The young black man, the skinny blonde, Julianna, and another student bantered back and forth in English.

It seemed no time had passed when the model stood, wrapped herself in her robe, stretched and yawned, then pulled a pack of cigarettes out of her pocket and walked out onto the balcony. Several others followed. They stood in a small group, laughing and chatting. Others gathered around a coffeepot. Julianna introduced Jake to Patrice, who explained how they figured the fee based on the number of students each evening. He filled out a registration card while Julianna wandered out to the balcony.

Jake poured himself a cup of coffee, then meandered about, looking at the work of the other students. He examined Julianna's canvas. She was painting in the style of the Cubists. He was curious as to how she had assisted the old man. Jake walked over to where the man still sat. There were several crumpled papers at his feet, but the paper on the easel was blank.

The man looked up. *"Comment commencer?"* he asked.

"Formes simples," Jake answered. "Break it down into the simple elements," he explained, continuing to speak to the old man in French.

"Je regarde et vois une femme. A beautiful, complex, mysterious shape, not a simple shape." The old man smiled. "Yesterday morning I came and there was an instructor. We drew apples, oranges, and wine bottles. But now . . . *c'est impossible!"* He shook his head. "You will advise me? Monsieur . . ." The man hesitated as if searching for a name.

"Jake Bowman," Jake said, extending his hand.

"Gaston Jadot. *Enchanté,* Monsieur Bowman," the man answered with a firm, strong hand. He looked directly at Jake. There was confidence in the handshake, a serious expression as if they were consummating an important business deal. The man wore an elbow-thin, threadbare sweater, a pair of faded slacks, but there was something about the way he took Jake's hand with such firmness, the way he spoke, that conveyed an elegance and refinement. Jake wondered where he had come from, what he was doing here at the studio. What would possess a man his age—Jake guessed him to be in his late seventies or early eighties—to embark on this creative endeavor so late in life?

The others came in from the balcony. The model took her pose and they commenced their work. Jake stood with Monsieur Jadot, suggesting how he might begin his drawing. "The human body is made up of spheres and cylinders—basic shapes."

"Like oranges and wine bottles," the man replied with a grin.

"Oui." Jake smiled.

The old man asked Jake if he might show him. Jake nodded, then left to get his own sketchpad.

He didn't touch the pencil or paper of the old man. He had

never believed in putting his own pen or brush to a student's work. After Jake demonstrated, the old man seemed more confident now as he began to draw, Jake explaining how he could start with basic forms, paying careful attention to proportions and relationships of shapes. It was easy if the figure was looked upon as just that—shapes and lines.

"You're a teacher?" Julianna asked.

Jake turned. She was standing behind them. "I've done some teaching."

"Where? In the States?"

"Yes."

"University?"

"Montana."

"Are you going back? To teach?"

"Probably not."

"You're working for the Cluny now?"

"Just the one job. An old friend works at the Cluny. She asked me to go down to Lyon to do the drawings."

"In the middle of the night?" Julianna smiled.

Jake nodded, but didn't answer.

"I'm curious," Julianna said. "What is the significance? One of the drawings represented one of the tapestries in the Cluny set, *The Lady and the Unicorn,* yet the second drawing was different. The woman was nude, and there was a knight in the drawing."

Again, Jake said nothing. He felt strangely as if he had betrayed Alex.

"Alexandra Pellier? Your friend?"

Shit, how did she know that?

"The check," Julianna said. "She signed the check."

He remembered now, it had been on his nightstand.

"Julianna," the young black man called from across the room, "you going with us tonight?"

"How about it, Jake?" Julianna asked. "We're all going out for a drink. Would you care to come along?"

Jake knew he should go back to his room, get some rest, rise early, and get to his painting. "Probably not."

"The night I opened the store for you, you said 'some other time.' This is it!" She reached up and touched him on the shoulder. "You're going with us. It'll be good for you. You're much too uptight to be creative." She gave his shoulder a little squeeze.

THEY WALKED TO a place just a block from the studio. It was small with a narrow bar and a few tables. Two old men sat at one table. A middle-aged man perched on a stool at the bar, a cigarette dangling from his mouth. He craned his neck and stared as they entered, then turned and snuffed his cigarette in an ashtray.

Julianna introduced Jake to the other students. The young black man with dreadlocks was Matthew Lewis and he was from Chicago. He wore a ring pierced through his left eyebrow, which seemed to bounce up and down every time he laughed. The long-necked blonde, with short hair that looked like it had been cut with a very dull scissors, was Gabby Mogenson. She was from someplace in New Mexico that Jake had never heard of. She worked as an artist's model to pay for painting lessons she took during the day. After they had ordered two bottles of wine, a dark-haired kid whose name was Brian joined them, and then a plumpish redhead with a hairdo tied up in a ponytail that reminded Jake of Woody Woodpecker.

They sat and visited and talked about their work. Matthew got up and went to the bar for two more bottles. It was cheap wine, like Jake and his buddies used to drink years ago by the gallon. He knew if he drank too much he wouldn't feel like painting the next morning, but something about being with this young enthusiastic group reminded him of his days as a student, his early days as a college professor. There was so much eagerness, youth, and creativity.

It was near midnight when they started to break up. Gabby, Matthew, Brian, and the Woody Woodpecker girl got up to leave. Matthew, who evidently had a car, asked Jake if he'd like a ride back to his place. Jake said no thanks, he'd catch the Métro. Then he found himself sitting alone with Julianna. "How about coming up to see my work?" she asked.

JULIANNA SHARED AN apartment with a girl named Michelle who was away for a few days. The place was small, one bedroom with a sleeper sofa in the living room, which was pulled out and covered with a pile of rumpled blankets. Canvases in a variety of sizes were lined up against the walls, the coffee table, and in the small kitchen on the table. Most were done in the style of the Cubists, like the work she was doing at the studio, but there were others that looked more like the work of the Impressionists. Several small sketches, in a realistic style that he rather liked, hung on the walls. They were all Julianna's work. He wasn't sure this would have been evident had she not signed each one with the single name *Julianna*.

She excused herself for a moment. Jake glanced around the room. He'd had too much to drink, he was tired, and he felt terribly uncomfortable because as he studied Julianna's work, he felt like a teacher. His natural impulse was to suggest ways in which she could improve her work, and he was pretty sure that wasn't what she wanted.

Julianna returned, then went into the kitchen and came out with a bottle of wine and two glasses. She poured them each a glass. She handed one to Jake.

"You haven't said anything about my work." Julianna took a sip of wine. "That's why I brought you up here." She laughed. "Surely, you didn't think I had other intentions." She leaned in close, her nose almost touching Jake's. It set him off balance. He felt dizzy. He sat down on the edge of the sleeper mattress, pushing aside a blanket, and set his wine on the table. Julianna sat down next to him.

"Your work," he said. "I like your sketches." He studied a large canvas propped against the wall. "You seem to be inspired by the Cubists right now, but I can see that some of your work shows the influence of the Impressionists."

"I was in love at the time," Julianna said. "Do you find your emotional state influences your work?" She leaned in close again, and placed her hand on his knee. Jake could smell her perfume, the wine and cigarettes on her breath. She was so near he could feel the warmth as she exhaled.

"Yes, I think it's got to."

"Are you in love now, Jake?"

"I'm engaged to a girl back home."

"That's not what I asked you."

"Yes, of course I'm in love."

"Then why are you here?" He wasn't sure if she meant here in Paris, when his fiancée was in Montana, or here in her apartment. Her hand moved slowly along the upper portion of his leg. She leaned in and kissed him, softly at first, then with greater force. His body responded, his lips as eager as hers. Jake pulled away and looked at her for a moment. She was very pretty. Her hands were on his shoulders. His body sank back into the mass of blankets, Julianna now loosening his belt with one hand, the other caressing his neck, moving down, working her fingers through the hair on his chest. He reached up, undoing the buttons on her blouse, revealing the soft flesh of her breasts.

16

JAKE TOOK THE Métro home from Julianna's Thursday morning. He felt like shit. His head ached. He'd had too much to drink the night before, a poor excuse for having slept with Julianna. Not a decision he'd made with his head or heart. No wonder women accused men of thinking with their dicks. But she'd been all over him. How could any guy have resisted?

She'd tried to talk him into taking the day off. "Let's go to some museums or something," she'd said.

"I should get to my painting," he answered.

"Aren't you the committed one," she teased.

Committed? What was it Alex had said about Jake's still not being big on commitment? And what the hell was she talking about? Was that what Alex had wanted years ago? Commitment? Shit, they were just a couple of kids.

Not big on commitment? Well, seems Alex was right. Here he was—Rebecca back home in Montana, ring still on her finger, and he was sleeping with Julianna.

What the hell was he doing?

The old bushy-browed man stopped him at the desk and told him he had a message. It was from Alex, dated last night, ten P.M. She'd left a phone number.

When he got up to his room he popped a couple aspirin and lay down on his bed. So Alex had finally decided to give him a call. He was curious about what she'd discovered, if she'd found any additional information regarding a seventh tapestry. And as much as he hated to admit it, he wanted to see her again. He rolled over, picked up the phone, and punched in the numbers. Alex's mother answered. He recognized her voice from when she'd picked Soleil up at the train station.

"Jake, so nice to talk to you again. Alex returned from Lyon late last night. We'd like you to come for dinner tonight if you don't have other plans."

"I could make it tonight." So Alex had been in Lyon all this time. She'd called last night. Right after she got home?

"About seven?"

"Sounds great."

"Sunny will be delighted. She's been drawing ever since your train ride back from Lyon. She's been asking when she might see you again."

"We had fun drawing," Jake said, surprisingly touched by the fact that Soleil was asking about him. "Did Alex mention how things had gone at the convent, Mrs. Benoit?"

"I'll leave that for Alex to tell."

He was definitely curious. "Then I'll see you at seven."

HE WENT OUT for a walk. It was too warm to run, but he needed to get out for some fresh air. He stopped for lunch. He didn't have much of an appetite, but he drank two glasses of tomato juice and a bottle of water.

He felt better when he got back to the room. He decided he would start a new painting, do some preliminary sketches rather than go right to the canvas. If he gave this some thought, more emphasis on the composition, maybe he would have better results. He had decided to give up on his first attempt, but he still wanted to use the window in the painting. He liked the lines of the shutter, the window ledge, the building across the street. But the emphasis would be on the woman, based on the sketches he'd done at the studio. He took out his sketchpad.

As he worked, a thought came to him. The pose of the

model from the studio drawing was similar to the nude maiden in the second sketch he'd done for Alex. If he moved the arm a little here, rotated the angle a bit . . . Quickly, he did several variations of the pose with slight differences in the position of the arms. He sketched in the outline of a small horse, front hooves perched on the woman's lap, added a sleek spiraled horn. Was this a bit too "New Agey"? Or cartoonish, like some fantasy poster tacked on the wall of a teenage girl? Maybe even corny? That was a word a college professor had used to describe one of Jake's paintings sophomore year. Jake hadn't been exactly sure what it had meant at the time, but he was pretty sure it meant shitty.

Shitty? He studied his drawings. No. He kind of liked this. He recalled what Alex had told him on the drive to the convent. Some of the interpretations of the unicorn in art. Purity. Innocence. Virgins. Redemption. Phallic symbols, symbols of Christ incarnate—eroticism and redemption. Carnal knowledge and knowledge of the divine. This idea—incorporating a unicorn in his painting—sounded so corny it almost turned around on itself to become something of substance. He rather liked this idea for a painting. Maybe even a couple of paintings. There were so many aspects of the concept to explore. He would start with a limited palette. Do this painting with the cool colors he had envisioned on his first attempt.

He came up with several different possibilities for the composition. Then he decided he would go to the Bois de Boulogne. He remembered there were stables at the park—he'd gone riding there years ago. He would sketch the horses. The unicorn would look so real it would fool anyone.

As he sat on the Métro on the way to the park, the image of the convent drawings kept playing in his mind, particularly the second with the maiden and the knight. As much as Alex had wanted this to be part of *The Lady and the Unicorn* set, Jake couldn't help but think how much it resembled the Pegasus tapestry he'd seen at the special exhibition at the Grand Palais.

He spent several hours sketching horses at the park, among them a pretty long-legged spring colt. He could easily envision this little fellow, with the addition of a sleek spiraled horn, cradled by a fair young maiden. Another thought came to him. His father. Wasn't this what his father had suggested? He'd been good at drawing horses when he was a kid. And now, here he was drawing horses again, horses with horns. Maybe his dad would think this was okay.

As Jake packed up his supplies, he decided, as long as he was out and about, he'd drop by the exhibition hall and take another look at *Le Pégase*. He still had a couple hours before dinner at Alex's.

He arrived and meandered through the first few rooms, glancing briefly at the early works. He wandered into the hall where the late Gothic works were displayed, and stood before *Le Pégase*.

It was a beautiful piece, the colors as rich and deep as those in the Cluny set. The knight mounted on the winged horse looked very much like the knight in the convent drawing. The three maidens were similar to the slender maidens in the unicorn tapestries, although they were not ornately garbed like the Cluny maidens. They were sleek and slender and naked, like the maiden in the second drawing, the maiden Jake had so carefully duplicated for Alex, the maiden he would use as inspiration in his painting.

"Très belle," a voice came from behind him.

Jake turned. Gaston Jadot, the old man from the studio, stood behind him gazing up at the tapestry.

"Monsieur Jadot, bonjour."

"Bonjour, Monsieur Bowman."

"Très belle," Jake repeated Gaston Jadot's words as the two men stood, looking up at the tapestry.

"It seems," Gaston said, "we have much in common, Monsieur Bowman. Perhaps our interest in tapestry."

"Oui," Jake answered. He did indeed have an interest in tapestry, although his was a recently acquired interest.

"La couleur," Gaston said, "the color, brilliant."

"La couleur, magnifique," Jake replied.

"Semblable à La Dame à la Licorne."

"Oui," Jake agreed once more. There were similarities in the tapestry and the unicorn set.

They visited for a few minutes. Jake asked if Gaston had seen the tapestry before. Gaston replied that it was in a private collection. This was the first time the work had been publicly shown. They talked a little about the similarities in this single tapestry with those in The Cloisters and the Cluny. Jake was surprised at the old man's knowledge, and in truth a bit amazed that he himself had acquired such knowledge of Gothic tapestries during his short time in Paris.

Walking home, Jake couldn't help but think what a strange coincidence this was—running into Gaston Jadot as he studied *Le Pégase*. He thought of his conversation with Julianna the previous evening, her questions about the drawings he'd done for Alex. They had spoken English, and Jake hadn't thought the old man understood their conversation, but now he wondered. Jake's trip to view the tapestry again was based on his curiosity, his desire to compare the second drawing from the convent to *Le Pégase*. How strange, he thought, that Gaston Jadot would be there too, looking at the very same tapestry.

17

THAT EVENING JUST before seven, a small bouquet of fresh flowers in hand, a bottle of wine tucked under his arm, the duplicates of the unicorn drawings folded, just as the original set, in the pocket of his jacket, Jake rode up on the elevator to Alex's apartment. At the door, he was greeted by an excited Soleil and the aroma of meat roasting in the oven.

"*Bonsoir,* Monsieur Bowman." The child clutched a tablet in her hands. Without another word, she held it out as he stood in the doorway.

He set the wine on the floor, adjusted the flowers under his arm, and opened the tablet. The pages were filled with drawings of unicorns, rabbits, dogs, even a monkey, which he recognized as one from the tapestry *Smell*. There were also imitations of the *mille-fleurs* scattered on the page.

"My teacher," Soleil said, "she told me they are very good."

"They are very good, Soleil. You show real talent."

"I want you to teach me how to draw the maidens. People are more difficult than flowers or animals."

"Yes, people are very difficult."

"Soleil, please . . ." Jake looked up to see Alex walking

toward the entryway where he still stood. She smiled. Her hair was tied back and she wore slacks and a pale pink blouse that matched the blush in her cheeks. She was holding a dishtowel and managed to look beautiful and elegant as she dried her hands. "Please, Soleil, it would be polite to invite our guest in before bombarding him with your drawings."

"Monsieur Bowman," the little girl said, "won't you come in." She lowered her head, a bit embarrassed, Jake thought. He stooped down, picked up the wine, and handed it, along with the flowers, to Alex.

"Oh, Jake, they're lovely," Alex said, smelling the flowers. "Thank you." She gave him a quick hug. "Now, please, come in."

He glanced around the room. It took him by surprise. For some reason he had expected Alex to live in a home surrounded by medieval treasures. The furniture was traditional— wingback chairs, an upholstered sofa, comfortable and homey. The pictures and paintings on the walls were an eclectic mixture. Most were original paintings, some abstract, some realistic, but certainly not what he had expected to find in Alex's home. A pile of colorful books—children's books, he thought—sat on a table.

"Please, sit down," Alex said. She looked much more relaxed than she had when he left her in Lyon. Her natural color had returned. She seemed happy to see him. "Mom and I are finishing up in the kitchen. May I offer you a drink?" She held up his bottle. "Wine?"

"Sure. Smells good in here," he said, sniffing.

"This looks delightful." Alex turned the bottle around in her hand. "*Châteauneuf-du-Pape*. Very nice. Shall I open it?"

"Will it go with dinner?" He wondered now if he'd spent too much on the wine, if he looked like a fool trying to impress her.

"Perfect," Alex said. She smiled at her daughter. "Perhaps Monsieur Bowman would like to look at your drawings now."

"*Merci,* Mama."

"Oh, I have something else for you." Jake pulled the drawings from his pocket.

Alex set the wine and flowers on the coffee table. She

unfolded the first drawing and studied it, then examined the second. "Jake, thank you so much."

"Mama," Soleil said, "can Monsieur Bowman look at *my* drawings now?"

"Yes, okay," Alex answered. "I should put *these* someplace safe." She held Jake's drawings up and offered her daughter a smile that carried a playful mixture of motherly warmth and admonishment.

Soleil returned a sheepish smile and Alex picked up the wine and flowers in one hand and left the room. Jake sat on the sofa. Soleil sat next to him. She opened the tablet to where they had left off. He looked at the drawings, turning the pages slowly. "Very nice, Soleil."

"Can you show me how to draw the maidens?"

"Sure."

"I'll get a pencil." She bounced up off the sofa. Alex came back into the room, carrying a glass of red wine. "Are you deserting our guest, Sunny?"

"I need to find a pencil."

Alex handed the wine to Jake, then sat down next to him. "How has your work been going since your return from Lyon?"

"Good," he answered.

"That's wonderful. See, I told you it would come."

Soleil scampered back into the room, carrying several pencils. Alex got up.

"I'm eager to know if you discovered anything more about the tapestry," Jake said.

Alex smiled. "I'll tell you all about it during dinner. Mom needs a little help in the kitchen right now."

Alex left the room and Soleil settled down on the sofa next to Jake. "Which maiden is your favorite?" she asked.

"Well, I guess I never thought about it." He assumed she was referring to the maidens in the unicorn tapestries. Undoubtedly Soleil had seen the resemblance in the drawings he'd done on the train, not to mention those she had destroyed, and the new set he'd brought this evening.

"I like *L'Ouïe, Hearing,*" she said. "She is the most beautiful."

Jake tried to picture the maiden in *Hearing*. He recalled she was playing the hand organ. He thought her hair was tied

up in an aigrette. She wore opulent, jeweled garments, as did
all the maidens.

Soleil smiled. "Do you think she looks like Barbie?"

"Barbie?" Jake asked, perplexed, then realized the little
girl was talking about a Barbie doll. "Maybe a little," he said.
The maidens in the tapestries all had the long, slender, elegant
bodies, the blond hair, the idealized vision of the medieval
maiden. None of them were as buxom as a Barbie, but that
had not been a fashionable image of women at the time. How
strange, he thought, that the little girl had compared the beautiful maidens to a modern-day cultural icon.

"The maiden in the seventh tapestry is naked." She said it
matter-of-factly.

The seventh tapestry? Had Alex found it? Had Soleil seen
it? Or was she speaking of the drawing?

"I like the beautiful costumes," Soleil said. "Do you?"

Little girls always preferred their Barbies in elegant, expensive designer clothes, Jake thought. It made him laugh to
himself. "Yes, I like the beautiful costumes."

Alex entered, carrying a tray of hors d'oeuvres. She was
followed by her mother, who carried two glasses of wine. The
two looked very much alike, Jake thought, though Sarah was
at least three inches shorter than her daughter. When Jake met
her at the train station, he was surprised she was so young. His
own mother was almost seventy, but Sarah Benoit looked
barely over fifty.

"Good evening, Jake," Sarah said. "We're so pleased you
were able to come."

"My pleasure." He stood. Sarah motioned him to sit. Alex
offered the tray of hors d'oeuvres.

Sarah handed Alex a glass of wine. "Would you like a
soda?" she asked Soleil. They both glanced at Alex.

"That would be fine," Alex said, nodding.

"Can I have a whole one?"

"Half. Pour it into a glass."

"Can I have the other half with dinner?"

"No. Milk."

"But what about the other half? The bubbles will all go
out," the child argued. "It will be ruined, wasted." She was a
spirited little thing, Jake thought, just like her mother.

"Half," Alex repeated.

"Oh, all right." Soleil gritted her teeth and left the room.

"Strong-willed child," Alex said and laughed.

"Like her mother," Sarah added.

"Nothing wrong with a woman who knows her own mind," Jake said.

Both women smiled and nodded. Jake took a bite of baguette spread with pâté.

"Tell me about your work," Sarah said.

"It seems the first week here in Paris, it just didn't come," Jake answered. "I started something this morning . . . I think it might work."

"I'd love to see it," Alex said.

"I'm just getting started."

Soleil came back, carrying a small plastic cup. Quietly, she sat on the floor next to the sofa and set her soda on the coffee table. She opened her sketch tablet and started to draw.

Sarah said, "I remember a drawing you did for Alex when you were students. A portrait. It hung in her father's office for years. It was lovely."

Again, Jake glanced at Alex. He sensed that this reference to a drawing he'd done years ago made her uncomfortable. It had been hanging in her father's office? Jake didn't even know Alex's parents were aware of his existence.

"Monsieur Bowman is going to teach me how to draw the maidens," Soleil said. "The ones with beautiful gowns and jewels."

"That's very nice of Monsieur Bowman," Alex said. "Did you know he's a teacher?"

"He's good at drawing."

"Yes, he is."

"I'd like to hear about your return trip to the convent," Jake said.

Sarah stood. "Dinner will be ready in just a few minutes."

"Need any more help?" Alex asked.

"No, you sit and visit. I imagine Jake is eager to hear about your discovery."

"Yes, I am," Jake said. "So, you did make a discovery."

"Yes." Alex grinned.

"Well, come on. Tell me."

"There is," Alex said, followed by a dramatic pause, "a seventh tapestry."

"You found it?"

"Yes, and it's beautiful. The colors are bright, vivid. It's perfectly preserved."

"And based on the drawing?"

"Yes."

"Colors similar to the Cluny's?"

"Very much, but little fading."

"Where? At the convent?"

"It was."

"Was?"

"Yes." Alex smiled.

Soleil looked up from her drawing. "I know where it is," she whispered.

"It was found in the wall," Alex said, "as they were working on the renovations."

"*Buried*—like in the poem?"

"Yes, and I can't help but think there's an additional tapestry—the poem seems to allude to the fact that there was an eighth tapestry."

"At the convent?"

"No, I don't think so. I'm trying to recall the words of the poem . . . something about the fruit of their creativity to be found in the village near . . ."

"In Vienne?"

Alex nodded. "After spending another day at Sainte Blandine's, going through the library again, I drove into Vienne. I talked to the parish priest and several of the elder citizens, then visited the museum. I found nothing to lead me to an additional tapestry, in the library or in Vienne, but I'm returning Friday after Soleil gets out of school."

Sarah came back in. "Dinner is served."

"I'm hungry." Soleil stood. Alex and Jake followed her into the dining room.

Dinner was a traditional American meal, served family style. Roast beef and potatoes, salad, and bread and butter. Jake loved French food, but it was nice to have an American meal.

"The Cluny has made an offer?" Jake asked as he served himself a large piece of roast. "On the tapestry?"

"It may not be as easy as I'd hoped. Sister Etienne has it in her head that if it brings a good price, they'll be able to stay at the convent."

Jake handed Alex the platter. "I thought they were moving to a retirement convent in Lyon." He scooped a large spoonful of mashed potatoes and covered it with gravy.

"That is the Archbishop's wish. I think he'd like to get them out of there as soon as possible, although, as I understand, the facilities in Lyon aren't quite ready."

"But he's already renovating the place."

"Yes, but Sister Etienne believes the upper level could still be used as a hotel, compatible with a convent on the lower level. They haven't used the upper level in years. If they sell the tapestry, the proceeds would allow nursing help, ramps for the nuns in wheelchairs, rent to the archdiocese. They've asked me to help make arrangements for the sale."

"Doesn't that put you in a bit of a spot?"

"I'm hoping it will work out for the nuns and the Cluny. I've contacted Elizabeth Dorling at Sotheby's in London. We could get the tapestry in auction late this summer."

"Are you concerned about that? The tapestry going on the block?"

Alex rubbed her temple and sighed. "The idea of a public auction concerns me. We have limited acquisition funds. We've made several major purchases this year. The timing is less than perfect. I've already begun my campaign to find the money. There are benefactors. But a public auction will bring in the private collectors."

"Rich people with money?"

"I'm afraid so. And even that darn Dr. Martinson." Alex made a face that reminded Jake of Sunny's reaction when her mother told her she couldn't have a whole soda. "You know *The Hunt of the Unicorn* series in The Cloisters came from a gift from the Rockefellers. Damned rich Americans."

Soleil giggled, then covered her mouth.

Alex cleared her throat. "*Darned* rich Americans."

"You will get it," Sarah said, quietly. "I know you will."

Alex sighed again, then glanced at Soleil, who was working very hard at cutting her meat into tiny bite-size pieces. "Do you need some help, Sunny?"

"I can do it," the little girl replied, smiling at Jake.

He smiled at Soleil.

"It belongs in the Cluny," Alex said.

"Does Sister Etienne understand," he asked, "that you think it's part of the Cluny set? Does she know how much you want to have it for your museum?"

"I *know* it's part of the set. I found something that convinces me it's part of the set. And Adèle Le Viste *did* design it. She and the *tapissier* were lovers. They belong together."

"The *tapissier* and Adèle?" Jake asked. "Or the seven tapestries?"

Alex laughed lightly. "Both. There's a hallmark, a tapestry weaver's signature, on the seventh tapestry. It's the same as the design on the band of *A Mon Seul Désir* in the Cluny. The same symbol intertwined with Adèle's A in the drawing. Don't you see?" Alex asked. "The tapestries must be together. Adèle and the weaver were separated because of the times in which they lived, because he was judged not suitable. And now . . ." Alex paused. "I know it seems silly, but I feel somehow if I can bring the tapestries together, Adèle and the *tapissier* will be together once more."

Sarah smiled. "Can you believe my logical, intellectual, pragmatic daughter is being motivated by romance?"

"Oh, Mom . . . am I being ridiculous? Do I want my way so badly, I'm becoming a fool? A romantic idiot?"

"And what's wrong with romantic idiots?" Sarah laughed. "What a dull world it would be without romantic idiots. Don't you agree, Jake?"

He nodded. "Yes, a very dull world."

After dessert, brownies and vanilla ice cream, Alex and Sarah left Jake with Soleil while they went to clean up in the kitchen. He offered to help, but Alex insisted he stay with Sunny and teach her how to draw a medieval maiden. The little girl had been patient throughout dinner, mentioning only once that she "sure hoped" he had time to show her how to draw the maidens. Alex noted this with, "I'm very proud of you," before she left the two of them alone in the living room.

"Which maiden shall we draw first?" Soleil asked. She sat on the floor again, pencil in hand, drawing tablet in front of her.

"Well, let's see . . ." Jake said as he sat on the sofa behind her. He didn't think he could duplicate any of the maidens from memory. Maybe one from the convent drawings. "Let's do our own maiden," he said. "We can do a medieval maiden and use the ones in the tapestries to help us out, for ideas on the costumes, but it's best to do your own drawing. Real artists don't copy."

Soleil looked up at him. "But *you* copied the drawings from the convent."

Jake smiled. The kid was right. "Your mother wanted to study the drawings. I did that to help her out."

"Okay," she said, agreeably, "but I don't want her to be naked. I want to draw a beautiful costume."

"I think we can do that."

They worked together for about ten minutes. Jake explained how the human body was perfectly proportioned, how Soleil could use the measurement of the head—he showed her how to use the pencil to measure—to determine the dimensions of the body. They did a rough outline sketch of the head and body, then filled in the facial features, as he instructed her again on the proper proportions. Jake urged her to create her own design for the maiden's costume, suggesting that the maidens in the Cluny set wore garments consisting of robes with underskirts, and jewels and turbanlike headdresses. Soleil wanted hers to have long hair, and Jake showed her how she could do the hair with a jeweled crown that he thought was similar to the maiden's in *Touch.*

"Do you know there's a secret," Soleil whispered, "a secret at Grandmère and Grandpère's in Lyon?" She looked up.

"No, what?" he asked. "What's the secret?"

"Are you telling secrets, Soleil?" Alex walked in and sat beside Jake. She looked at the little girl's drawing. "Sunny, that's beautiful."

Proudly, Soleil handed the drawing to her mother.

Alex studied the drawing, then, affectionately, she stroked the little girl's head. "It's beautiful, Sunny. Which maiden is it?"

"Monsieur Bowman says real artists don't copy."

"Yes, I can see now. It's your own design. It's lovely."

"Thank you." Soleil smiled at Jake.

"Are you ready for bed?" Alex asked.

"Can't I stay up and draw some more?"

"I'd like to visit with Jake. But perhaps he could come again sometime. Please tell Monsieur Bowman thank you and good night."

The little girl closed her tablet. She stood. "Thank you very much, Monsieur Bowman. You will come again?" She reached out and hugged him.

"Yes," Jake answered, struck by the child's affection. "I'd like to."

"Could we draw the costumes in color next time?"

"Yes, we could," he answered.

"Good night, Mama." Soleil hugged her mother.

"Grandma will pray with you tonight. Okay?"

Sarah appeared in the doorway. "It's been a pleasure seeing you, Jake."

Jake stood. "Dinner was great. Thank you."

Soleil handed the tablet to her grandmother. "I want you to see my beautiful maiden," she said as they started out of the room. "Next time we are going to do them in color."

"So, did she spill the beans?" Alex asked.

"The secret at Grandmère and Grandpère's in Lyon?"

Alex smiled and nodded. It looked like she might burst out in giggles of delight.

"The tapestry?"

"Yes."

"Then, you've got it?"

"Yes and no."

"I don't understand."

"Sister Etienne asked me to take it."

"But I thought she wanted to offer it at auction."

"She does. But she said she didn't think it would be safe at the convent, with the renovations and all. I think she's actually afraid the Archbishop will want to claim it. She asked me to take it to keep it safe. She didn't even ask where I would take it."

"It's in Lyon? At the Pelliers'?"

"Yes. Sister Etienne seemed anxious to remove it from the convent. I would have preferred to have it properly crated and shipped, but we rolled it, covered it with canvas, doubled it over, and strapped it to the top of my car. Quite a sight. And me—nervous as hell, bumping up and down on that horrible road, then the highway to Lyon, stopping every few miles to make sure it wasn't shifting or coming loose. There was no way I was going to drive all the way to Paris like that. But it's safe now in Lyon. I think it's best to leave it there until we arrange proper transportation to the auction house in London. When I go this weekend, I plan on taking photographs for the catalogue."

"What about the Archbishop, does he know about it?"

"His men found it, but Sister Etienne said she doesn't believe they even looked at it. They just turned it over to the nuns."

"So she's going to try selling it without the Archbishop's knowledge?"

"We've both agreed it's best to keep it under wraps for a time. We made a deal—Sister Etienne and I. I'll help her sell it, get the best price. And she's agreed there will be no formal announcement until the auction catalogue comes out late this summer. That will give me time to get the finances in order and give the Cluny a better shot at it."

"But what about the Archbishop? What will happen if he gets word of this?"

"I seriously doubt the Archbishop makes a habit of reading auction house catalogues. And right now, no one knows about the tapestry. No one other than the nuns, the Pelliers, Madame Demy, Mom, Soleil, you, and I. And you can keep a secret, can't you, Jake?"

18

A SECRET? JAKE thought as he sat in the cab on the way home from Alex's that night. Of course, he could keep a secret. He didn't mention that Julianna had seen the drawings and noticed the similarities to the Cluny tapestries, that she was aware he'd gone down to Lyon to do some work for the museum. And then there was the old man. Was it just a coincidence that he had shown up at the tapestry exhibition the following day? Was it possible Gaston Jadot, or anyone else in the studio, for that matter, had heard and understood Jake and Julianna's conversation about the drawings?

Another thought on Jake's mind that evening, as the cab bumped along Rue des Ecoles on the way to his hotel, was the feeling that something he couldn't control, something he hadn't planned on or prepared for, was slowly moving within him—his growing affection for Alex's daughter, Soleil. He'd spent little time around children. He wasn't sure he even liked kids. He and Rebecca had talked about having a family. She wanted four. He had agreed on two. Rebecca said he would make a good father; he was patient and kind. His reluctance, she was sure, was based on fear of the unknown.

Now, his thoughts turned to Rebecca as the cab pulled up

in front of his hotel on Rue Monge, and Jake couldn't help but think that, as each day passed in Paris, his feelings and his future became more and more blurred and confusing.

He called Rebecca and then his mother. Rebecca wasn't in. Jake guessed she was at the hospital. He left a message, said he'd call back. His mother was delighted to hear from him. He told her about his work, going to the studio, how much he was enjoying being in Paris, visiting the museums again. And because he knew it would please her, he told her he got a small job, doing some sketches for a museum. When she asked, he said it was through an old friend from school, Alexandra Benoit. He didn't describe the drawings or mention the tapestry.

THE FOLLOWING EVENING he went again to the art studio. Julianna approached as soon as he entered. "I thought maybe you'd phone or come up."

"I've been busy the last couple days . . ."

"We need to talk," she said. "About the other night."

He didn't want to have this discussion here. Who knows who might be listening.

He hesitated. "The other night, Julianna—"

"I know, I know," she said, holding up her hand. "You told me about the fiancée. I understand. But that doesn't mean we can't have a good time. Your honesty is refreshing, compared to some men I've known. But 'Miss Montana' won't be showing up until August." She moved in closer. "You did enjoy the other night?" she whispered.

What man wouldn't? A beautiful woman, so eagerly jumping his bones. And now she seemed to be telling him there were no strings attached, no emotional commitment required. He liked Julianna—her in-your-face bluntness and sexuality—but he knew she wasn't a girl he could fall in love with. Maybe that's why he didn't have stronger feelings of having betrayed Rebecca. He really didn't, and that fact alone made him feel like shit. If there was any betrayal, he knew it had to do with Alex.

"You want to go out after?" she asked.

"Well, I—"

"Are you afraid to be alone with me?" She grinned. "Actually we're all going. TGIF."

Thank God it's Friday? Jake wondered. As if this group of carefree young artists needed to unwind after a stressful week.

The model was disrobing now, and the others were starting to work. "Think about it," Julianna said.

"I should get home early. The painting is going well. Staying out late partying isn't in my best interest right now."

"Yes, you should spend your time painting when the inspiration is there." Her smile softened. "When are you going to invite me up to see your paintings?"

"There's not much to show right now."

"When you've got something, I'd love to see it." She stood waiting for a moment, then said, "Well, I expect we should all get to work."

HE TOOK HIS time that evening, putting his things away, getting ready to leave. Everyone had left the studio except Jake and Gaston Jadot.

"Voulez-vous," Gaston asked, *"prendre un verre?"*

Would he like to go for a drink? Somehow the invitation didn't seem quite so threatening coming from Gaston. *"Oui, merci,"* he answered.

The two men left the studio and found a small bar just down the street. They ordered a carafe of *vin ordinaire.*

They talked about the class. Gaston said they would be getting a new model the following week. Then, out of the blue, he said, *"Très intéressante, cette découverte les deux dessins."*

The discovery of the two drawings? The old man was commenting on what an interesting discovery this had been. Jake smiled slowly. He had guessed correctly—the old man did understand Jake and Julianna's conversation. Yet he was talking about a "discovery." Jake couldn't recall that either he or Julianna had referred to a "discovery."

Jake looked closely at the old man. *"Parlez-vous anglais?"*

"Un peu." Gaston lifted his wine to his lips and sipped.

More than a little, Jake guessed.

The old man chuckled. "Yes, I speak English." He spoke in

English now with very little accent. It sounded like a confession.

"You speak English well."

"During the war, I was a liaison officer working with the Americans."

"Why didn't you say something?" Jake asked. "You've never joined in the conversations in English."

"We are in France," the old man noted. He sounded very serious, but then he grinned.

"Oui," Jake agreed. *"Nous sommes à France."* They were indeed in France, something the French would seldom allow their foreign guests to forget.

The old man drank again, slowly. "An old man is not unlike a small child, sitting in the corner, listening to the adults, the grown-ups unaware that the child understands everything. One might learn a great deal from sitting silently in the corner." He chuckled again.

And what have you learned? Jake wanted to ask, but felt he should proceed with caution. The old man was definitely curious about the drawings. And he definitely had an interest in medieval tapestry. Jake wondered again about the meaning of Gaston's visit to the tapestry exhibition. Coincidence?

"This is interesting," Gaston said. "The drawings. They must have significance if this friend, this Alexandra, asks you to rush to Lyon to do the drawings."

Jake nodded, listening, trying to be noncommittal. Was it just curiosity on the old man's part?

"What is the significance?" Gaston asked.

Jake hesitated. "Perhaps I'll call on the artist's code of honor and confidentiality." He laughed as if making a joke. *Proceed with caution,* Jake told himself again. Gaston seemed perfectly harmless—an old man shuffling about the art studio in a tattered, elbow-worn sweater. Yet there was a certain refinement, a subtle elegance about the man. He was interested in art, medieval tapestries. Just how interested? Jake wondered. He had the feeling Gaston Jadot might be more of a threat to the secrecy of Alex's discovery than Julianna.

"Might the drawing represent an additional tapestry?" Gaston asked. "It's believed by some that the Cluny set is incomplete, that other tapestries might have existed at one time."

Jake didn't answer.

The old man smiled and nodded.

Jake took a drink of wine but said nothing.

Monsieur Jadot was gracious enough to let the subject drop. He asked about Jake's painting, said he too would be interested in seeing some of his work. He was always interested in seeing the work of promising new artists. Jake said he was working on something he hoped might turn into a series of paintings.

They finished their drinks, then walked together to the Métro station. Gaston told Jake he lived with his sister's daughter. She would probably be concerned about his being late. He should have called. He laughed and said sometimes he felt like a child who had to report in, call home if he was going to be late. Jake said it was nice to have someone to worry about you. The old man nodded.

They visited as they bumped along in the dark tunnel. Jake asked Monsieur Jadot how he had become interested in learning to draw. He explained that he had always been interested in art. He enjoyed the beauty of the artist's creation and had always felt it might be something he would enjoy himself. But he was too busy. He had worked until just a few years ago in the family business, until his wife became very ill. He had spent the last three years of her life taking care of her. He was alone for two more, then his sister's daughter had asked him to move in with her. It was at her urging that Gaston had found the studio and started coming to classes.

"And do you enjoy it?" Jake asked.

"*Oui*—" Gaston looked up as the train came to a halt. "I must transfer here, Monsieur Bowman." He stood, held out his hand. "It has been a pleasant evening. Will you return to the studio next week?"

"Yes, I'll see you then."

THE FOLLOWING MORNING, Jake went out for a run. When he got back to the hotel, Andrè stopped him at the desk to tell him he had a message from Alex, and she wanted him to call right away.

It wasn't seven yet. Jake couldn't imagine why Alex would

call this early unless it was an emergency. He asked to use the desk phone.

Alex answered on the first ring. "How would you like to drive down to Lyon this morning?" she asked.

"I thought you were leaving yesterday. Is everything okay?"

"Soleil's come down with a cold, so I decided to wait until today. She seems fine, but I don't think the trip would be the best for her right now, and I don't like to take her to the Pelliers' even if it is just a little sniffle. Pierre is so frail. How would you like to take a drive, help me with the photographs for the catalogue, do a little exploring in Vienne? Could you spare a couple days?"

"Sure."

HE WAS STANDING outside the hotel when she arrived, his thumb cocked like a hitchhiker. She couldn't help but smile.

"Thanks for coming with me," she said as he threw his bag in the backseat and hopped in next to her.

"I think I'm involved here."

She looked at him perplexed. "Oh, you mean with the mystery of the tapestries?"

"Yes, with the tapestries. And professionally. You are paying me for this trip?" he asked with a grin.

She smiled and nodded. "Why, yes, of course."

They moved through the early-morning traffic. It was Saturday, the streets free of the usual weekday commuters. They chatted as they drove out onto the Périphérique, then headed south toward Lyon.

"I want to thank you again," Alex said, "for duplicating the drawings, *again*."

"I didn't know if you'd find much use for them now that the tapestry's been found."

"Oh no, the drawings have been extremely helpful. I stayed up last night studying them. There's something in the first that seems to confirm the notion that the woman is returning the jewels to the casket in *A Mon Seul Désir*, rather than taking them out. On the border to the left, in one of the smaller sketches, I noticed she's *wearing* the jewels, then to the right in a drawing of the woman's head and shoulders, her neck is bare. A confirmation, I believe, that she's giving up these earthly pleasures. And then, in the drawing representing the newly discovered seventh tapestry, there's something that might support an interpretation."

"Which is?"

"The tapestry itself is large, and without hanging it and stepping back it's difficult to study the entire piece. But in the small drawing I noticed something about the angle of the knight's lance. At first it appears to be aimed at the unicorn's heart, but I believe it's actually directed toward the maiden, her maidenhood to put it delicately."

Jake didn't say anything, but he was getting the picture. Even after he'd done the drawing twice, he hadn't noticed this, but he understood what Alex was talking about. Who would have thought these ancient tapestries were so darned sexy?

"If the sixth tapestry, *A Mon Seul Désir,*" Alex continued, "can be interpreted as free will obtained by denial of the sensuous pleasures, couldn't the seventh represent just the opposite—freedom obtained through surrender to passion? Has the knight come to claim the maiden, to awaken her passions?"

"The knight being the tapestry weaver?"

Alex nodded. "In the seventh tapestry, the garden island has expanded into a more realistic setting. Has the surrender to passion, the surrender to love, opened up a whole new world to the young maiden? No longer confined to the garden island of her father's château?"

"The surrender to earthly pleasures?" Jake asked.

"Not exactly medieval thought." Alex grinned. "But I think Adèle was a woman ahead of her time."

"Who, unfortunately, ended up without her true love."

"Ah, yes." Alex sighed. "I'm afraid she did."

Jake asked about the weaver's mark on the tapestry, if it appeared on any of the others, the six tapestries in the Cluny.

"No, but there was severe damage to the selvedge and borders of all six pieces in the Cluny set. Most of them have had portions rewoven at some time. And it wasn't until 1528 that the workshops of Brussels were required to include a weaver's mark."

"But weren't the Cluny tapestries created earlier? Late fourteen hundreds?"

"Probably. The weaver's mark could have been used earlier. And maybe this seventh tapestry wasn't actually woven until later. But, it was definitely designed before 1491."

"The date of Adèle Le Viste's death?"

"Yes." Alex paused. "You know, when I was looking through the records of the Sisters of Sainte Blandine, I noticed there were patterns. Sometimes several deaths were reported within a short period, almost as if a plague, an epidemic had hit the convent."

"They certainly didn't have the preventive medicine we have now."

"No." Alex shook her head. "Now and then a single death would be reported. Generally an older nun, but then, the young Adèle Le Viste . . ."

"And you wonder how and why she died?"

"Yes. The thought is always on my mind. Can one die of a broken heart?"

"It usually mends," Jake said. "Over time. You get over it."

Alex looked at Jake.

"There's no cure," he said. "Maybe you get used to the pain."

"I suppose," Alex said. She wondered if they were really talking about Adèle Le Viste. Had she broken Jake's heart years ago when she married Thierry? And had his heart mended? Was he over her now?

Alex picked up speed and passed several slow-moving vehicles on the highway.

After a while he asked, "How do you think the tapestry arrived at the convent, and how did it end up in the wall?"

"We may never know the answers to those questions. It's not unusual to find pieces when ancient buildings are destroyed— under floorboards, behind walls, in cellars, even in tombs. Monasteries and churches have on occasion turned up unknown pieces, hidden away for centuries. Perhaps they were concealed intentionally, priceless treasures to be recovered at a later date, then forgotten when those who had hidden them died. Or perhaps they were simply used for other purposes when a particular style was no longer in fashion, stuffed inside walls for insulation, fill between floorboards. At times there wasn't much respect for tapestry. The Verteuil Tapestries in New York, *The Hunt of the Unicorn* series at The Cloisters, were used for storing potatoes. A peasant's wife came to Madame de la Rochefoucauld at the Château de Verteuil one day in the mid-1800s, aware that the family was searching for family possessions that had been lost during the French Revolution. She informed Madame de la Rochefoucauld that her husband had been using some curtains to cover potatoes in the barn during the winter to prevent them from freezing. The 'curtains' were the now famous Verteuil Tapestries and were returned to their owners." Alex sighed. "And of course, our own *The Lady and the Unicorn,* two of them were rolled up in the Hôtel de Ville, chomped by rats for years, rotting from the moisture. Amazing they survived."

"And now, a seventh piece."

"Yes." Alex smiled. "The seventh unicorn."

WHEN THEY WERE about halfway to Lyon, Jake said, "I went back to the tapestry exhibition."

"You *are* getting involved," Alex said, pleased.

"I wanted to take another look at *The Pegasus,* particularly after I'd done the sketches."

"You saw similarities in the nude maiden and knight?"

"Yes," he answered, strangely relieved that Alex had come up with this observation herself. "Do you think there's any connection?"

"I've always held a strong belief that *The Pegasus* was done in the same workshop as the unicorn tapestries."

"By the same designer?"

"Highly unlikely. I do believe that Adèle designed *The Lady and the Unicorn* tapestries, at least the original concept."

"What do you mean?"

"The production of a tapestry or set of tapestries is an involved process in which many artists and craftsmen take part. An original design would be produced, then a painting, a cartoon."

"A cartoon?" he asked. "Oh, the large drawing used behind the loom as a guide."

"Yes." Alex went on to explain that a design was often based on something smaller or simpler like a manuscript illumination, an artist's print, an illustration.

"Or a pen sketch?" Jake asked.

"Yes," Alex replied. "Just putting the pieces of what I know together—the poem, the drawings, my knowledge of tapestry history and production, I believe Adèle did the original designs, but the cartoons were most likely done by an artist in Paris. The cartoon itself would become the property of the workshop's master, to be used or altered as he wished."

"So a tapestry could come up later, inspired or influenced by an earlier design?"

"Exactly," Alex answered. "So maybe Adèle did have some influence on the creation of *Le Pégase*." She smiled at this thought.

WHEN THEY ARRIVED in Lyon, Simone asked about Soleil, and Alex said she was doing fine, just a cold, but she thought it best if she stayed home and rested over the weekend. Madame Pellier said that was probably wise. She said she would put Alex in Soleil's room and Jake in the guest room if Alex didn't mind taking the smaller. Jake was shown to his room to drop off his bag, then they were taken to the dining room where Marie served a lunch of *boudin blanc,* veal sausage, bread, and salad. Again, Pierre was not well and did not join them.

Alex was eager to show Jake the tapestry, but didn't want to offend her mother-in-law, so she sat and ate. Conversation was strained at first, and Alex found herself talking too much. Simone was gracious, as always, but Alex wondered what she thought about Jake—this was the second time he had been with her at the Pelliers'.

After lunch, she went to sit with Pierre, leaving Jake to visit with Simone in the living room.

Alex could see Pierre was slipping each time she visited. He lay in bed, his eyes open, staring at the ceiling. She sat and took his hand, wondering if he was even aware of her presence. "Soleil sends her love, Grandpère."

Alex told him about the little girl, what a fine artist she was becoming. She spoke of the tapestry, her desire to have it for the Cluny. He would have enjoyed hearing this a short time ago. But now, Alex wasn't sure he could even hear her. As she gazed down at Pierre, she felt a tightness in her chest, an itching in her eyes. She loved this old man so deeply. Perhaps if it hadn't been for Simone and Pierre, she would have left Thierry. And now here she was at the Pelliers' with Jake. She wondered what Simone thought, sitting now, visiting with Jake. But Simone was aware only that Jake had come to help her with the tapestry, to photograph it for the catalogue. It was not like she was bringing an old lover into the home of her dead husband.

As Alex rose, she bent over and kissed Pierre on the forehead. She stood, gazing down at him for a moment, then returned to the living room where Simone and Jake sat, engaged in what appeared to be a comfortable conversation. This was something she had always admired about him. He could spend days alone, completely isolated, working on a painting, yet he always appeared to be comfortable, at ease, even with someone he barely knew.

Simone looked up and smiled. "I suppose you young people need to get to work now."

"Yes, we probably should."

Jake stood, smiled at Simone. "*Merci,* Madame Pellier," he said before leaving with Alex.

"He looks awful," Alex said quietly as they walked down the hall to the library. "I don't know that he's going to be with us much longer. Even after the second stroke, when he couldn't speak, there was something in his eyes, and you just knew he understood. But now . . . I sat and visited . . ." Her voice caught as she spoke. "I wish you could have met him when he was well."

"Yes, I wish I'd met him then."

They entered the library. Jake flipped on the switch and Alex led him to the far side of the room where the long bundle lay rolled on the floor. Without speaking, they untied the ropes securing the protective canvas, and then they unrolled it. It was so large they had to drape it over the table and butt it up against the bookcase to display the complete piece.

Alex smiled as she watched Jake examine the tapestry. He glanced back at her and grinned. "It's beautiful . . . Wow, amazing . . . It looks like it's fresh off the loom."

"Gorgeous, isn't it," Alex whispered, leaning in close to Jake.

"Yes, it is." He gazed at the tapestry, then looked at her again and they stared at each other as if they were sharing something very intimate and personal. "Yes, beautiful," he said.

Alex took a deep breath, then looked back down at the tapestry, although she felt Jake was still staring at her. She could almost feel his breath on the back of her neck.

"Guess I'd better go get that camera," she said, "so we can get to work."

"Good idea."

Alex left, returning to her bedroom to retrieve the camera she'd brought from the museum in Paris.

When she came back to the library, Jake still stood, staring down at the tapestry. He looked back at her. "I can certainly see why you want to claim it for the Cluny."

"Yes," Alex said, smiling. "I think we need to hang it." She could hear that let's-get-down-to-business tone in her voice. "Don't you? To do the photo?"

"That would work best."

They rolled the tapestry, then carried it into the living room, where Alex explained that she would like to remove an Aubusson that covered a good portion of one wall and hang the unicorn tapestry. As she took several photos of the weaver's hallmark on the back, Jake measured the two tapestries and informed her they would have to make some adjustments for the tapestry to hang properly. This involved a trip to the hardware store, then Jake's working on the supports used for hanging. They brought a ladder in from the library and borrowed another from the building supervisor and removed the bulky Aubusson. The unicorn tapestry was even heavier—Jake guessed at least sixty pounds—a challenge to hang. He suggested Alex climb up the ladder on the left. He would take on the weight, lifting as Alex reached the top, then go up the opposite ladder and secure the right side.

"I surely didn't anticipate this much trouble," Alex said as she started up the ladder.

"What trouble?" Jake replied.

"Oh right, men like these complicated challenges." She looked back at Jake, who gazed up at her, grinning as if he hadn't had this much fun in a long time, and she couldn't help but smile too. "I had hoped to run down to Sainte Blandine's later today. This is taking much longer than I'd planned."

"Sometimes things take a bit longer than planned. If you want to do the job right."

"Well, let's do it right." Alex nodded in agreement, then continued up the ladder.

After the tapestry was secured, they stood back to admire their work.

"Perfect," Alex said. "We make a good team."

"We always did," Jake replied.

For several moments it seemed they were each waiting for the other to add something to this reflection. Finally she said, "Guess I'd better get the camera set up."

Jake helped with the camera. Alex took one roll of film, then another.

"Do you think you're getting enough shots?" he teased.

"I certainly hope so . . . I don't want to go through this again." Although, in truth, she would have to admit she was having fun too.

By the time they finished, Marie was ready to serve dinner.

After they ate, Alex called home to check on Soleil, then went in to visit once more with Pierre. Jake sat in the living room with Madame Pellier. Marie served coffee. When Alex returned, Simone asked about Soleil, who was doing fine, then the older woman said good night and excused herself. Alex poured a cup of coffee from a carafe Marie had left. She sat.

"Soleil asked about you. She likes you, Jake."

"I like her too."

"You're good with children. You seem to have that gift of patience, which I must admit I'm sometimes lacking. Do you and Rebecca plan on having a family?"

"We've talked about it."

He seemed uncomfortable having this discussion, about his and Rebecca's plans. Maybe Alex shouldn't have asked. Maybe it was none of her business. She was prodding him. She wanted him to tell her about Rebecca, to say that she was a good woman, that he was madly in love with her. Or maybe what she really wanted was for Jake to say, *I'm having second thoughts. That's why I'm here . . . I'm not really sure about Rebecca anymore.*

"We'd like to have two," he said, "a boy and a girl."

"You'll be a good father." Alex smiled. "Sunny would love to have a little brother." Why was she telling him this? Although it was true. Sunny often told her mother she would like a little brother.

"You're planning to marry again?"

"Oh, I don't know. I've become rather independent over the past few years."

"You always were, Alex." He laughed. So did she.

They sat, drinking coffee, talking, mostly about the tapestry. Alex refilled her cup, brought the carafe over, and refilled Jake's. She told him she'd like to go to the convent early in the morning, then drive into Vienne. Father Maurin from Saint Pierre had given her the name of a woman whose family had lived in the area for years, and he thought if anyone might be able to track down an ancient tapestry, it would be Madame Gerlier.

ALEX LAY IN bed that night, unable to sleep. She could hear the creaks and groans of the ancient building, and then she imagined she could hear him, creeping down the hall, quietly opening the door to her room, sliding into bed beside her, whispering into her ear—a confession that he had made a terrible mistake, that he should have put up a fight for her years ago, that he knew the moment he saw her again in the museum that they were meant to be together. And then she would make her own confession—she would tell him how deeply unhappy and empty her marriage had been.

Finally she drifted off into a bumpy sleep, wondered what was going through his mind as he lay in bed just down the hall.

* * *

THE IMAGE OF Alex invaded Jake's futile attempts at sleep. He could see her smile, how she'd absolutely glowed when she showed him the tapestry. Then a replay flashed through his mind—Alex climbing up the ladder to hang the tapestry. If he had let go of reason for even a second, he might have yanked her off that ladder and pulled her down to the floor, made love to her right there on the oriental carpet in the living room of her rich in-laws.

It seemed he was waiting again for Alex. Waiting for some indication of where they were to go from here. She wasn't a woman with whom a man could easily initiate any emotional or physical intimacy. He remembered years ago how he had waited, and then feeling it was something she wanted, he made a move, an awkward attempt, touching her soft, sweet-smelling body. A recollection that could still humiliate and arouse him at the same time. She'd said, "I want to wait until I'm married." He remembered clearly she hadn't said *we*. That had stuck with him all these years. And something else had stuck with him—the thought that she was *out of his league*.

Now here he was, alone in this big fancy bed—hell, he'd had to clear off a ton of tasseled silk pillows just to crawl under the covers—wondering again, how did he fit into all this? Alex's world.

Was he nothing more than an old friend? A professional colleague? Tonight Alex had asked about Rebecca and Jake's plans for children. What did she want from him? Was he merely a tagalong on her tapestry excursions? He didn't understand Alex any better now than he had years ago.

THEY LEFT EARLY the following morning for the convent. They spoke little as they drove. Jake waited out in the vestibule while Alex went in to talk to Sister Etienne.

After leaving the convent, as they drove into Vienne, Alex told Jake about her conversation with the nun. Sister Etienne was pleased they would be able to get the tapestry into a late-summer auction. She had already had a discussion with the

Archbishop, who wanted to move the nuns out within the next two weeks. Sister Etienne had told him of their wish to stay, if they were able to raise enough from the proceeds of the sale of their property. The Archbishop had agreed, putting off the move. Sister Etienne thought he probably suspected there would be no great amount, but was merely pacifying the nuns for the time, as he was behind schedule on his renovations anyway.

In Vienne, Alex called the number given to her by Father Maurin. They made an appointment to visit with Madame Gerlier at two, then stopped at a café for lunch.

MADAME GERLIER WAS a large, buxom woman, with bleached blond hair that Alex guessed had probably gone gray decades ago. Bright red lipstick comically enlarged her wrinkled little mouth. Her skirt was too short and her heels too high, causing her to walk with an unsteady gait along the stone floors of the château that, according to Madame Gerlier, had been in the family since the late fourteenth century. The woman reached out and put her arm through Jake's. As she explained the family history, she seemed to be addressing her remarks to him, although she would turn and include Alex now and then. Madame Gerlier looked like a woman who in her youth had possibly been beautiful and was not quite ready to let go of the idea. Alex couldn't help but think of her mother-in-law, whose beauty was so natural, part of her beauty being the fact that she had accepted her age.

As Madame Gerlier led them down the hall and into a living room decorated in garish red velvet, she spoke of a set of tapestries that had also been in the family for hundreds of years. She turned to Alex. "Father Maurin says you are interested in tapestries."

"Yes, particularly medieval. I'm looking for one woven perhaps in the late fourteen hundreds, probably in Brussels, with a deep red background, with *mille-fleurs* design. Are you aware of any such tapestries in the valley?"

"The Vérons had some tapestries. I'm trying to think now, as I recall there was some red, or was it green, and I think they were done in Aubusson, not Brussels." She smiled at Jake.

"They paid a fortune for them, and why, you know, they can hardly keep the place up, and it's well known"—she turned back to Alex once more—"I'm not one to spread gossip, like I said, it's well known Monsieur Véron is a drinker and a womanizer too."

Alex glanced around the room as Madame Gerlier went on and on, with this story, then another, none of them having anything to do with medieval tapestries. The room was filled with dust-covered, ancient-looking urns and vases, silk flower arrangements, and large, cumbersome, antiquey-looking furniture, none of which Alex found particularly attractive. A young woman served coffee, and Jake and Alex were forced to listen to more stories. Jake listened courteously, but now and then he'd glance over at Alex, his head tilted, his eyebrows rising discreetly. She could see he was getting almost as impatient as she.

"Perhaps you could show us the tapestries," Alex suggested, after Madame Gerlier offered them the third refill and about the fiftieth story.

"*Oui, oui,*" Madame Gerlier replied. She rose slowly, almost losing her balance once more on the too-high-heeled shoes. "The nicest is in the master bedroom." She blushed, then smiled at Jake. She led them down another hall, into a bedroom with a massive canopied bed. A large tapestry hung on one wall. It was a mythological scene depicting a partially clad maiden seated on a rock, Cupid peeking out from behind a tree to the right, Bacchus hiding behind a tree to the left. The border was filled with putti holding enormous flower-filled baskets. The predominant colors were blues and pinks, somewhat faded.

"My husband, Henri, loved it. He always thought I resembled the Diana." Madame Gerlier turned to Jake, then looked up at the tapestry. "The goddess Diana, goddess of the hunt. What better place for a hunt than in the bedroom, Henri used to say." She smiled at Jake, then covered her mouth to suppress a giggle.

"It's lovely," Alex said. "Probably mid–seventeenth century, a little later than what we're looking for."

"It's not for sale," the old woman said, as if Alex had just made an offer. "It has been in the family for years."

"Yes, what a treasured family heirloom."

They were led to a second, smaller bedroom and shown a second piece, most likely part of the same set as the first. Again Alex remarked how lovely it was. They returned to the living room, where Madame Gerlier offered more coffee. From Jake's frequent glances and fidgety shifting in his chair, Alex could see he'd definitely had enough—both coffee and Madame Gerlier.

"*Merci,* Madame Gerlier," Alex said, "but we must return to Paris this evening and have quite a drive ahead of us. Thank you for showing us your tapestries." She stood. So did Jake.

When they were outside, walking to the car, Alex said, "Sorry. I didn't know what I was getting you into. These tapestry-hunting expeditions turn up all kinds of surprises." They exchanged glances and both burst out laughing. "Oh, Jake, you're still quite the charmer. Madame Gerlier was obviously taken with you."

"I think she's just a lonely old lady."

"A horny, lonely old lady," Alex replied. "Thank you for giving up your weekend to help me out. It's been fun—hanging tapestries, hunting tapestries."

"It would have been nice," he said seriously, "if we'd accomplished more."

"Oh, we did. We got the photos. I talked to Sister Etienne. The Archbishop has agreed to let them stay a little longer, evidently without any curiosity about their discovery."

"It would have been nice to find that eighth tapestry."

"If there is such a tapestry."

Alex unlocked the car door, and Jake held it as she slid in on the driver's side. Suddenly she felt very tired. She looked up at him.

"May I make a suggestion," he said, squatting down so their eyes were level. He raised his arm and gripped the seat-back behind her to keep his balance.

"What kind of suggestion?" The words came out in a tone so embarrassingly flirty and teasing she could feel herself blush.

"Nothing illicit." He smiled slowly.

She smiled. "Of course. Nothing illicit. Yes, go ahead. Make a suggestion."

"You look tired. Do you mind if I drive us back to Paris?"

"I like that idea." She held the keys out to him in the palm of her hand. He reached over and slowly removed them, the warmth of his touch lingering for a moment.

"Yes," she said. "I'd like that very much."

19

THE FOLLOWING MORNING, Alex woke with an itch in her throat. She had caught Soleil's cold. She drank a glass of orange juice, took two cold tablets, the nondrowsy kind, packed her purse with tissues, cough drops, and extra cold tablets, and then left for the museum. She felt awful, but she had so much to do. Luckily, the Métro was not crowded and she was not forced to stand.

After visiting with Madame Demy, filling her in on the events of the weekend, Alex spent the rest of the morning on the phone. She called Monsieur Bourlet, the trustee of Thierry's estate, to set up a lunch appointment. He was always helpful in money matters. Then she called Madame Genevoix to invite her and her husband to dinner Friday evening. They were extremely wealthy and generous in supporting the arts. Alex wanted to present them with her discovery in hopes they could see the value of the Cluny's acquisition of the tapestry.

Madame Genevoix said they would not be available Friday, but perhaps sometime the following week. Alex hated to put it off that long, but didn't want to discuss the motive for her dinner invitation over the phone. They settled on the following Friday night. Madame Genevoix, as usual, was in a chatty mood. Before they said good-bye, she asked about the American artist they'd met at the reception.

"Jacob Bowman," Alex said.

"*Oui,* Monsieur Bowman. I would like to see some of his work."

"I'll invite him for dinner next Friday evening."

"We'll look forward to that."

Madame Genevoix ran a gallery in Paris, showing the work of prominent contemporary artists. Now and then she sponsored an up-and-coming artist. It was a mere hobby for the woman, introducing new artists, but Alex knew it could be helpful for Jake, and it would be a perfect reason to invite him for dinner.

She phoned him at his hotel.

"Alex, you sound awful," Jake said. "Are you okay?"

"I think I've caught Sunny's cold."

"All the excitement over the weekend—hanging tapestries, running around chasing after tapestries—probably lowered your resistance to that cold bug."

"I was tired when we got back, even though I slept most of the way. Thanks for driving, and thank you for going with me."

"It was fun."

"I had a nice time too," she said, followed by an awkward little gap in the conversation. It sounded like she was thanking him for a nice time on a date. "Anyway . . . the reason I called, I've got some exciting news. Remember meeting the Genevoix at the tapestry exhibition?"

"There were so many people that evening."

"Older couple, we met them when we first walked in."

"Yes, I remember you introduced them as great patrons of the arts. And the good news is they've agreed to purchase the tapestry for the museum?"

"Not yet. But I've invited them for dinner and I'd like you to come too. Madame Genevoix owns a gallery here in Paris. The location is great, by the river. And . . . the exciting part . . . she'd like to see some of your work."

"You're kidding? When?"

"Come for dinner a week from this Friday night. You can charm the lady, set something up. Why don't you bring a painting. I'll hang it. I'm sure she'll like it and you can schedule a showing of additional work."

"Additional?" Jake laughed.

"What?" Alex asked. "There is no additional?"

"I have a painting I wouldn't show anyone. I'm working on another. Next Friday?"

"I know you work well under pressure. I remember back in the good ol' days. You could always meet a deadline."

"Pulled a few all-nighters."

"Yes, I do recall."

"You haven't seen any of my work for over fourteen years."

"True, but I'm confident in your talent and eager to see what you're doing now."

"Thank you, Alex, for setting this up. I'll have something for you to hang."

ALEX LEFT WORK early that evening to take Soleil to her ballet class. The studio was just a short distance from their home.

Soleil carried her ballet slippers in a small backpack that looked like a fuzzy rabbit. She bounced in an excited skip, the backpack bobbing up and down, the rabbit's ears flapping. Alex took her hand as they waited at the light to cross the street.

"Will Monsieur Bowman be coming again soon?" Soleil looked up at her mother. "He said we could draw the maidens in color."

"Monsieur Bowman is very busy, Sunny. He has work to do." Alex had hoped when she called that afternoon Jake would suggest they get together, but he hadn't. She felt disappointed, but she knew he had to dedicate his time to his painting, particularly now that she had set up this meeting with Madame Genevoix.

"But he went to Lyon with you," Soleil said.

"Yes. He was helping me with my work for the museum." They crossed the street.

"With the new tapestry at Grandmère and Grandpère's?"

"Yes."

"Will it hang in your museum soon?"

"Yes, it will."

"I like Monsieur Bowman," Soleil said. "Do you like Monsieur Bowman?"

"Yes, I like Monsieur Bowman. Do you know we went to school together here in Paris many years ago?"

"Do you love Monsieur Bowman?"

Why would Sunny ask such a question? Alex wondered. What did a little girl know about love between a man and woman? "He's a special friend," she answered.

Shit, Alex thought as they walked into the building, what did she herself know about love between a man and woman? They started to climb the steps to the second-floor studio.

"I would like him to be my special friend too," Soleil said.

"Yes, I'm sure he would like that."

Alex was tired when she went to bed early that evening, but she couldn't sleep. Sunny's question kept playing in her head. "Do you love Monsieur Bowman?" she had asked. "I would like him to be my special friend too."

Special friend? Hadn't they been more than that? They were so young and they had never used the word *love.* If he had loved her, wouldn't he have come after her? Wouldn't he have at least replied when she wrote to tell him she was marrying Thierry? Perhaps it wasn't love at all. Or could it have been the most perfect kind of love? The innocent, unknowing, foolish, lustful, unrealized love of youth.

Yes, what did she know about love? Did she know any more now than she had as an awkward teen? She'd gone to an all-girls high school, and the few dates she'd had then were arranged by her brother—with one of his friends—or her mother—with the son of a friend. She didn't have a real boyfriend until her freshman year in college. There were other boyfriends in college, nothing serious. Then Jake. Then Thierry.

And with Thierry everything seemed to go so fast. Before she knew it, he had flown to Baltimore one weekend and asked Alex's father for her hand in marriage, which, at the time, she found old-fashioned and romantic. Of course, her father said it was Alex's decision. Her mother was concerned that Alex was too young, that she hadn't experienced enough on her own, although Alex's mother herself had been young.

It *was* Alex's decision, but it seemed she was suddenly swept up in something she hadn't quite had time to fully ponder. The invitations were printed, the caterer arranged, flowers ordered, the cathedral reserved. She was getting married!

Thierry was in a hurry. Of course, he was . . . They'd had
heavy sessions of touching and kissing, and Thierry said he
would go mad if he couldn't have her. She tried to explain
why she wanted to wait. It wasn't even something religious,
although it was what she had been taught by the Sisters of St.
Francis at her high school in Baltimore. A virtuous woman
was to save herself for marriage.

No, it wasn't a religious thing, though Alex knew it was
something spiritual. Body and soul. Flesh and spirit. One
man, one woman, united forever.

Alex had vivid memories of the wedding night. She and
Thierry were both exhausted. After a few kisses, he climbed on
top of her and was pushing himself inside her. Within seconds,
it was done. Then he rolled over and went to sleep. Alex lay
awake. Was this it? Was this what she had saved herself for?

Later in their marriage, Alex had tried talking to Thierry,
tried to tell him kindly that she was not satisfied, although she
didn't use that word. It would have crushed his ego, which
was much more fragile than she would have ever imagined.
He seemed insulted, as if his good looks and money should
have been sufficient in themselves to bring her to a full earth-
shattering climax. He made her feel it was her fault. He told
her she was cold and unfeeling and often she believed him.

After Thierry, there were other men and meaningless sex. After Thierry, why not? She had slept with men she didn't even
like. About a year ago, at a conference in Berne, she had stopped
for a drink at the hotel bar, to unwind after a long day of meetings. She met a man, an American, nice enough and interesting
to talk to. He'd come up to her room, a thought that made her
shudder now. They had a few more drinks. The sex was hot and
quick and a little rough. When she woke the next morning he
was still there. She felt cheap and dirty, but at the same time
grateful that she was still alive. He could have been some
weirdo, a serial killer. They didn't have a lot to talk about that
morning. She gave him a fake name and number. He said he'd
call the next time he was in Paris. She was relieved when he left.

She'd pretty much sworn off men after that. Wasn't she
better off without them? And wasn't her life full enough, with
her work, her daughter?

Now, here Jake was again. But engaged to a sweet little

nurse, waiting for him back home in Montana.

Alex wondered if she was making a mistake, letting Soleil become so fond of Jake. And then she questioned the wisdom of her own growing attachment to him.

AFTER SPEAKING WITH Alex, Jake felt doubly motivated. He painted all morning, then late into the afternoon.

He liked this new piece. He'd used the model from the studio, the window in his room, the unicorn from the drawings he'd done at the Bois de Boulogne. That vacant, faraway look on the young woman's face seemed to take on a new significance when he placed her in the scene with the unicorn, both sitting before the window, open to a world in which neither of them was involved. Her expression now seemed not one of disinterest or boredom, but of youthful unknowing, and her nudity looked not at all seductive or sexual, but innocent, like the nakedness of a newborn child. He had used soft, cool colors that had turned out just as he had intended.

By evening, he was putting on the finishing touches. The figures of the maiden and unicorn came to life as he added details and highlights, darkened shadows. He set the canvas on the dresser and stood back. This was pretty damn good.

The next morning, he went to Musée Gustave Moreau on Rue de la Rochefoucauld. The artist Moreau was known for his symbolic works in depicting mythological fantasies, with several pieces featuring unicorns. His work was part of the Romantic movement of the late 1800s. Jake didn't particularly care for the style. There was little depth to the work. But in a way it did inspire him. He found it interesting—obviously some influence from the unicorn tapestries. The maidens were decked in jewels and fancy turbans like the young women in the Cluny tapestries, although several of them were nude.

He spent the afternoon at the library, doing research on the unicorn in art. He made copies of reproductions of several medieval and Renaissance works, some depicting the unicorn and Virgin in Annunciation scenes, and several allegorical representations. He found a reproduction of a Raphael, *Young Woman and Unicorn,* and a Moretto da Brescia with a Renaissance city as landscape in the background.

He rushed home and began sketches for a new painting. He worked late into the night on his new drawing—a young woman holding a small unicorn in her lap, similar to what he was now referring to as his "first painting," but inspired by the Raphael. According to his research, the small unicorn in this piece could be seen solely as an attribute—chastity or modesty. He would use a pose similar to Raphael's, but instead of the Renaissance-type costume, he would dress the woman in a contemporary costume, and instead of the hills framed by two columns in the Raphael, he would use a modern-day scene of Paris in the background.

Wednesday morning, he transferred his drawing to canvas. He liked what he'd come up with. The woman wore jeans and a T-shirt. The tiny unicorn sat in her lap, like a pet—a kitten or puppy. The scene in the background, with the Eiffel tower, repeated the vertical lines of the window, the unicorn's horn. He laughed a little at the interpretations a critic might give the painting, which he had decided to call *Chastity*.

As he worked, he gave the woman a sweet, yet slightly smug Mona Lisa smile, which also reminded him a bit of the lion in *Touch*. He liked it, and as he painted, he laughed with delight, working alone, giddy over the power, the self-control, the motivation he felt.

That evening, he called and spoke with Alex to thank her for her inspiration. She seemed as busy as he, and as involved in her own project—obtaining funds to purchase the seventh tapestry. As much as he wanted to see her again, he knew he should continue working. And she didn't suggest they get together. Was she growing tired of him again already?

Thursday morning as he worked, he started to plan his next painting. He wanted to do some glazing on this second piece, which he couldn't do on the wet canvas, so he would work on a third composition. That afternoon he went to the co-op to purchase a larger canvas. The store was crowded, and though Julianna waved from across the room where she was helping a young man, Jake didn't hang around to chat after he'd paid for the canvas.

When he got back to his hotel, he did several sketches, preliminary drawings. He decided he would incorporate at least two figures into this painting, and also a more involved landscape, a forest with a lake in the background, similar to Moreau's *Ladies and Unicorn,* which had also reminded him of Manet's *The Picnic.* The piece had stirred up quite a scandal when it was presented at the Salon des Refusés in the mid-1800s. The viewers were perplexed by Manet's painting, although it was actually a reworking of *Concert Champêtre* by the sixteenth-century Venetian artist Giorgione.

Jake would incorporate a figure similar to Manet's nude woman, another female figure and a unicorn, this time a full-bodied, muscular animal using some of the sketches from the Bois de Boulogne.

Friday he decided he would go to the studio that evening. For the past few days he had spoken to no one other than Alex. He was lonely and he also needed a model to use for his third painting.

Monsieur Jadot was not at the studio that evening. A somewhat subdued Julianna suggested he was ill, that there had been something going around, the flu, summer colds. Both Matthew and Brian were sick that week, she said. Jake had noticed that neither of the two young men was there that evening.

They had a new model, Gabby, the friend of Julianna and Matthew whom Jake had met last week. Since there were so few students that evening, it was easier to agree on a pose, and Jake was able to get one he could use in his new painting. The idea also came to him that he could probably get Gabby to come pose for him.

During their break, Julianna walked over and stood beside Jake as he poured a cup of coffee. "You could have said hello the other day."

"You looked pretty busy."

"How about you? I saw you bought a new canvas."

"I'm getting some work together for a local gallery."

"A local gallery? You *are* doing well. Any more work for the Cluny? Madame Pellier?"

"Haven't done anything but paint all week." No way he was going to mention his second trip to Lyon.

"Well, sounds like your painting is coming along. I'm looking forward to seeing your work. Which gallery?"

"Nothing's set yet. I'm hopeful."

"Let me know when you schedule your first show."

Jake couldn't quite interpret Julianna's tone. She didn't seem upset or pissed off at him. "I will," he said and smiled.

AFTER THEIR SESSION, Jake approached Gabby and asked if she'd be willing to come pose for him. She said she would be free all weekend, and they agreed on a time and price.

When Jake returned to his hotel, there was a message from Alex. Had she dropped by? It appeared to be in her handwriting. She and Soleil had gone to Lyon. "Will miss you," the note said, "but we know you're busy with your painting. See you next Friday evening at 7:30."

She would miss him? Alex or Soleil? Or both?

He wished she had called and invited him to go along. But Gabby was coming the next day. He had work to do.

Gabby arrived Saturday at nine A.M. They worked through the morning, stopped for a brief break and lunch—they had fruit, bread, and cheese that he'd purchased early that morning when he'd gone for a run. Gabby was very quiet. Jake didn't feel an obligation to chat with her or entertain her, although they visited during their lunch break. Gabby seemed to open up a bit, telling Jake how people thought all you had to do to be a model was throw your clothes off and sit still. She laughed shyly. "The sitting still isn't all that easy."

"I don't know how you do it," Jake said.

"Mind control," Gabby answered.

They went back to work and continued through the afternoon. She agreed to come again the following morning at ten.

On Sunday, Jake completed one of the figures on his third painting. For the next two days, he worked on the unicorn and the background, a forest and lake. He added a picnic lunch, similar to that in Manet's *The Picnic,* using a still life of apples, oranges, and grapes in a basket, a loaf of bread, and a bottle of wine. Then he ate the fruit and half the bread and drank two glasses of wine as he sat admiring his most recent effort, getting up now and then to add a little touch of color here, darken a shadow there.

He spoke with Alex on the phone. Her cold was much better. Her trip to Lyon and Vienne had been uneventful. She had visited with the Vérons, whom Madame Gerlier suggested she contact, and found nothing. "I don't think there is an eighth tapestry. At least no longer in existence, not in Vienne anyway. Perhaps I should just concentrate on obtaining the seventh."

"And how's your campaign to raise funds going?" Jake asked.

"Slowly. Monsieur Bourlet has put me in contact with several promising prospects. It isn't easy raising money while trying to keep the discovery hush-hush."

"No, I don't suppose so."

"Will you have something for me to hang Friday night?"

"Yes. It's coming along."

"Then I should leave you to your work."

"And you to yours."

JAKE FINISHED THE third painting, which was larger and much more detailed than his first two, early Friday afternoon. It was very good, he thought. He would take it to Alex's that evening, although he was working in oils, and it wasn't dry. He went to the co-op to buy a frame and also pick up a set of colored pencils for Soleil. He didn't see Julianna and guessed it was her day off.

When he arrived at Alex's apartment that evening, carrying his not-yet-dry painting, the box of pencils in his jacket pocket, Alex greeted him at the front door. She wore a sleeveless summer dress with a scooped neckline revealing a good portion of her creamy pale skin. She looked beautiful. He had been so busy with his work over the past few days that at times he had successfully pushed her out of his mind. But now, seeing her again, he wondered how he had been able to accomplish that and how he had been able to work with such intense concentration.

He was disappointed to find that Soleil had gone to the movies with her grandmother. "I brought her a gift," he said, pulling the box of pencils out of his pocket.

"How sweet of you, Jake. She'll be delighted." Then Alex explained briefly that she wanted to create a pleasant, but semibusinesslike atmosphere that evening and didn't believe the presence of a six-year-old, complaining about the tomatoes in the salad, would be appropriate. In addition to Jake and the Genevoix, she had invited another couple, the Barbiers. Alex took Jake's painting. "Come, let me see it." She set it up against the wall and stood back.

"It's still wet," he said.

"I won't touch it." She examined it up close, then stepped back and looked at it for several minutes from a distance. Jake held his breath. She smiled. He exhaled.

"It's very good," she said. He could tell she was sincere. "I like the theme, the maidens and unicorn. It's turned out very nicely." She nodded and smiled. "Inspired by Manet?" she asked. "Yet, it's got a very contemporary feel about it—the young woman with the short cropped hair. A model from your studio?"

Jake nodded. "Her name's Gabby." He laughed. "Although she doesn't talk much, which is a fortunate trait in a model."

"Yes." Alex smiled. "A good trait in a model, I'm sure." She picked up the painting. Jake followed as she carried it into the dining room. "Here," she said, pointing at a landscape in dark colors hanging on the wall above the buffet. "Let's hang it here so our guests will be able to see it as we eat. I'll put Madame Genevoix right there." She gestured to the far side of the table.

A woman in a black uniform and white apron entered the room carrying a bouquet of fresh flowers. Alex smiled and nodded toward the table. The woman arranged the centerpiece in the middle of the table, which was set with full china, silver, and crystal.

"I've hired some help for the evening," Alex said. "Why don't you take the painting down and we'll hang yours."

She adjusted the lighting as Jake hung his painting. It looked good, the colors terrific. He hoped Madame Genevoix would be intrigued and ask to see more. Jake laughed to himself, because other than the two smaller paintings, there was no more.

The Barbiers arrived precisely at eight. The Genevoix were fashionably late. Cocktails and hors d'oeuvres were served in the living room, accompanied by general conversation about the weather, the latest happenings in Paris. They didn't discuss the tapestries or Jake's painting. Shortly before nine, Alex escorted them into the dining room.

Madame Genevoix noticed the painting right away. "It's quite nice," she said. "Do I know the artist?"

"That's Monsieur Bowman's latest work," Alex said.

Madame Genevoix studied the painting from across the

table. Jake sat next to her. After a few moments the woman reached out and placed her hand on his arm. *"Oui, très agréable.* The theme of the unicorn. Not unlike the French painter, Moreau, a Romantic, although your style is very different. Do you know his work, Moreau?"

"Yes," Jake answered, "I'm familiar with his work."

Madame Genevoix smiled. "We French have always been intrigued with the mythical beast. Quite popular in medieval art and literature too."

Might this be the perfect opportunity, Jake wondered, for Alex to present her case, her discovery of the seventh unicorn tapestry?

"I was quite sure," Alex said, "you would be delighted with Jake's work." She smiled at him.

He smiled too, mostly because, less than two hours ago, Alex had no idea what the painting even looked like.

"I'd like to see more of your work," Madame Genevoix said. "I have a gallery here in Paris. I think your work would show nicely. Perhaps you could bring four or five more pieces by sometime soon so I might take a look."

"Eh bien, merci, Madame Genevoix," Jake said. "I'd be pleased to bring something by," he added, wondering how quickly he could paint a couple more pieces. He'd never produced such satisfying work this fast in his life. But could he keep up the pace?

The meal was served in the traditional French fashion, the entrées all French, very different from the American meal Jake had been served the last time at Alex's. After the *plat principal,* a delicious *agneau chilindron, salade* was served, followed by an assortment of *fromage,* then dessert, tasty little strawberry tarts, and fruit with *café.* As they were finishing, Alex's mother appeared with Soleil. Alex introduced her mother and her daughter, and asked about the movie. Soleil said it was wonderful. She smiled shyly at Jake. "Will you help me with my drawing tonight?"

Alex said, "Grandma will help you get ready for bed. Monsieur Bowman has brought you a gift. Perhaps if you get ready, brush your teeth, he could come in and tell you good night."

The child grinned. "Okay," she said and gave her mother a hug.

As she left the room with her grandmother, Madame Genevoix commented on how much the child had grown since she had seen her last. Madame Barbier said what a beautiful little girl she was, how much she looked like her mother. Alex suggested they go to the living room, and asked if anyone would care for more coffee, or a *digestif,* an after-dinner drink.

They sat sipping coffee and Cognac. Alex had still not brought up the subject of the tapestry. Sarah came in and told Jake that Soleil was ready for bed, then led him to her room. The child was already tucked into her small, white-framed bed with a ruffled pink canopy. A lamp sitting on the matching white dresser cast soft shadows of stuffed animals perched along the bottom of the bed. Sarah stood in the doorway while Jake went in and sat next to Soleil. She sat up and smiled. "I'm so happy to see you again."

"And I'm happy to see you, too."

"Did you bring me a birthday gift, Monsieur Bowman?"

"Is it your birthday?"

"Next Friday, July second. Will you come to my party?"

"How old will you be?"

"Seven."

"Seven? A lucky number." Jake pulled the box of pencils out of his pocket. "I didn't know about the birthday, I just brought this because I thought it might be something you could use." He handed the pencils to Soleil.

"Oh," she squealed, "thank you so very much." She reached out and gave him a hug. "Can we draw tonight?"

"It's very late," Sarah said.

"Will you come another day?" the child asked. "Tomorrow?"

"Yes, I'll come again. Tomorrow? Maybe I'd better check that out with your mother."

"We're going shopping for your birthday presents tomorrow," Sarah said. "Maybe Monsieur Bowman can come back a different day. Please say good night now, so he can go join the other guests."

"Good night, Monsieur Bowman," she said, "and thank you very much." She gave him another hug.

"Good night, Soleil, and thank *you.*"

"For what? I didn't give you anything."

"For being such a delightful little girl." He got up to leave.

"Monsieur Bowman," the child said.

"Yes, Soleil?" He turned.

"It would be all right if you call me Sunny."

"I'd like that very much," he answered. "Good night, Sunny."

When Jake returned to the living room, Alex had finally introduced the topic of the mysterious unicorn tapestry.

"And where was it found?" Madame Genevoix asked.

"I can't reveal that just yet," Alex said. "But I assure you it's an authentic late-medieval tapestry. And it appears to be part of *The Lady and the Unicorn* set."

"But I thought," Monsieur Barbier said, "it's been established the six pieces are a complete set."

"Yes," Madame Barbier added, "hasn't it been accepted there were only six pieces found at Boussac?"

"Yes, but as you might recall," Alex said, "the tapestries had been hanging at the château in Boussac for two hundred years. They had been moved there, probably from one of the estates of their original owner, Jean Le Viste." Alex got up. "Will you excuse me for a moment."

She returned with an envelope. She opened it slowly and dramatically and placed a photo on the coffee table in front of the two women.

"Beautiful!" Madame Barbier cried out with astonishment.

"Magnifique!" Madame Genevoix exclaimed.

AFTER HER GUESTS left, Jake and Alex sat in the living room. Sarah joined them.

"Overall," Alex said, "I think we could call it a successful evening."

"Did your guests seem interested in financing the tapestry?" Sarah asked.

"I think I've enticed them to consider it," Alex replied. "I don't have a definite commitment."

"She was very subtle," Jake said, "but I'm sure they got the idea that the museum wouldn't be able to make the purchase without some help."

Alex slumped down in the chair and threw her long legs over the side. "I'm exhausted," she said. "This fund-raising is hard work." She smiled at Jake. "And what about you? Now wasn't our Madame Genevoix just tickled with your work?"

Jake sighed, then laughed. "I should go home and lock myself in my room. No food, no drink, no phone calls, no company. Nothing but me, my paint, canvas, and inspiration." He sat up straight in his chair. "But first, I believe I have an obligation to one little girl."

"Yes," Sarah said, glancing at Alex. "Your daughter has invited Jake to come give another drawing lesson."

JAKE RETURNED SUNDAY morning for brunch. Alex had taken Sunny to Mass and wasn't home yet. Sarah Benoit, who said she'd been up for early Mass—she had trouble sleeping late—invited him into the kitchen and offered him coffee, motioning for him to sit.

They visited as she sliced oranges and arranged them on a platter alongside both green and purple grapes. "The painting you brought Friday night is lovely," she said. "You seem to have found your inspiration."

"Thank you. Yes, I think I have."

"You're working in a studio here in Paris?"

"Right now my room is doubling as my personal studio, though I'm going to a place up at Montmartre for live models."

"Where are you staying?" Her voice had a casual but interested tone that reminded him of his own mother.

"A little hotel on the Left Bank, *Le Perroquet Violet.*"

"Perroquet?"

"Parrot."

"A violet parrot?"

"Actually there is a parrot, sitting right at the front counter, but it's red, yellow, and green."

"Lots of color, good for an artist." Sarah grinned.

"Maybe so." Jake smiled too. A warm, comforting aroma now filled the room. "Sure smells good. What's in the oven?"

"Cinnamon rolls."

"My favorite," Jake said, sounding like a kid, thinking again of his mother, and being back home in her kitchen at the ranch. He'd come in from school, she would be baking cookies, or maybe bread or pies, and she'd pour him a glass of milk, and he'd sit with her as she gently quizzed him, carefully coaxed him into a discussion of the day's events.

"Is there anything I can do to help?" he asked.

"No, just sit. Everything's about ready."

Sarah pulled a small carton of strawberries from the refrigerator and arranged them on the fruit platter. "Sunny seems quite taken with you," she said.

"I'm growing fond of her too."

"Will you be staying in Paris long?"

"At least until August," he answered. He'd been vague when the question was asked before. But now, he knew he needed to take it seriously. His visitor's visa was good for three months. He had been in Paris for one. If he could get Madame Genevoix to show his work, sell a few paintings, maybe he should look into legalizing his long-term status. Rebecca would be coming in less than two months. Would she be expecting him to return with her?

"Alex says you're engaged to a girl back home, that she's coming to visit later this summer. More coffee?" Sarah asked.

"I can get it," he said.

The kitchen timer went off. Sarah pulled the rolls out of the oven. "Alex and Sunny should be home soon." She drizzled frosting over the rolls. "You know, Jake . . ." Sarah hesitated, as if reluctant to say what she was about to say. "You can break a little girl's heart just as easily as a big girl's."

What was she talking about? Did Sarah think he was getting too close to Soleil? And what was this "big girl" business? Did Alex's mother think it was Jake who had broken her daughter's heart? Alex had married Thierry. Alex was the one who had broken his heart. He heard the front door open, then tiny footsteps as Sunny rushed into the kitchen. She gave Jake a hug.

Alex walked in. "Mmm, smells good, Mom." She reached out and embraced Jake so lightly and briefly, he barely felt her touch.

They had brunch in the dining room, then Alex said she and her mother would clean up in the kitchen. Sunny was anxious to try out her new pencils. Alex said she'd done nothing but stare at them, removing them one by one, examining them, but she had waited for Jake to help her. She hadn't yet used the pencils.

They settled down in the living room, Soleil on the floor by the coffee table, Jake sitting behind her.

She slid the pencils out of the box and arranged them in an even row on the table. "Which colors shall we use?"

Jake picked out a dark blue, a red, and yellow.

"That's all?" She gave him a puzzled look.

"Think of the tapestries in your mother's museum. *The Lady and the Unicorn*. What colors?"

"Red, gold, . . . blue," she said slowly. "But there's green too."

"Let me show you something." He picked up the blue pencil. On the corner of the paper, he drew a leaf, colored it in lightly on one side, darker on the other. Then he picked up the yellow pencil and colored over the entire leaf.

"It's magic," Soleil said. "You've made green." She grinned broadly.

They decided on a garden scene with a maiden, not unlike the Cluny tapestries. Soleil drew an outline of the maiden, then picked up the red pencil.

"The maiden is a virgin, isn't she," Soleil said as she filled in the overgarment. "Do you know what a virgin is?" She asked the question matter-of-factly. "Well, do you?"

Jake hesitated. "Well . . . uh . . ." Wasn't this a discussion she should be having with her mother?

"I do," she announced proudly.

"Oh?"

"It's a maiden who hasn't had a seed planted in her garden."

Jake smiled. Soleil turned and smiled too. She went back to her drawing. She asked, "Do you know what grows out of the seed?"

"A flower?"

"No." She stared at him as if he were the dumbest person on Earth. "A baby."

And suddenly, it came to him—Alex was wrong about the eighth tapestry. The poem, the allusions, the garden metaphors. The fruit of their love to be found in the village near. It wasn't a tapestry at all. There wasn't an eighth tapestry.

Alex walked into the room

"I've just had an inspiration," he said.

"What is it?"

"The eighth tapestry. I think you're looking for something that no longer exists. What you're looking for died hundreds of years ago."

20

ALONE, ALEX LEFT early the next morning for Vienne. She didn't know exactly what she was looking for, but she knew Jake was right. Had she been so determined to believe that the poem spoke of an eighth tapestry that she had completely missed what should have been obvious? It was a child. The child of Adèle Le Viste and her lover, the *tapissier*.

Alex wondered if Adèle had been unaware as she left for the convent that she was carrying his child. She had died a short time after her arrival at St. Blandine's. Alex suspected she'd died in childbirth. Had the child been taken to the village, raised by a loving peasant family? Or had Adèle watched as the child had been taken from her? Such a possibility made Alex shudder.

Alex thought of her conversation with Sister Anne, the old nun's being "called" at a young age, yet having the ability to answer or reject the call. But a woman in the Middle Ages—did she have any choice? Surely, this was not Adèle's true calling, or her true choice. And then Alex reflected on her own choice. She had married Thierry. Even with freedom to choose, one does not always choose well.

Alex stopped at the convent to visit with Sister Etienne and to check on the nuns. Now that they would be staying on at the convent at least until the middle of August, without any help, Alex was concerned. The Archbishop probably had good reason for wanting to move them to the retirement home. As far as Alex knew, they didn't have any means of contacting the outside world if an emergency arose. What if one of the elderly nuns became ill? She would talk to Sister Etienne and suggest they ask the Archbishop for some additional help.

Sister Etienne was pleased to see Alex. Sister Anne brought tea, lemon, and a pot of hot water wrapped in a cozy into the office. She smiled and nodded, then left the two women to visit.

"The Archbishop has asked for a copy of the inventory in his attempt to determine if sufficient proceeds would allow us to stay," Sister Etienne said. "He wants an account of the items that have been sold, or have had an offer made. I'm afraid he won't be terribly impressed." The nun smiled. "Of course, the inventory does not include the tapestry."

"He has no idea?" Alex asked.

"I don't believe so."

Alex squeezed lemon into her cup, stirred, then took a sip of hot tea. "I wonder if this is wise," she said, "your decision to stay here without any help. What if an emergency should arise?"

Sister Etienne reached deep into the pocket of her habit, rattling her rosary beads as she pulled out a small cellular phone. "The Archbishop evidently had the same thought as you, Alexandra."

Alex smiled. "Perhaps you could give me the number?"

Sister Etienne wrote the number on a notepad, then handed it to Alex.

"*Merci.*" Alex slipped it into her purse.

They talked about the auction. Alex told Sister Etienne about her plans to have the tapestry shipped to London, how it would be described in the catalogue, which would be coming out in less than three weeks. The photos had been sent and the price estimated, Alex told Sister Etienne, based on the price of several tapestries that had been previously sold. A tapestry depicting a woman riding a unicorn, probably woven in Tournai in the fifteenth century, had been sold last May at Sotheby's for 128,000 British pounds. The tapestry had extensive damage and reweaving. "Of course," Alex said, "your tapestry will most likely go for much more. As far as I know, there's been nothing quite like this offered at public auction, nothing from this time period in such perfect condition."

"And will the ownership be noted in the catalogue?"

"No," Alex answered, "that will remain confidential."

"So the Archbishop will have no way of knowing?"

"I imagine he might become suspicious, after the sale of the tapestry. Might he become suspicious when you are unable to show where the funds came from, based on your inventory? Or will you be willing to reveal it then?"

"But doesn't the tapestry rightfully belong to the order?"

"Yes," Alex answered, "it does."

The nun nodded and picked up a pencil, twisting it nervously in her hand.

Alex wondered if they could really pull this off, the Archbishop unaware until after the deed was done. And could Alex come up with the funds to purchase the tapestry for the Cluny?

Sister Etienne poured more hot water for Alex, then herself.

"I wanted to ask," Alex said as she dunked the tea bag in her cup, "about the legend regarding the tapestry, the poem." She placed the tea bag on the saucer. "Was there ever a thought, a story that the *tapissier* and the young woman conceived a child?"

"There are always legends, not just the legend of the young woman and the *tapissier,* but these stories are always coming up. A young woman sent to the convent because of an illicit love affair, or even a rape. She is with child. She has disgraced her family. Then, of course," the nun said with a smile, "the stories about the immaculate conception, once she's here at the convent."

"And what would become of the child?" Alex asked. "A child born here at the convent."

"A good family would be found."

Alex nodded. Had the child been aware of his or her heritage? And what did Alex hope to find? Someone who had lived and died almost five hundred years ago? Even if she discovered something, what significance would it have? Were there still descendents of Adèle Le Viste living in the village?

Sister Etienne reached down and slid out a lower drawer of the desk. She bent over, pulled out a book, and placed it on the desk. Alex immediately recognized it as the medieval prayer book.

"For you," Sister Etienne said. "For your museum. I know you said it is of some value, though not of great value. I do appreciate the help you are giving us, and we would like you to have it."

Alex hesitated. It would mean a great deal to her to have Adèle's prayer book for the museum. She was touched by Sister Etienne's offer and the nun's realization of how much this meant to Alex.

"Please," Sister Etienne said, "I know that in a special way you feel connected to the young woman. We would like you to have the prayer book."

Alex had shared with Sister Etienne during their last visit her theory on Adèle Le Viste, her discovery of the young woman's name in the book of records, the tiny signature *Adèle* on the drawing. Alex remembered how the nun sat, listening attentively, nodding as if she were taking it all in, as if she understood this was proof the tapestry was part of the set designed for Jean Le Viste, as if she understood it must be displayed in the Cluny with the others. But the nun had said nothing. Perhaps the good sister, whose earlier observations had certainly implied her belief that the tapestry was one of the Cluny set, didn't want to admit it belonged with the others in Paris.

Yet now Sister Etienne was acknowledging Alex's feelings by offering her the prayer book. The nun must have understood how deeply Alex believed it had at one time belonged to the young Adèle Le Viste, the woman she believed had designed the tapestries.

Alex reached out and took the book. *"Merci."* She opened it and slowly turned the pages. She wasn't consciously checking to see if the drawings were still hidden in the middle of the book, but she knew as soon as she looked up that this was exactly what Sister Etienne thought.

"I think we'll keep the drawings for a while," the nun said, "at least until after the tapestry is sold."

Alex felt embarrassed, and a little ashamed. "Thank you so much for this gift. We will treasure it at our museum."

ALEX STOPPED TO see Madame Gerlier, who seemed pleased to have company, although she inquired about Jake, and Alex guessed the woman would have been much more pleased if Alex had brought him along. She asked Madame Gerlier if she'd heard a legend about a baby being brought from the convent to live with a family in the village. It seemed this was a common story. Myth or truth, there was nothing unusual about it. The woman had stories, dozens of them, the majority relating to twentieth-century events and families still living in Vienne.

After visiting with Madame Gerlier, Alex went to see Father Maurin. While driving, she had come up with the idea that there would be records, much like those she had discovered at the Convent of Sainte Blandine. Some fifteenth-century recording that would provide a clue. Father Maurin suggested baptismal and matrimonial records and let Alex pore over several large books. What was she expecting to find? She had no name for the *tapissier*. Even if she did, it would most likely have no value in her search. And a child adopted by a local family would not carry the name Le Viste. What did Alex expect to find?

As she studied the records, Alex was touched with a little flutter of excitement as she came across the name *Benoit,* her family name. She knew it was not an uncommon name, but she wondered if she was looking at a small part of her own history. She had often considered doing some type of research, tracing her roots, but she knew a genealogical study could be difficult and time consuming. She certainly didn't have time to pursue this now.

As interesting as the records were, recording baptisms and sacramental marriages, they provided no clue as to the identity of the child of Adèle Le Viste. Alex thanked Father Maurin and drove to Lyon, where she spent the night at the Pelliers'. The following morning she returned to Paris.

Sunny was in an unruly prebirthday mood, eager for her party, excited about the presents she, her mother, and her grandmother had picked out the previous weekend. There were others she had not seen, gifts her mother had bought as a surprise. Soleil was not at all happy that she would have to wait until Friday. Couldn't she just have one? Now, before her birthday?

Alex called to talk to Jake, but the man who answered the phone at his hotel said Monsieur Bowman was not taking calls. Alex guessed he had locked himself in his room, frantically painting to have something to take to Madame Genevoix.

WEDNESDAY MORNING, SOLEIL sat, moving her scrambled eggs around on her plate with her fork, eating nothing other than a few bites of toast. She glanced up at her mother, who was reading the morning newspaper. "Will you call Monsieur Bowman to make sure he knows what time my birthday party is?"

Alex looked up from her newspaper. Sarah placed her coffee cup in her saucer and looked at the child, then at Alex, who asked, "You invited Jake to your birthday party?"

"I want him to come," Soleil replied. "Will you call him?"

Alex glanced at her mother. "Well . . . yes, I guess I could."

Sarah said, "Are you finished with your breakfast, Sunny? Why don't you take your plate and cup back into the kitchen."

After Soleil had left, Sarah asked, "Are you sure this is a good idea?"

"What?" Alex replied.

"Inviting Jake. Letting him become so much a part of your daughter's life."

"Why? Jake is fine. He's grown very fond of Sunny."

"And she of him."

"So what's the problem?"

"Oh, Alex, for such a smart girl, sometimes you aren't very bright. The problem is that she becomes attached. Then he leaves."

"Eventually, yes. He's engaged to a girl back home. And isn't this the way it works? They leave." It came out almost snotty, as if it were her mother's fault that Jake would be leaving. Alex wanted to take the words back, but with the angry words came the realization of an emotion that in the vaguest way had been playing restlessly in every corner of her mind and heart for the past fourteen years—it wasn't Alex who had deserted Jake, but Jake who had left Alex. He had let her go off with Thierry without the slightest protest. He hadn't even come to tell her good-bye when he left Paris that spring. When she wrote to tell him she was marrying Thierry, he hadn't replied.

"And who will miss him more when he leaves?" Sarah asked. "Sunny or her mother?"

Alex didn't answer. But the thought would not leave her, then or as she rode to work that morning. Why had she let him come so easily back into her life, and why had she let him become so friendly with her daughter? She knew he didn't plan to stay. He had a fiancée waiting for him back home in Montana.

Alex didn't call him that day, though she had told Soleil she would. She wanted to talk to him, to tell him about the prayer book, her gift from Sister Etienne, her most recent trip to Vienne. But she couldn't bring herself to pick up the phone.

That evening Soleil asked if she had called.

"I was very busy today," Alex answered.

"Well, then," Soleil replied angrily, "if you won't do it, I will. Tell me his phone number."

"I'll call tomorrow."

The following morning, as they ate breakfast, Soleil commented that it was just one day until her birthday. She reminded her mother again that she had promised to call Jake.

"Yes, I told you I would call." Alex turned to the second page of the newspaper. Her eyes stopped abruptly. She couldn't believe the words she read. The headline—*"Les Religieuses et l'Archevêque de Lyon Se Disputent une Tapisserie Ancienne."* "Nuns and Archbishop of Lyon Battle over Ancient Tapestry."

21

ALEX SCANNED THE article quickly. An ancient tapestry had been found in a convent south of Lyon. The nuns were claiming it, but the Archbishop was disputing the ownership, as the archdiocese had purchased the building and grounds years ago. The convent was not identified as Sainte Blandine's. The present location of the tapestry was unknown. It had been removed from the convent and was being held by a trusted friend. The "trusted friend" was not named. There was nothing in the article about the upcoming sale at Sotheby's.

Alex read the article once more, slowly. Why hadn't Sister Etienne called? Alex wondered if the nun herself had told the Archbishop about the tapestry, overcome with guilt from keeping the discovery a secret. Had the nuns been forced to turn the drawings over to him? Or had the Archbishop become aware of the tapestry's existence from another source? Had the men working on the renovation come forward?

"Will you call him, Mama?" Soleil interrupted her mother's thoughts.

"Yes, Sunny, I'll call him." Yes, she would call Jake. And she would call Sister Etienne. She glanced at her watch and realized, if she didn't hurry, she would be late for an early

meeting scheduled for that morning. She ripped the small article out of the paper. She would call from her office.

As soon as she arrived at the museum, Alex picked up the
phone and punched in the number Sister Etienne had given
her. No answer. She tried again. Still no answer. She called Simone Pellier in Lyon. First, she asked about Pierre. Simone
said he was about the same. Then Alex asked if her mother-in-
law had seen the article. She had not. Alex asked Simone if
anyone had contacted her about the tapestry. Simone said no,
it was perfectly safe. But Alex was concerned. Had she put her
in-laws in a dangerous or compromising position, harboring
the tapestry? No one knew it was there. No, that wasn't true. Simone knew. Alex's mother knew. Soleil. Even Marie. Madame
Demy, the Director of the Cluny, knew where it was. And Jake
knew. Yes, Jake knew. But Jake would not betray her.

She was late for her meeting. As soon as the last item on
the agenda was discussed, Alex rushed back to her office. She
tried calling the convent a third time without success, then dialed Jake's number. The man at the desk said he was still not
taking calls. Alex sat, wondering what she should do next.
The catalogue for the sale at Sotheby's would come out in two
weeks; the auction was scheduled for the thirteenth of August.
Six weeks away. Friday the thirteenth. Should she have taken
this as a bad omen?

She paced back and forth in her small windowless office,
then picked up the article and read it again. Even if the Archbishop took possession of the tapestry, was it likely he would
sell it? Maybe the Cluny still had a shot at it. But what about
the nuns? Had they already been thrown out of their home,
forced to take up residency in the retirement convent in Lyon?

Alex sat at her desk. She should return to the convent, drive
down to see Sister Etienne. She had three appointments that
morning, but she could cancel them. That afternoon she was
teaching a seminar to a group of college students, a commitment she'd made months ago. Perhaps Dominique could take
the class. No, she remembered, Dominique left yesterday for a
week in Provence to visit family. Alex would have to take the
seminar. And she still had to pick up favors and decorations for
Sunny's party tomorrow. Maybe she could take the high-speed
train down that night or early the following morning, rent a car.

No, Sunny would be up early. Alex had promised her she could open some of her presents before breakfast. There was no way she could take off now or tomorrow. And wouldn't Sister Etienne call if there was a real problem? Could it all wait until this weekend? What could Alex do about it anyway? If the nuns wished to turn the tapestry over to the Archbishop, they would have to contact her. She had the tapestry. Sister Etienne didn't even know where it was.

She went in to see Madame Demy, who hadn't read the paper yet that morning. Alex handed her the article. The Director reached for the reading glasses hanging from the gold chain around her neck and settled them on her nose. She motioned toward the chair in front of her desk as she read the article, but Alex was too nervous to sit.

"Have you spoken with the nuns at Sainte Blandine's?" Madame Demy asked.

"I've been trying to call. The Archbishop has given them a cell phone in case of emergency, but I'm not sure they even know how to use it. Maybe it doesn't transmit this far."

"Do you want to go down again?"

"Yes, but I have a seminar this afternoon and Sunny's birthday tomorrow."

"If it's rightfully the property of the archdiocese, it will have to be turned over."

Alex stared at the woman. She couldn't believe Madame Demy was being so casual about this. But then, she had never shown the enthusiasm over the discovery Alex felt she should. She had never even asked to see the tapestry and was only mildly enthused about the gift of the prayer book. Was the woman jealous? Jealous that it had been Alex's discovery?

"You know, Alexandra . . ." Madame Demy had never called her Alexandra before; it had always been *Madame Pellier, Madame Demy*. Business had always been conducted in a businesslike manner. "Even if the nuns are able to prove ownership, even if it goes to auction, there is no guarantee we will get it."

Alex didn't know what to say. She stood staring down at the Director. "I'll go to Blandine's early Saturday morning and sort things out."

Madame Demy nodded and said that would be fine.

Just before eleven, Alex told Sandrine she would be out for
a while. She had to pick up some things for Sunny's party. She
would also go see Jake. Maybe he could tell her what to do.

JAKE STOOD BEFORE the mirror and rubbed his fingers
over the stubble on his chin. He hadn't taken time to shave
since Sunday morning. Maybe he'd just leave it, create a
whole new image, impress Madame Genevoix—avant-garde
artist from Montana. He had completed two additional paintings in the past week and had started another. He'd set up an
appointment to meet with Madame Genevoix Monday afternoon at her gallery.

Since early Saturday, he'd done nothing but paint. Sunday
evening he'd called Rebecca, then his mother, to tell them he
had an opportunity to meet with a gallery owner to show his
work. He also wanted to let them know he'd be taking no calls
for the next week. He didn't want either of them to be concerned if they tried calling. Rebecca told him she had made
her reservation. She'd be arriving in Paris on August thirteenth. Friday the thirteenth, but she saw that as her lucky day.
Then she said, "Isn't it nice you're getting these opportunities
in Paris."

"It's going well," he agreed.

"Your mother told me you'd done some sketches for a museum."

"Yes."

"For your friend Alex?"

"Yes." Could he detect the slightest irritation in her voice?
He hadn't told Rebecca about his trips to Lyon, his doing the
sketches for Alex. In fact, he had actually told Rebecca very
little about his past relationship with Alex. In a conversation
about former romances, he'd mentioned her as a girl he'd had
a crush on at his school in Paris, and Rebecca had wanted to
know more. He told her it had never developed into anything.
She'd married a wealthy Frenchman.

"Alex has been helpful," Jake said. "In fact, it's through
Alex I'm having this opportunity to meet with Madame
Genevoix."

"I didn't realize she was still in Paris."

"She married a Frenchman."

"Oh, yes," Rebecca replied. "And she and her husband live in Paris."

"He passed away a couple years ago, but Alex has stayed. She has a young daughter. She's established herself here at the Cluny. Her reputation and connections have been extremely helpful."

"Well isn't that nice."

AFTER HIS SUNDAY calls, he had painted. All week he painted, slept little, neglected to shave. He grabbed something to eat now and then, but he could tell he'd dropped several pounds. He hadn't gone out to run, although he tried to do at least fifteen to twenty minutes of sit-ups and push-ups each day. Yet the intensity of his work had become almost a physical exercise in itself.

Gabby had come up two days to model—Monday and Tuesday—and arranged for a friend to come all day Wednesday. In the evening and at night when he was alone, he worked on backgrounds and unicorns. With the new model he'd started what he was referring to as his *rouge,* his red series. The first paintings had been done in cool colors, predominately blues, his *bleu* paintings; but the warm colors had begun to take over his palette and canvas.

He couldn't believe it was Thursday already. He wanted to drop by the museum to see Alex, let her know how the painting was going, and find out about her latest trip to Lyon and Vienne. He wanted to ask her about Soleil. What did a seven-year-old girl want for her birthday? He had not forgotten Sunny's birthday was this Friday.

He showered and dressed. He needed to get out for a while. The temperature had risen considerably the past few days. There was no air-conditioning in his cheap hotel, and by midday his third-floor room was often stifling.

Jake glanced in the mirror over the dresser. Maybe he should shave if he was going over to see Alex, and comb his hair. It was sticking up all over the place. He heard a knock on the door.

He opened it. It was Alex.

"Have you seen the paper today?" she asked.

"I haven't read a paper for over a week." He could see she was upset. She reached in her purse, pulled out a clipping, and handed it to him.

"How did this happen?" he asked as he read.

"I tried calling Sister Etienne, but no answer. I wonder if she was overcome with guilt and confessed that the tapestry had been found."

"But doesn't it belong to the nuns?"

"It's my belief it does. Yet if Archbishop Bonnisseau contests the ownership—"

"It could really mess up the Cluny's acquisition?"

"Yes, it could."

"And this article might stir up some interest from other museums and collectors?"

"I had hoped to keep the discovery under wraps for a couple more weeks, at least until the catalogue comes out. And I'm somewhat concerned about my reputation, if this should interfere with the auction at Sotheby's." She took a deep breath and continued. "The description in the article is rather vague—'A valuable medieval tapestry.' What does that say? And the convent isn't named. How many convents are there south of Lyon?"

"I'd guess a few. There's nothing here to suggest Sainte Blandine's."

"And the trusted friend, the expert on medieval tapestries in Paris? How many of those are running around in the city?" Alex took the news clipping from Jake and put it back in her purse. "I should probably go back to Sainte Blandine's, talk to Sister Etienne, find out what's going on. But the timing on this whole thing is terrible." Alex threw her head back and laughed as if she might cry. "Soleil's birthday is tomorrow. I can't leave now."

"And why should you? They can't do anything about it without you anyway. The nuns don't know where it is. Do they?"

Alex shook her head. "No, they don't."

"There's no reason you need to rush off right away, Alex. Enjoy Sunny's birthday."

"Yes, I should." Alex smiled. "She's very excited. A birthday party is quite an event for a seven-year-old."

"I would imagine. I wanted to ask you about that—her party."

"She'd like you to come."

Jake realized they were still standing in the doorway. He invited Alex in, then suddenly was aware the place was a mess. He probably didn't look so great either. He ran his finger through his hair, rubbed his chin.

The room was so hot. He imagined it didn't smell very good either. Dirty clothes, unmade bed, soda bottles, banana peels, apple cores. And paintings everywhere—up against the walls, leaning against the bed, the dresser.

Alex glanced around the room. "Oh, Jake, you've been working. They're wonderful." She smiled up at him. "No time to shave?"

"What do you think?" he said, scratching his chin. "Maybe I should grow a beard?"

"Looks like you've got a good start. And it might go with your new hairstyle."

For a moment he thought she was going to reach over and touch his hair, brush it off his forehead, but she didn't. He pushed it back, combing again with his fingers.

"Your paintings, they're wonderful," she said again, her eyes moving from canvas to canvas.

"I've got an appointment with Madame Genevoix on Monday. I want to thank you again."

"It's your talent that got you the notice." Alex knelt on the floor in front of Jake's most recent painting, probably his best, yet still unfinished. It was set in a garden, the colors similar to the Cluny tapestries.

"Blue series . . . and now, red series," Alex said. "Very nice. Just like the Verteuil tapestries and the Cluny set." She turned and looked up at him. "Do you know that the set in The Cloisters is often referred to as the *Blue Series,* and the Cluny set, the *Red Series*?" She sat back on her legs and stared at the painting. "Red, like the tapestry from Sainte Blandine's . . . Oh, Jake." She sighed. "What is the matter with me? Is it wrong to want something so badly?"

She rose to her knees, then stood. As she turned, a banana peel stuck to the narrow heel of her shoe. She reached down to remove it, lifting her foot, losing her balance. Jake reached over to help her.

"Sorry," he said, holding Alex's arm. He could smell her again, that delicious fresh scent. They stood silently, as if paralyzed, his hand on her arm, Alex staring at him, her eyes filled with some kind of fear. Jake had a sudden urge to take her in his arms, to soothe her, to tell her she would have the tapestry, that she would have anything she wanted. He wished his room were clean, his bed made with fresh sheets.

"Like a slapstick cartoon—woman slips on banana peel." Alex laughed nervously and handed him the banana peel. She'd regained her balance, and he released her arm.

He looked around for the trash can. He had no idea where it was. "I would have cleaned house if I'd known company was coming." He was sweating. He could feel drops forming on his forehead. It was so damned hot.

"I called," Alex said, "but you weren't taking calls."

"No. I figured I'd get more work done this way."

"And it's certainly paid off." She looked around the room again, then at Jake. They stared at each other again as if neither of them knew quite what to say now. "I'm sorry to bother you," Alex apologized. "I can see how busy you are. I guess I just wanted your opinion."

"Enjoy your daughter's birthday. If you haven't heard from Sainte Blandine's by this weekend, you'll have time to go down and see what's going on." He smiled. "I know you'll get the tapestry. We both know it belongs in the Cluny. It will work out."

Alex smiled too, but not with great enthusiasm, and he didn't think he'd done much to put her mind at ease.

"Sunny's party starts at five," Alex said. "I should get back to work now." She started out of the room, then turned. "You didn't tell anyone, did you, Jake? You didn't mention the tapestry to anyone?"

22

"YOU ARE SO stupid," Jake muttered to himself as he walked down the street. He shouldn't have said anything. But when she turned and asked, "You didn't tell anyone, did you, Jake?" she must have seen something in his eyes. Betrayal? No. He would never betray Alex. Guilt? He did feel guilty, even though he *hadn't* told anyone, he hadn't mentioned the discovery of the tapestry to anyone. He'd told his mother he'd done some drawings for the museum, and now, evidently, Rebecca knew, but he'd never mentioned they might have something to do with a set of tapestries. And he should have guarded the drawings more closely. He shouldn't have let Julianna burst into his room that night.

So he confessed to Alex that a friend from the studio had seen the drawings, that she'd come by one evening while he was working on the second set and walked right in. Before he knew it, she was standing over them, admiring the drawings, asking more questions. But he hadn't told her anything.

Jake didn't mention that Julianna had wanted to talk about the drawings one night at the studio. He didn't tell Alex about Gaston Jadot listening in on the conversation, or about running into Monsieur Jadot the following day at the tapestry exhibition.

"How could you, Jake?" Alex had demanded. "How could you have been so careless when you know how much this means to me?"

She stomped out of the room. Damn her anyway. Where did she get off, blaming him?

He was on his way to buy a fan for his room and also a birthday gift for Alex's daughter. He assumed he hadn't been *uninvited* to the party, although Alex was extremely upset when she left. Did she really think Julianna had somehow alerted the Archbishop of Lyon to the discovery of the priceless tapestry? Jake wasn't the only one who knew. He'd told Alex as much. What about all those so-called art patrons she'd been wining and dining? All her rich friends. She'd been showing those photos of the tapestry around to anyone who could pay the price. She claimed she'd been careful about exactly what she'd told them concerning the discovery of the tapestry. But wasn't it possible that one of these people had become curious and started a little investigation of their own? Alex had shown them a photo of the tapestry. All Julianna had seen were the sketches.

"Stick it, Alex," he said as he walked. Alex and all her rich friends could roll the damn tapestry and stuff it.

It was so blasted hot, the noon sun blazing down, reflecting off the concrete and stone. He'd go get the fan for his room, but first he'd get Sunny's birthday gift. He was going to her birthday party, despite Alex's unfair accusations. He wasn't going to let Sunny down.

What should he get a girl for her seventh birthday? More art supplies, maybe a beginner's set of watercolors or acrylics? Maybe he should get her a toy. A doll. Didn't little girls love dolls?

He found a toy store off Rue des Ecoles. He went in and walked up and down the aisles. The toys looked like those you'd find in any toy store in America—Star Wars, Mickey Mouse, Barbie dolls. Barbie dolls? What would Alex think if he bought her daughter a Barbie? He'd always seen Alex as a bit of a feminist, not a mother who would easily consent to her seven-year-old daughter owning a doll that, when enlarged to real-people size, would have a bust of something like thirty-eight inches and a waist of maybe about eighteen inches. He remembered that Sunny had compared Barbie to the lovely maidens in the Cluny. He knew she'd love to have a beautiful blond Barbie. And suddenly he had an inspiration he was sure would please both mother and daughter.

·ALEX RETURNED TO her office. *What is the matter with me?* she asked herself. *Am I losing my mind?* She'd actually accused Jake of being the reason the information got out, and he'd come back with accusations of his own.

She'd stomped out, furious with him. But as she ran back to her office, she knew that she had been unfair, and she wondered if her anger had anything to do with the tapestry. Did she need this anger to feel safe? Did it provide the distance, the space, she needed to keep from admitting her true feelings?

When they were alone in his room, before the fight, she had sensed that he wanted to take her in his arms, to kiss her. But he hadn't. Was this all in her imagination, because it was what *she* had wanted? He looked so damned sexy—his dark stubble, his hair going all this way and that. She'd wanted to touch him, but she hadn't. She could tell he'd just showered; he smelled clean and fresh, like hotel soap, and his room—such a mess, yet filled with beautiful paintings. Such beautiful paintings. She was so proud of him. But then, somehow, they had gotten into this ridiculous fight.

Alex tried to push all this out of her mind and forget about Jake. She had other problems to deal with. She picked up the phone and called the convent. Again, no answer. If she didn't hear from Sister Etienne by Saturday, she would leave early that morning.

Her seminar started at one. She tried to muster her usual enthusiasm. It was a good group—intelligent, curious students with lots of questions. Alex tried to keep her mind from drifting. By four-thirty when the last students left, Alex was exhausted.

That evening before returning home, she picked up the birthday decorations for the party and stopped by the market to buy groceries for Soleil's special birthday dinner. She would pick up the cake she'd ordered the following afternoon.

At dinner, Soleil asked, "Did you talk to him?"

"Yes," Alex answered. "In fact, I went over to see him."

"He's coming?"

"Yes." Would he decide not to come because of the way she'd treated him? No, he would be there; Alex was sure he would show up. He wouldn't disappoint Sunny, even though Alex had treated him so poorly. She would talk to him then. She would apologize.

THE FOLLOWING MORNING, Soleil was up early. She crawled into bed with her mother.

"Happy birthday," Alex said.

"I'm seven!"

"Yes, you are. Happy birthday, seven-year-old."

Soleil jumped up. "Can I open some of my presents?"

Alex got out of bed. "Yes, you may."

As she sat watching Sunny open gifts—a new dress to wear to her party that night, a game, some books, a jewelry craft set her grandmother had picked out the previous weekend—Alex wondered if they had gotten the child too many gifts. There were even more to open at the party. She tried so hard not to spoil her daughter, but always seemed to overindulge on special occasions. She wondered if it would be different if Soleil had brothers and sisters. Alex didn't want her daughter to grow up to be a spoiled only child, like her father, Thierry.

"Oh, thank you, Mama. Thank you, Grandma." Soleil gave them each a hug. At least, Alex thought, she did seem to have a sense of gratitude.

ALEX DIDN'T HAVE time to read the newspaper until she was on the Métro on her way to work. On the second page, another article appeared. This one was more detailed. Sainte Blandine's was identified as the convent. The article described the tapestry, even compared it to the Cluny set. Although it did not name Alex as the trusted friend, it did state that the tapestry had been based on a drawing found in a medieval prayer book that had been donated to a museum in Paris. That pretty well narrows it down, Alex thought. "The Cluny set . . . donation of a *medieval* prayer book to a museum in Paris." Would there be any doubt? Would she receive a call from the Archbishop of Lyon soon, demanding the return of the tapestry?

She went in to see Madame Demy. The Director had read the morning paper and had seen the article. "I think it would have been unrealistic not to have expected something like this."

Alex was so angry she couldn't reply.

"This doesn't mean the Cluny won't have the tapestry," Madame Demy said. "However, the path to its acquisition might be more difficult than we had originally anticipated."

We? Alex wondered. As if Madame Demy had been involved or concerned in any way. Why hadn't she taken a more active role in this quest? Didn't she realize how important it was that the tapestry hang in the Cluny with the others?

"Even if the Archbishop proves ownership," Madame Demy said, "it's possible he'll want to sell it."

"Yes," Alex answered, her voice surprisingly calm. "There's always that possibility."

When she returned to her office, there was a message from Elizabeth Dorling from Sotheby's, requesting that Alex call. Had Elizabeth read the articles? Had she recognized the description of the tapestry as the same one that would be included in auction the following month in London?

Alex picked up the phone and dialed. She was put on hold for several long minutes, waiting for Elizabeth to come to the phone.

"Is it just a coincidence," Elizabeth asked, "or does this tapestry described on page two of *Le Journal Parisien* bear a close resemblance to the one that is going to be listed in our catalogue, the catalogue that goes to the printer in five days?" Elizabeth did not sound pleased.

"It is the same," Alex answered. "But it belongs to the nuns. They have every legal right to sell it. You saw the contract, the letters in Archbishop Bonnisseau's own handwriting."

"It doesn't appear the Archbishop agrees. Even if the nuns are the legal owners, it could create somewhat of a problem if

the Archbishop contests the ownership. What do you suggest
I do?"

"Five days?" Alex asked. "It won't go to the printer for five
days?"

"Yes."

"Will you give me five days?"

Elizabeth hesitated. Alex took a deep breath.

"Yes. I'll give you five days."

After she hung up, Alex tried once more to call Sister
Etienne. She wondered if the Archbishop had confiscated the
nuns' phone. Was he now keeping them prisoners at the convent or had he already transferred them to the retirement convent in Lyon? Damn, she should have dropped everything,
gone down there yesterday. Now there was no way she could
leave until the following morning.

Alex worked for two more hours, finishing a report. She
wrote two letters. It was difficult keeping her mind on her work.
An image of Jake kept popping into her head—she would see
him tonight. Then the tapestry, pushing its way into her
thoughts. Five days. Just five days to straighten this out. Suddenly, it came to her—a brilliant inspiration. She pulled out
the phone book, flipped pages over until she found the number
of *Le Journal Parisien*. She picked up the phone and punched
in the numbers.

23

ALEX STOPPED BY the bakery to pick up the birthday cake. When she arrived home, Soleil was beyond excited as Alex lifted the lid to show her the cake—white with pink frosting ballet slippers and roses. Sarah helped them decorate and set out the party favors.

Simone Pellier called to wish her granddaughter a happy birthday. She had sent a beautiful hand-knit sweater back with Alex the previous weekend. Grandmère told Soleil she had another present waiting for her the next time she visited. Alex took the phone and talked to her mother-in-law for a few minutes about Pierre. Simone said there was no change. "About the same."

Alex asked if there had been anyone inquiring about the tapestry. There had been no inquiries. Alex said she would be down the following morning and move the tapestry to another location. She didn't think the Pelliers were in any danger, and didn't want Simone to be alarmed, but in light of what might come out the following day in *Le Journal Parisien*, Alex wanted to move the tapestry. She hoped she could ship it off to London.

The next day's *Journal* . . . Alex knew she had taken a chance calling the reporter. But if the article came out the way she hoped, it just might help her cause, or at least the nuns'. She wished she could have talked to Sister Etienne first.

At ten to five the birthday guests—eight little girls from Soleil's school—began to arrive. Just before five, as Alex worked in the kitchen, getting out the plates and cups for the children's dinner, she heard Jake's voice. Something clamped inside her chest. She took a deep breath and went out into the dining room where the little girls gathered around admiring the decorations, balloons, and cake. Soleil walked in holding Jake's hand and introduced him to her guests.

He glanced at Alex and smiled, apologetically, she thought, his big brown eyes looking at her like a puppy who'd chewed up his master's favorite slippers. He'd shaved and his hair was neatly combed, as if he'd done it to please her. He had a little nick on his chin. How could he look so damned vulnerable and sexy at the same time?

Soleil whisked him away to participate in the games set up in the living room.

After a game of *cache-cache,* the guests were all herded back to the dining room. The children sat at the table. Soleil began to open her gifts, which she oohed and ahhed over and, much to Alex's delight, thanked each guest for coming and for their wonderful gifts, even when two of them turned out to be the same—colorful fingernail polish with sparkles, that Alex, quite frankly, thought was a dreadful gift for a seven-year-old, or for anyone, actually.

"Just what I wanted!" Soleil squealed as she opened the pair of in-line skates from her mother. She jumped up from the table and gave Alex a hug.

Soleil saved Jake's gift until last. She opened it slowly, looking up and smiling at him as she did. Her eyes grew wide as she pulled the box out of the paper. "Oh, it's lovely, Monsieur Bowman. It's the most beautiful gift I have ever received in my entire whole life."

Alex stood over her daughter, staring down. It *was.* It was the most beautiful gift ever. It was a doll dressed in gold brocade, with a red velvet overgarment with long, loose sleeves of a soft transparent muslin, very much like the maiden in *A Mon Seul Désir.* Long blond hair fell down her back like the maidens in *Sight* and *Touch,* and a portion of it was braided and twisted into an aigrette with a jeweled, veiled turban like the maiden in *Hearing*. The belt was a gold plaited cord, the necklace a double strand of tiny pearls, sewn to the upper portion of the dress like the young woman in *Sight*.

"Look, Mama," Soleil said. "Isn't it the most beautiful gift?"

Alex nodded, speechless.

"C'est très belle," said one of the guests, a pudgy little girl with dark hair.

"C'est la plus jolie Barbie du monde!" Another little blond girl stood and walked over to get a better look. The most beautiful Barbie in the world.

"It's exquisite, Jake," Sarah said. "Where did you find it? I think we went to every toy and department store in Paris last weekend, and we certainly didn't see a doll like that."

"I got the doll at a toy store just a few blocks from my hotel."

"And the costume?" Alex asked.

"I made it."

"You made it? How?"

"Fabric, needle, thread, some miniature fake jewels, gold cord."

"You sewed it?" Alex asked incredulously.

"I've done some fiber collage, fabric sculpture. Sewed on a few buttons. I know how to use a needle and thread."

"C'est magnifique," Soleil exclaimed. "It's the most beautiful ever," she said, switching back to English. She got up and walked over to Jake and gave him a hug. "I love you very much, Monsieur Bowman."

THAT NIGHT, WHEN Alex put Soleil to bed, the little girl was exhausted. She insisted on taking the doll to bed with her, although Alex would have preferred she put it back in the box and set it up on the shelf. It was much too beautiful to play with or take to bed.

"We had a good day," Soleil said and yawned.

"Yes, we did."

"Do you know," she said slowly, rubbing her eyes, "the best part?"

"What was the best part?"

But before Soleil could answer, she had fallen asleep.

Alex stared down at her perfect little daughter with a brief prayer of thanks. Then she reached over and touched the doll. She picked it up and ran her fingers over the soft, red velvet skirt. What kind of man would sew a gown for a doll, a precious gift for a seven-year-old child?

She had wanted to talk to him, but there had never been the opportunity. She hoped he'd stay after Sunny's guests left, but when parents started coming to pick up the little girls, there was plenty of confusion, and Jake was gone.

"I don't know what's going on with you and Jake," Sarah said softly as she entered the room, "but I certainly noticed the tension this evening."

Alex stroked the velvet fabric but said nothing.

"You know, Alex, in so many aspects of your life, you've been unafraid to take charge, to forge ahead, to go after whatever it was you wanted. But in your private life, it almost seems you purposely construct false barriers. What are you afraid of? Why is it you are so afraid to go after what you really want when it comes to your heart? Are you afraid of being hurt?"

Alex stood. She placed the doll next to Soleil and pulled the covers up, then looked over at the dark, shadowed figure of her mother. "And what is it you think I want?"

"Only you can answer that question, Alex. Only you."

ALEX COULDN'T SLEEP. Shortly before midnight she rose. She dressed and called a cab. She knew where she was going, but didn't know exactly why, or what she would tell him when she got there. She would apologize. She knew it had been wrong to accuse him. It was ridiculous to blame him, insane to think this marvelous discovery could have been kept a secret forever. She wasn't sure how the information got out. But did it even matter?

There was something else she wanted to tell him, Alex thought as she gave directions to the driver. But what was it she wanted to say? She knew, for her daughter's sake, she needed to decide for herself just what it was she wanted from Jacob Bowman. Could she possibly tell him she loved him?

Could she open herself up to what might come of such an admission? Or what she might lose? And what about Rebecca? How did Jake really feel about Rebecca? Could he have left her back home in Montana if he truly loved her?

Alex's heart thumped as the cab turned onto Rue des Ecoles. What was she doing, going to him in the middle of the night? What if she told him she loved him, and he replied, "How very touching, Alex, but I'm in love with someone else. Don't you realize you're fourteen years too late?"

Alex thought about what her mother had said. Ever since she was a child, she had been encouraged to go after what she wanted, to make her own decisions and work toward a goal.

She thought about an incident years ago. She was in high school, just a sophomore. Her brother, Phillip, was a junior. He'd broken curfew and been grounded.

"You're being unfair," Phillip had shouted at their father. "You're always coming down on me, and Alex can do anything she damn well pleases."

"It's a choice you made, Phillip," their father replied calmly. "You know the rules, and you chose to break them." And, then he said—and Alex still remembered his words clearly—"Alex can do what she wants, because I know she will make the right choices."

It was true. She always did. Her father had never even mentioned curfew; she knew what time she was expected home. Her father trusted her completely. It had become a burden rather than a freedom. She could not allow herself to make mistakes. At times she longed to do something "bad," something against the rules, something she hadn't thought through, something spontaneous and adventurous.

Even now—she was an adult, her father was gone, and there was still that ridiculous fear of making the wrong choice, of displeasing someone. She had made a bad choice with Thierry, and she had displeased him. Sometimes she feared that she was incapable of pleasing a man.

Why was she going to Jake in the middle of the night? What did she want and what did she want from him? "Only you can answer that question," her mother had said.

When she arrived at Jake's hotel, paid the driver, and got out of the cab, the thoughts coursing through her mind had still not formulated into words. She still didn't know exactly what she would say.

HE HAD LOST the day sewing, so he painted after returning from the party. It was still warm in his room, unbearably hot, even with his newly acquired fan, so he had stripped down to his undershorts.

He should have spent the afternoon painting, but it had taken over four hours to finish that little dress. What would rugged ol' John Bowman think of this? Now his son was not only paintin' those pictures, he was sewin' doll clothes. The thought made Jake laugh. But that afternoon, once he'd started sewing that tiny, delicate costume, constructing the jewels, the miniature turban, he was filled with an emotion close to the joy he felt when he was painting. He didn't think it was the activity itself, but the thought of what it would mean to Sunny. And then, when he saw the expression on her face as she opened his gift, he knew it had all been worth it. The little girl was overjoyed. Alex was more difficult to read. She had smiled at him when he arrived, and he could see she was touched by the gift he'd given Soleil, yet Alex barely spoke to him all evening. Admittedly, she'd been busy, with the children, supervising the games, and serving the dinner—American-style hamburgers and French fries, cake and ice cream.

He mixed more paint, a deep dark red. Just as he started to lay a stroke on the canvas, he heard a knock on the door. The unexpected pounding startled him. His hand jerked, running a blob of red paint across his bare chest. He looked at his watch as the knocking continued. It was half past midnight. Who would be at his door at this hour? He slipped on his jeans and went to find out.

When he opened the door, he was surprised to see Julianna standing there. She wore low-slung cut-off jeans and a cropped tank top no bigger than a postage stamp. In her pierced navel she sported a silver and turquoise ring.

"So where have you been?" she asked, leaning up against the doorjamb, her thumb hooked in the loop of her jeans. "It's Friday night. Not coming up to the studio anymore?"

"I've been busy."

Julianna leaned in close and he could smell she'd been drinking. "You missed TGIF," she said.

"Doesn't appear you did."

She laughed and walked in, closing the door behind her. "Aren't you going to invite me in?"

"Looks like you're in."

"Am I?" Her eyes moved slowly around the room. "Nice painting. You *have* been busy." Then she looked back at him. "Do you know you've got red paint on your chest?"

He glanced down, then at Julianna as she walked closer. She extended her finger and touched the spot of red paint. Her finger moved, a curved, circular motion, then another. Jake looked down. She had drawn a red heart on his bare skin.

Someone rapped on the door again and Jake jumped.

"Expecting company?" Julianna asked. Before he could answer, she had walked to the door and opened it.

Jake looked over. "Alex!"

"Alex?" Julianna said.

Alex looked too shocked to say anything. She stared at Julianna, then at Jake. The fan hummed.

"Well," Julianna said after a moment, "come on in, Alex dear." She motioned with her finger. "Come in and join the fun."

Alex stared at Julianna's finger, the tip covered with red paint. She looked up, her gaze meeting Jake's. As her eyes dropped, he sensed that the red heart Julianna had drawn on his bare chest might as well have been the scarlet letter on Hester Prynne.

Alex said nothing. She stood paralyzed. Then, suddenly, she turned and ran.

24

•

JAKE RAN AFTER her, through the hall, down the stairs. "Alex. Alex," he shouted. He caught her by the arm. She twisted, turned. Then she shoved him hard, broke loose, and ran. He lost his balance and fell, landing on the rough wooden steps, stunned.

She was gone. Jake gazed down the stairs, then stood and ran to the ground floor. When he got to the street, he looked up Rue Monge one direction then the other. No Alex. He ran a block, then stopped, trying to catch his breath. A couple, walking along the street, turned and looked, then whispered to one another. The man had a strange expression on his face; the woman giggled, and Jake realized he was barefooted, wearing only his jeans, a red heart painted on his chest. He turned and walked back to the hotel and climbed the stairs to his room.

Julianna sat on the bed. Jake sat next to her and buried his face in his hands.

"Alex? Alexandra Pellier from the museum?" Julianna asked.

He looked up, nodded. He was sweating. He could feel the moisture in the palms of his hands. The fan hummed.

"It's Alex, isn't it?" she asked.

He looked at her, puzzled.

"It's Alex, isn't it?" Julianna asked once more. "It's not that fiancée back home in Montana."

He didn't answer. They sat together silently.

Julianna stood. Jake looked up at her. "Did you talk to anyone?" he asked. "Did you mention the drawings to anyone?"

"From the studio?"

"No, no." Maybe he should just leave it alone. But he wanted to know. He wanted to make things right with Alex, and first he needed to know if he'd had anything to do with the Archbishop's becoming aware of the tapestry.

"Oh," she said, "you mean those drawings, the unicorn drawings? Alex wants to know what I know about them?"

"Did you mention them to anyone?"

"What would I have mentioned? I didn't know much about them. When I saw them, I noticed right away that one looked like it had something to do with *The Lady and the Unicorn* tapestries in the Cluny. The other, with the knight and nude woman, seemed quite mysterious, but I could see you weren't about to tell me anything. But no, I don't think so. I don't think I mentioned them to anyone."

"Are you sure?"

"Well . . ." she hesitated. "I might have said something to Matthew."

"Might have?"

"I can't remember for certain." She sounded a little angry that he was interrogating her. "We talk all the time. I might have said something."

"Do you read the newspaper?"

"No, I don't often read the newspaper. Should I?"

He sensed she was telling the truth. She didn't seem to be aware of the articles concerning the tapestry.

Julianna gazed down at Jake's most recent painting, the first of the red series, propped up against the wall. "It really is incredibly lovely, Jake." She looked at him and smiled, then walked toward the door. "I'll leave you to your work."

ALTHOUGH SHE HAD crawled into bed after she returned from Jake's Alex was unable to sleep. She felt betrayed, and she knew it had nothing to do with the tapestry. As she lay in bed, the feeling grew and intensified, the image of the beautiful young Asian girl floating through her head. And Jake, his bare chest inscribed with a red heart. The same red on the girl's finger as she motioned Alex into the room. Abruptly, she sat up in bed. Why should she feel this way? If he had betrayed anyone, it was Rebecca.

She got up and made a pot of coffee. She sat in the kitchen, drinking. To hell with Jake. Her concern now was to mitigate the damage done, the problem with the tapestry. She had four days. Four days before the catalogue would go to the printers. Four days to let Elizabeth Dorling know if the tapestry could be offered at the auction in August.

She would wait until six that morning to leave for the convent. The newspaper usually arrived by six or shortly after, and she wanted to see the paper before she took off. If only she could have spoken with Sister Etienne before she'd talked to the reporter. But time was running out, and if the article came out the way Alex hoped, surely it would help. But had the reporter listened to her? Would he use the information as she intended? Or would her plan backfire and make things worse?

Shortly after six, the paper arrived. Alex started to turn the page, then stopped. It was on the front page. Quickly she scanned the article. She smiled and laughed out loud. It couldn't have been better if she'd written it herself.

The article told the story of the convent, how it had become the property of the archdiocese years ago, how the contents had remained the property of the nuns. It was the intention of the Sisters of Sainte Blandine's to sell the tapestry so they might remain at the convent, which had been home to some of the nuns for more than seventy-five years.

Perhaps Alex had exaggerated a little with the numbers, but hadn't Sister Anne told her she'd been there for over sixty-seven years? And she wasn't even the oldest.

The article mentioned the nuns ranged in age from sixty-nine to ninety-two, although, in truth, Alex knew it was the Mother Superior who had been ninety-two. And she was dead. Alex didn't know for sure the age of the oldest remaining nun.

The proceeds from the sale of the tapestry would be used

to defray the cost of renovations to accommodate the elderly
nuns, to provide for nursing care. Rent would be paid to the
archdiocese. The article suggested the tapestry was the most
valuable late Gothic ever discovered, in near perfect condition, something never seen in a tapestry this old. A similar
mille-fleurs allegorical tapestry, probably from the same period, had been sold just over a year ago at Sotheby's for
128,000 British pounds. That particular tapestry was in poor
condition, with extensive reweaving. Sainte Blandine's would
most likely bring at least twice, possibly three or even four
times this amount. The proceeds could be set up in a trust. If
properly managed, the nuns' care could be paid for from the
interest alone. On the death of the last nun, the ownership of
the trust could be transferred to the archdiocese.

Alex had never discussed this with the nuns, but it sounded
feasible. And she had exaggerated the value, which she realized could make it difficult for the Cluny's acquisition if anyone actually believed it, if anyone would pay that price. She
was amazed the reporter, whose name was Georges Gaudens,
had accepted what she'd told him. Perhaps he had checked her
reference to a similar tapestry having been sold at Sotheby's
last year.

The reporter had agreed his source would be protected.
Alex's name appeared nowhere in the article. And, just as she
had hoped, the whole story made Archbishop Bonnisseau
sound like a heartless fool. How could he possibly not relent?

Alex folded the newspaper and placed it beside her briefcase. She swallowed the last of her coffee. The phone rang.

The Archbishop? Jake? Someone who had read the article
and realized it was Alex who had the tapestry?

She picked up the phone.

"I have some sad news," Simone Pellier said with a catch
in her voice. "We lost Pierre early this morning."

Alex woke her mother and told her about Pierre. Simone
had asked that Alex come alone to help with the arrangements. Sarah could bring Soleil down for the services later.
Alex called Madame Demy at her home. She debated whether
she should wake Soleil. Would the child understand? Alex
knew she had no memory of her father's death.

She went into Soleil's room and walked over to her bed.

She was asleep, Jake's beautiful birthday doll snuggled at her side.

The child opened her eyes and looked up. "What's the matter?" she asked.

Alex sat down on the bed. "I'm going to Lyon this morning."

Soleil sat up. "You already told me that last night."

"I just spoke with Grandmère. She had some sad news this morning."

"Has Grandpère gone to heaven to be with God?"

"Yes." Tears formed in Alex's eyes as she reached out and put her arms around her daughter. The tears filled her eyes, but they would not fall.

Soleil patted her mother on the back as if to console her. "Grandmère says Grandpère will be happy now. He doesn't hurt anymore. He will be very happy with God in heaven."

How wise and kind Simone had been, Alex thought. She had prepared Soleil for this loss.

"Can I come with you?" Soleil asked, releasing the embrace, looking at her mother.

"Grandmère needs my help right now. I'm going this morning to help with the arrangements."

"For Grandpère's funeral?"

Alex nodded. "Grandma will bring you down for the services in a couple days. Is that all right?"

"Yes," Soleil said. "That's all right."

ALEX LEFT FOR Lyon. How strange, she thought, that Pierre's loss would come on this day. Would she lose the tapestry too? The thought frightened her. Not the thought of losing the tapestry, but the thought that she could equate losing a precious human life with the loss of an ancient weaving made from threads of wool. The tears streamed down her face, and barely let up until she reached Lyon.

25

ALEX CONTACTED THE newspaper with the obituary notice. She spoke with the funeral director and Father Varaigne about the services scheduled for Wednesday. Most of the details had been previously arranged, and Simone had prepared for this. The simple tasks she asked of Alex were difficult only in that they were part of her farewell to Pierre Pellier. Neither Pierre nor Simone had any living siblings, but Alex called nieces, nephews, and twice-removed cousins as Simone sat by her side. Some of them Simone wished to speak to, others she did not.

Simone was doing as well as could be expected, although she looked tired. She wore no makeup and her normally coifed white hair looked as if it had not been styled in days.

Several visitors came by the apartment—Father Varaigne, a couple of women from Simone's parish.

Alex called home and spoke with her mother and Soleil. She told them the services would be Wednesday morning and requested that Sarah bring Sunny down Tuesday afternoon. Alex told her mother which dress she wanted Sunny to wear for the funeral and suggested what other clothes she should pack.

"Simone, she's doing well?" Sarah asked.

"Worn out, but yes, she's doing well. She was prepared for this. As much as one can be prepared for such a loss."

"Give her my love."

"I will."

"Alex . . ." Sarah hesitated.

"Yes?"

"You had several calls this morning."

From Jake? Alex wondered with a touch of panic. Had it been only yesterday he had come to Soleil's party? Only last night she'd run from his room?

"After reading the article in today's paper," Sarah said, "I wasn't entirely surprised."

"You read the article?"

"Sunny had to help me with the translation." Sarah laughed. "But I got the general drift."

"What did you think?"

"I think the Archbishop has no choice but to give in, unless he wants to be mistaken for Satan himself."

Alex laughed too. "Who called?" She couldn't bring herself to ask if it had been Jake. She didn't think her mother even knew she'd left in the middle of the night.

"Two reporters," Sarah answered, "one from *Le Journal Parisien,* a Georges something-or-other—"

"Gaudens?"

"Yes, I believe that was it, and a reporter from a television station. I told them you were out of town. They both asked if you'd gone to Sainte Blandine's, and I said no. And another call from a Paul Westerman. He said he was an old friend, though I suspected that was just a line. Do you know a Paul Westerman?"

"We were in school together in Paris. But I haven't seen or heard from him in years."

"He had all kinds of questions about the tapestry and wanted to know if you had any knowledge of it. I said he'd have to talk to you. I told him you weren't available, that he should call you at your office in Paris next week."

"No other calls?"

"Just those."

Alex wondered if Jake had seen the article. She also wondered what he was thinking now about her running away last night, shoving him, knocking him down on the steps. Even with all that had happened since, Alex found herself turning the event over in her mind, replaying it, trying to imagine she hadn't behaved so immaturely. If she had it to do over again . . . she was shocked, unprepared to see him with that beautiful young woman . . . Did he wonder why she had come to him in the middle of the night? If he cared at all, wouldn't he have called?

"Thanks, Mom," Alex said. "We'll see you and Sunny Tuesday."

"Yes, we'll see you then."

AFTER LUNCH, AS her mother-in-law napped, Alex went into the library. She was eager to examine the tapestry once more, but until now had not been able to leave Simone. She was shocked when she walked over to the corner where the tapestry had been sitting, wrapped and tied, for the past several weeks. It wasn't there. She walked around the room. The tapestry was large; it could hardly be hiding in the room without Alex finding it. Her heart went *thump, thump, thump,* then seemed to stop completely for a moment. Had Simone moved it? She hadn't said anything, but Alex was sure her mother-in-law had other things on her mind. Alex sat, trying to calm herself. She heard a knock on the door. It was Marie.

"Is there anything I can get for you, Madame Pellier?"

"Marie, did Madame Pellier move the tapestry?"

"*Oui.* She didn't want it sitting out in the library, not with all the recent publicity. I assure you it is safe. Madame Pellier will let you know, perhaps it slipped her mind with . . ." The words caught in her throat.

"I see," Alex said. She hesitated. "It's been moved. Where?"

"Madame Pellier will let you know." Marie stared at Alex for a moment, then nodded and left the room.

Alex didn't like this, not knowing, not having control. But then, what kind of control did she have over any of this anymore? She no longer knew where the tapestry was. She had no idea what was going on at Sainte Blandine's, if the nuns were even still there at the convent. And now—calls from reporters, and Paul Westerman, of all people. Alex remembered Jake telling her that Paul was working in London for a company involved in art acquisition and appraisal. What interest would Paul have in the tapestry? Was he looking to buy it for some wealthy investor or art lover?

Alex glanced at the phone sitting on the desk, then picked it up and dialed the number she had memorized. Much to her surprise, there was an answer. The tiny voice she immediately recognized. "Sister Anne?"

"Oui."

"This is Alexandra Pellier. I've been worried. I couldn't get through, and I couldn't come down until today. You're still at Sainte Blandine's?"

"Oui. And what a commotion. What activity we have out here. People everywhere. Reporters."

"Reporters?"

"From *Le Journal Parisien,* from the newspaper in Lyon, from London, from Rome. They all want to tell our story."

"What about the Archbishop?"

"We didn't tell him. We didn't tell him you have the tapestry. And it wasn't a lie when we said we didn't know where it was."

"I want to come down, see what I can do to help, but I'm here in Lyon with my mother-in-law now. My father-in-law passed away this morning. She needs my help and I can't leave right now."

"Eternal rest grant unto him, O Lord, may perpetual light shine upon him." Sister Anne rattled the prayer off quickly. Alex could see the old nun crossing herself. "With the story in the paper, how can the Archbishop take the tapestry away?"

They had seen the article, then. Good. "Is Sister Etienne available?"

"She's getting everyone gathered for the photographs."

"Photographs?"

"For the newspapers."

That would be perfect, Alex thought. The old nuns, their picture splashed on the front page. *Be sure to get Sister Eulalie and Sister Philomena in their wheelchairs,* she wanted to say. How could the Archbishop throw them out now? "Then you're doing all right? The Archbishop isn't ready to force you to leave Sainte Blandine's?"

"On the contrary." There was a hint of a giggle in the nun's voice. "I think he's about ready to grant us what we wish. He brought in a nurse, and we're getting all kinds of attention." Alex got the feeling Sister Anne was quite enjoying all this attention. "Could I have Sister Etienne call?" she asked.

"Yes, please." Alex gave Sister Anne the Pelliers' number in Lyon.

SIMONE SPOKE LITTLE at dinner that evening. Alex could see she was very tired. She had spent the past several years tending to Pierre, an emotionally exhausting task, but now the enormous void in her life seemed to have drained her completely.

"Have you spoken to the nuns at Sainte Blandine's?" Simone asked as they sat with coffee. This was the first time the subject had come up. Alex guessed Simone had been too preoccupied to have seen the latest article. Alex had wanted to ask her about the tapestry, but felt uncomfortable bringing it up.

"Yes, I spoke with Sister Anne this afternoon."

"They are doing fine?"

"They seem to be."

Simone must have sensed an uneasiness in Alex's voice. "We could probably get along just fine tomorrow, if you'd like to drive down to Saint Blandine's."

"Perhaps I should. You're sure you'll be all right?"

"Yes. Marie is here, and Madame Le Quieu and Madame Deville from church are coming by tomorrow after Mass." She added a cube of sugar to her coffee and stirred it slowly, her eyes downcast. She looked up. "You're wondering about the tapestry?"

"Yes."

"It's safe."

Alex waited.

Simone smiled. "Just trust me, Alexandra. It is safe, but I don't believe I'll tell you where it is just yet."

Alex stared at her mother-in-law, trying not to show how upset and shocked she was.

"If I tell you where it is, you'll just want to move it, and I don't think that's necessary. When Philippe Bonnisseau gives in, we'll take it out of hiding."

"The Archbishop? You think he'll give in?"

"Oh, Philippe is a stubborn man, but I think he has sense enough to know this fight with the nuns is not good for the Church." Simone took a sip of coffee. "Spiritually or economically."

"Philippe?" Alex wondered why she hadn't considered this—that Simone and Pierre might be friends with the Archbishop. The family had lived in Lyon for years. "You know Archbishop Bonnisseau?"

"Quite well. Pierre and I have always been involved in the Church here in Lyon." Simone stirred her coffee. She looked up and there was a slight movement across her face, a tightness about her eyes, that sent a chill through Alex because she was unable to read the thoughts behind it. She'd always felt that she and Simone had an unspoken connection. They never talked about the unhappiness in Alex's marriage, though she was sure Simone knew, and often Alex wondered if it was a thread of common guilt that held the two women together. *If I'd been a better mother . . . Thierry would have been a better man. If I'd been a better wife . . . Thierry would have been a better husband.* Yet sometimes Alex felt that Simone might blame her for Thierry's death. Would he still be here if Alex had provided a loving home, the excitement Thierry seemed to crave? And now a horrible thought entered her mind—Simone had an influence that could possibly sabotage Alex's chances of getting the tapestry. No, no, she pushed these thoughts out of her mind. Simone loved Alex as if she were her own daughter.

Now as Alex looked at her mother-in-law, she could see it was pain and fatigue that had settled in her eyes. Simone rose from the table. "If you don't mind, dear, I think I'll go to bed." She walked slowly, her shoulders stooped, looking for the first time in Alex's memory like the old woman that she was. "Thank you so much for coming, Alexandra. You and Soleil are my only real family now." She bent over and kissed Alex on the forehead.

"Good night." Alex reached out and held her *belle-mère*'s hand for a moment. "Good night, my dear Simone."

That night, Alex watched a Paris newscast. She seldom watched television, but had for the past few nights, ever since the first article appeared. There had been no mention of the tapestry or the situation at Blandine's either night. But now, with the front-page article and the call from the TV reporter, she guessed there might be something on the evening news.

There was a brief story with basically the same information that had appeared in the three articles. Fortunately, again, there was no mention of Alex's name. The emphasis seemed to be more on the fate of the nuns than the fate of the tapestry.

The next morning, another article appeared in the newspaper—front page—and a photograph of Sister Eulalie, Sister Philomena, Sister Etienne, and the wrinkled little doorkeeper, who was identified as Sister Venantius. The nuns didn't look particularly pathetic; in fact they looked almost happy—those two little nuns grinning out from their wheelchairs, Sister Etienne with her plump, jolly face. From the photo, one would think they had already won the battle with the Archbishop. Except for Sister Venantius, who wore her customary scowl. Alex wasn't sure if this would evoke much sympathy. But they all looked old—ancient—and maybe that was enough. The photo was accompanied by a story about the nuns, telling how long each had been at the convent, what a move like this might mean to their physical and emotional health. There was a separate article, a man-on-the-street-type poll, asking opinions on who should have the tapestry—the nuns or the Archbishop. Of course, everyone, except some jerk who felt it was a question of legal ownership, said the nuns should be allowed to sell the tapestry and stay at the convent. *Perfect,* Alex thought, *just perfect.*

The front-page article on the nuns referred to another story on page eight. Alex flipped the pages quickly. It was an article on unicorn tapestries, describing the Sainte Blandine's tapestry as a unicorn tapestry. The article said the Cluny Museum possessed one of the most famous sets, *La Dame à la Licorne,* and that another famous set, *The Hunt of the Unicorn,* was owned by The Cloisters in New York. Both museums had loaned pieces for a special exhibition currently showing in Paris at the Grand Palais through August sixth. The treasure found at Sainte Blandine's was purported to be similar in color to the Cluny set, often referred to as the "Red Set." Alex wondered where this information had come from—so few had actually seen the tapestry. The colors and style, according to the article, if similar to the Cluny's, might also be similar to those in another verdure tapestry from the same time period, probably the late 1500s. The article said *Le Pégase* was from a private collection and could also be currently viewed at the special exhibition. The story noted that it was the first time this particular tapestry had been publicly displayed. Now where, Alex wondered, did this comparison to *Le Pégase* come from?

The article reiterated what the story from the previous day had implied—that the tapestry, which had been authenticated by a medieval art specialist, might prove to be one of the most valuable ever found, and that if it were allowed to go to public auction it would most likely bring a record price.

Had Alex been instrumental in creating this belief that the tapestry could go for an unheard-of price? Would the publicity inflate the price? Now that the nuns' story had moved onto page one and the evening newscast, would the price go up? Could it really go for over five hundred thousand British pounds, as this article stated? Over nine hundred thousand American dollars? Had Alex contributed to creating what might well be the barrier to the Cluny's acquisition? Would she save the nuns and lose the tapestry?

Alex walked with Simone to Mass. Neither woman mentioned the article or the tapestry. In fact, conversation was almost nonexistent. Alex tried to engage her mother-in-law in light conversation—what a beautiful day it was, although in fact it was quite warm. The elder Madame Pellier wore a sweater, and Alex wondered how she could tolerate the heat.

At Mass, Alex prayed. She prayed Sister Anne's prayer— *Eternal rest grant unto him, O Lord, and may perpetual light shine upon him.* She prayed for Simone, and as she looked over at her mother-in-law, Alex saw how tired and old she was, and wondered if Simone herself would give up, now that her beloved Pierre was gone.

Then Alex said a prayer to Adèle Le Viste. *Dear Adèle, please protect the nuns, please allow them to claim the tapestry. And, please, guide me in my own quest.*

Alex wondered if Adèle could really hear her. Was there

truly a communion of saints—a belief that after life, the good and the holy sat with the Almighty Father, whispering requests from friends below who had sought their intercession? Adèle had been a nun, a woman of the spirit, although a reluctant one. As Alex prayed, a calm came over her, as if Adèle were truly present, comforting Alex, assuring her that everything would work out just fine.

On the way home, Simone mentioned that Monsieur Henri Sauvestre, Pierre's attorney, would be dropping by the following morning and she would like Alex to be present.

When Simone's friends came to visit shortly after they returned from church, Alex felt she could leave for the convent.

"Are you sure this is all right?" she asked.

"Yes, you go ahead, dear," Simone said. "I'll see you this evening."

AS ALEX DROVE, she wondered what she would find when she arrived. More reporters? She wasn't even sure what kind of reception she would get at the convent. Sister Etienne had never returned her call. And would she be recognized by someone? Her name had not been mentioned in any of the articles, but the reference to a trusted friend, a medieval art expert, the comparison of the tapestry to the Cluny set, the fact that the prayer book had been donated to a museum in Paris— surely the Archbishop was at least suspicious someone from the Cluny was involved. And the calls from the reporters. But no one would know she was from the Cluny. Maybe she could just pass as another reporter or interested party.

When she arrived at the convent, she could see what Sister Anne had been talking about. There were at least six or seven cars parked out front. One, a van, was from the local TV station. Alex parked, adjusted her sunglasses as if they would offer some protection, and then got out of the car, took a deep breath, and walked up to the convent through a small group of people gathered at the front door. No one tried to stop or question her as she knocked. The window slid open. Sister Venantius's wrinkled little face appeared. She gazed out at Alex, then she actually smiled. "Madame Pellier, come in. We have good news this morning."

"Madame Pellier?" Alex heard a voice from behind her.

She turned. Suddenly, she heard the whir of a camera. "Alexandra Pellier? From the Cluny in Paris? Do you have the tapestry?"

Sister Venantius opened the door and Alex rushed inside.

"The Archbishop has agreed to our claim of ownership," Sister Venantius said as she led Alex down the hall. "But then I should let Sister Etienne fill you in on the details."

Sister Etienne appeared in the hall, walking toward them. The nun looked like she hadn't slept in days. It appeared she had lost weight. Her face didn't seem quite so round, not even as plump as it looked in the photograph in that morning's paper. The nun squinted, then smiled. "Alexandra." She embraced Alex. "I must apologize for not getting in touch, but I didn't want to put you in danger. Those phones—why, anyone at all can listen in." Sister Etienne breathed deeply as if she were trying to catch her breath. "Did Sister Venantius tell you?"

"Yes. It's true?"

"Yes, Archbishop Bonnisseau has agreed to let us send the tapestry to auction." Sister Etienne motioned for Alex to follow.

"Did you get that in writing?"

They arrived at the nun's office, walked in and sat.

"Something to drink?" Sister Etienne asked.

Alex shook her head. "Does the convent have an attorney?"

Sister Etienne laughed. "No. I thought you might be able to help us out. I've set up an appointment with the Archbishop in Lyon Wednesday morning."

"He knows my name? He knows I have the tapestry?"

"No. I told him we would send a representative. I agree with you. We need it in writing. Could you take care of that?"

"Yes." She could speak to Simone's attorney tomorrow. Tomorrow . . . tomorrow was Monday. Alex rubbed her head and tried to think. How could she take care of everything she had to attend to—Simone, the attorney, Pierre's funeral, the tapestry, the Archbishop, the nuns, Sotheby's? Simone had asked her to meet tomorrow with the attorney regarding Pierre's estate. Soleil and her mother would arrive Tuesday. Wednesday was the deadline to contact Elizabeth Dorling at Sotheby's. Wednesday was Pierre's funeral.

"Tuesday morning," Alex said. "We'll have to meet Tuesday morning. I'll have my attorney draw up an agreement." She hoped, she could get Henri Sauvestre, Pierre and Simone's attorney, to get something drawn up by then.

Sister Etienne nodded, then sat back, dug into her pocket, and pulled out the phone. She dialed. "Sister Etienne from Sainte Blandine's. I wish to speak with the Archbishop." The nun smiled at Alex while she waited. She wore the expression of a woman in control now. Her fatigue seemed to have taken on an almost victorious glow. A woman who had just competed in a strenuous athletic event, who had risen triumphant.

"*Oui, bonjour,* Archbishop Bonnisseau. Sister Etienne from Saint Blandine's. . . . Yes, I'm well this morning. . . . Our representative would like to meet sooner. Tuesday morning." Sister Etienne looked at Alex. "Ten A.M.?"

Alex nodded.

"*Oui.*" The nun smiled. "Ten A.M. will be fine."

Alex stayed and ate lunch with the nuns, then returned to Sister Etienne's office, where the two women spoke again of the arrangements for the sale of the tapestry.

"Will it really bring the price mentioned in the article?" The nun asked. "When we talked about this before, you said a similar tapestry had gone for one hundred twenty-eight thousand pounds over a year ago."

"Yes, but your tapestry is in much better condition. Perhaps the article exaggerated the value, but the media is a powerful influence. All this attention might inflate the price."

A broad grin flashed across Sister Etienne's face, then quickly settled into a composed, appreciative smile.

The two women discussed the proposed contract, outlining the components, based on the nun's earlier conversation with the Archbishop. The proceeds would be placed in a trust, administered by a trustee appointed by the convent, and anything that remained after the demise of the last nun would be transferred to the archdiocese. Alex assured her the attorney would include these points in the agreement. Sister Etienne said she would release this information to the press, almost as if she were an old pro.

A reluctant Alex put on her sunglasses and left the convent, walking out into the glaring sunlight. She knew someone had recognized her when she entered and wondered if he might be lurking, ready to pounce. What type of inquisition might await her? Did she have anything to fear, now that the Archbishop had agreed to legally turn the ownership of the tapestry over to the nuns?

There were still several reporters milling about. Alex walked quickly toward her car.

"Madame Pellier," someone shouted. The voice was familiar. Alex turned, but kept walking. She didn't recognize the man. Then, it came to her.

"Madame Pellier, Georges Gaudens from *Le Journal Parisien.* We spoke."

"*Oui,* Monsieur Gaudens. Perhaps you should speak with Sister Etienne. She is ready to release additional information on the fate of the tapestry." Alex unlocked her car door and got in. She pulled a business card out of her purse, wrote the Pelliers' number in Lyon, and handed it to him. "My number in Lyon." He took the card and nodded.

Several minutes later, as Alex turned off the gravel road onto the highway, she got the feeling she was being followed. She had not actually seen anyone in her mirror, but something told her she was not alone. As she approached Vienne, she noticed a dark-blue Peugeot behind her. Had it been parked outside the convent? She pulled off to fuel her car, but also to determine if she was being followed. The blue car had fallen several cars behind, and she didn't think it had turned off. She drove around for a while, turning abruptly here, then there, in an attempt to lose the blue car, although she didn't see it behind her. She found a fuel station. As she filled her tank, she looked around and didn't see the blue Peugeot. Then, just as she was about to leave, she noticed the familiar vehicle pull in. Quickly, Alex pulled out and drove toward the freeway.

Back on the highway, she looked in her rearview mirror. No blue car. Was she just imagining she was being followed? She drove about five miles, looking back more often than forward. Then, suddenly, there it was again, three cars back. By the time she reached the outskirts of Lyon, there was only one car between Alex and the blue car. She entered the city, taking a zigzag path, running two red lights. Surely she had lost him. She parked several blocks from the Pelliers' apartment. No sign of the blue car. She walked rapidly toward Simone's apartment. It was broad daylight, people walking down the boulevard. Surely she was safe. What was she afraid of anyway? Would someone harm her over a tapestry? Here on the streets of Lyon in the middle of the day?

"Madame Pellier," she heard a man calling from behind her. Without stopping, she looked back. She could see now, it was Dr. Henry Martinson. And then, behind him, huffing and puffing and out of breath, another man, short and stout, wearing large dark sunglasses. The man grabbed Martinson by the shoulder, and as he whirled him around, Alex heard herself scream.

26

JAKE WORKED THROUGH the weekend. By late Sunday afternoon he had six paintings, four of them framed. He would go to the co-op the following morning and buy frames for the remaining two. His appointment with Madame Genevoix was at one P.M. Monday. He would need help transporting his work to the art gallery. He could call a cab, but several of the canvases were still wet, and he wanted someone who could help him carry them down from the third floor, someone who would take some care.

At one time, Jake would have considered asking Alex to help him take the paintings over to the gallery. Hadn't he helped her out every time she snapped her fingers? But now . . . now, he didn't think they were even speaking. He'd started to call a couple times after the fiasco late Friday night, but couldn't bring himself to do it. Was he supposed to apologize to Alex? For what? The more he thought about it, the angrier he got. To hell with Alex. She was obviously shocked to see Julianna in his room that night, but even if he had been entertaining a lady friend, having an intimate little rendezvous, as he was sure Alex had interpreted Julianna's late-night visit, it was none of Alex's business anyway. Yet he couldn't help but wonder why she'd come up to see him so late that night. Had she come to apologize? But why in the middle of the night? Maybe she had come for more than that, a fantasy he'd played through his mind more times than he could count.

He kept seeing her face. The expression of utter disgust and betrayal. Maybe he should give her a call, explain about Julianna. But there was still the matter of the tapestry. Jake wasn't completely sure he hadn't had something to do with the information getting out. He didn't think Julianna had said anything, yet she said she might have mentioned it to Matthew. There had been another article in the paper that morning. Someone was obviously leaking information to the press. That morning's article was complete with pictures of the nuns from Sainte Blandine's. The story was definitely sympathetic toward the sisters' cause. Jake didn't think the article, along with another on unicorn tapestries, comparing the convent tapestry to the Cluny's, The Cloister's tapestries, and even *Le Pégase* at the Grand Palais was publicity Alex would greet with great warmth. Now if all that didn't stir up enough interest to boost the asking price sky high, Jake didn't know what would. Even if the Archbishop allowed the nuns to sell the tapestry, all this interest and publicity might put it out of Alex's reach.

He'd had a strange call from Paul Westerman that very morning. Paul said he was looking for Alex. He'd called her home, got some runaround about Alex being out of town. He was sure Jake would have contacted Alex in Paris, maybe would know if Alex was involved in this mysterious tapestry thing.

"Tapestry?" Jake had asked, perhaps with a bit too much innocence in his voice.

Paul laughed. "You do read the newspaper, don't you, Jake? And you have been in touch with Alex since your arrival in Paris?

"Yes, I've seen Alex."

"Happen to know if she's involved in this tapestry discovery down in Lyon?"

"I'm sure Alex would be interested in any discovery of a medieval tapestry," Jake answered. "She works for a medieval museum." He wasn't good at lying, but he sure as hell wasn't going to tell anyone, even Paul, anything about Alex's involvement.

"Just passing through Paris on my way south," Paul said. "Train leaves in five minutes. Thought I'd give you a ring. Maybe we can get together for dinner next time I'm in Paris."

"Give me a call."

"How's the painting going?"

"Going good."

"Good."

After he hung up, Jake wondered about Paul's interest in the tapestry. Probably some collector hired him to check it out.

He called Gabby to get Matthew's number. She wasn't in, but her roommate gave him the number. She seemed to know Jake, and he wondered if she was the Woody Woodpecker girl.

When he called Matthew, Jake tried to sound casual. "Do you recall," he asked, "did Julianna happen to mention anything about a tapestry or some drawings?"

"Is that the one on the news the other night? The one found in that convent down by Lyon? She was talking about it. Said your lady friend had some connection."

"She mention it before?"

"Don't think so. Just last night when it came on the tube."

Could he eliminate Matthew now? Jake thought so. The only one left was Gaston Jadot. Jake would go to the studio the following evening and talk to Monsieur Jadot. He would find out if the old man had something to do with the articles in the paper or the Archbishop's knowledge of the tapestry discovery.

27

"WHAT THE HELL?" Martinson yelled, pushing the man who'd come up behind him.

"You all right, Alex?" the stout man shouted as he gripped Martinson by both wrists. And then she realized who it was. She hadn't seen him in over ten years, but the voice she would know anywhere, a gravelly voice, thickened through a serious nicotine habit. He'd put on a few extra pounds—although he'd always been rather plumpish—and his brown scraggly beard, which had given him a hippie-artist look, was gone. He still sported a mustache, now neatly trimmed.

"Paul?"

"You okay, Alex?"

Alex nodded. Martinson struggled, and though he was much taller than Paul, Paul's thick hands easily encircled his wrists. "Let me go, you imbecile. I'm not trying to shoot her or anything. I just want to talk to her."

Paul glanced at Alex, who nodded. Paul let go and Martinson straightened himself, adjusting his tie and then the lapels of his jacket. The anxiety that had built up in Alex seemed to dissipate, and her relief came out in a strange, nervous laugh. Martinson shot her an annoyed look, and Alex said, with a little bow, aware of the waggish dignity she was adding to this bizarre scene, "Dr. Martinson, may I present Paul Westerman, an old friend. Paul, Dr. Henry Martinson, curator from The Cloisters Museum in New York."

Paul offered his hand, and reluctantly Martinson took it.

"Just want to talk?" Paul said. "So, talk."

"What are you?" Martinson demanded. "Some kind of bodyguard?"

Paul folded his arms over his wide chest. "You followed her from the convent."

"And you," Martinson snorted, "followed me."

Strangely, Alex hadn't picked out either of them in the crowd outside the convent, but she had rushed in and out as quickly as possible. She took a deep breath.

"I saw you go into the convent, Madame Pellier," Martinson said. "It's obvious you have some influence where the tapestry is concerned. There was mention of a public offering. Surely you are not planning to dissuade the nuns from doing what would be in their best interest." He was wearing a suit and tie, though the weather was hovering somewhere in the nineties. A bead of sweat had formed on his brow. "The Cloisters is prepared to make a substantial offer on the tapestry. I would like the opportunity to present our offer. I take it you are a woman who believes in fair play."

When Alex did not reply, Martinson added, "We're not going to let this opportunity pass without a fight." He glanced at Paul. "Well, not that kind of fight."

"No, assuredly not," Paul said with a shake of his head. He pulled a pack of cigarettes from his pocket and tapped one out.

"You do have the tapestry?" Martinson asked Alex. *"Trusted friend? Medieval art expert?"* he prodded. "If the glove fits."

What kind of idiot expression was that? Alex thought. "Descriptions that might fit many. Obviously you've been following the story. The convent was crawling with reporters today, and I believe the nuns were ready to release additional information. Perhaps you should have stuck around." Alex knew it would all come out in *Le Journal Parisien,* that Martinson would have as good a chance at acquiring the tapestry as anyone, including the

Cluny, but she didn't want to give him the satisfaction of knowing that just yet. "I might suggest you read *Le Journal Parisien* tomorrow," she snapped, feeling a warmth rise up the back of her neck.

Paul let out a puff that encircled all three of them in a cloud of smoke. Martinson cleared his throat, pulled a white silk handkerchief from his breast pocket and wiped his forehead, then fastidiously folded and replaced it, all the while staring at Alex. She stared back, and wondered why she disliked this man so. He was doing no more than she—chasing after something they both wanted. But she wasn't going to tell him a thing. Not a darned thing.

"Now, if you'll excuse me," she said, "I have a private matter to attend to."

"We shall meet again, I'm sure, Madame Pellier." Once more Martinson straightened his tie, then turned and started down the street.

"Nice guy," Paul said as they watched him turn the corner. "Could we go somewhere and talk?"

"I really need to get back."

"Back? Back to Paris?"

"No, my mother-in-law's here in Lyon." She motioned down the street. "My father-in-law just passed away."

His eyebrows twisted a little, an expression that seemed so familiar to Alex. He was always inquisitive, questioning, never accepting anything at face value. She just knew he was wondering what she was doing, running around chasing after tapestries when her mother-in-law was in mourning.

"Hey, thanks for coming to my rescue," she said, giving him a quick hug. "Good to see you, Paul." And then, with another anxious laugh, she added, "I think." She started to walk, Paul moving along beside her, taking a hasty drag on his cigarette.

"So, what were *you* up to at the convent?" Alex asked.

Paul grinned. "I called your number in Paris. Got the runaround. I had no idea about . . . about your family situation." His expression took a somber turn. "I called Jake. He was rather evasive, so I knew something was going on with you. Been seeing much of Jake?"

"Now and then." She didn't want to talk about Jake. She didn't even want to think about Jake. She had more than enough on her mind right now. Paul was huffing and puffing, trying to keep up with her. "That's not good for you," she said, nodding toward his cigarette. She didn't slow down.

"Yeah, I know." He coughed. "So, what *do* you know, Alex?"

"What's your interest?"

"Maybe we're all after the same thing. You, me, Dr. Martinson."

"Maybe."

"A client hired me to check out the authenticity of the tapestry. He's interested. Without seeing it, this might be difficult—verifying it's a genuine late-medieval tapestry, similar in style to the set that hangs in *your* museum." Paul's mouth turned up into an impish, mischievous grin, and Alex couldn't help but think of all the tricks and jokes he'd played years ago when they were students. And she also remembered how competitive he'd been. He was a bit of a jokester, but he always liked to end up on top with grades, accomplishments, and awards when they were in school.

"It *has been* authenticated?" Paul asked. "By a medieval art expert? Has it not, Madame Pellier?"

Alex continued to walk. "As I told Dr. Martinson, you might check out the—"

"Ah, come on, Alex, for an old friend . . ."

They had arrived at the front door of Simone's building. Alex pointed up. "This is where I get off."

"Could we get together?" Paul asked. He took a deep pull on his cigarette, then turned his head and blew out a puff of smoke.

"It's just not a good time." Alex felt like her brain might cave in. She needed to contact Elizabeth Dorling at Sotheby's, needed to talk to Simone's attorney, meet with the Archbishop. Was Paul's showing up just one more problem she'd have to deal with, not to mention Martinson? "Call me next week at the Cluny." She dug in her purse and pulled out a business card. Paul stuck it in his shirt pocket.

What harm would it do to tell him now? she thought. "Yes, it has been authenticated. It will be offered at auction at Sotheby's next month. The Archbishop has agreed to the nuns' proposal to sell the tapestry and allow them to stay at the convent."

"And the tapestry, when might it be viewed?"

"The catalogue should be out late next week, and a viewing prior to the auction, which will be August thirteenth."

"Is it as exquisite as we've been led to believe?"

"I'll leave that for you to decide."

He snuffed his cigarette out on the sidewalk. "Good to see you again, Alex. Sorry about your father-in-law. I'll call you next week then?" He didn't move, as if he were waiting for something more. Did he expect a private viewing? He knew she had seen it. Most likely, he knew she was in possession of it. But suddenly, Alex became aware once more of something else she had tried to push out of her thoughts for the past twenty-four hours. Right now, she didn't even know where the tapestry was.

28

EARLY MONDAY MORNING, on the way to the co-op to purchase his frames, Jake grabbed a cup of coffee and stopped to pick up a paper. Standing in front of the newsstand, juggling his coffee in one hand, he unfolded the paper. There on the bottom portion of the front page was a picture of Alex, wearing sunglasses and a startled expression. The headline read, "Collectors and museum officials gather as mystery of tapestry unfolds." Alex was identified as Alexandra Pellier, curator at the Musée National du Moyen Age, Thermes de Cluny in Paris.

Jake scanned the article. The Archbishop had agreed to allow the nuns to sell the tapestry and remain at the convent. The upper floors could still be used as a hotel, and the Archbishop's representative said rooms would be available late this fall. The tapestry would be auctioned at Sotheby's in mid-August. Alex was identified as one of many who would be interested in obtaining the tapestry, and also as the trusted friend who had assisted the nuns. Sister Etienne said if Madame Pellier had not been so honest, she could have obtained the tapestry for a fraction of its true value. The sisters of Sainte Blandine were grateful Madame Pellier had put the nuns' welfare above her own desires.

Well, Jake thought, *everyone is a winner here. Alex looks like a saint, the nuns get to stay, the Archbishop gets publicity for his new hotel, and some museum or lucky collector gets the tapestry.* Yet, perhaps in the end—Sainte Alex and the Cluny would turn out to be the only losers in the whole ordeal. Even if Alex was a heroine to the nuns, it was highly likely her museum would lose the tapestry. The price of sainthood!

It would have happened anyway, Jake told himself, even if the tapestry had remained a secret a while longer. Surely the discovery would have gotten out to the art community, although most likely not with all the publicity generated by the controversy over the ownership. All this attention would most likely inflate the price, making it more difficult for Alex. But she was resourceful. She would figure out how to get the tapestry for her museum. Alex would raise the money one way or another. Yet he still felt he had to clear his name with her.

Jake went to the co-op and purchased two new frames. It was early and Julianna wasn't in yet. He hadn't seen her since Friday night. He returned to his hotel and framed the last two paintings, then lined them up and examined them.

Pretty damn good! He hoped Madame Genevoix would think so too. If he could get her to show his work, maybe he could sell a few paintings. He'd already made a substantial investment in canvases and frames, and while his savings were holding out, he knew at some time he would have to produce some income.

Just before noon as he waited for Matthew, who'd offered to help him take the paintings to the gallery, Alex's mother, Sarah Benoit, called.

"I thought you might want to know," Sarah said. "I don't imagine Alex called. Pierre Pellier passed away this weekend. Alex has gone down to Lyon to be with Simone. Sunny and I are leaving early tomorrow afternoon."

"I didn't know," Jake said. "Thank you for calling. Please extend my condolences to Simone."

"Yes, I will," Sarah answered.

"And Alex," Jake said. "And Sunny for the loss of her grandfather."

"Yes," Sarah replied. Then an awkward silence as if they

were each waiting for the other to speak. "Have you been following the story in the news?"

"Quite the publicity."

"Perhaps it's not good for Alex."

"Alex will get what she wants. She always does." It came out with a sarcastic edge, which he really hadn't intended.

"I'm not sure Alex always knows what she wants," Sarah said. "Well, I just wanted you to know about Pierre."

"Thank you for calling, Mrs. Benoit."

ALEX MET IN the library with Simone and her attorney late Monday morning. Henri Sauvestre was the second Henri Sauvestre to act as legal council for the Pelliers. His father had been Simone and Pierre's attorney for over thirty years; for the past twenty years, the younger Monsieur Sauvestre had served in this capacity. He was probably in his late fifties or early sixties, although Simone always referred to him as the Young Henri Sauvestre. He was not particularly handsome, but nice looking in a put-together sort of way. He dressed impeccably—starched, crisp white shirt, monogrammed French cuffs, gold cuff links, polished Italian leather shoes. Alex guessed that next to Father Varaigne and Alex herself, he was the person Simone most trusted and relied on.

There were no great surprises in Pierre's will. The bulk of his estate went to Simone—the apartment, the bank accounts, and the more valuable pieces of art. There were sizable contributions to various charities, a generous gift to the Church. He had set up a second trust for Soleil, which Alex had been aware of for some time. It would again be administered by Alain Bourlet. Alex was the beneficiary of several paintings and sculptures that she had always admired. Some, she knew, were valuable, others potentially so.

After the meeting, Alex asked if she might speak with Monsieur Sauvestre about an urgent matter. Simone excused herself and left the two alone.

"I don't know," Alex started out slowly, "if you've been following the events that have taken place recently at the *Couvent de Sainte Blandine*."

"Avec beaucoup de intérêt," Monsieur Sauvestre replied.

With great interest? Had everyone in France been following the story? Alex wondered.

"La photographie in the paper this morning," Monsieur Sauvestre said. "You have become somewhat of a *héroïne."* He looked at Alex with what she saw as admiration. Surely she didn't deserve this.

"The good sisters of Sainte Blandine's have asked me to meet with the Archbishop tomorrow," Alex said. "He has agreed not to contest the nuns' legal ownership of the tapestry, to allow them to stay at the convent, under certain conditions for the sale and management of the funds. We need help in drawing up a legally binding document. I know this is very short notice, but I need some help. I thought maybe . . ." Alex felt so foolish—as if this busy attorney had nothing to do the following morning—but she desperately needed something right away to assure Elizabeth Dorling the catalogue could go to print on Wednesday. She had to get this taken care of by tomorrow.

Monsieur Sauvestre rubbed his chin and thought for a moment. "Tomorrow is not good," he said. *"Mais oui,* we can work something out. *A quelle heure,* what time is your meeting?"

"Ten A.M."

Again Monsieur Sauvestre rubbed his chin, as if this were part of the thinking process. *"Dites-moi"*—he looked at Alex intently now—"tell me exactly what the Archbishop has agreed to."

Alex reiterated what she had discussed with Sister Etienne. She explained the matter was urgent, as she wished to have something for Sotheby's by Wednesday. Monsieur Sauvestre listened with great interest, and, although he took no notes, Alex knew he was taking in every detail. He asked if Alex had power of attorney to sign for the nuns. She told him no. Why would she have thought of this? Now, even if they reached an agreement in writing, would she have to run down to the convent to get a signature from Sister Etienne?

Before leaving, Monsieur Sauvestre told Alex he would be unable to meet with her tomorrow, but he would send a representative from the firm. Perhaps she could come by his office tomorrow about nine-fifteen, so she could go over the agreement before meeting with the Archbishop. He suggested, if Alex would get in touch with the nuns, he could have a courier sent down to the convent the following afternoon for a signature. He realized Simone needed her right now. How kind, Alex thought, but realized, of course, he was providing extra service because of Simone.

Alex called Elizabeth Dorling in London. Yes, she had been following the story. She was pleased things had turned out favorably for the nuns, and, as Alex suspected, she wanted something in writing to confirm the legal ownership. Alex said she would have a document faxed over no later than Wednesday morning.

She spoke with Sister Etienne to let her know a courier would be coming out the following afternoon for a signature. She asked if things were going well, and the nun said they had quieted down considerably.

That afternoon, Alex sat with Simone, then suggested they go for a walk. Alex was going nearly crazy just sitting.

The warm air had cooled considerably. They walked along the river, a soft breeze blowing off the water. People hurried about—a young mother pushing twin babies in a double stroller; a middle-aged woman with several long, crusty baguettes protruding from her grocery bag; a briefcase-carrying businessman rushing to a late-afternoon meeting. People engaged in the normal routines of their daily lives. These people did not know that Simone's life would never be the same, that her ordinary, daily activities would never again follow the customary routine. And Alex, her life was certainly about to make a turn also—she was on the verge of either losing or obtaining possibly the most spectacular late-medieval tapestry ever discovered. Her picture had appeared in the paper that morning. Last night Georges Gaudens had called. He told Alex the reporters from Lyon and the local TV station were aware she was involved in the tapestry discovery, although they did not know she was at the Pelliers' in Lyon. When she explained the situation with her family, he agreed he would not reveal her whereabouts. She hadn't heard any more from Martinson or Paul.

Just as they were returning to the apartment, Simone said, "I'm pleased things have worked out with the nuns. Was Monsieur Sauvestre able to help you with the legal aspects?"

"Yes. I have a meeting tomorrow at nine-fifteen. I may be gone most of the morning."

"That's fine. Soleil and Sarah will be here tomorrow afternoon. I'm glad we got our business taken care of."

Alex assumed her mother-in-law was talking about the arrangements for Pierre's services and the meeting with the attorney. She wondered if it had even crossed Simone's mind that Alex would like to know where she'd hidden the tapestry. "I'd like to relieve you of the burden of the tapestry as soon as possible. I'd like to ship it to London."

Simone hesitated. "I might ask that you wait until after the services, after things have settled down. I just don't want you fussing with it right now."

Alex took in a deep breath and felt her heart pumping rapidly. Again she pushed her frustrations aside. "Yes, of course, Simone."

MONDAY AFTERNOON, MATTHEW helped Jake take his paintings to the gallery. Madame Genevoix examined each carefully, asking that several be moved to various locations, adjusting the lights, smiling and nodding, obviously excited about what Jake had produced. She told him she had an opening in mid-August—the scheduled artist had cancelled out, or more precisely, they'd had a falling-out when she requested an exclusive showing, to which the artist would not agree. She wanted to know if Jake would be interested, under these conditions—that he not show at any other gallery in Paris prior to the showing in August. Would he be interested?

Certainement! There was no way Jake would have enough work for more than a single show anyway—in fact, he would have to work nonstop to have enough for a show in August. Madame Genevoix asked if she might keep the largest painting to display now, to create some interest.

Matthew nudged Jake and grinned. "Hey, go for it, man. Then we won't have to carry it back."

As they walked around the gallery, Jake felt elated. He was painting, filled with a creativity he hadn't known in years. And now, an opportunity to show in a prestigious Paris gallery. He liked the layout of the gallery, the location, Madame Genevoix's enthusiastic attitude.

Madame Genevoix said she would need a photo of Jake, a bio, any information he might want to use in the brochures and postcards that she always sent out to her patrons prior to the opening. Also his own mailing list for anyone he wanted to include. The woman carried on a bit about opening night, how she always had something catered.

As he and Matthew were about to leave, Madame Genevoix said, "You're following all this excitement with Alexandra Pellier and the unicorn tapestry?"

"*Oui.*" Jake nodded.

"The publicity might be a nice tie-in for your show, the theme of the unicorn." Madame Genevoix smiled broadly.

Again Jake agreed. It was a thought that had crossed his mind more than once.

"Wouldn't it be lovely," the woman declared, "if we could obtain the tapestry for the Cluny?"

"*Oui, très agréable.*" Well, there, Jake thought. With enthusiastic, wealthy supporters like Madame Genevoix, Alex would get her money. "The tapestry belongs in the Cluny with the others. *N'est pas, Madame?*"

On the way back home, Jake thanked Matthew for his help and asked if he'd be willing to pose for a painting. Jake had been thinking for several days about doing an Annunciation scene, again incorporating the symbolic unicorn. He could use Gabby for the Virgin—with her long neck he could get a nice Parmigianino thing going. But he'd need a male model for the Angel Gabriel. He knew the studio had male models on Monday nights, but when the idea first came to him, he thought Matthew would be perfect.

"You want me to model for an angel?" Matthew asked with a big grin, then broke out laughing.

"Would you do it?"

"Sure. Cool . . . a black angel from Chicago? Yeah, man, I'll do it."

"Could you come by tomorrow?"

"No problem," Matthew said as they pulled up to Jake's hotel.

"I thought I might drop by the studio tonight." Jake got out and started to unload the paintings. "I need to talk to Gaston Jadot."

"Monsieur Jadot hasn't been at the studio for the past few weeks."

"Well, maybe I'll just drop by anyway."

Jake called Rebecca after Matthew left. It was just past six A.M. in Montana, and she sounded groggy. He tried to blame her lack of enthusiasm when he told her about the gallery show on the fact that she wasn't quite awake.

"This means you'll be staying in Paris this fall?" she asked.

"Yes."

"I thought . . . well, I thought . . ."

"It's a wonderful opportunity, Rebecca. And I'm painting. You just don't know how it feels to be painting again. Producing something I feel good about. And now, the opportunity to show, maybe sell some of my work."

"I understand," she said. But he wasn't sure she did.

GASTON JADOT WAS at the studio that evening. He said he'd come down with a bout of *la grippe,* that it was hard on an old man, but he was feeling fine now.

Jake spoke with Julianna for a few moments. She was friendly, but not flirty. Jake sensed that something had changed since last Friday night when both Alex and Julianna had paid him an unexpected late-night visit. Julianna mentioned she'd seen his *girlfriend* in the paper, and wasn't this all so exciting about the tapestry. And wasn't it incredibly exciting to be in on this discovery?

Exciting was hardly the word for it, Jake thought. He glanced at Gaston Jadot to see if the old man was listening. He was putting his supplies away for the evening, but Jake got the feeling that he was listening.

"Would you like to go for a drink this evening, Monsieur Jadot?" Jake called across the room. Gaston turned and nodded.

They went to the same bar near the studio where they had gone before. Gaston asked about the gallery show—he'd obviously been listening in on that conversation too. Jake explained how his old friend Alexandra Pellier from the Cluny Museum had helped him make the connection. Jake watched the old man's expression, which could best be described as poker face, at the mention of Alex's name.

"This Alex, she is your lover?"

Again, Jake wondered if the old man had heard Julianna refer to Alex as his *girlfriend*. "No. Friends. We were students here in Paris years ago."

"And you were in love with this Alex then?"

Jake didn't answer. What business was it of Gaston's, or Julianna's or anyone else's for that matter?

Jake took a slow drink of wine, then asked about Gaston's family business. He had mentioned in an earlier conversation that he'd been involved in a family business until just a few years ago.

"Les objects anciens," Gaston replied. *"Antiquités."*

Oh, great, Jake thought. If he was going to mention the discovery of ancient drawings, possibly relating to the discovery of a priceless Gothic tapestry, he might as well mention it in the presence of a dealer of antiques.

Gaston went on to explain how his father had started with a small shop in Paris, how the business had expanded, a shop in Lyon, how the family had become involved in international antiquities trade. They had done well. The family was comfortable.

Jake nodded. "Would the family be interested in the discovery of a late-medieval tapestry?" he asked.

"I read the newspaper," Gaston replied. "Interesting . . . the discovery at the convent, the drawings . . . then the tapestry."

Jake knew Gaston could have read all of this in the paper. But he also knew the old man had been listening in on the conversation with Julianna, long before any of this hit the news.

"Did you mention to anyone the conversation with Julianna about the drawings?"

Gaston smiled, not the guilty smile of a thief who had been caught, but almost a smile of satisfaction, the expression of one who had the upper hand. "I have friends," he said, "men not unlike myself, retired, but still interested in the arts, interested in what is going on in the world."

"And you said something?"

Gaston nodded.

"Is there any way this could have triggered the publicity, the Archbishop's knowledge of the discovery?"

The look on Gaston's face now carried a trace of guilt. "My friend, Marcel Bonnisseau," he said as if confessing.

"Bonnisseau? Like in Archbishop Bonnisseau?"

"They are brothers." The old man nodded.

This wasn't what Jake wanted to hear. Not at all what he wanted to hear.

TUESDAY MORNING, ALEX noticed Simone wore a little makeup. She looked like she had slept last night, and for the first time since Alex arrived, she'd had Marie do her hair. Simone spoke of her excitement to see Soleil that afternoon and mentioned she had another birthday gift for her, a carriage for her doll.

At eight-thirty Alex left for Henri Sauvestre's office. She met with a young attorney who had been assigned to write up the agreement for the nuns. He looked barely old enough to be out of law school—so young, in fact, Alex wondered if he had to shave more than once a week. He had such an eager, wanting-to-please demeanor about him and treated Alex as if she were some sort of celebrity.

She looked over the agreement. It contained everything she had discussed with Monsieur Sauvestre the previous day. He hadn't missed a detail. Hopefully, this would be agreeable to the Archbishop and everything could be taken care of quickly.

The young attorney, whose name was Hervé Haye, accompanied Alex to the meeting with the Archbishop, which turned out not to be a meeting with the Archbishop at all. The address that Sister Etienne had given Alex was the address of a law firm in Lyon. They met with an attorney representing the archdiocese. A few minor changes were made to the agreement. At Alex's insistence, she and Hervé waited while a secretary typed it up, and the attorney agreed it would be sent over immediately to the Archbishop for his approval and signature.

"I need this completed and signed by this afternoon," Alex said.

The Archbishop's attorney looked at her with a brow that wrinkled, an incredulous wrinkled brow, the same dubious brow that had twitched when Alex insisted the agreement be typed up right away while they waited. Alex knew that in France everything tended to be *en cours*—in process—but she needed this now.

Alex felt the young attorney reach out and touch her lightly on the arm. Reassurance from a child? He looked at her and nodded as if to say, *I'll take care of this for you.* Then Alex heard Simone's words in her head. *Trust me.* Why was it that everything in her life right now was based on trusting someone else? She wanted to scream, *Let me take care of all this myself,* but she knew she was at the mercy of others.

On the way back to his office, Hervé Haye assured Alex he would have something signed and ready to send to Elizabeth Dorling early the following morning. Alex explained that her father-in-law's funeral was the next morning, that she would have no time for chasing after contracts or signatures and was relying on him. She gave him a business card on which she'd written her number in Lyon and the fax number at Sotheby's in London.

That afternoon, Alex drove her mother-in-law to the station to meet Soleil and Sarah. Simone seemed completely in control now, as if the past three days had provided the time she needed to put herself back together and prepare for guests. There would be others arriving—nieces, nephews, cousins—although they would all stay at hotels in Lyon.

As soon as they got back to the apartment, Simone presented her granddaughter with her late birthday gift. Soleil ran to the bedroom to retrieve the doll, then put her in the carriage along with Jake's beautiful Medieval Barbie, which she had carried with her on the train from Paris. She pushed the carriage about the apartment from room to room.

The three women sat in the living room, visiting. Mostly they talked about Soleil, the one thing all three had in common. Sarah's French was improving, and Simone spoke some English, so the conversation was carried on in a mixture of the two languages. Alex was amazed at how well the two women communicated, and she realized how much they shared. Sarah expressed her regrets on Simone's loss of her husband, and Simone said, yes, surely Sarah understood—she had gone through the same loss. Realizing all three of them were widows, although her mother and mother-in-law had had long, loving relationships, the painful truth came to Alex once more—she had never truly loved her husband. Was it a much sadder tale to lose a husband from a loveless marriage? Alex got up to go look for Soleil.

She found her in the hall, coming out of Simone's bedroom, using the long corridor as a walkway for her carriage. The carpet runner had been shoved and partially rolled into a corner. "What are you doing, Soleil?" Alex tried to keep her voice calm.

"It's too bumpy."

"So you're just rearranging things to suit your fancy?"

"Grandmère doesn't mind."

"Your mother minds. Let's put things back in their proper places." Alex bent down and unrolled and smoothed the carpet runner. "Were you in Grandmère's bedroom?"

The little girl looked down, obviously aware her mother was not pleased.

"Did you mess anything up?"

Soleil nodded. Alex took her daughter's hand and led her into the bedroom, an enormous room with sitting area filled with an antique sofa, two chairs, several small tables, and a fireplace. A large Persian rug, which covered a good portion of the room, had been pulled back on one corner. "At least you didn't shove it into a corner," Alex said.

"I couldn't. It's too heavy."

Alex tried to suppress her smile. She walked to the carpet and started to turn back the corner. Sunny was right—it was very heavy. Heavy, even for a large wool carpet. And terribly bulky. Then Alex noticed that the back was covered with fabric. She knew authentic oriental rugs never had cloth backing; this was always a warning sign that something was hidden—imperfections, flaws. Everything in Simone and Pierre's home was authentic and of the highest quality. Alex pulled the corner back farther. The fabric backing was hand-stitched along the border. She knelt down on the floor and turned it back farther, then picked at the stitching, which started to unravel. She stuck her finger under the fabric and felt a faintly rough, familiar texture. Yes indeed—the cloth backing had been added to hide something.

29

AFTER PIERRE'S SERVICES, family and friends gathered at Simone's. Several ladies from the church had set up a buffet. As Alex visited with a woman from Grenoble, Thierry's cousin, she caught the eye of Henri Sauvestre across the room. He smiled and nodded, then walked toward them.

Alex introduced him to Thierry's cousin. They visited for a few minutes, then the cousin left to check on her children.

"Everything has been taken care of," Monsieur Sauvestre said, reaching out, touching Alex reassuringly on the shoulder.

"*Merci*," Alex said, and she could hear her own sigh of relief. "Madame Dorling at Sotheby's?"

"*Oui. Tout.*"

"*Merci, merci beaucoup.*"

That evening, Simone again seemed very tired. Alex had planned to leave the following day, if the tapestry matter could be resolved, but now she was concerned that Simone might still need her. She had said nothing to her mother-in-law about discovering the tapestry hidden under the rug. But why hadn't she told Alex where it was? Simone had said she didn't want Alex fussing with it right now.

Alex put Soleil to bed, then sat in the living room with her mother and Simone.

"Thank you, Alexandra," Simone said. "You've been such a big help, but I know you have to return to work."

Alex nodded.

"I'll be fine," Simone said reassuringly. "Marie is here. I have my friends from church. My life will change now. I realize that, but I'll be fine. *Merci*, Sarah," she said, turning to Alex's mother. "It's helped that we've been able to talk."

Sarah smiled. "Yes."

Simone rose. "Come, Alexandra. I know you're anxious to get the tapestry shipped off to London."

Alex stood and followed Simone down the hall. The older woman motioned for Sarah to come too.

The three women entered the bedroom. Simone walked to the Persian rug and asked Alex to turn it back. Alex knelt down and pulled back the corner. She felt the bulk of the two woven fabrics joined together as Simone instructed her.

"The tapestry," Simone said proudly.

Her mother-in-law seemed so pleased that Alex said nothing about her earlier discovery. And somehow she knew now what Simone had told her was true. Why had Alex been so unwilling to trust her?

The next morning, Alex called Elizabeth Dorling at Sotheby's. The paperwork had been received, and the catalogue had gone to print.

Alex insured the tapestry and had it packed and crated and shipped to London. Unsure of how much she should insure it for—it was priceless; if lost or destroyed it could never be replaced—she had purchased a 1.5 million Euro policy, considerably more than the price that would be listed in the catalogue.

Early that afternoon, Alex, Sarah, and Sunny returned to Paris. After dropping them off at home, Alex went immediately to the Cluny. The museum was closed, but Madame Demy was still in her office. Alex spoke to her, filling her in on the latest details. Now they just had to raise the money.

Alex spent the following morning on the phone. She spoke to Madame Genevoix, who was extremely enthusiastic about the tapestry. She and her husband had discussed the matter, and they would be willing to make a donation. Madame

Genevoix said Alex must be pleased about Jake's upcoming show at her gallery. Alex didn't mention that she hadn't spoken to Jake in almost a week. She said he was a talented artist and she hoped the show would be successful for both of them.

Alex sat for a moment after she hung up. Jake. He'd sent a brief note saying how sorry he was to hear of her loss. Should she call him? She was happy for him about the gallery show. The Genevoix was a wonderful opportunity for any artist. As she thought about Jake, Alex realized how much she missed him. She thought of their evening together at the tapestry exhibition, his rushing to Lyon to help her with the drawings. She smiled as the thoughts entered her head—going down to the convent, discovering the name *Adèle Le Viste* in the convent's records, hanging the tapestry, visiting with Madame Gerlier in Vienne in their quest to find an eighth tapestry, which Jake had later suggested wasn't a tapestry at all, but a child. And Soleil had grown fond of Jake. At her birthday party, she told him she loved him, the words so innocent and natural, as if the utterance of those three simple words—*I love you*—were not capable of shaking the entire universe.

He'd created the lovely medieval doll for her daughter. This thought filled Alex with a feeling so tender it made her ache. But then—the image of Jake with the beautiful Asian girl. And the warmth of that tenderness heated to a burning sense of betrayal.

THAT AFTERNOON, ALEX spoke to several other benefactors from whom she had solicited donations earlier. Each of them had been following the publicity concerning the tapestry, and they were all aware that this was *the* tapestry she'd spoken of when she'd told them of her plans to acquire a recently discovered Gothic piece for the Cluny. It seemed everyone was eager to take part in the Cluny's acquisition of the beautiful, now famous, tapestry.

By five, Alex had verbal commitments for donations of eight hundred thousand Euros, the equivalent of almost one million American dollars. She felt she should continue to raise funds, to have a comfortable cushion. Her plan was to have everything arranged by the last week in July, when she, her mother, and Soleil would be taking a holiday in Italy. She knew she would feel comfortable about leaving only if she was certain everything had been taken care of.

The following afternoon, Dr. Martinson called from New York.

"Isn't it a shame," he said, "the nuns, letting the tapestry go to auction. It would certainly have been a fine donation to some medieval museum. Now, just about anyone could have a shot at it."

"Yes, what a shame," Alex replied, her voice filled with mock graciousness.

"And drawings in a prayer book? The book that was donated to a medieval museum in Paris?" Martinson's tone suggested he thought Alex also had the drawings, which she did not. "Yet there was only one medieval prayer book on the list," he mused. "Nothing remarkable, surely not museum quality."

Alex said nothing.

"August thirteenth?" Martinson said. "Friday the thirteenth—now won't that be the lucky day for some fortunate collector or museum."

"Yes, lucky indeed," Alex replied. "I'm sure we'll be seeing you in London, August thirteenth."

"Wouldn't miss it for the world."

After she hung up, Alex sat thinking. Martinson didn't have a chance, not a chance in hell.

JAKE HAD BEEN working furiously. Madame Genevoix was encouraging, and he felt genuinely good about his work. He had started a new painting, his Annunciation scene on three panels, large enough to show on one wall in the gallery. Matthew came over for several sittings. They draped him in a white sheet, and he looked downright angelic. Jake sketched in an arched portico on the three panels with angel, unicorn, and Virgin. It would be an impressive piece.

He went to the Louvre to check out the Renaissance section for angel wings and did some sketches, but knew he hadn't found exactly what he wanted. He envisioned a certain texture, like real feathers. On the way back from the museum, it had come to him—right there at his hotel, *Le Perroquet Violet,* he had feathers. So he spent the afternoon with his sketchpad on the reception counter in front of his model, *Le Perroquet,* who seemed quite pleased with all this attention.

Now, alone back in his room, he was putting the finishing touches on Matthew-Gabriel's wings. He stepped back, and felt a well of satisfaction rise within him. A fantastic, realistic texture. He wished he could share this with someone. He wished he could share this with Alex. She'd get a kick out of his parrot wings transposed to his angel.

Maybe he should give her a call. Pierre's funeral had been three days ago. He wondered if she was back in Paris. What would he say if he called? Just called to tell you about my fantastic angel wings? Or how about—Sorry for telling Gaston Jadot about the drawings of the tapestry, sorry he told Marcel Bonnisseau, who just happens to be the Archbishop's brother? Yet Jake was still trying to figure all this out himself. Even if Gaston had passed the information on to the Archbishop's brother, how did he connect this to the convent of Sainte Blandine's? Julianna knew he'd gone down to Lyon and so, obviously, did Gaston, but there had never been any mention of the convent. So what would he say to Alex? Maybe just address the other problem—Julianna. He could tell Alex they were just friends—isn't that what they were now? He also had a question for Alex—what was she doing out so late, dropping by his room well after midnight? That question had been playing repeatedly in his mind for the past week.

Jake looked at his watch. Almost two A.M. He couldn't call Alex tonight. Maybe tomorrow. Then again, maybe he wouldn't. Maybe he didn't need the confusion of having Alex in his life again. Maybe he was better off without her.

30

EARLY THE FOLLOWING week, Alex received an advance copy of the catalogue. It would be available to the general public at the end of the week. The printer had done a wonderful job—the colors in the photographs, the tapestry and a small insert of the hallmark on the back, appeared as bright and clear as the true colors. The text noted that, based on the style, the *mille-fleurs,* and the texture and dye of the wool used in the tapestry, it had most likely been woven in Brussels in the late fifteenth or early sixteenth century, possibly in the same workshop as the Cluny's unicorn tapestries. The description in the catalogue included comparisons to the Cluny set and a brief history of unicorn tapestries.

Alex sat and stared at the photos in the catalogue, and wondered once more—would she be able to acquire it for the museum? It was strange how all along, from the first trip to the convent, the discovery of the drawings, and Sister Etienne's disclosure of the treasure, Alex felt in some inexplicable way as if she had been chosen. Sister Etienne told her the nuns prayed for guidance the night they found the tapestry. Then Alex arrived, uninvited, the following morning. Sister Etienne said she had been sent to help them. But sent for what? And

how mysterious, Alex's recurring thought that by bringing the
seventh tapestry to the Cluny to hang with the others, the passion and creativity of the artist Adèle and the *tapissier* from
Brussels would be given a second chance. A second chance
for love.

THE PUBLICITY OVER the tapestry had died down when
the catalogue came out officially on July sixteenth. A brief article appeared, tucked inside the arts section of the newspaper.

Alex spoke several times with Sister Etienne, who informed her, modestly but with some joy—as it acknowledged
that the Order of Sainte Blandine had been infused with new
life—that her official title was now Reverend Mother Etienne.
The nuns had held an election and chosen her as the new
Mother Superior. The Archbishop's renovations were coming
along. He had constructed ramps. Sisters Eulalie and Philomena were now able to go outside for fresh air without great
difficulty. Sister Etienne expressed her gratitude to Alex for
all the help she had given the nuns in arranging the sale of the
tapestry. They had a little gift for Alex and would like her to
stop by soon.

Alex spoke often with her mother-in-law. Simone was getting out now and then—dinner one evening with friends, a
night at the theatre, which Pierre had always loved when he
was well. She asked when Alex would be coming down again.
It had been almost two weeks now and Alex had been so busy,
having missed almost a week of work while she was with Simone, and with her fund-raising efforts, that she had not returned to Lyon. She wondered if perhaps her mother-in-law
would travel to Paris now. Or maybe . . .

"We've had a trip planned since last winter for the final
week in July. I'm taking Mom and Soleil down to Florence
and Rome for a little holiday. Would you consider going with
us?"

Simone hesitated. "I haven't been to Italy for years. I've always loved Florence. Will you let me think about it?"

"We'd love to have you come along, Simone."

The following day, Simone called and said she would like
to go with them. Alex spent the next several days finishing

projects, making more calls about the tapestry. Before she left for her holiday in Italy, she had raised almost one million three hundred thousand Euros, the equivalent of over one and a half million American dollars. It was an unheard-of price for a tapestry. She had no doubt that come August thirteenth, the seventh unicorn tapestry would be on its way to the Cluny.

BY THE THIRD week in July, Jake had finished the three large panels and several smaller paintings and started a double-paneled painting. He had never felt so good about his work and had never produced so much so quickly. His tiny room at *Le Perroquet Violet* had become too cramped and cluttered, and he'd rented a second room to store his paintings.

Friday nights he went to the studio, mostly for the companionship. Sometimes he would drop in during the week. Now and then he would go for a drink with Gaston. He liked the old man. They would visit, generally about art, about what was going on at the studio.

One evening, the old man asked about Jake's friend Alex. He hadn't heard Jake mention her lately, and apologized if his discussing the drawings, the tapestries, with his friends had jeopardized this friendship.

"No, it isn't that," Jake replied. He knew it was much more than that. Maybe if he and Alex couldn't be lovers, they couldn't even be friends. Maybe that's what it was all about that evening when she had found him with Julianna. Still, he missed Alex, and he missed Soleil. Often he thought of the child—why couldn't they be friends, even if he and Alex were not? Yet he knew that was up to Alex. In fact, the whole thing was up to Alex. She would have to come to him.

Once in a while, Jake would go out with the younger students. Julianna was always friendly, but that was it.

At least twice a week, Jake called Montana and talked to Rebecca. The conversations had become strained and distant. She was not pleased about his decision to stay on that fall. He wondered if she should cancel her trip, even suggested this to Rebecca.

"You don't understand what I'm going through here, Jake. It's as if everything revolves around your world, what's happening with you. You don't seem to realize I'm over here, trying to lead my own life."

"I'm sorry, Rebecca." And he was, but for what he wasn't sure.

She questioned him about Alex, and he said there was nothing going on between them, that he hadn't seen her in weeks. Rebecca cried and said she was confused—they needed to get together in person and talk about their future.

Their future? If Rebecca couldn't understand about his painting, that he had to stay in Paris, maybe they didn't have a future.

ALEX BARELY THOUGHT of the tapestry or Jake during her week in Italy. She enjoyed the time with her daughter, mother, and mother-in-law. People would stop and stare as the four of them walked down the street. Alex wondered if they thought, *Why, isn't that lovely—four generations.* Simone was old enough to be Sarah's mother—she was in her mideighties, Sarah just fifty-six. Alex felt comfortable being part of this intimate little group, and pleased Simone had decided to come along.

But now and then, she would catch a glimpse of a couple sitting in a dark, intimate corner of a little trattoria; throwing coins in a fountain, making shared wishes; exchanging a kiss in the middle of a piazza in Florence with no shame or embarrassment—the Italians had no inhibitions and no shame in public displays of affection—and Alex would wonder if there wasn't more. Did she really want to be one of the three merry widows for the rest of her life?

An image would come to her. A family, a real family. Herself, Soleil, a father, and a little boy. A boy with dark hair and deep dark eyes.

31

WHEN ALEX RETURNED to Paris, the auction at Sotheby's was less than two weeks away. Her feelings now were much like the final two weeks of her pregnancy. She was ready, completely prepared. There was nothing to do but wait, nothing she could do to hasten it.

As Alex sorted through her mail, she came across an envelope with the return address of La Galerie Genevoix. She tore it open. It was an invitation to Jake's opening, Thursday the twelfth of August. A colorful brochure, with a picture of Jake and several photos of his work, was included. He had written a note on the bottom of the invitation. It was brief—"Would love to see you, Soleil, and your mom opening night. Thanks again for all your help." She looked at the note, examined the handwriting, which in a way seemed more intimate and personal than the photo of Jake himself, or even his paintings. She wondered what he was thinking as he wrote it. Had he included a handwritten note with all his invitations? Or had he spent hours trying to decide what to write, trying to make it sound so casual, when what he really wanted was to see her again?

The paintings reproduced in the brochure included the piece he'd brought to her home, the painting that had reminded her of the Manet, the one she'd hung on her wall the evening she invited the Genevoix. There was also a painting of a woman and a unicorn, one Alex thought she had seen in his room the day she went over to tell him about the Archbishop and nuns' battle over the tapestry. Now as she examined the small reproduction, she could see that the pose of the woman and unicorn was based on the seventh tapestry, Adèle's drawing. It was beautiful.

A sudden pang of pride throbbed inside her. She knew how much work he would have had to put into preparing for a show in such a short period of time. She hoped he would do well. Perhaps she should show her support, at least on a professional level. But that Thursday was the night before the auction at Sotheby's. She was scheduled to leave for London that evening.

ALEX CALLED THE bank and checked the total in the escrow account for the tapestry purchase. Several of her benefactors had already deposited the promised funds. Most had agreed the money would be in the account no later than Monday of the following week. If the Cluny was unable to purchase the tapestry, a notion Alex was barely able to consider, the funds would be returned.

By late Friday afternoon, most of the money was in the account. The auction was just one week away. The largest benefactors, the Genevoix, were contributing five hundred thousand Euros, and Alex knew their money would not reach the account until the middle of the following week.

On Tuesday, she received a call from Madame Genevoix. At first, Alex couldn't understand what the woman was saying. She was crying. Then the words came through. "He's left me. He's left me for another woman."

"You and Monsieur Genevoix have been together for many years. I'm sure he'll realize what a mistake he's made and come back begging your forgiveness." Alex had no idea how to comfort a woman who had been dumped by her husband after so many years—should she say, *Oh, I'm sure he's coming back,* or should she say, *Why the dirty rat, you're much better off without him*?

"No, he's not coming back. And I'm so sorry, Alex."

Sorry, Alex? And it came to her suddenly—Madame Genevoix had called to tell her he had also run off with the money.

"He's emptied the accounts, hidden assets. Oh, Alex, I'm so sorry."

Alex felt a sudden rush of heat, then a numbness that seemed to take over her entire body. "Surely this is just a fling. He will come back," she heard herself saying, in a soft, sympathetic voice, when in her own head she was shouting, *No. This can't be true. Surely you're not telling me we won't have the funds to purchase the tapestry.*

There was a long pause; neither woman spoke.

"I'm so sorry," Alex repeated.

"Oh, Alexandra, surely there are others who have contributed."

"Yes, of course, there are others."

"Will you be coming to Monsieur Bowman's opening Thursday?" This delivered with a note of cheerfulness.

"I'm leaving for London Thursday evening. I wish you both well."

"Thank you, Alexandra. The work at my gallery, this is the only thing saving my sanity now."

And what is to save my sanity? Alex wondered as she told Madame Genevoix once more how sorry she was, that she was sure everything would work out.

After she hung up, Alex sat staring at the phone for several minutes. Then she picked it up and dialed Alain Bourlet. She asked if they might meet for lunch.

At lunch, Alex explained that her major benefactor had pulled out. She was desperate for funds. Might he consider a donation from the trust?

Monsieur Bourlet scratched his white goatee, cleared his throat. "I've been entrusted to invest, to make wise financial decisions."

"Will you consider it?"

The man scratched his beard again and nodded, yet not with the enthusiasm Alex had hoped for.

She spent the rest of the afternoon and evening on the phone, successfully increasing several of the patrons' gifts, finding other smaller donors. But nothing near the amount promised by the Genevoix.

Early the following morning, Alain Bourlet called.

"I must apologize, Alex, but I'm afraid this contribution would not be a wise fiduciary decision. It has been difficult, separating my personal feelings from my professional. I hope you understand."

"Yes, Monsieur Bourlet. I appreciate your considering it." Alex paused. "How long will it take to liquidate my own investment account?"

"A good portion of it within a day or two. Are you sure this is what you want? The portfolio has done well, but there are a few investments I'd advise you to hold."

"Do it," Alex said.

Alex was furious when she hung up. She stood and paced the floor. Her own investments were nowhere near a fraction of the funds promised by the Genevoix. If she had known this was going to happen, she could have attempted to sell some of the paintings and sculptures she had inherited from Pierre. Everything was still in storage in Lyon. There was no way she could sell any of it on such short notice. She would call Simone. No, she would go down to Lyon. She would have to ask her mother-in-law for the money. Simone would help her.

She had never asked Simone for money. Her mother-in-law had always been generous, but, in truth, didn't have a great understanding of finances. Pierre had handled everything, and then as his health deteriorated he had turned his affairs over to trusted advisors.

Simone had never asked Alex about her plans to finance the acquisition of the tapestry, but Alex imagined she thought the funds for the tapestry would come from the Cluny itself, as if the museum had millions sitting around in petty cash.

Alex called her mother at home to tell her she would be leaving for Lyon that afternoon. It was now Wednesday, two days before the auction. She called Simone, but didn't want to explain her intentions over the phone. When she told her mother-in-law she would be visiting that afternoon, Simone replied, "How very thoughtful of you, Alexandra. I'm feeling rather lonely today. I knew you would call, but I know how busy you are and I never imagined you would come to Lyon. Thank you, dear, thank you." There was a catch in Simone's voice now, almost as if she might cry.

She had been doing so well, Alex thought—after Pierre's death, during their trip to Italy—but now, she sounded so emotionally fragile. Alex remembered it was months after her father's loss that her mother had done her real mourning, and even after Thierry's death, the truth of it hadn't hit Alex until weeks after the funeral.

It didn't occur to her until she was in the car on her way to Lyon why Simone had sensed that Alex would call today, when Alex herself didn't know until shortly before she picked up the phone. It had nothing to do with the tapestry. Today was Simone and Pierre's anniversary.

SHE ARRIVED IN Lyon late that afternoon. Marie prepared one of Pierre's favorite meals—*bœuf bourguignon*. They toasted him with a bottle of rare vintage Burgundy that had been in the cellar for years. Pierre had been saving it for a special occasion. Simone spoke of the day she and Pierre met when he came to the theatre and a mutual friend brought him backstage. "So many years ago," she said, her eyes shimmering. And then, for the first time since Pierre's death, Alex sat with her mother-in-law and held her hand as she cried.

The following morning they went for a short walk and returned to the apartment. Marie brought coffee and fresh brioches as Alex and Simone sat in the *salle de séjour*. Alex knew she would have to leave soon. It was a long drive to Paris, and she was scheduled to catch the shuttle for London that evening.

Alex spoke of Soleil, the one thing that always seemed to perk Simone up. They talked about Soleil's ballet classes, and Alex told Simone about the day she'd taken her daughter to the park to try out the new skates she'd received for her birthday.

"She's becoming a wonderful little artist," Simone added with a smile. "She showed me some of her drawings. Monsieur Bowman has been instructing her. A nice young man."

Alex nodded, searching for the right response. "He's been very kind to Soleil." She poured more coffee, stirred in milk, and added sugar, though she never took sugar with her coffee. She lifted a brioche from the tray and spread it with butter.

After a long silence, she said, "Perhaps you'll come visit us in Paris when I get back."

"Back?" Simone asked.

"From London. I'm going to London this evening for the auction."

"Oh, yes," Simone replied with a shake of her head. "Yes, I'd forgotten." She wiped a crumb from her lips, folded her napkin, and placed it on the table alongside her empty coffee cup.

Alex knew if she was to ask for the money she should do it now.

Simone gazed blankly about the room, and then with a wave of her thin arm and a deep sigh she said, "Look around this room. What do you see?"

Alex studied the room, not sure what Simone was asking. The art, the Aubusson, the Persian rugs, the antique furniture. "Beautiful art, beautiful furnishings," she answered.

Simone nodded. "Pierre and I enjoyed life . . . together . . . all the comforts and beauty we had. I know I should take some joy in life again, but—"

"It will come again," Alex offered hopefully.

Simone shook her head. "I'm an old woman. Perhaps I have had my life."

"Please, . . . Simone." Alex reached for her hand.

"Oh, I know I still have much to enjoy—you and Soleil. Do you know my own mother lived until she was ninety-seven? I could be around for some time," she said with a sad laugh. "I should look forward to watching Soleil grow into a beautiful young woman, as thoughtful as her mother."

Alex didn't feel particularly thoughtful. If only Simone knew the real reason she had come to Lyon.

"And perhaps, someday she will have a brother or a sister. I would hope for that . . . for both of you. Oh, I know they won't be mine in the sense that Soleil is—"

"Simone, you will always be *belle-mère, Grandmère*."

Marie came in to check on their coffee, refilling each of their cups. When she left, Simone said, "I know you must return to Paris. You're leaving this evening for London?"

"Yes."

Simone took in and released a deep breath and again her eyes moved slowly about the room. "The tapestry, Alexandra, do you think having it in your museum will bring you happiness? Perhaps for a while. A sense of accomplishment, surely." She picked up her cup and took a slow sip of coffee, then with moist eyes fixed on Alex, she said, "But true happiness comes from loving and, sometimes even more difficult, opening ourselves up and accepting love."

ALEX LEFT LYON without asking for the money for the tapestry. When she arrived in Paris, she went directly to the Cluny. She called her mother and told her to get out her party frock and Soleil's new birthday dress. They were going to Jake's opening at La Galerie Genevoix that evening.

32

JAKE SPENT WEDNESDAY evening, Thursday morning, and the early afternoon at the gallery, setting up the show. Matthew and Brian came over to help, along with another young man employed by the gallery. Madame Genevoix supervised, commenting on how pleased she was with Jake's work. Matthew strutted around, a big grin on his face as if this were his show.

"Are we gonna be famous now?" he asked Jake as they stood gazing at his angel portrait hanging on the large wall in the entry. "Never thought I'd sprout a pair of wings."

"Lookin' good." Jake couldn't help but smile himself.

After the paintings were hung and the lighting adjusted, Jake took a final look, feeling quite proud of his accomplishment. It was the best work he'd ever done. It would be a terrific show. Matthew had brought his camera and was taking shots for Jake's portfolio. Jake would send some photos home to his mother. He had invited her to fly over, but she'd decided the trip might be a bit much for her, and maybe Jake and Rebecca needed some time alone together.

He would be picking Rebecca up at the airport that afternoon. She'd originally planned to come in Friday morning, but had rescheduled so she could be there for his opening.

Just after three, he rented a car and drove out to the airport.

ALEX MADE A few more phone calls. She had collected
over one hundred forty thousand Euros in additional funds
since Madame Genevoix's call, a large part of this coming
from her own investments, a check that Alain Bourlet had
dropped off at the office that day. It appeared he had not completely liquidated her account. But even now, she had the
equivalent of over one million American dollars. A medieval
tapestry had never gone for that much.

She went home and packed a bag for her trip to London.
She would take an early-morning train to London, rather than
the 8:07 she had planned that evening. After rummaging
through her closet, she decided on a short, sleeveless, pale-
blue silk shift for Jake's opening that evening. She slipped it
on and stood before the full-length mirror on her closet door.
The dress fit snugly and showed a fair amount of leg. Sophisticated, but sexy.

Shoes? She opened the closet and pulled out a pair of
pumps, then considered a strappy pair of narrow, silver, very
high-heeled sandals. She seldom wore them because they were
rather uncomfortable, and she couldn't wear pantyhose, which
made her feel quite bare. But she slipped them on anyway and
stood tall and straight, her shoulders thrown back. Yes, just
right!

ALEX, HER MOTHER, and an excited Soleil took a cab to
La Galerie Genevoix. A large three-paneled painting hung in
the entry—an Annunciation scene with a beautiful young
black man as the angel Gabriel, an elegant long-necked Virgin, and a unicorn. It was done in a realistic style, the shadows
and light so brilliantly rendered that the forms nearly came to
life. It was very good, and it made Alex smile. The angel wore
dreadlocks. Alex felt as if she personally had been involved in
its creation, although she had never seen the work.

"Very nice," Sarah said and nodded.

"I want to see Monsieur Bowman," Soleil said.

As they entered the main exhibition room, Alex looked around, feeling an emotion that was a mixture of joy and pride. He had done it! The gallery was filled with the usual opening-night art crowd, many familiar faces—patrons, collectors, artists, people like Alex who loved art for the sake of art. She glanced into the atrium where waiters glided by with trays of drinks and hors d'oeuvres. Madame Genevoix knew how to do it right. But where was Jake?

"There he is," Soleil shouted. "Monsieur Bowman."

Alex looked across the room. Their eyes met and he smiled. So did she. He was delighted to see her and she was so glad she had decided to come. He walked toward them.

Soleil let go of her mother's hand and ran to Jake. "I am so happy to see you, Monsieur Bowman." The little girl reached out as Jake bent down on one knee to give her a hug.

"And I'm so happy to see you," he said. Jake looked up as Sarah and Alex approached. "And I'm very happy to see your mother and grandma." He stood and smiled at Alex again.

"A lovely show," Sarah said. "Congratulations."

"Thank you for coming."

Alex glanced around the room. "Your work, it's wonderful. I knew you could do it."

"Your being here means a lot to me, Alex." Then he turned to the woman standing next to him, a woman Alex hadn't even noticed when she saw him across the room. He had been standing alone. Hadn't he?

"Alex, I'd like you to meet Rebecca Garrett," he said. "Rebecca, I'd like you to meet Alexandra Pellier; her daughter, Soleil; and Alex's mother, Sarah Benoit."

"Oh yes, the tapestry lady," Rebecca said, reaching out for Alex's hand. Her touch was delicate and soft, the hand of a nurse. She smiled at Soleil, then took Sarah's hand.

Alex stood, stunned. The tapestry lady? Is this what she was—the tapestry lady? She tried to regain her composure. Could Rebecca see that Alex was about to fall apart? Yet what had Alex expected? She knew Rebecca was coming to Paris. Of course Jake's fiancée would show up for his opening night.

Alex tried to smile, to appear as if she were not examining every detail, every feature of this woman, Jake's fiancée. She was very pretty, with thick, natural, not-from-a-bottle auburn hair, green eyes, her skin pale and slightly freckled. She wore a pastel floral summer dress with a lightweight peach-colored jacket. Pretty and wholesome, the kind of woman who would make a good wife, a good mother. And petite, delicate, causing Alex to feel huge and awkward, towering over her.

Madame Genevoix approached, greeted Alex, and then whispered something to Jake, who excused himself. Soleil was attempting to drag her grandmother toward the atrium.

"Why don't you go ahead, Mom," Alex said, then asked Rebecca, "Are you enjoying your stay here in Paris?"

"I just arrived this afternoon," Rebecca said. "A little jet lag maybe. Not quite sure I can believe I'm really here yet. And the excitement of the show."

"You must be very proud."

"Proud?"

"Of Jake, his work."

"Oh, yes." Rebecca laughed. A little embarrassed, Alex thought, that she wasn't showing more enthusiasm. "His work has certainly been inspired since he's been here in Paris." And then, Alex could see, Rebecca was sizing her up too. Was she perhaps more than the tapestry lady?

"You and Jake have known each other for a long time," Rebecca said.

"Yes. We were students together here in Paris fourteen years ago."

"That was a special time in his life."

"Yes, mine too."

Rebecca glanced around the room, as if searching for an excuse to leave, to end this terribly awkward conversation. "Well, it's been nice meeting you," she said with a smile.

"Nice meeting you too, Rebecca. Enjoy your stay here in Paris."

"I'm sure I will. Thank you for coming this evening." Rebecca turned and walked off in the direction Jake had been escorted by Madame Genevoix. Alex stood for a moment in the middle of the room, then slowly she walked from painting to painting, stopping at each to examine Jake's beautiful work. She felt both involved and completely unattached as she moved about the gallery.

She walked into the atrium where people stood, visiting,

drinking wine and champagne, nibbling on hors d'oeuvres. She didn't see her mother and Soleil. A waiter walked by. Alex pulled a glass of wine off his tray and gulped it, draining half of it in a matter of seconds, and then she heard a voice from behind her.

"Alex, hi."

She turned. It was the Asian girl.

"Julianna Kimura," she said. "Remember me?"

Alex nodded and took a drink of wine, then another. What could she say? How could she not remember? "Alexandra Pellier," she replied, wondering if she was going to feel more and more uncomfortable as the evening progressed.

"Yes, I know who you are. So tomorrow is the big day—the auction."

"Yes." Alex put the wineglass to her lips, then realized it was empty.

Another waiter walked by balancing a tray of drinks. Julianna took two and handed one to Alex, who replaced her empty. "And tonight is Jake's big night," Julianna said.

"Yes, a very nice show."

Raising her glass in a toast, Julianna said. "To Jake. I predict big things for Jacob Bowman." Reluctantly, Alex too raised her glass. Julianna's eyes darted around the room. "So, what do you think?"

"Very nice."

"No, I mean the fiancée." Julianna motioned across the room as Jake and Rebecca entered. Jake's eyes again met Alex's. A small group had gathered around him and his attention shifted to a man standing in front of him.

"She's very pretty," Alex said.

"Pretty," Julianna said, "but they don't look like they go together. Look at them. Do they look happy? Does she look remotely thrilled to be here?"

Alex hesitated, took another gulp of wine. She looked over at Jake, who again gazed at her over the man's shoulder. Rebecca stood fidgeting with the strap on her purse. "No," Alex admitted.

"I knew it that night, which, by the way, was very innocent. I'd just dropped by to see why Jake hadn't been coming to the studio. He'd been working. He's been working very hard, which is quite evident tonight." Julianna looked at Alex as if expecting a reply or confirmation.

Alex nodded.

"He's very talented," Julianna said.

"Yes, he is."

"Nothing was going on between the two of us that night."

"You don't owe me an explanation, Julianna."

"Well, somebody needs to do something about it. I could see that night it wasn't Rebecca he was in love with. It was so obvious, the way he looked at you, the way you stood there saying nothing. Jake is so clearly in love with you. And you're in love with him. And both of you are incredibly stupid if you don't do something about it."

Alex couldn't think of an appropriate reply. She swallowed the last of her wine. "I'd like to take a look around."

"Good luck," Julianna said. "I hope you get that tapestry tomorrow."

"Thanks, Julianna."

Alex wandered off by herself and walked through the gallery, stopping to look at each of Jake's paintings once more. Yes, Julianna was right—big things from Jacob Bowman.

Alex got another glass of wine, then found a waiter with hors d'oeuvres, realizing three glasses of wine on an empty stomach wasn't a good idea. When she raised the glass to her lips, she was suddenly aware she was shaking, not just her hand, but her entire body. Was Julianna right? Did Jake really love her, not Rebecca? And was she so incredibly stupid she couldn't see the truth? Or was she so stupid she was unable to do anything about it? What should she do? March right up to him, right here in front of hundreds of people, Rebecca included, and say, "I love you, Jake, and you love me, and we should be together?"

"Mama, Mama."

Alex looked down and saw Soleil holding her grandmother's hand.

"I saw all the beautiful paintings, and I got some punch and cookies."

Alex smiled. She could see from the red mustache.

"Is Monsieur Bowman a famous artist now?" the child asked.

"Well on his way, Sunny. Big things for Jacob Bowman, I predict."

Alex felt a hand on her shoulder. She turned to see Madame Genevoix. The woman held a champagne flute in one hand. "I just want to thank you," she said, "for bringing Jacob to me. I know the show will do well. Even tonight we've had an enthusiastic response. We've already sold two of the larger paintings." The woman was almost giddy, a little drunk, actually, Alex thought.

"Wonderful," Alex said. "I'm so pleased to hear that."

"Well, yes, yes, very good." The woman reached down and patted Soleil on the head. "And what do you think?"

"I'm very pleased to hear that too," the child replied.

Alex, her mother, and Soleil walked once more together through the gallery, visiting with several other acquaintances. Alex looked around for Julianna, but didn't see her anywhere. When they were ready to leave, Sarah suggested they congratulate Jake again on the success of his opening. Jake stood across the room, a small crowd gathered around him. Rebecca was standing off to one side, looking as if she couldn't wait to get out of there. Alex glanced at her watch. "We probably should get Soleil home to bed. And I'd better get some sleep if I'm going to catch that early six-thirty-seven train to London."

Outside the gallery, Alex hailed a cab. She got in with her mother and Soleil. The little girl was asleep within minutes.

"Quite an exciting evening," Sarah said.

"Yes, quite." They sat without further conversation. Was Julianna right? Alex wondered. And what about Simone? She said true happiness could be found only through love, that even if Alex got the tapestry for her museum it would only make her happy for a short time. There would be another challenge after that, and then another. A constant search for happiness and fulfillment. And what if she didn't get the tapestry? She thought of the young Adèle Le Viste. All along, Alex felt that in some way she had been chosen to reunite the tapestry with the others in the Cluny, that in this she would somehow give Adèle and her lover another chance. But had she completely misinterpreted why the events of the past few months had taken place? Events that might be little more than a series of coincidences? Was Adèle trying to tell Alex to take another look at her own life? Was it Alex, not Adèle Le Viste, who was being given a second chance?

"Merci," Alex told the driver when they arrived at the apartment. She dug into her evening bag and pulled out the fare, then handed it to the driver. She picked Soleil up in her arms as Sarah held the door. They started toward the building. Then, abruptly, Alex turned. *"Attendez,"* she shouted at the driver, who had just started to pull back onto the street. Alex ran over and lightly kicked the car door, Soleil still in her arms. *"S'il vous plaît,"* she shouted, *"attendez."*

The man turned and stared, then rolled down the window.

"S'il vous plaît, attendez."

The driver nodded and pulled over to park.

Alex looked at her mother, who was shaking her head. They walked into the building and went up to the apartment in the elevator. Alex put Sunny to bed, then got her briefcase and the bag she had packed for her trip. She dumped the contents of her small evening bag on the bed, picked out several items, and stuffed them in her purse.

Her mother was standing outside her door.

"I'm leaving for London," Alex said.

"I didn't realize there was a train this late."

"I have some things to take care of first."

"Things?" Sarah smiled.

Alex kissed her mother on the cheek. "I'll call."

"Good luck."

"Thanks, Mom."

The cab driver waited down on the street in a no-parking zone. Alex got in. "La Galerie Genevoix," she said.

The driver looked back, snuffed his cigarette out in the ash-tray and they took off.

When they arrived at the gallery Alex paid the driver, but didn't wait for change. *Am I crazy?* Alex asked herself, as she walked up to the entrance. What was she going to tell Jake when she found him?

The gallery crowd had thinned, though there were still small clusters of people milling about. Alex walked through the first room, the second, then the third. She carried her bag in one hand, her briefcase in the other, her purse strapped over her shoulder, and must have looked ridiculous. Jake was nowhere in the building. Neither was Rebecca. Then she saw Madame Genevoix in a corner chatting with a tall, thin man. Alex walked over and the woman introduced him, but Alex barely heard the words.

"Jake?" she asked.

"I'm afraid he's left. Mademoiselle Garrett was very tired from her travels."

Alex turned and left the gallery. She walked along the river. She was headed toward the Latin Quarter, Rue Monge where Jake lived. Yes, she was crazy. He'd probably left to be alone with Rebecca, to celebrate their reunion, his opening night. What was Alex going to do—burst in on them? Pound down the door, screaming, "You can't marry Rebecca"? But the image of Jake and Rebecca standing together in the gallery came back to her. Julianna was right. They didn't belong together. They didn't even look good together. And the image of Jake, smiling at her as she entered the gallery, as if she and Jake were the only two people in the world.

She moved along the river, through Place Saint Michel, down the boulevard, past Saint Germain, on to Rue des Ecoles. Maybe she should call a cab. It was probably at least two miles to Jake's hotel, not a particularly good idea to walk alone late at night, although the streets were well lit and there was still a fair amount of traffic moving up and down the boulevard. But her shoes—those stupid, skinny, strappy, high-heeled sandals were the most uncomfortable things she'd ever worn. She pulled them off, then stood on the corner until a cab stopped and picked her up.

She arrived on Jake's street, paid the driver, got out, and walked into his building. She climbed the stairs, barefooted, bag in tow, her shoes and briefcase in one hand, and stood at his door. Then, as if someone else, someone much braver and much more sure of herself and her feelings, were inhabiting her body, Alex knocked.

There was no answer. She knocked again. Still no answer. Were they inside? Making love? Or had they gone out somewhere to celebrate? She knocked again. Still no answer. She turned and started down the steps. She was too late. Why hadn't she done something sooner? Before Rebecca arrived in Paris. She felt the tears well up in her eyes. She was a complete and utter fool. She sat on the steps, opened her purse, pulled out a tissue, and dabbed at her eyes. After a few moments, she stood, walked back to the door, and knocked again. "Jake," she shouted, "it's Alex. I have to talk to you." Still no answer. Surely no one was inside. Jake would answer if he heard her, frantic, pounding on his door late at night. She sat again. She would wait for him. She would sit and wait until he returned.

She must have fallen asleep. When she woke, it was half past four. Had Jake returned? Had he and Rebecca walked right over Alex, not even noticed her slumped there on the steps? She laughed at the thought. Had she sunk so low? Like a drunken bum, sleeping it off on the rough, slivery steps of a cheap hotel. She stood, brushed herself off, and readjusted her dress, which had twisted around her waist. She could still go to the auction. The train wouldn't leave for another two hours. She put on her shoes, picked up her bag, briefcase, and purse, and walked down to the street and hailed a cab.

At the terminal, she bought her ticket, got a cup of coffee, and went to the restroom. She changed her clothes and shoes, washed her face, and reapplied her makeup. After attempting to fix her hair, she went back out to the terminal, through security and passport control, and entered the boarding area.

A loud voice announced that 9005 was now boarding, and Alex followed the crowd onto the train. She pulled out her ticket and checked her seat assignment. The train was full, people pressing up against one another as she moved through the first car. She walked through the second car, checking her ticket once more. As she replaced it in the outside pocket of her purse, she looked up. Her heart took a sudden leap. There was Jake, smiling at her.

33

ALEX STOOD IN the aisle, paralyzed.

"Good morning, Alex."

"Jake? What are you doing here?" Juggling her bags, dropping one in the aisle, she reached up and attempted to comb through her hair with her fingers. She must look awful, yet he gazed up at her, still smiling, staring at her as if she were some kind of vision.

A large man with a small bag pushed, trying to get through. Alex didn't move. "What are you doing here?" she asked again.

"This *is* the train to London?" Jake answered.

"*Pardon,*" the large man said in a deep voice as he pushed again, forcing Alex over in the aisle against the seat. Jake grabbed her bag, motioned her to sit, then pulled her by the hand into the seat next to him as a crowd of people moved down the aisle.

He drew her closer and kissed her. And she kissed him. They kissed for a long time as the train jerked and started to move out of the terminal.

She was shaking, then laughing. "What the hell are you doing here? And was that a hello kiss, or a good-bye-Alex-I'll-never-see-you-again kiss?" She reached out and grasped his arm, attempting to compose herself. "Why?" She shook her head, trying to shake out her confusion. "Why are you here?" She released his arm and glanced around the train. "And where is Rebecca?"

"At her hotel in Paris."

The train swished along the track. A family in the seat in front of them—a father, mother, and small child—settled noisily into their seats.

"In Paris? The day after your fiancée arrives, you're taking off for London?"

"We called it off."

"Called what off?"

"The engagement. We've probably been breaking up ever since I made the decision to come to Paris. It was a mutual decision."

"You left her alone in Paris?"

"Matthew and Julianna are going to take her out this weekend, show her the sights. She won't be alone."

Alex stared at him. "Why did she come over if you're no longer together?"

"We needed to talk. And she had that nonrefundable ticket." He smiled. "And then . . . last night at the opening . . . Rebecca could see . . . she said it was obvious."

"Obvious? What?"

"That it was over."

"You're going to London?" Alex only dared to believe what this might mean. "Why?"

"I thought I might take in an auction. Your mother said you'd left for London hours ago. I was surprised when I saw you walk onto the train."

"*You* were surprised. You talked to my mother?"

"Where have you been?" Jake asked.

A young woman stopped in the aisle, examined her ticket, and held it up to Jake and Alex, pointing at the seat number. Jake reached over and pulled the ticket out of the pocket on Alex's purse, then exchanged it with the one the woman was holding in her hand. *"Ma femme,"* he said, *"s'il vous plaît?"*

The woman looked startled, but examined the ticket Jake had handed her. She glanced at Jake, then Alex. She smiled, shook her head, and walked away, fanning herself with Alex's ticket.

"Your woman? Huh?" Alex asked. "And we're on our way to London?"

Jake nodded.

The family had settled in. The mother pulled out a brown paper bag. The scent of citrus began to fill the stale air. She handed an orange section to the child who was standing up in the seat, staring back at Jake and Alex.

Alex's heart thumped. Her body felt weird and detached and silly—like she might burst out into uncontrollable giggles at any moment. She stared across the aisle, out the window. The early-morning sun glowed on the buildings as they moved through the city. She looked at him to make sure he was still there. Yes, he was here with her, and they were on their way to London. Together.

"Tell me again," Alex said, smiling at the child, then turning to Jake, her expression serious now. "Tell me again, Jake, why are you here?"

The mother reached up. *"Pardonez-nous,"* she said as she settled the child back into the seat.

"I thought you might need me," Jake said.

"Need you?"

"Yes, Alex, 'need me.' Some people do need other people. It isn't considered a weakness by everyone."

"No, I suppose that's a belief held by some." Her lips slowly moved toward a smile.

"Where were you?" he asked. "Where have you been all night?"

She hesitated a moment before answering. "Sitting on the steps of your hotel on Rue Monge."

He couldn't hide his surprise.

"I wanted to tell you something," she said.

"What did you want to tell me?"

"I wanted to tell you . . . I wanted to tell you I love you."

"But I wasn't home?"

She shook her head.

"So you couldn't tell me?"

She shook her head once more, as tears slipped down her cheeks.

"And do you still?"

"Yes," she said. "I love you."

He cupped her face in his hand and stared into her eyes as if he could see deep within her. "I love you too, Alex." He wiped the tear from her cheek. "It came to me so clearly last night. There I was—star of the show, center stage. But I knew it wasn't complete. I knew when I saw you . . ." He kissed her again, then whispered, "I promise, Alex, I will never let you go again."

THEY SAT ON the train for the next few hours, holding each other, kissing and caressing as they had done years ago in the TV room in her pension in Paris when they were students. They talked about the auction of the tapestry. Alex told him about Martinson and Paul following her from the convent, how both were intent on claiming the tapestry. Jake told her about Gaston Jadot, the possibility that the old man had somehow been involved in the Archbishop's knowledge of the tapestry. Alex said it didn't matter. She told him about losing the money from the Genevoix, and Jake said he knew; he wished there was something he could do about it. Alex said she was hopeful she could still get the tapestry, that she had far more than any tapestry had ever brought at auction. Then she told him what Simone had said about true happiness.

"Could you be happy even if someone else got the tapestry?" Jake asked.

Alex hesitated. She told him about Adèle le Viste—something she had shared with no one else—how she felt at times the young woman was speaking to her. Not in words, there were never words, only a feeling, a calm that would come over her. "I always thought she was trying to tell me that despite all the obstacles, I would get the tapestry, that in some way this would reunite Adèle and her lover. But then, for the past few days, it's come to me. Perhaps I have been misinterpreting the reasons for what has been happening, if there are reasons why things happen. Is it Adèle who has made me take another look at my life? If there is a purpose to what has happened in the past few months, was it not for Adèle, but for me—to realize what true happiness is?"

"And what is it?"

"I feel happy now, here with you."

"But if you don't get the tapestry?"

Alex looked out the window into the dark tunnel. They would soon be in London. She turned back to Jake. "I don't want to imagine that, not yet."

THEY ARRIVED IN London at Waterloo International at eight forty-six A.M. The auction of Italian and French Furniture and Tapestries was scheduled to begin at ten A.M. The unicorn tapestry was lot number 233, and Alex said it wouldn't go on sale until late afternoon, but she wanted to arrive on time, check out the crowd, find a seat at the back of the auction room so she could keep track of who was there and who was bidding. They took a cab into the city shortly after nine.

Jake had never been to an art auction in a prestigious auction house. He'd been to cattle auctions with his dad years ago in Montana when he was a kid, and he'd loved to go then. As he explained about Montana cattle auctions, Jake dramatized, trying to imitate the fast-paced rhythm of the auctioneer's voice. Alex laughed, which made him feel good. Although she had seemed relaxed on the train after they were together, as soon as they pulled into London, she appeared again overcome with a nervous apprehension.

Jake told Alex how he remembered sitting with his dad, not even aware he'd bought anything. Later, when he'd asked, Jake learned his father had bought several hundred head of cattle. He asked his dad how he'd done that without Jake even realizing, and his dad had raised his hand and just barely touched his Stetson to demonstrate.

"Is that how it's done here?" Jake asked Alex. "If I accidentally scratch my nose at the wrong moment, will I have bought a priceless unicorn tapestry?"

Alex laughed. "Oh, Jake, will you? Buy the tapestry for me?"

"If it would make you happy, if I could, yes, I would."

She smiled. "It works very similar to those cattle auctions back in Montana. Just like that cattle auctioneer, who was probably well aware of your daddy and other ranchers who'd be in a position to buy, Sotheby's will be familiar with potential buyers—dealers, museum representatives, collectors. On a priceless work such as the seventh unicorn tapestry, they generally know beforehand who the primary bidders will be. So, yes, a bid could be made with a mere touch of the hat, a nod of the head."

"Then you know who the primary bidders will be?"

"The Cluny, of course."

Jake nodded.

"Ferguson from Victoria and Albert, Martinson from The Cloisters. I'm sure with all the publicity there will be a slew of private collectors and dealers, Paul Westerman among them."

"Ah, yes, Paul."

Alex seemed to relax again as they talked, but then, as they turned onto New Bond Street, where Sotheby's auction house was located, she looked out the window and Jake could hear her taking deep breaths.

"You okay?" he asked.

Alex laughed. "Just putting in my final prayer to Sainte Adèle."

The cab pulled up in front of the building. "Kiss me one more time," she said. "Jake, please, kiss me once more."

He pulled her close and kissed her and didn't stop until the cab driver cleared his throat for the second time.

They walked into the building. A woman in a dark suit, sitting at a desk off to their left, greeted them. Alex smiled and nodded. Jake said, "Good morning." They walked through a wide corridor, past a small tearoom, up the stairs to the second level.

Because of the publicity surrounding the auction, the sale was ticketed. Alex had reserved two. She'd explained on the train that she thought Madame Demy might want to attend. The Director had declined, not particularly surprising Alex because the woman had taken an inexplicably detached role in the discovery from the very beginning.

"Maybe she sees this as your acquisition," Jake said. "Maybe she wants you to take full credit when the tapestry is hung in the Cluny."

"I'm not sure," Alex had replied. "She's always been rather guarded with her feelings."

They entered the main gallery through two enormous wooden doors with shiny brass knobs. Jake signed up at a reception desk in a lobby just outside the salesroom and got a paddle with a number on it. Alex had explained that, because it was ticketed entrance only, he would have to establish an account, which he did by presenting a single form of identification—surprising Jake by how easy it was to gain entry.

"You're all set to bid now," Alex said. As an established bidder, she was not required to fill out the registration card.

Just before ten, they walked into the gallery where the auction would take place. It was an unexpectedly small room, well lit, with a high decorative skylight and track lighting running the length and width of the room on both sides. Three wooden podiums stood at the front of the room—two small ones equipped with computer desks and a larger, more ornate one that looked almost like a pulpit, where, Alex explained, the auctioneer would soon appear. A long, high, three-person podium ran along the right aisle. Folding chairs were arranged in even rows, covering the floor. Alex placed her briefcase and bag on two chairs toward the back.

A cacophony of light chatter, a mixture of conversations from several small groups, filled the room, an undecipherable blending of several different languages. Most of the men wore business suits, as did many of the women. Some were dressed more casually, a few more formally, in sparkling jewels—it was too hot for furs. None of the women wore those large hats like Jake had seen in the movies. It didn't appear Paul had arrived yet, and Jake didn't recognize any of the people he had met at the tapestry exhibition at the Grand Palais in Paris.

"Martinson," Alex whispered and nodded toward the door.

Dr. Martinson walked over. "*Bonjour,* Madame Pellier," he said, "and Monsieur . . ." His puzzled expression told Jake the man did not remember his name, maybe not even Jake himself.

Jake held out his hand. "Jake Bowman. We met in Paris, then again at the Convent of Sainte Blandine."

"Ah, yes," Martinson said with little interest, although he did shake hands. He looked at his watch. "The auction will soon begin."

Alex nodded and smiled. "Perhaps we should take our seats."

Martinson stared at Alex for a moment, then said, *"Oui. Bonne chance."* He smiled, then turned and walked toward the middle of the room where he found a single empty seat.

"Bonne chance?" Alex whispered to Jake as they sat. "He'll need more than *bonne chance*. There's no way Sainte Adèle is going to allow Martinson to get hold of that tapestry." Alex smiled and so did Jake.

The auctioneer, in dark suit and red striped tie, a tall, angular man, mounted the rostrum. It was exactly ten A.M. The gavel fell and the sale commenced.

The first few lots were antique Italian furniture, purchased mostly by a few gentlemen sitting toward the front of the room. Alex told Jake they were all dealers. He followed along in the catalogue, which she'd handed him shortly after they sat. The auctioneer pointed here and there. "Ah, yes, the gentleman on the aisle wearing the paisley tie . . . do I hear thirty thousand pounds . . . will you cover the bid, Lord Wilmington?"

Jake's eyes bounced back and forth from catalogue to auctioneer and about the room, in an attempt to determine exactly who was making each bid, how close the final prices were coming to those listed in the catalogue. He glanced up now and then at the electronic board hanging above the auctioneer. Numbers flashed on the board, tracking the bidding price in pounds, dollars, and Euros.

Sometimes the bidding appeared to be between just a couple of bidders. Other items stirred up a bit of a contest between several different people in various locations in the room. When bidding slowed, the auctioneer would add a little interesting descriptive banter to get the crowd going: "For such an excellent example, this lovely seventeenth-century Italian carved giltwood mirror . . . note the finely carved scrolling acanthus leaves, surely I hear six thousand for this fine work . . ." At times bids seemed to be made, then raised within seconds. Often, Jake couldn't determine who had put in the final bid before the auctioneer lowered his gavel and moved on to the next item.

Just before noon, the auctioneer announced a break. The auction would resume at two-thirty P.M.

Alex and Jake left the building for lunch. Alex was too nervous to eat, although she ordered a sandwich and sat staring at it as Jake quickly finished his. She suggested they take a walk. They spoke little, other than commenting on what they saw in store windows—jewelry, designer clothes, antique furniture, and art prints. Jake sensed this was what Alex wanted; she did not want to talk about the tapestry or anything else of importance. There were so many things he wanted to tell her. He felt exuberant just being with her, but he remained silent about these thoughts and feelings that were shouting inside him. Just after two they headed back to the auction house.

As they entered the building, a familiar, gravelly voice called out. "Jake, Alex." They turned as Paul Westerman approached, panting, out of breath.

Alex gave him a hug. The two men shook hands.

"You're too late," Jake joked, cuffing Paul on the shoulder. "Alex and I bought the tapestry this morning."

"You and Alex?" Paul grinned. "Is this a group thing?"

"Not a group thing." Alex looped her arm through Jake's. "Just the two of us."

"The two of you?" Paul's smile broadened. He looked at Jake. "The two of you? Together at last, after all these years?" He glanced over at Alex.

"Yes," she said and smiled. "Together at last."

"Well, great," Paul said. "That's great," he repeated as they walked through the hall toward the stairs to the second floor. "I hate to take away from your obvious happiness by pulling that tapestry out from under you." He laughed.

"We'll see," Alex replied with a grin.

They entered the auction hall and Alex and Jake resumed their positions. Paul stood at the back of the now packed room. It appeared several others had joined the group since the morning session and the small gallery was now overflowing. Alex pointed out reporters from Paris and Lyon, standing in the back.

Once more, the auctioneer lowered his gavel. At two-thirty P.M. the auction continued. For the first hour, the remainder of the furnishings and decorative objects were sold. At about three-thirty the first tapestry, a historical narrative fragment depicting a hunting scene, came on the block. It was a piece measuring, according to the catalogue, eight-foot-six by five-foot-seven, a portion of a much larger tapestry, obviously worn and faded. The catalogue noted extensive restoration and reweaving. It went for just over nine thousand pounds, the gavel price falling about midway in the estimated price range.

It was followed by a Flemish historical narrative, then a late Louis XIV verdure landscape tapestry. As Jake watched and listened, it became obvious how well preserved, bright, and vivid the colors of the unicorn tapestry were, how wonderfully preserved and just how rare and valuable such a piece truly was. Those on the block now were often mere fragments of larger pieces. Even those that were complete tapestries were generally faded, and restorations and reweavings were always noted in the catalogue. Jake flipped the pages and glanced at Alex. The unicorn tapestry was now just three lots away. He took Alex's hand. She smiled, but he could feel the tension in her tight grip.

When the Aubusson listed just before the unicorn tapestry came on the block, Alex released his hand and kissed him lightly on the cheek. The gavel fell once more. And then, the large, beautiful red tapestry appeared. There was an audible gasp from the crowd.

It was evident now how perfect it was, how miraculously preserved, how beautifully designed and woven. Jake realized that until just a few days ago, when the tapestry went on display at Sotheby's, no one in the crowd had seen it. Only he and Alex. She looked at him and smiled, almost relaxed, as if she were thinking the same thoughts, as if the appearance of the tapestry, created by the union of two people who had loved one another completely, could bring a feeling of calm to one man and one woman over five hundred years later.

The bidding began slowly, starting out well below the catalogue's lowest estimated price. The auctioneer, composed through the earlier part of the auction, seemed visibly shaken by the beauty of the work, and stumbled in his attempts to describe it. Didn't it speak for itself?

The initial bids came from the group in front, those Alex had earlier identified as dealers. When the bids approached the midlevel of the estimated prices, the museum people, at least those Jake had remembered meeting, those Alex had pointed out earlier, began to nod and raise hands and paddles to place their bids. It was getting serious now. The auctioneer had ceased his descriptive banter. "Yes, I have two hundred thousand now from the Met, Dr. Martinson. Do I hear two twenty?"

Alex raised her hand.

"Madame Pellier from the Cluny." The auctioneer acknowledged her bid with the slightest nod and smile. "Do I hear two thirty?"

A bid came from the back of the room. Jake looked back and guessed, from the grin, that it had come from Paul.

"We have two thirty now, ladies and gentlemen, do I hear two forty?"

Martinson nodded.

"Ah, yes, two forty from the Met. Two fifty?"

Alex raised her hand.

"Two fifty from the Cluny. Two sixty?"

The bidding continued, picking up speed. A bid from the man from the Victoria and Albert in London, at two sixty, then Martinson at two seventy, Paul at two eighty, then Alex, two ninety. A bid again from someone in the front of the room. As Alex had told him, the auctioneer was well aware of those bidding, addressing them now by name—no *man in the paisley tie,* or *lady on the aisle.* The bids moved quickly, soon reaching three hundred sixty thousand, the amount listed as high estimate in the catalogue. Jake knew from what Alex had told him that she had the equivalent of just over a million American dollars. A tapestry had never gone at auction for anywhere near that amount. He knew, in British pounds, adding on the buyer's premium, Alex could afford to go as high as five hundred sixty thousand pounds.

There was a bid coming in from the aisle now, a middle-aged bald man, a representative, as Alex had explained earlier, of the auction house, placing bids for someone who was bidding by phone. This somewhat reduced the theatrics, the drama of the live bidding, not being able to see or determine who was placing the bid.

"We have three seventy," the auctioneer announced. "Do I hear three eighty?"

Martinson nodded, and Jake thought he heard him grunt.

"Three ninety?" The auctioneer looked at Alex, then glanced to the back of the room. "Yes, Mr. Westerman at three ninety. Will you cover the bid?" The man's eyes moved to Martinson, then Alex. The number of bidders had thinned considerably and the auctioneer was well aware. He glanced at the man representing the phone bidder. The man nodded. "We have four hundred now," the auctioneer announced. "Four hundred thousand. Do I hear four ten?"

Martinson waved.

"Four ten. Will you cover that, Madame Pellier?"

Alex nodded.

"Four hundred twenty from the Cluny. Four thirty? Four hundred thirty thousand, Mr. Westerman?"

Jake looked back at Paul who smiled and shook his head. He'd dropped out. It was now just Martinson, Alex, and the mysterious phone bidder.

"Four twenty now. Do I hear four thirty?"

Again, a grunt and wave from Martinson.

The bidding bounced from Alex to Martinson to the phone bidder, until it reached five hundred twenty thousand.

Jake knew they were getting close; he knew Alex couldn't go much further.

"Five hundred thirty?"

Alex raised her hand. She was a pale, almost translucent white, perhaps truly aware for the first time that she might lose the tapestry.

"Five hundred thirty from the Cluny. Will you cover, Dr. Martinson?"

"Five thirty-five," Martinson grunted, reducing the increment by half. Did this mean they were getting to the final bid? Jake wondered.

"Five forty?" the auctioneer looked to the aisle. The man in the aisle nodded. The auctioneer did also. "I have five forty."

With her left hand, Alex touched Jake's arm. Her hand was shaking violently, though when she raised her right hand, it appeared firm and steady. "Five forty-five."

"Five hundred forty-five thousand pounds from the Cluny." He looked once more to the aisle, then to Martinson. "Will the Met cover?"

"Five fifty," Martinson said, not quite a grunt.

"Five fifty-five?" the auctioneer asked, glancing again to the aisle. Jake looked over too. The man seemed to be conferring with the client, speaking into his headset. He nodded.

"Will the Cluny cover?"

"Five sixty," Alex came back.

The auctioneer looked to Martinson, who sat stiff in his seat. "Five sixty-five?"

Martinson nodded, then looked back at Alex, who sat staring up at the tapestry.

Jake knew she was done.

A hush filled the room and it seemed several long seconds before the auctioneer said, "Do I have a cover?" He glanced over at the representative in the aisle. No response. Had the phone bidder also dropped out? The auctioneer looked at Alex, who sat frozen. She did not respond.

"All done?" the auctioneer asked.

Finally, "Five seventy," from the aisle, the unidentified bidder through his representative.

"Will the Met cover?"

Martinson sat, looking around the room, as if somewhere hidden he could discover who was bidding against him. Jake wasn't sure if he was out of money or just irritated. Long seconds passed.

Then Jake did something that even he couldn't believe. He raised his paddle high, like some amateur bidder. He raised his paddle as the auctioneer looked down in disbelief. Alex turned and stared at Jake.

"Five seventy-five," he croaked.

34

AND THEN, EVERYTHING seemed to Jake as if it moved in slow motion. All eyes in the room turned to him as he sat, his paddle extended like the Statue of Liberty holding her flame. Alex stared at him, her expression moving from shock to amazement to delight. The auctioneer announced, in a voice that sounded like an old-fashioned phonograph record playing on slow speed, "I have five hundred seventy-five thousand, ladies and gentlemen, from the man in the brown jacket at the back of the room."

Alex touched Jake's arm once more, and he heard the auctioneer, speaking now in a normal voice coming from a real person, "Will the Met cover that bid, Dr. Martinson?"

It didn't surprise Jake when Martinson offered five eighty, and the bidding continued, with new momentum, bouncing back and forth again like a Ping-Pong match between the unknown phone bidder and Martinson.

"Five ninety."

"Six hundred."

"Six ten."

The bidding slowed down as the numbers soared to eight

hundred fifty thousand pounds. Martinson pulled a handkerchief from his breast pocket and wiped his forehead. "Eight hundred sixty," he said.

The phone bidder covered with an offer of eight hundred seventy.

It was quite obvious Martinson was getting near his final bid. The back of his head was damp with sweat, his hair curling into little swirls. Jake looked at Alex, who sat erect in her chair, her expression now unreadable. The phone bidder he could not see.

Martinson put in a bid of eight hundred seventy-two thousand. His opponent came back with eight seventy-three.

"Will the Met cover?"

Total silence from the room, as if everyone were holding their breath. Moments passed. The auctioneer looked down at Martinson. "Fair warning . . . final bid?" He raised his gavel. Not a sound from the crowd. "All done?"

Martinson rose and stomped out of the room. The auctioneer announced, "Selling at eight hundred seventy-three thousand pounds," as he lowered the gavel.

The beautiful unicorn tapestry had sold for eight hundred seventy-three thousand pounds, just over one and a half million dollars, to an unknown bidder.

Jake glanced at Alex to see if she was ready to leave. She sat stiff in her chair, staring straight ahead. The auction continued, the auctioneer appearing drained of energy as he attempted to sell the next tapestry, which drew little interest or excitement from those still in the gallery. When the next item came up, Alex nodded at Jake, picked up her bag and briefcase, and, without speaking, they left the hall. Reporters had gathered outside.

"Madame Pellier," one of them shouted, "are you disappointed the Cluny was unable to obtain the unicorn tapestry?"

"Yes, of course, I'm disappointed," Alex said in a voice so calm and controlled it surprised Jake.

"Do you really think it's a seventh piece to the set in the Cluny?" a voice from the crowd.

"Who do you think purchased it?" another voice shouted.

"A private collector who I'm sure will wish to remain

anonymous." Alex looped her arm through Jake's and they pushed through the crowd. Jake looked around for Paul, but didn't see him. "Let's get out of here," Alex whispered.

They moved quickly down New Bond Street. Alex looked out toward the street. Jake guessed she was looking for a cab, but they kept walking. Neither spoke for several blocks. He loosened his tie, pulled it off, and stuffed it in his pocket.

"Let's go get something to eat," Alex said. "I'm starving."

"Sure," Jake replied.

They walked until they found a pub. It wasn't until they were inside sitting at a table and had each ordered a beer and fish and chips that Alex asked, "What were you doing back there?" She didn't look angry or upset, just curious.

"My bid?"

She nodded.

"I have some savings. I sold two paintings. If I was doing the math correctly, converting the American dollars, the Euros to British pounds, I thought . . . well, I thought together, with what you raised, with my money . . . well, together we could buy the tapestry."

She smiled. "You're still a little crazy. Aren't you?"

He smiled too, then nodded.

The bartender delivered their beers. Alex took a sip, emitted a little moaning sound.

"Are you going to be okay?" Jake asked.

Alex took another drink. "I'm not sure right now. It may take a while."

"In shock?"

"Not really. I know what happened. I know we didn't get it."

"Who did?"

"Like I told the reporter, a private collector, someone who might just hang it on the wall and admire it. Beauty for the sake of beauty."

"Then you don't think it's another museum, a dealer or investor who will lock it away in a vault?"

"No. A museum would want to publicize the acquisition, make the public aware. An investor, I'm not sure. But for some reason, I know it went to someone who will cherish the beauty and creativity."

"I like that idea."

Alex nodded and took another sip of beer. She stared down at her mug. Music played lightly in the background, a woman singing a ballad in a low voice, nearly drowned out by the chatter of a group of men playing a game of darts in the back of the pub. The smell of fried food wafted in the air.

"It was strange," Alex said, "sitting there, the tapestry on the block. A feeling came once more—Adèle was there, then even the *tapissier.* And you"—she looked up at Jake—"and me. And I knew then, even if we lost it, we would never lose Adèle, the *tapissier,* each other, that somehow their love, their creation will always be a part of *us* . . . is that terribly strange?"

"No," Jake said. "I had that feeling too."

"I'm going to be okay. Disappointed. You know how much I wanted the tapestry. But I'm going to be okay." She took Jake's hand, held it to her lips, and kissed it. "Thank you for coming to London. Thank you for bidding on the tapestry. Thank you, Jake, for everything."

"I love you, Alex."

They sat staring at each other for several moments. Then Alex said, "Will you stay with me tonight? Will you stay here in London with me?"

"*With* you?"

"*With* me."

"This isn't some kind of consolation prize? Girl loses tapestry? Girl substitutes boy?"

"No." Alex said, stroking his hand. "This is something I've wanted for a long time, long before the tapestry."

THEY PAID THE tab and left the pub before their meal arrived. At the nearest hotel, on Albemarle Street, they rode up to their room holding hands in the elevator. Alex was so cold she shivered, yet her hand grew warm as he tightened his grip on hers.

He was nervous too—she could tell by the way he grasped her hand, as if she might disappear if he let go, the way he fumbled as he put the key in the door. They entered, dropped their bags, and stared at each other for several moments. She kissed him. On the neck first, then the chin, rough with his late-afternoon stubble.

"Maybe I should shave," he said.

"No, no, no," she whispered, her fingers pressed to his lips. She kissed him again, on the mouth now, her hands moving through his hair, down his face, his neck. He pulled her close, their kisses deep, long, and slow. His hands moved over the pearl buttons on her blouse. He unhooked her bra, slipped the straps off her shoulders and ran his fingers over her breasts, sending a surge of heat coursing through her. She clutched the buttons on his shirt, working them undone, then pushed his jacket off his shoulders.

He carried her to the bed, and slowly they finished undressing each other. Then, as bright shafts of late-afternoon sun fell into the room through the louvered shutters, they made love for the first time. And she felt her senses, distinct and different, and then together, culminating in their union, also come alive for the very first time. The taste of him. His smell—a mixture of soap and sweat and something so uniquely Jake it made her shudder. The texture of the dark, coarse hair on his chest, the feel of the muscles, tight and firm along his neck, his shoulder, his arm. She looked up into his eyes and felt lost in the depth of them, yet so very safe. She guided him inside her as she lay beneath him. His eyes were open, looking at her as he entered. And then, the sweet low sound of his voice. "I love you, Alex."

She closed her eyes and the sensation of him inside her intensified. His heart pounded as she tightened her grip on him, drawing him closer, their hearts beating together, their bodies moving rhythmically together. And then for the first time, giving herself to another, she felt, not hollow and empty, but full and complete.

IN THE MORNING, they made love once more, then lay together. "Could you stay again tonight?" Alex asked.

"Yes. And tomorrow?"

Alex laughed. "I do have a daughter in Paris. A job."

"I don't suppose I'll be able to give up my work either, just because I sold a couple paintings."

"Would you mind terribly, Jake?" Alex sat up in bed. "I need to make a couple phone calls."

He nodded. "That's fine."

Alex rose and went over to the phone. She sat, naked, as she dialed, and he thought how much he wanted to hold her again, how much he wanted to spend the rest of his life loving her.

"In the paper, yes," Alex said. "I'm sorry, Mom. I should have called last night." Alex hesitated, looked over at Jake. She smiled, then said, "Yes, Jake's here with me . . . Yes, I'm very happy too. May I talk to Soleil?"

Once more, Alex looked at Jake and smiled as she waited for her daughter to come to the phone. "Yes, sweetheart . . . no, we didn't get the tapestry . . . but it's okay . . . you don't always get everything you want. . . . Yes, Sunny, I do love Monsieur Bowman, and yes, he will come to see you when we get back to Paris. . . . I love you too . . . We'll see you tomorrow."

The second conversation was brief. Madame Demy at the museum.

Alex got off the phone and shrugged her shoulders. "Of course, she knew. It was in the paper this morning. She said she hoped I wasn't too disappointed. She knows I did everything I could to get the tapestry for the Cluny."

"You did, Alex."

She crawled back in bed with him.

He held her close and stroked her hair. "I'm starving," he said. "Should I call room service, have them send something up?"

"We missed dinner, didn't we?" She laughed.

"Yes, I think we did." He kissed her, then got up and walked to the phone. He picked up the receiver and looked at Alex. "I probably should make another call too. I really should call her—Rebecca. Just to make sure she's okay. Make sure things worked out with Julianna and Matthew."

Alex sat up and stared at Jake. "This is just one of the things I love about you. You are a good, kind, thoughtful man."

35

JAKE AND ALEX returned to Paris late Sunday. They got a cab at the station, then he dropped her off at her apartment and returned to his hotel. He had been in Paris by himself in this tiny room now for almost three months, yet that night he felt as if he had never been so alone. He knew Alex had to return to her daughter, but he also knew they would be together soon.

She called him early Monday morning before leaving for work, just to tell him she loved him, to invite him for dinner that night. The sound of her voice thrilled him, and he wondered how he could bear to wait until that evening.

He went down for breakfast, then walked to La Galerie Genevoix.

Briefly Madame Genevoix expressed her disappointment that the Cluny had not obtained the tapestry, but she was chiefly consumed with her delight over the success of Jake's opening. She showed him the review in *Le Journal Parisien*.

A new talent arrives on the Paris scene . . . how timely, the romantic, mystical theme of the unicorn, recently popularized by the discovery of a Gothic tapestry sold Friday at

auction for a record price at Sotheby's in London. . . .
Monsieur Bowman's realistic style, with emphasis on light
and shadow, his skillful use of color, so adeptly renders the
unicorn that one might believe such a mythical creature truly
exists. . . . Yet this medieval theme takes on a fresh perspec-
tive under Monsieur Bowman's brush. . . . the human figures
and faces might well be inspired by any modern Parisian . . .
a trendy young girl shopping at Marchés aux Puces de St.
Ouen, an artist sipping wine at an outdoor table in Place du
Tertre, a woman picking over the fruit and vegetables on
Rue Lepic. No ethereal Virgin Mary, or celestial Gabriel.
Is that a golden ring pierced through that dreadlocked
Gabriel's right brow? Remove the spiraled horn from the
unicorn and such a creature might as likely be found in a
rodeo, as in a garden under the spell of a nubile medieval
virgin. . . . well worth a stroll down to La Galerie Genevoix.

Madame Genevoix said the review brought record crowds
Saturday and Sunday. She sold three more paintings and received inquiries on several others. Hubert Lafontaine had expressed an interest in having a portrait of his wife done. He
loved the women in the unicorn paintings, and wanted his
wife portrayed in such a setting.

After lunch, Jake returned to his hotel and called Monsieur
Lafontaine and arranged to meet with him Thursday afternoon.

Later that evening, Jake took a cab to Alex's. Soleil greeted
him at the front door. "Monsieur Bowman, I'm so happy to
see you."

"And I'm happy to see you too." He pulled the little girl up
into his arms and gave her a hug. "And, I think, Sunny, it
would be all right if you call me *Jake*." Alex entered the room
and hurried over to him, catching the little girl in the middle
of their embrace. "That is," Jake said, "if it's all right with
your mother."

"Yes." Alex nodded and smiled at Sunny. "I think that
would be just fine."

THE FOLLOWING MORNING Jake called and suggested
she come over on her lunch break. He said he'd cleaned his

room, and he could go out and pick up something to eat.

Alex said she'd come by about noon. She'd bring dessert.

At half past two as they sat on the rumpled bed, propped against the headboard in a pile of pillows, eating chocolate cake, Alex said, "I have something to tell you."

"What is it?" He took her hand in his and licked the frosting off her fingers.

"We're going away this weekend. That is, if you're available."

"We? You and me?"

"Madame Demy invited us to have lunch with her in the country Saturday. Her uncle has a château in the Loire Valley where they often spend weekends. As far as I know, this is the first time anyone from the museum has been invited. Perhaps she's feeling guilty that she offered so little support in my attempt to get the tapestry. So she's invited us to spend Saturday. I thought since we were taking a drive . . ."

Jake grinned. "We might as well find an intimate little inn or château and get a room for the weekend. We could leave Friday night. Good idea?"

"Brilliant idea."

THURSDAY AFTERNOON, JUST after Jake returned from meeting with Monsieur Lafontaine to discuss his wife's portrait, Alex called.

"Oh, Jake, you'll never believe what I received by special courier this afternoon."

"What?"

"A gift from the Sisters of Sainte Blandine—Adèle's drawings, along with the poem and a letter from Mother Etienne, thanking me for what I have done for the convent. She called me a special blessing. Can you imagine that, Jake?"

"Yes, Alex, I can."

AFTER WORK FRIDAY, Alex and Jake drove south from Paris, where they had reserved a room for the weekend at a sixteenth-century hunting lodge now converted into a hotel.

They skipped dinner in the dining room that evening, eating a picnic supper in the privacy of their room. In the morning, they had a breakfast of coffee and croissants, then drove through the valley admiring the numerous châteaux perched on green hillsides, the River Loire meandering through the valley, the fields full of enormous, bright yellow sunflowers. Colorful hot-air balloons dotted the cloudless blue summer sky.

Just before one, following directions Madame Demy had given Alex, they arrived at *La Château de la Vallée Verte*.

"Impressive," Jake said as they parked. They walked up along a path carved through the perfectly trimmed lawn. The building with a neoclassical façade of light-colored cut stone was elegantly symmetrical, a dome topping each side wing. Decorative carvings appeared over the many windows. A small bridge arched over a dry moat, now carpeted with the same lush green as the lawn, and led up to the front entrance.

Madame Demy came to the door, greeting both Alex and Jake with a kiss on each cheek. She wore slacks and a cotton blouse, her hair pulled back loosely, a contrast to the prim suits and tight little bun she always wore in the museum.

She asked if they had any trouble with the directions.

"No, not at all," Jake answered, "and what a wonderful drive."

"A beautiful time of year in the valley," the older woman agreed.

"Your home is lovely." Alex said. A dark parquet floor graced the entry. The portrait of an ancient-looking ancestor, in a gold gilt frame, hung above a heavy wooden console table with a marble inlay top on which a large bouquet of fresh flowers sat. To the left, a carved white limestone staircase led to a landing where a full set of armor, appearing as if it might contain a medieval knight, stood with lance in hand. "Thank you so much for inviting us."

"We're pleased you were able to come." Madame Demy motioned them through the entryway, past the large stone staircase into a formal living room. As they entered, Alex's

eyes immediately locked on the far wall. She grabbed Jake's
arm and pointed.

On the wall, brilliant and as beautiful as it had been in the
exhibition at the Grand Palais, but appearing much more as if
it now found itself in its natural environment, hung *Le Pégase.*

"Le Pégase!" Alex gasped. She released Jake's arm and
walked closer. She stood silently gazing at the tapestry. It covered a good portion of the wall and was framed by a wood
molding, obviously constructed specifically for the tapestry.
"You, Madame Demy?" Alex asked. "You are the owner? *Le
Pégase*?"

"Someday," a voice came from behind them. Both Alex
and Jake turned. "A family heirloom," the man said.

"Monsieur Jadot!" Jake exclaimed.

"Alexandra," Madame Demy said as she approached Alex
and touched her lightly on the arm, "I'd like you to meet my
uncle, Gaston Jadot."

The old man moved slowly, shuffling across the parquet
floor, his steps softening as he walked onto the carpet.

"Monsieur Bowman," Madame Demy said, "I believe you
and my uncle have become quite good friends over the past
few months."

Gaston reached out as Alex extended her hand. He held it
for a moment. *"Enchanté,"* he said, then turned to Jake. "So
good to see you again, Monsieur Bowman."

"What a nice surprise," Jake said, taking the old man's
hand.

"You, Monsieur Jadot," Alex asked, "you are the owner?"

"Le Pégase has been in the family for many years," Gaston
said.

"It's beautiful," Alex replied.

"A true masterpiece. Perhaps from the same workshop as
La Dame à la Licorne, a theory held by many."

"Yes."

"I read an article several years ago," Gaston said, "a comparison of *Le Pégase* and the Cluny tapestries. A well-
thought-out piece. The author believed the tapestries were
done in the same workshop. Even an admission that *Le*

Pégase was a more refined work, produced at a later date."

Alex smiled. She knew he was referring to an article she'd written.

"Quite a brilliant comparison," Gaston said. "Amazing actually, as I knew it had been written based only on photographs, and I knew the author had never seen *Le Pégase*." He chuckled.

"Until the Grand Palais exhibition," Alex said. "A generous gesture, allowing the tapestry to be viewed by the public."

"*Oui, oui,* perhaps true art should be shared."

"Might you share with me any knowledge you have of the tapestry's origin?"

"In truth, little is known, as great a mystery as your unicorn tapestries. There are papers from when the tapestry was purchased, I believe in the files in Paris. Although, as I recall, there was little information other than the purchase date, the previous owner." Gaston turned back to Madame Demy. "Am I correct, Béatrice?"

"Yes, very little information," Madame Demy answered. A young woman came in and whispered something in her ear. "Perhaps we could continue our discussion in the dining room," Madame Demy said. "Monsieur Bowman." Jake offered his arm and they started down the hall, Alex and Gaston following close behind.

"It's nice to have you here with us," Gaston said as they walked. "It's such a pleasure to have such a fine young couple as guests in our home. We seldom have company anymore."

As they entered the dining room, Alex tightened her grip on Monsieur Jadot. "*Oh, mon dieu!*" she gasped.

"Is it so wrong," Gaston said softly, "an old man's wish to be surrounded by beauty in his final years?"

On the far wall hung the seventh unicorn tapestry.

"You, Monsieur Jadot," Alex said, "you were the mystery bidder?"

Gaston nodded.

Alex let go of his arm, then walked across the room and gazed up at the tapestry for several long moments. "I knew it would go to someone who would cherish it, appreciate the work for its beauty." She turned, a satisfaction slowly spreading over her. "And you will, won't you, Monsieur Jadot?"

"*Oui*. Yes, I will." Gaston stood beside Alex now, staring up at the tapestry. "I've always been intrigued," he said, "with the similarities between *Le Pégase* and *La Dame à la Licorne* in your museum. And when this came up, the possibility of a new discovery . . . why, that was enough to make an old man giddy. How could you blame me?"

"Uncle Gaston," Madame Demy said, "overheard a phone message concerning your discovery at Sainte Blandine's, and though it was very vague . . ." She glanced at Gaston, her expression conveying affection rather than displeasure or betrayal. "And, then, I was puzzled when he started asking questions about a set of drawings. I had never mentioned the drawings, or the fact they might be related to the Cluny's tapestries."

"I'm afraid I was the one who supplied that information," Jake said, "when Monsieur Jadot overheard my conversation with Julianna about the drawings."

"It wasn't my intention to have all this information become public," Gaston said. "But it came to me, offered, it seemed, as a gift." He shook his head, apologetically. "Perhaps I spoke too much. It wasn't my intention to stir up such a commotion, this business with the nuns and the Archbishop." The old man sighed. "Then when it went to auction . . . What choice did I have?" He turned to Alex, as if she should answer his question. "I had to buy it, to save it. We couldn't allow it to be shipped off to America, now could we?"

"No, we couldn't." She smiled. "It should remain here in France." She wasn't angry, but felt a growing connection with the old man, who seemed to love the tapestries as much as she.

"Perhaps it is selfish, not to share this beauty," Gaston said, waving his arm. "But a few more years . . . soon I will be gone, and then perhaps there will be no shouts of condemnation, no accusations of selfishness, but whispered words of praise for an old man who shared his love for beauty. Yes, it won't be long. The tapestry will one day soon hang in the Cluny with the others."

"In the Cluny?" Alex asked.

"*Oùi,*" Gaston answered.

"The Cluny," Madame Demy said, "has been named beneficiary of the tapestry in Uncle Gaston's will."

IT WAS PAST four when Alex and Jake started back to their inn. After a lunch of pheasant, bread, salad, fruit, *fromage,* and *tarte tatin,* along with wine, which Monsieur Jadot had explained was from a nearby vineyard, Madame Demy had escorted them on a tour of the grounds and gardens. Gaston had invited them to come visit in Paris.

As Jake drove, Alex gazed out the window, blissfully full and content. Bright yellow sunflowers, against a cobalt sky, glowed in the late-afternoon sun.

"Happy?" Jake asked, reaching over touching her shoulder.

"A perfect afternoon." She turned and smiled. "Good food. Good drink. Good company and good news. Yes, frightfully happy."

"It is rather scary. Isn't it? And we've just begun."

She grinned, then took his hand and pressed the palm to her lips. "I'm still having a time grasping the idea that the tapestry will hang in the Cluny, though I hope it isn't soon. I like Monsieur Jadot and hate to think it's his passing that will unite the tapestry with the others."

"He seems healthy enough. I don't think it'll be that soon, but nobody, including Gaston, will be here forever."

"It all passes, doesn't it?" Again, her eyes met his.

Jake nodded.

"Do you think they're together?"

"Adèle and the *tapissier?*"

"Yes, do you?" she asked seriously.

"In their creation, the tapestries, yes, they're together."

"Yes, but maybe even in a more profound sense . . . in a spiritual sense. Don't you believe two people who love each other will always be together? True love surely transcends this . . . this temporal world."

"This garden of earthly pleasures?" Jake ran his fingers along her neck.

"Yes." Alex relaxed, melting into his touch. "This garden of earthly pleasures." She closed her eyes and a wonderful calm came over her, a presence of someone or something greater than this moment. And then . . . nothing more than the abundance and completeness of this.

EPILOGUE

HE CAME IN the night, pounding violently on the convent door. "Adèle Le Viste," he shouted. "I must see Adèle Le Viste."

The old nun was not asleep. She had risen with the others a short time ago for the Matins and always had difficulty returning to her slumber; often she was awake until the early-morning Lauds. She lit a lantern and left her room. As she passed through the hall, she could hear the man, still shouting, pounding. Several young novices stuck their heads out through the doors of their tiny cells. She told them to return to their beds, which they did obediently. When the old nun got to the door, she opened the window on the upper portion.

"Adèle Le Viste," he shouted once more.

At first she thought he was drunk, but then she realized, by the glassy look in his eyes, it was madness, a madness that possesses one overcome with grief.

"I must see her," he said, his voice softening now.

She knew who he was. It was the *tapissier*, Adèle's lover, the father of the child.

"She is not here," the nun said. She could see in his eyes not only grief, but love, a love that had turned to sorrow.

"I have been searching for many years. She must be here. She must be. I must see her. I have something to give her."

The nun opened the door and stepped outside. "She lived here long ago, but she is gone now."

The man refused to move.

"I will take you to her."

"Wait, wait," he said. "The gift." He pointed beyond the gate of the convent, where a horse stood outlined in the moonlight. The nun could see a small cart attached to the horse, a long bundle tied to the cart. The man walked over, untied the bundle, then hoisted it onto the animal and secured it. He released the horse from the cart.

Together, they walked up the path—the old nun, the man, leading the horse through the wildflowers that sprouted in early spring on the hillside. The flowers were light with dew, and the woman could feel the moisture against her hand. A gentle breeze rustled her habit as they approached the top of the hill. She carried the lantern, looking back at him as he followed. Did he understand?

When they reached the top of the hill she led him to a simple grave with a plain wooden cross. The nun turned to the man. "She rests now with our Father in heaven."

He lowered the bundle from the horse, placed it beside the grave, then knelt down in front of the marker. The old woman knelt also. She prayed aloud, "Almighty Father, Adèle Le Viste rests with you now, protect and guide those she loves who remain here on earth." She was praying now, not only for this man, but also for the child.

"She's gone?" he asked, sounding like a child himself.

"*Oui,*" the nun answered.

He began to weep. His body trembled as he knelt, his head bent in sorrow. And then he was still. Finally he rose and unrolled the large bundle. The nun stood and raised the lantern. It was a tapestry, an enormous tapestry, covering not only the resting place of Adèle, but also spreading out over the adjoining plots. The old woman knew at once it was the seventh tapestry, the final piece in the set created for Adèle's father. Even in the faint light of the lantern, she could make out the detail—a rich red background, fruit trees, small animals, a beautiful maiden, a unicorn, a knight. The nun had never seen anything so exquisite.

She knew how the young woman and the weaver had worked together on the tapestries, how Adèle had designed them, how they had been woven in his workshop in Brussels. They had met first in the garden, then, as they worked together, they had fallen in love. Adèle Le Viste had told her these things during the short time she had been at Sainte Blandine's. When her father discovered their love, he was furious. The young Adèle had been promised to another, a man of high social rank and wealth.

When Adèle came to the convent, the seventh tapestry had not yet been finished. Yet here it was now, rolled out on the young woman's grave.

"You will take it then," the man said. "It belongs here at the convent."

"Oh, no," she answered.

"You must," he said. "It must remain here."

"This is a magnificent work. It should hang in the château of a lord or prince. It does not belong in a convent."

"Sell it then," he said, his voice filled with a mixture of grief and anger. "Sell it. It will bring a great price."

"No, no," she protested. "We live a simple life. We produce what little we need. We are self-sufficient at the Convent of Sainte Blandine."

"Then take it and wait until such time when you are in need." He knelt once more, bowed his head. The nun knelt beside him and, silently, they prayed together.

After some time, neither speaking nor moving, the woman heard the chant of the nuns coming from the convent. She rose. Gently she touched him on the shoulder. The man did not move. Not knowing what else to do, the old woman returned to the convent.

After she prayed with the others in the chapel, she returned to the cemetery. It was daylight now, a lovely spring day, the wildflowers in shades of lavender blooming on the hillside. When she arrived at the grave of Adèle Le Viste, the man was no longer there. But the tapestry remained, rolled out on the grave. In the sunlight, she could see more clearly the magnificent colors. For several minutes she stood staring. What should she do? She prayed once more, for guidance, then returned to the convent.

The men from the village had started to arrive. The convent was being enlarged—there were many young women now, dedicating themselves to the service of the Lord. The small building was filled with nuns, some two to a cell. Soon there would be more rooms.

"Bonjour," one of the men greeted the old nun. His name was Bernard. He was a simple man, a large awkward man, but a skillful builder. It was said he was slow, but he followed directions. He was a good worker.

"Bernard," the nun said, "will you help me?"

"Oui," he replied.

Again, she took the path up the hillside where she had left the *tapissier* the previous night, where she had returned early that morning. Bernard followed.

As they walked, the man hummed a familiar tune. He seemed always happy, pleased with each new day.

The nun asked, "The miller's son, is he growing into a good strong boy?"

"Oui, a good, strong boy."

She would always ask—when a new girl came to the convent, when someone arrived from the village to pick up produce or perform a service for the nuns. When the village priest came to hear confessions, to say Mass. This day, thoughts of the boy weighed heavy on her mind. She had said nothing to the *tapissier.* She had not told him of the young boy, his son, Adèle's son. And now, the man was gone.

They stood before Adèle's grave, the simple man and the nun both staring down at the tapestry.

"Très belle," he said.

"Oui, très belle." Once more she prayed, and then she asked, "Will you help me?"

"Oui."

Together they rolled the tapestry, then carried the heavy, awkward bundle slowly down the hillside. The *tapissier* had told her it should remain at the convent. They should sell it if they found themselves in need. What to do? What to do? the nun asked herself. Then it came to her . . . they should hide it someplace. Perhaps there would be a time in the future when the nuns would be in need.

They carried it to the second floor of the new building.

The nun looked around. It was a large room with the beginnings of an interior wall. Stones and timbers lay in stacks. Additional walls would be added to further divide the structure into smaller cells. Could the tapestry be placed in the wall, hidden and protected for the time?

The nun bent down and began to unroll the tapestry. *"S'il vous plaît."* She looked up at Bernard, who knelt to help her. They rerolled the tapestry as tightly as possible and secured it with a rope on each end.

"Merci," the nun said. "In the wall, Bernard. It must be placed in the wall."

He looked at the woman, puzzled, and scratched his head.

"C'est possible?" she asked.

Bernard continued scratching his head, then he smiled. He held his large flat hands together in front of him as if praying, then slowly he spread them apart. *"Oui, deux murs."*

The nun smiled. Yes, two walls.

THAT NIGHT, AS the old woman knelt in her cell, she wondered if she had done the right thing. She thought of Adèle, the *tapissier,* their child, the boy in the village—the miller's son, ten years old now, the young Jacques Benoit. They said he was a good strong boy, a happy child. Had she done the right thing?

She was an old woman. Soon she would be gone. She must leave something to point the way to the tapestry. Someday, at the proper time, someday when the nuns were in need. That's what the *tapissier* had wanted. She rose, walked over to her desk, and took out pen and parchment. She would write a poem. It would tell the story of the love of Adèle and the *tapissier.* It would lead the way to the tapestry.

Putting pen to parchment, the words began to flow, as if directed by another.

"She met him in the garden . . ."